It did to belie make it

Ma bedroom when I returned, her arms folded across her chest. That T-shirt of hers was a bit baggy but did little to hide the curves beneath.

Curves I'd felt pressed up against me only moments ago.

Curves I intended to explore with my hands again at some point.

Curves that were mine to keep.

An intriguing concept. I'd explore it more later.

"Ready?" I asked her.

"Waiting for you, Prince Charming," she drawled.

"*Prince Charming?*" I repeated, arching a brow.

"You just wasted ten minutes of my life getting dressed, brushing your teeth, applying deodorant, and doing whatever else just happened in there."

"Combing my hair," I said, completing her list and removing the innuendo from the latter part of her statement. "Had I wanted to jerk off, you would have been waiting for a bit longer than a handful of minutes. I also would have ensured that you could watch." I winked at her and moved around her in the doorway. "Stop staring at my ass, sweetheart. And let's go."

She muttered something unflattering at my back.

*Definitely going to be a challenge.*

I grabbed my keys and wallet and met her at the front door. "After you, *princess.*"

She snorted.

I smiled.

*Let the chase begin.*

# CROSSED FATES

## A KINGDOM OF WOLVES NOVEL

USA TODAY BESTSELLING AUTHOR

# LEXI C. FOSS
# ELLE CHRISTENSEN

This is a work of fiction. Names, characters, places, and incidents are either the product of the author's imagination or are used fictitiously, and any resemblance to actual persons, living or dead, business establishments, events, or locales is entirely coincidental.

*Crossed Fates*

Editing by: Outthink Editing, LLC

Proofreading by: Katie Schmahl & Jean Bachen

Cover Design: Covers by Aura

Cover Photography: CJC Photography

Models: Jackie & Stephen

Published by: Ninja Newt Publishing, LLC

Print Edition

ISBN: 978-1-954183-36-0

# KINGDOM OF WOLVES

## KINGDOM OF WOLVES: A WORLD WHERE ALPHAS RULE

Enter the Kingdom of Wolves, a shared universe created by a set of fantastic authors that feature psychotic and possessive wolf alphas, intoxicating relationships, fated mates and strong badass heroines. Kingdom of Wolves will keep you up all night, addicted for more.

Make sure to leave your manners at the door, these wolves don't play nice when it comes to the women they want.

These stories are all set in the same world and can be read in any order. Some books are standalones and some are the start of a series.

### This shared world will bring you books by the following authors:

**Wild Moon** by C.R. Jane & Mila Young
**Lost** by M. Sinclair
**Torn to Bits** by Katie May
**Crossed Fates** by Lexi C. Foss & Elle Christensen
**Shift of Morals** by K Webster
**Rabid** by Ivy Asher & Raven Kennedy
**Alpha's Claim** by Amelia Hutchins
**Lunacy** by Lanie Olson

## A Kingdom of Wolves Novel

*Welcome to the Kingdom of Wolves.*
*Careful. These alphas bite.*

### Alaric

Here's the thing about alphas—we don't submit. It's how I ended up as a lone wolf without a pack. I refused to challenge my older brother for the alpha throne, and now I slay monsters for a living.

So the hot little redhead I just saved on my latest mission? Yeah, I have no problem taming her. Except my wolf thinks she's my fated mate.

No, thanks. I'm good.
Only, fate has other plans for us both.

My older brother's just been poisoned, so I'm headed back to a family I no longer know. And the gorgeous female my wolf wants to claim is in the driver's seat beside me. Why? Because she f*cking stabbed me.

Fated mates? Yeah, more like fated hate.

### Makayla

One day, you're hunting a jackhole hybrid with a penchant for abducting women. And the next, you're staring into the eyes of your future mate.

At least that's what this alpha wolf seems to think.

He's tempting, sure. But I'm not interested in anything long-term.

Sometimes, love can be worth the risk.
And sometimes, it'll kill you.
Let the mating games begin.

**Authors' Note:** *Crossed Fates* is a standalone shifter romance with dark undertones. Alaric is all possessive alpha wolf, and Makayla is all fiery stubborn female. Together, they're explosive and passionate. There will be heat. There will be death. There will be biting. Enjoy.

# CROSSED FATES

## A KINGDOM OF WOLVES NOVEL

VAMPIRE DYNASTY

## A Note from Sapphire

Meddling.

Hmm. Yes, I do enjoy it. And in the case of Makayla, I'd say she deserves it more than most. She's a lone wolf lost in the wrong world. So I gave her a little push. I can't wait to see the results.

Her alpha mate is no Prince Charming, and he's going to require a hell of a lot of work. But he'll be worth it in the end.
Assuming he bites.

Ah, stubborn males. They're so much fun to tame. Only, this one thinks the game is the other way around. Makayla will show him.

I hope, anyway. For the true threat can only be resolved if they work as a team.

*Good luck, young wolves. I'm rooting for you both.*

# Prologue

## Makayla

Here's the thing about fate.

One day, you're hunting an asshole hybrid with a penchant for abducting women. And the next, you're staring into the eyes of your future.

It's a momentary distraction. Look the wrong way, and your destiny is forever altered. Look the right way, and you just might miss the life-altering event.

Will I pick the correct path?

There's really only one way to find out.

Whatever happens, it won't be conventional. It'll be violent, hungry, and *raw*. We're both alphas. We're both lone wolves. We're both in for a world of pain and suffering.

But sometimes, love can be worth the risk.

And sometimes, it'll kill you.

Welcome to my future. I'm playing in a world that isn't my own, and just like back home, these alphas bite. Someone should probably warn Alaric that I have every intention of biting back. Or maybe not.

Let the mating games begin.

# CHAPTER 1

## MAKAYLA

*Present Day*

BLOODSUCKER SERIAL KILLER.

I considered the nickname, then peered through the bars at the hulking beast seated by the desk. I wasn't impressed. The media had made this guy sound like some sort of mastermind lunatic. That was why I'd chosen the kidnap approach for this case. It seemed like the best way to make the arrogant jackhole talk.

But now I wondered if I should have just knocked him out, handcuffed him in silver chains, and interrogated him the old-fashioned way.

A sigh escaped me. *Better luck next time,* I thought.

I fiddled with the cuffs in front of me. They were made of silver, which burned my wrists, but they wouldn't be difficult to unlatch in a pinch. The bars would be more of a problem. I didn't have a key, so a wire would have to do.

*Thank God for bras.*

Hulk—my nickname for the Bloodsucker Serial Killer because it was far more appropriate—shifted, his muscular body way too big for his tiny stool. He really should consider some upgrades around this shithole. This underground dungeon of his was more like a glorified basement.

Of course, this was just the holding cage.

Maybe things would be more interesting once he moved me to my upgraded digs. Then we'd get to the heart of this trafficking matter.

Or I'd kill him.

The decision remained to be seen.

*What kind of shifter are you?* I wondered. He had this weird smoky stench around him that didn't match what I knew about the shifters in this realm. As far as I knew, dragons didn't exist here. Although, that would be pretty cool if they did.

The hint of blood on the air suggested he might be part vamp as well.

So a hybrid of some kind.

*Interesting.* I'd spent the last three years traversing realms and had never heard of a hybrid before, much less encountered one.

My alpha, Nathan, would definitely be intrigued. Marc, too. I'd have to report this back to them once I finished up here. Not that I worked for Nathan's black ops agency anymore. I'd gone freelance after the job that had originally brought me to this realm. Then I'd stayed because the people of this world clearly needed my help.

And if hybrids were a thing now, then I was *definitely* needed here.

I rolled off my cot and started to pace the small space of my cell. Dusty cement floor. Small windows near the high ceiling. Sports bar above us—something I'd sensed more than observed from my fake unconscious state when the hybrid had taken me down the single set of stairs.

I cataloged every detail and frowned at the summary in

my head. "Yeah, I gotta be honest with you, Hulk. This place is roughly a two-star rating in my book."

He ignored me, his focus on his screens.

Small talk clearly wasn't in this guy's repertoire. I drummed my fingers against my thighs, considering him. This situation required a delicate touch, maybe some coaxing, or I could do what I happened to be really good at—just plain piss him off. *With finesse.*

*Yes, I like this plan.*

I heaved a dramatic exhale and lounged against the wall beside the door to my cell.

"You know, there are several deteriorations you could make to this place that would lower your rating," I advised him. "I mean, I travel *a lot* and stay in a *ton* of different styles of accommodations, and, to be honest, this isn't the worst place I've spent the night. Hence the two-star rating."

Hulk merely snorted, unamused.

I kept expecting him to pull out a cigarette, to go with the whole smoky aura thing.

But those screens had him captivated instead.

*I'm starting to take offense to this silent treatment, big guy,* I thought, deciding to up my game. He obviously needed a more thorough lesson on polite conversation.

"Don't get me wrong, you nailed the whole musty dungeon atmosphere, but I just don't *believe* it, you know? I want to; I'm really trying here. It's not that the cot is too lumpy or the toilet bowl is too clean, but"—as suspected, when I paused, he glanced at me over his shoulder, so I gave him two thumbs up and a big, toothy grin—"major props for the silver bars. Those are how you lost your third star."

Of course, he gained a star with the cuffs. Like, who

decided to chain a victim's hands in front of them? That rookie move served as a clear underestimation of my abilities—an underestimation that was, frankly, offensive. My brother had taught me to pick handcuffs before day one of enforcer training. Then my alpha's black ops agency had refined the skill after recruiting me.

"Shut up," Hulk grunted.

"No problem." I wandered to the other side of the bars caging me in and tapped one with my finger. "Ouch!" The fiery pain on the tip of my digit zinged across my nerve endings, but I managed to contain my shudder. I did, however, make a high-pitched yelp, rattle my cuffs around, and hop from foot to foot while cradling my "poor, abused" hand.

As I'd hoped, the man whipped his head around to take a gander at what had caused my outburst. After a quick assessment, he rolled his eyes so hard that he could have checked out his own ass, and went back to his paperwork. "Had to be an airhead," he muttered in a low, exasperated tone.

"I was just curious," I said, pretending to defend myself. "Besides, if I don't thoroughly inspect the accommodations, how will I know what to put in my review? Oh, that reminds me, is there a continental breakfast? I hope you don't just serve moldy fruit. I do a lot of yoga and shit, so I can enjoy a morning pastry. Provided it's not filled with anything delicious. Wouldn't want to boost your—"

He twisted around and glared at me. "Shut. Up." The words held a bit more bite this time.

"Sure, sure. Sorry about that." I mimed zipping my lips and walked with deliberate slowness toward said lumpy cot until he'd turned his back again. Halting in my tracks, I pivoted and studied my captor.

I'd taken on this hybrid asshole pro bono after I saw the news about Valaria Crimson's death. The famous heiress had made all the headlines, but that wasn't why I took on her case. No, I had two reasons.

First, Valaria Crimson was a shifter. Not that humans knew that about her—mortals had no idea supernaturals existed around them.

And second, the moniker the news agencies had given the culprit had piqued my interest.

But this guy was so not living up to the *Bloodsucker Serial Killer* title.

I expected something grander after all my digging into his background. He was supposed to be some sort of human trafficking king. As someone who had studied multiple cases like this—and solved them—I was seriously unimpressed.

I could only imagine what my mentor would say right now. Probably something snarky about this being a colossal waste of time. I agreed.

*Speaking of...*

"You know, actually, this sort of reminds me of my first visit to this, uh, city. Only, that dungeon had torture devices and a witch in it." One I'd helped save and return to her appropriate realm—*my realm.* "Maybe you should consider acquiring a witch? Might knock you down a quarter star or so. I wouldn't suggest letting her be rescued, though. That's how that dungeon gained stars. Shame, really, as they had such potential. So that's why—"

Hulk shoved his chair back from the table, sending it flying out from under him, and stalked over to stare at me with a thunderous expression. "I said, *shut it.*"

I put my hands up in a surrender pose. "Shutting it." I only paused for a second before adding, "Except, um, just wondering, what are you going to do with me? I can't exactly rate my stay if I'm dead."

"Oh, we're not going to kill you."

*We. Interesting.* I'd noticed a plethora of lackeys, but his use of the word *we* seemed to imply he had partners.

His reddish eyes flashed black, his animal near the surface. *Totally a wolf under that skin.* He scanned me from head to toe, and back up, lingering on my breasts before returning to my face.

I had to hold in a snort. *Bad idea, dude.* There were two killers in this room.

"Does the carpet match the drapes?" he asked in a slimy voice before licking his lips.

Years of self-control kept me from delivering a swift dick punch for that shitty-ass line. I didn't trust my sharp tongue, though, so I kept silent.

"Too bad I won't have the opportunity to find out. You're slated for review tomorrow. Then you'll likely go to auction soon after."

*Now we're getting somewhere.* I opened my mouth to push for details, only to be interrupted by the door opening at the top of the stairs.

The sound of hurried feet on metal steps followed.

My nose twitched, my inner wolf groaning in irritation. *Vampire. Ugh.*

A short, scraggly guy with a head slightly too big for his body appeared a second later. His eyes went straight to me, and his pupils flared with lust—or hunger—I couldn't tell which reaction was more prevalent.

I cocked my head to the side and stared at him coolly, deciding to drop the act and step up my game. Pissing off both jackholes would lead to more informative verbal vomit. "Bleed out, Sir Wanna-Bite." Seemed like an appropriate nickname. "Never going to happen. Not even if my life depended on it."

He scowled at me, his face warped by his frown and lowered brows. "Watch it, bitch. It just might," he snarled.

"I'll never understand why people think it's an insult to call me exactly what I am."

"A female dog?" He rolled his eyes.

"No." I let my wolf close to the surface, allowing the little shit to see her in my eyes as she pushed to be released. "A vindictive, aggressive woman with deadly aim. *And* a female wolf."

Sir Wanna-Bite opened his mouth to issue a rebuttal but was cut off when the hybrid spoke. "Enough, Luther."

*Luther?* I rolled my eyes. *"Sir Wanna-Bite" is so much more fun.*

The vamp sneered at me, his eyes blazing with a mixture of hatred and lust. I simply smiled pleasantly, needling him because that was how I got my kicks.

Hulk's phone rang, interrupting my witty repartee. He retrieved it from his pocket and answered immediately. "Vex."

I blinked. *Seriously? Why are you all ruining my nicknames?*

"Is it safe to talk?" the caller asked.

"Yeah, it's just Luther here right now," Vex—*ugh*—replied.

*And me,* I thought with a mental wave. *But yes, please continue treating me as insignificant. Just a shifter with wolf hearing over here.*

Hopefully, this caller would finally give me something to work off of.

"Good. The silver package has been delivered," said the caller. "They should be dead by morning."

*Silver? What the hell does that have to do with auctioning girls?*

7

"Did you let the boss know?" Vex asked.

"Yeah."

*Ah, shit.* Those were words I didn't want to hear. I thought the hybrid was the boss. Now I had to go through him to find out who really ran this show. *Fuck a duck.*

I added the boss's identity to the information I intended to extract from these gullible idiots. I also wanted more details about the silver package. It seemed strange that a shifter, half-breed or not, would mess with something so toxic. Which meant it had to be important.

"Anything else?" Vex asked.

"Yeah. Boss saw your new catch on the surveillance feed. He says he wants you to hold on to her for him. Something about striking a chord of familiarity, if you feel me."

Vex glanced at me and grunted. "The chatty one?"

The caller chuckled. "Pretty redhead."

"Her mouth isn't all that pretty." Vex's irises flared an eerie red color as he studied me. "But all right."

"I'll be in touch." The caller hung up.

Vex set the phone on the table and then lifted his chin at Luther. "Go get Neo."

Luther threw me what I assumed was supposed to be a threatening scowl but looked more like a pout, then scampered up the stairs.

"I assume that all means you can't sample the goods?" No sense in hiding my enhanced hearing now that he'd finished talking.

Vex's shoulders stiffened, and he grunted as he stomped back over to his seat at the table.

"That's unusual, huh?"

He grunted again, and the muscles in his back tightened.

"Ooooh, am I special? Please say yes. A girl always likes to be special."

Vex turned in his seat and glared at me. "I wouldn't be so mouthy if I were you. The boss wants you for himself, and trust me, he'll cut off that tongue if you don't keep it in your mouth."

Two sets of feet scurried down the stairs, interrupting me. *Again.*

*I'm going to kill you just for being a pest*, I decided as Luther came into view. *I mean, honestly, how is a girl supposed to work around here with all these constant interruptions? And could you not scurry? It makes you sound like a damn mouse.*

The newcomer—Neo, I presumed—stood at least six inches shorter than Luther.

*How strange for a shifter*, I mused, catching his scent as he hit the bottom step. Perhaps he worked for Vex because he wanted to feel like a bigger man.

Because it was true what they said—size really did matter, especially for a wolf.

Neo's gaze went right to me as though he could hear me mocking his petite frame. I merely smiled in response. He eyed me curiously for a moment, then walked toward my cage, stopping a foot away.

"What breed of wolf are you?"

"What *breed* are you?" I countered. But I already knew. *Bitten wolf.* His smell and the lack of a feral animalistic gleam in his eyes gave him away. Totemic breeds typically had their beasts lurking in their gazes, Lycans were a distinct two-legged shifter type, and Fenrir weren't real wolves—only their eyes shifted.

"Neo, take this to the warehouse on Grand," Vex said, drawing Neo's attention away from me as he handed him a sheet of paper.

Neo snatched it and glanced at me curiously one more time before departing.

Apparently, he was just as bad at small talk as the other two.

I sighed. *This is going to take me all night at this rate.*

Luther's red eyes locked onto me again, and he inched closer. "I should taste her to make sure she's good enough to be sold." His mouth curved into a greasy smile.

*Ew.*

Also, I was a little offended at the implication.

"My blood is like heroin, vamp," I taunted. "One taste and you'll be hooked. But you should have some self-control. Didn't anyone ever teach you to say no to drugs?"

Vex made a sound that might have been a chuckle. If so, he was rusty at it. "Feisty," he grunted. "It's a pity I won't be the one to bring you to heel."

"Sir Wanna-Bite isn't enough of a challenge for you?" I drawled. "Imagine that."

Luther's face turned red, and he took a threatening step forward, but Vex—who remained deadpan—yanked him backward just as a commotion broke out upstairs.

Vex stood, looking closely at the camera feeds. "Fucking E.V.I.E.," he growled. He spun around and pointed a finger at Luther. "Watch her," he commanded as he stalked toward the stairs. At the last second, he narrowed his gaze and added, "No biting."

Luther double-blinked and nodded. "Of course."

*Liar, liar, pants on fire.*

Vex jogged up, leaving me alone with the weak little shit.

*Well, I tried to do this the easy way.* I began fiddling with my cuffs. *But it seems a simple interrogation is just not going to work here.*

Luther's stare turned menacing as he approached.

"If you're going for intimidation, you might want to grow a foot or so," I jibed. Honestly, the insult would be better served to his buddy Neo, but the little pip-squeak had run off with his tail between his legs, ready to do Vex's bidding.

Luther sneered and sibilated, "I'm going to make you bleed."

I rolled my eyes skyward. "Really? I thought maybe you were going to eat my brains like a zombie. A vampire make me bleed? I'm shocked!"

Luther's face turned purple and mottled with rage.

Perfect. *Time to stop pretending I'm not in charge.*

I popped the clasp on the cuff, ready to kick some ass and demand some answers, but a body flying down the stairs distracted me.

*Okay, seriously. Someone up there is messing with me. Three interruptions in, like, ten minutes? This can't be… hold on… Is that Vex?* I glared at the ceiling. "Are you fucking serious right now?"

Some asshole just killed my target!

I glared at the male descending the stairs.

Then my lips parted.

Because holy wow, someone had sent me a fallen angel dressed in black leather and jeans. I looked up again. *All right. Not as mad now.*

Except the godly male walked straight up to Luther and drove a stake through his chest, taking down yet another one of *my* targets. *Shit!*

Piercing blue eyes landed on me, causing my wolf to perk up with interest. *Oh, yes,* she seemed to be saying, her proverbial purr vibrating me to my core.

I nearly growled in response. *Not fucking happening. He killed our targets. The only action we'll be seeing is his blood painting the walls.*

My cuffs were already unfastened.

Now all I needed was to escape this cage.

Then I'd return the favor by killing this intruder for interrupting my interrogation. I would have taken it out on Luther, but this hot wolf had beaten me to the punch. So I'd take out my frustration on his beautiful face instead.

# CHAPTER 2

## ALARIC

*MATE.*

*She's my fucking mate.*

Of all the places to stumble upon my fate, it had to be here—in the basement of a Mets fans bar. I nearly groaned, but the blue fire dancing in her pretty gaze suggested that would be an unwelcome greeting. So instead, I cocked my head to the side and asked, "Need a hand, sweetheart?"

"Sweet? Do I look goddamn *sweet* to you?"

I allowed my gaze to roam over her T-shirt and jeans, noting the curves beneath. She was stunning. Perfectly proportioned. Athletic. Tall for a female, but I still had about seven inches on her. And she possessed an alpha air.

Definitely an ideal mate.

Too bad I didn't want one.

"Well, you certainly smell sweet," I murmured. At least to my wolf. The beast prowled inside me, begging to be unleashed. He wanted to claim what was rightfully his—a treat he'd been waiting his lifetime to find.

I didn't share the sentiment.

Sure, she was hot. I wouldn't mind a quick fuck up against the bars. But I didn't have time for an entanglement.

"Yeah, that's not happening," she said, clearly picking up on the vibes from my hungry wolf.

I arched a brow. "I don't recall offering." A groan sounded from the bottom of the stairs while I spoke, causing me to curse out loud. "Damn hybrid." The son of bitch refused to *die*.

"Wait!" the pretty, redheaded female called.

I ignored her, pulling out my gun again, and aimed at the asshole's head. Blood pooled between the creature's eyes, stalling his shift to monster-form. I'd come face-to-face with that bullshit last night at Blood Thirteen and had no intention of doing it again.

"Eat wood," I said, whipping out a stake and kneeling to drive it through his chest.

A growl sounded from behind me, causing all the hairs along my arms to dance. I left my stake in the hybrid's chest and spun to face a fuming redhead. She'd not only lost her cuffs but had also opened her cage.

"Impressive," I admitted, re-holstering my gun.

"*Imbecile*," she tossed back, causing both my eyebrows to shoot upward.

"Excuse me?"

"I was in the middle of interrogating that guy!" She pointed at the very dead hybrid—seemed my stake did the trick, *thank fuck*—and then shoved that finger in my chest. "You have no idea what you've done."

I glanced at her blunt nail, then back up at her, amused. "What kind of wolf are you?"

She startled at my change in topic. "Excuse me?"

"What kind—"

"Yeah, I fucking heard you," she snapped, dropping her hand and starting to pace.

I folded my arms, my leather jacket creaking a bit with the sound. "Seriously, where are you from?" Because she wasn't a Bitten wolf, which meant she might not even feel the whole fated-mates call between us. Totemics, Fenrirs, and Lycans all had their own mating rituals, most of which weren't controlled by soul bonds.

But I didn't catch any sort of familiar vibe from her, marking her as decidedly other to my wolf's senses.

She said nothing, walking over to pick up a tablet from a table, then started going through papers and scattering things all over the floor.

"First crime scene?" I wondered out loud. Because she was doing a shit job of keeping her prints off of everything. Not that it mattered. I'd call up a crew from headquarters and have them clean it all up in thirty minutes.

"Nothing," she said to herself. "*Shit.*"

"What are you looking for?" I asked, walking toward her.

She spun on her heel and threw up a palm. "Don't. You've already screwed this up enough."

"Right." My fated mate was insane. Fantastic. I pulled out my phone to pull up the contact *Cleanup Bitches of Eliminate Vampiric Influences Everywhere*, abbreviated as *E.V.I.E. Cleanup Bitches* in my address book, and shot them a text with my location.

My boss, Jude, would be pleased that the hybrid mess had finally come to an end. The bastard had been terrorizing New York City, earning himself the nickname of Bloodsucker Serial Killer. Never a good thing in a world where humans didn't know vamps or shifters existed. The reporters were far too close to the truth on this one.

The curvy redhead wandered over to the hybrid to search him, her delectable ass a beacon in the air as she bent.

My wolf growled in approval, the sound touching my chest, but I swallowed it before she could hear it.

Although, the look she flashed me over her shoulder suggested she'd *sensed* it. She also muttered something under her breath that sounded like "Horny wolves," amusing me further.

"Do you have a name?" I asked her.

"I do." She pulled a mobile from the hybrid's pocket and used his thumb to unlock it, then started looking through it.

"And what's your name?" I pressed when she didn't elaborate.

"None of your business," she replied sweetly.

I grunted. "Fate strongly disagrees with that." Unless I could just make up whatever name I wanted for my supposed mate. But then I'd like a chance to craft her, too. I'd absolutely give her this woman's body, face, and hair. I'd nix the attitude, though. Make her a little more submissive and needy. Definitely wet. Hard nipples. Mmm, she'd crawl for me and beg to suck my cock, too.

The redhead rolled her eyes as if she could hear my thoughts and grunted. "I think you've done enough to ruin my evening. Feel free to see yourself out."

I chuckled. "Not happening, sweetheart. The cleanup crew will be here in thirty to pick these guys up." I knew that because a buzz had just landed on my wrist with an ETA. The lab was eager to play with the hybrid and determine his origin.

"To go to E.V.I.E.?" she asked.

I frowned. "How do you know that?"

"Hybrid called you out when he caught you on the security cameras." She nodded to a set of monitors, then tossed the creature's phone onto the table. "Well, this was a bust. All blocked numbers and no contacts." She started muttering to herself again, something about having to find another *in*.

"Who are you?" I asked, my amusement starting to take a back seat in the face of suspicion. She ignored me again, causing my wolf to pace in irritation. Neither of us took lightly to being disregarded or pushed to the side. I might have been born a human, but I'd very much grown into my alpha soul over the last decade. And I didn't appreciate this woman acting like I lacked authority in this situation.

"I asked you a question, *mate*." I enunciated that last word with a force I felt to my very core, my wolf snarling in agreement. *Heel*, he wanted to say. *Roll over. Beg.*

It was a new desire, one I'd hoped never to experience.

Alas, fate had played her hand.

And now I was staring at my destiny.

Assuming I chose to accept it. Most wolves in my position wouldn't be able to choose, but I'd never wanted a mate. Of course, it was going to play hell with my ability to fuck. So we might have to come up with some sort of arrangement.

"Mate?" she repeated with a snort. "Not even close to my real name."

"It's what you are." The growl in my voice reverberated in my chest as I narrowed my gaze at her. "Don't tell me you can't sense it."

She finally paused to look at me. *Really* look at me. A glimmer of approval flashed in her gaze, her wolf peeking out to admire what she likely already considered hers.

Our animals recognized our fate.

They connected on a soul-level, their need to rut a sharp instinct that proved difficult to ignore. At least for lesser wolves. But the female before me certainly wasn't that.

*Alpha*, my animal recognized. *Ideal alpha mate.*

I disagreed.

An ideal mate would be on her knees already, begging me to take her.

This woman obviously missed that memo. Maybe I'd hand it to her later. *After* I figured out who she was, and her heritage.

"You're a Bitten wolf," she said after a beat.

"I am."

"I'm not," she returned.

"Clearly." I leaned against the wall near the hybrid's corpse, both blocking her exit and waiting for my team to arrive. I also intended to handle any issues that might come flying down the stairs in the interim.

I'd learned my lesson last night—the hybrid bastard had friends. *A lot of them.* Which was how I'd ended up in a chair, wrapped up in silver chains, in the late evening hours. Fortunately, my slayer partner, Violet, had an obsessive vamp admirer who'd helped free us.

Then she'd run off and left me to clean up the mess.

*Fine by me*, I thought. I'd always preferred to work alone. Just wasn't expecting to find a pretty shifter waiting for me in a cage. Maybe I'd craft one for her later and make it a playpen she couldn't break out of.

"We're not mates." The redhead uttered the words slowly and precisely, her tone grating.

"We are mates," I corrected. "But if it's any consolation, I'm not thrilled about it either. Yet, here we are."

"No, I don't accept."

"There's nothing to accept." Our connection snapped into place the moment I caught her scent—a flowery aroma that seemed to wrap a vise around my neck and balls. Had I known I would be castrated tonight, I would have gone out for a good fuck before chasing down the hybrid.

*Damn, I'll never desire another female again.* A definite downside to the whole fate process. I'd honestly never expected to run into my other half, because I tended to avoid shifters. The alpha in me had a penchant for taking charge, which caused boundary issues when near a pack.

Hence my lone-wolf status.

"That's where you're—"

My phone's ring cut her off, the sound shrill in the otherwise quiet, dungeon-like room. I pressed my finger to my lips, telling her to be quiet without words, and put the phone to my ear. "Calder," I said, using my last name.

The female rolled her eyes and started toward me, her destination clear as her eyes drifted up the stairs. I caught her by the arm. *Stay*, I mouthed as the caller said, "Son," over the line.

I blinked, surprised to hear my father's voice. I pulled my phone away to check the time, noting the postmidnight hour. "What's wrong?" I immediately asked. Not only did he rarely call me, but he also never phoned this late.

The woman beside me twisted out of my hold, causing me to growl in annoyance. "Stop," I demanded, grabbing her harder this time. "We're not done yet."

She snarled.

I replied by squeezing harder, holding her in place. "Sorry, in the middle of a mission and one of the caged animals is overreacting," I muttered, refocusing on my dad. Then I repeated, "What's wrong?"

The words had barely left my mouth when the she-devil grabbed a knife from my belt and thrust it into my shoulder before I could even think to react.

My phone fell from my hand as my father's reply floated in the air between us.

"It's your brother." My phone clattered to the ground, my wolf senses picking up the words that followed as agony ripped down my arm. "Alaric, Tyler's been poisoned."

# CHAPTER 3

## MAKAYLA

"FUCK!" Alaric shouted. At least, I assumed that was his name because his father had called him that over the phone.

Right before saying his brother had just been poisoned.

*Fuck*, I echoed in my head, eyeing the furious shifter in front of me. He hadn't crumpled to the ground in defeat or cried out beyond the curse, just stood there bleeding and glowering at me with an expression that said he sincerely wanted to repay the favor.

I ripped the blade from his joint and jumped backward out of his reach, which was the exact opposite direction of what I'd originally intended. *Up*, I reminded myself. *I meant to go* up *the stairs and run.*

Only now I was well and truly blocked by an alpha male with an axe to grind.

*Awesome. Well done, Makayla.*

He slowly bent to pick up his phone with his good arm, his now-black eyes on me the entire time. I still held his knife in my fist, but he wore a gun on his belt. While I had good aim for a throw, I suspected he'd be faster, even without the use of his dominant hand.

Rather than place the phone at his ear, he put his

father on speaker and held it in a way that suggested he would drop it in exchange for his pistol if I so much as moved. "Poisoned with what?" It came out in a grated tone that sent a shiver down my spine. My wolf practically purred in response, intrigued by the rumbly voice.

*We are so not going there,* I told her.

Not that she had any intention of listening. When she sensed an attraction, she dove headfirst into it. Which was usually fine because I didn't mind hot one-night stands. But something about this male told me it wouldn't be just a night.

Probably because he appeared to be under the dubious impression that I was his mate.

Damn Bitten wolves, always talking about fate. They didn't believe in the concept of choice—a fact that was really too bad for him because I had every intention of making my own decisions, and I did not choose him. Or anyone.

Some wolves were made for mating. And I most certainly was not one of them.

"Silver," his father said, drawing me back to the conversation with another shiver.

*Silver poisoning. What are the chances of that being a coincidence?* I wondered, sighing to myself. *Definitely not high.*

Damn it, that meant I needed to help this jackass now. After his bout of manhandling, I wasn't very keen on that idea.

Although, I did stab him.

And from his expression, he wasn't likely to forgive that anytime soon. Despite the fact that my action had been justified. *Mostly. Okay, it might have been a little harsh.*

Bitten wolves didn't heal the way my kind did. I was immortal, but I could be killed if injured severely enough. Meanwhile, his kind were practically human. They aged normally and could die from natural causes—apart from disease. However, they typically healed faster than a mortal. He'd probably be good as new in a day or so.

*Besides, it's not like I stabbed him in the damn chest. Why is he being so grouchy about it?*

"Silver?" Alaric repeated, sounding doubtful. "How?"

"We suspect it was from his visit to the city this morning," his dad replied, a note of irritation in his tone. "As you know, he had a lunch appointment."

Alaric's jaw ticked, highlighting the light dusting of dark hairs along his chiseled jaw. "Yes. I meant to meet him there, but I found myself otherwise detained." He glared down at the hybrid as though to blame him.

I frowned. As he'd just arrived, it seemed an unfair correlation, unless he'd been hunting Vex all day. *Why did you come barging in here to kill him?* I would have opened my mouth to ask, but I didn't want to interrupt his conversation with his dad.

"I need you here," his father said, ignoring the excuse. "Now."

The wolf flashed in Alaric's eyes, reacting to the command in that single word.

*Definitely an alpha*, I realized. His size already sort of gave him away with that over-six-foot-tall frame and broad shoulders. Although, he had an athletic litheness to him that reminded me of a runner's build. Sleek and trim, but definitely strong. And I had no doubt his endurance in a fight lived up to his muscular build.

*Probably has decent endurance in bed, too*, I thought, allowing my gaze to drop to his tapered hips and strong thighs.

I was a wolf; therefore, I naturally noticed these things.

It didn't mean I wanted to test the theory. Of course, my wolf vehemently disagreed. *Tramp.*

Some of the ire had bled from his eyes as I returned

my focus to his face. His full lips even quirked up on one side, my appraisal having not gone unnoticed.

Because yeah, he was a wolf, too. Hence, he also noticed these things.

But the amusement quickly died as he shifted, flinching from the stab wound in his shoulder. Yeah, I'd be paying for that in a few minutes.

I swallowed, considering my options.

He had the upper hand with that gun. He also outweighed me by a lot. I was tall for a woman, making it difficult to squeeze by someone of Alaric's stature. However, I was fast. Especially in wolf form.

Of course, I couldn't exactly run around New York City with my fur on. And if I were to shift here, I'd end up naked when I switched back to my human skin later.

Which meant I had to fight him like this. *Ugh.*

"I need to wrap up this scene," Alaric finally said, the gravel in his tone remaining harsh and unmoving.

*Definitely still pissed.*

*I can't really blame him.*

"I'll be there by sunrise, or just after," he added.

"Good. The pack needs you, son."

Alaric's wolf took over his gaze again, his jaw clenching once more. "I'll do what I can."

"Do more," his father returned before cutting off the call.

Alaric just stood there for a minute, his anger tangible. Then he slowly returned his phone to the pocket of his jeans.

I considered apologizing, but it wouldn't be heartfelt. He'd deserved a blade to the shoulder for grabbing me like some sort of omega in need of a stern lesson.

However, I really didn't want him to return the favor.

*Okay. Maybe I should offer a different sort of olive branch here.*

I cleared my throat, considering what to say. "So, um, I'm Makayla." Seemed like a good idea to give him the answer he'd wanted from me earlier.

Although, I wasn't going to elaborate.

Explaining my origin would lead to a lot of questions I really didn't want to answer. It didn't seem all that right to tell a wolf I'd just met the truth when not even my pack knew about my job as a freelancer, let alone that I did it while jumping realms. Besides, it wasn't really his business.

"Makayla," he repeated, and hell if that didn't make my thighs clench. Did he have to say it in that sexy-as-sin tone? Like he wanted to chain me to a bed and ravage me as punishment for stabbing him?

I mentally shook myself, trying to rid myself of the lustful thoughts.

But they came back with a flourish as he took a menacing step toward me.

*Move,* I ordered my legs.

They didn't listen, my wolf perking up at the sight of the approaching alpha. She wanted to shift out of my skin and play with his animal.

I swallowed the urge and held his gaze, feigning a confidence I didn't quite feel.

He took another step, his black pupils flaring to hide his sapphire irises. Energy hummed across my skin, anticipation curling in my belly.

His woodsy scent swirled around me in a welcome caress that taunted my senses, urging me to kneel in an uncharacteristic display of submission. *What the hell?* I never knelt for anyone. Well, except for maybe Nathan. As alpha of my pack, he could control his wolves and command them to do whatever he wanted. Not that he ever would.

But Alaric didn't have that same power over me.

*I'm not his.*

I stood my ground, my spine elongating as I engaged in a battle of wills with the seething male before me. "If you weren't my destined mate, *Makayla*, I would consider killing you right now."

*Harsh words.*

*True words.*

*Angry words.*

My heart skipped a beat. "Are you expecting a display of gratitude?" Because if he was, he'd be waiting for a hell of a long time.

His gaze fell to my mouth, his fury lashing out at me in a palpable wave of heat. It sent a quiver through me, the brunt of it culminating in my lower belly.

Fighting always turned me on—especially when I had a decent partner—and I had no doubt this wolf would live up to my every expectation.

I licked my lips, and his nostrils flared in response.

"Kiss me and I'll forgive you."

"Kiss me and I'll kill you," I returned. I wasn't sure if I meant it, but I tightened my grip on the hilt of his knife just in case.

He smiled. "You know, I never wanted a mate." His blue irises bled through his black pupils, providing me with an unfettered glimpse at his stunning eyes as they slowly looked me over. "But I think I'm going to enjoy taming you, baby."

I snorted. "Good luck with that."

A set of dimples indented his cheeks, giving him a boyish charm that was severely at odds with the rest of him. "Keep talking," he murmured. "You're just turning me on more."

I rolled my eyes, but inside, I felt a similar pull to

demand he continue speaking, too. Because his voice reminded me of home. A strange sensation because he wasn't anything like the wolves of my usual acquaintance, and yet, I felt an odd sort of kinship to him.

*No, that's not right. It's just my wolf wanting me to roll over and let him have his wicked way with me.* A fantastically dirty idea, to be sure, but not one I wanted to entertain.

*Besides...* "Shouldn't you be focused on your brother right now?"

That wiped the grin from his features, his jaw hardening all over again. "You know, I would, but someone stabbed me." He gestured angrily to his shoulder. "How the hell am I supposed to drive up to Silver Lake in this condition, *Makayla*?"

"If that's your way of asking me to help you, it's not a good approach," I drawled, folding my arms.

His gaze immediately went to the knife in my hand, his stance tense. "As though I'd trust you to help me."

A fair reply. But I sort of wanted him to ask me anyway.

*Silver poisoning,* I thought again, mulling over the conversation Vex had engaged in with his unnamed colleague. Could this all be related somehow?

*But what did silver poisoning have to do with trafficking innocent girls?* I asked myself again.

My gut said it was somehow linked to whatever had happened to Alaric's brother. Vex's conversation clearly tipped off the suspicion.

However, if I were being completely honest, I did feel sort of bad about stabbing Alaric right as his father delivered earth-shattering news.

So I didn't have a choice, really.

*It's the honorable thing to do,* I realized with an internal sigh. "Look, I'll drive you. But we need to get that wrapped up first." I gestured to his injury with my chin. It looked pretty ghastly, and yet he didn't even seem to feel it.

*Strong wolf*, I mused. *Hot wolf.*

That last phrase obviously came from my animal side. Not that she spoke in full sentences, more in feelings. But yeah, I blamed her for the electric sensation humming through my veins.

I blamed him, too.

Just for existing.

His smolder wasn't helping. "Careful or I'll think you're apologizing."

"If you consider that an apology, then you should go back to grade-school English and request a lesson on apologetic terms. Pretty sure they come in the form of *I'm sorry* or *please forgive me*, not *I'll drive you.*"

The muscle-clenching in his jaw abated a little, his mouth twitching.

He obviously found me amusing.

Too bad the feeling wasn't mutual.

"Seriously, do you want a ride or not?" I demanded.

Now that pretty mouth turned upward in a panty-melting smile.

*Holy shit*, I thought. *That's not fair at all. He shouldn't just unleash that thing on unsuspecting women!*

"Oh, I absolutely intend to take you up on a ride," he replied, his tone shifting from gravelly to liquid sex in an instant. "But I need to heal first to give you a proper ride in return." He winked, then caught my wrist in an expert move and twisted the knife from my fingers.

I'd still been standing with my arms folded, and the sharp edge came dangerously close to my breast; only, he raised it to my throat and backed me up against the wall, his expression lethally serious.

"Stab me again and I'll lock you in a cage you can't escape from." The words were a breath against my mouth, our position change knocking me entirely off-kilter and leaving me weak and defenseless against him. He even had my thighs pinned beneath his.

*Well, this is embarrassing. Nathan and Marc would be chewing me out for letting this sexy shifter distract me enough to get the drop on me.*

I panted against him, not out of fear, but from a different sensation entirely.

He'd just disarmed me and pinned me with only one working arm.

And fuck if that wasn't the sexiest move I'd ever experienced.

*I really need to get laid more,* I realized.

My arms hung at my sides, useless to his overpowering masculinity. I knew exactly how to break his hold—by digging my thumb into his wound and squirming out of his reach—but another idea crossed my mind. A dangerous one. A notion that I knew would bring him to his proverbial knees, similar to what he'd just done to me.

He released me before I had a chance to act on it, his narrowed gaze telling me he'd read the intention from my expression. "I have supplies at my place, as well as a car." He slid the dirty blade into the hilt attached to his belt and pulled out his phone again to type something into it. "Cleaners will be here soon. Once they arrive, I'm leaving." His sapphire eyes captured mine. "If you're serious about helping me, feel free to follow."

The invitation hung between us as a choice, one he turned his back on as he started up the stairs.

*Help or leave.*

I knew my decision before he reached the top stair.

If there was a link between the silver poisoning and the girls, I had to know.

*Follow it is,* I thought, trailing after him.

# CHAPTER 4

## ALARIC

My thighs burned with restraint.

*Don't move.*

*Don't touch.*

*Don't fuck.*

I didn't have time for this madness. But I couldn't concentrate on anything beyond Makayla's medical ministrations.

She'd *stabbed* me. And now she was playing nurse in my apartment. Just without the appropriate outfit. She still wore her T-shirt and jeans, her long, dark red hair pulled high into a messy bun, as she bent over my shoulder and focused on stitching me up like some sort of damn quilt.

It infuriated me.

And it made me want to bend her over my bed and drive into her from behind. My shoulder would protest, but I'd welcome the pain as I unleashed an equal amount of agony into her pretty little body.

She deserved it and worse.

I wanted to make her crawl, beg, and mewl, all in that order. And then I'd consider letting her come. Maybe.

Her sweet scent slithered around me in a taunt, her fingers brushing my overheated skin as she finalized the last of her handiwork. "Almost done," she whispered, her throat bobbing as she swallowed.

She stood between my sprawled legs, my upper body shirtless as a result of her destroying my jacket and shirt. Blood was a bitch to clean, so I'd just tossed both items into the bin, then I'd kicked off my jeans and boxers and had washed up in a quick shower.

Which left me clad in only a towel.

A *tented* towel.

Because my intended mate was scant inches from my groin and drowning me in her sensual perfume. It'd be so easy to grab her by the hips and pull her into my lap. She'd protest, but only for a minute. One kiss was all I needed to subdue the stubborn female inside and call upon her wolf.

Shifters were always easy to seduce.

We were sexual by nature, our animals very much in charge of our instincts.

Which was why I had to ignore the inclination, because if I started playing with her now, I'd never make it up to Silver Lake by dawn.

Besides, she didn't deserve my cock. *Because she fucking stabbed me.*

Why was that such a damn turn-on? I should be furious—and I was—but I also wanted to drag her onto my bed and dare her to use that knife again.

A growl lodged in my throat, my wolf riding me hard.

I'd heard rumors about fated mates and what it did to the male. Those rumors weren't wrong. My drive to take her and mark her as mine nearly surpassed all reason.

*I don't know her.*

*I don't want to keep her.*

*Therefore, I will not have her.*

My wolf snarled in protest. I ignored him. He could

rant and rave later. Maybe I'd even take him for a long run through the woods up at Silver Lake.

He calmed a little at the thought, freedom a gift we rarely indulged in as a result of living in New York City. It was hard to find a place to shift and run without being seen. I managed it every now and then, especially when I couldn't take the itching sensation beneath my skin anymore.

Bitten wolves could shift at will, but that didn't mean we could go without our wolves for long periods of time. I pushed it on occasion, which always ended in a bad bout of aggression.

Which explained my mounting annoyance now.

It'd been at least three weeks since my last run. And after last night's date with silver chains, I felt a little cagey at the moment. That, coupled with the beauty standing between my legs, nurturing a wound she'd inflicted, and it was no wonder I craved a hard fuck.

*Mate,* I thought, tasting the word. *Damn it.*

I still didn't know what kind of wolf she was or what she'd even been doing locked up in the basement of that bar. Although, *locked up* seemed like a bit of a stretch, as she'd pretty easily freed herself.

"What were you doing there?" I wondered out loud. "At Bob's Bar, I mean."

*Yeah, Bob's Bar—a classy name for a classy establishment. Fucking Mets fans.*

"What were you doing there?" she countered, her voice huskier than before.

It had my gaze trailing over her to land on the apex between her thighs. *She's totally wet for me.* Just as I was hard for her.

Any other day, any other time, and I'd silence the

conversation with a kiss and work through our mutual attraction in an entirely different way.

Our animals didn't overthink a damn thing; they just wanted to fuck and coexist.

No emotions.

No strings.

Just pleasure.

At least for me.

Only that wasn't our situation at all. She was meant to be mine, whether I wanted her or not.

"Well?" she prompted when I didn't reply.

"I asked first." A childish response, but true. "Besides, you already know I work for E.V.I.E. So what do you think I was doing there?"

"I thought you slayers focused on vamps, not wolves."

"He was part vamp," I pointed out. "And I had a favor to return after what he did to me and Violet last night." I flinched as the needle slipped, puncturing my wound.

And my dick pulsed in response.

*Damn.*

Makayla cleared her throat. "What did he do to you and, uh, Violet?"

"Ambushed us and a bunch of humans at a nightclub," I muttered. "He had an army of vamps lying in wait, and they shut the doors and turned the place into a damn bloodbath. Then they knocked us out, and I woke up chained to a chair." If Violet's royal vamp boyfriend—or whatever the hell she considered him to be—hadn't shown up, the night might have gotten worse.

But the vamp had helped remove the silver holding me down, leaving me just enough slack to free myself after he'd disappeared with Violet.

"Needless to say, I wasn't pleased, and I've been hunting his ass all day to ensure that didn't happen again."

I met her blue gaze. "Your turn, sweetheart. How'd you find yourself locked in a cage?" Because the bar had been mostly quiet, from what I'd seen of it. No signs of vamps hunting for prey, just a few lackeys who made poor guard dogs.

"First of all, I'm not your sweetheart." She punctuated that with a particularly painful swipe of the needle. "And I didn't *find* myself locked up. I purposely let them catch me."

"Yeah? Why?"

She shrugged. "A new challenge."

Shifters might not be able to scent lies, but I caught hers from a mile away. "Liar."

Makayla merely smiled. "I didn't promise you the truth."

"No, you didn't," I agreed as she finished her last stitch. "But now you've just made me curious."

"Sounds like a you problem, not a me problem." She took a step back.

Or she tried to, anyway.

Because I caught her hips before she could complete the movement, and I yanked her forward instead. Her hands went to my shoulders, which stirred a hiss from me in response.

*Okay, grabbing the woman was a bad idea.*

But my instincts had fired, and I'd not been ready for her to leave my space yet. *Mine,* my beast demanded.

I ignored him again and focused on the female standing before me. "What kind of wolf are you?"

"One who doesn't appreciate manhandling."

My lips curled. "I blame my animal. He's rather keen on the idea of mounting you." I felt her responding shiver through my fingertips, her wolf reacting to my statement.

*Yeah, you definitely want me,* I thought at her animal. Not that she could hear me. That wasn't a mating trait for my kind. But perhaps it was for hers because I swore her animal peeked at me through those pretty blue eyes, approval radiating from within.

*Fascinating.*

"That's not going to happen," Makayla gritted out, her hands falling to my wrists to give them a threatening squeeze.

I tightened my grip in response. "You're the one who offered me a ride," I reminded her.

"Yeah. *Home.* Because you can't drive in this state, but I'm seriously considering making you try now." Her nails dug into my skin, yet she didn't tell me to release her. No, it was almost as though she was holding on instead. I wondered if she was even aware of it or if her wolf had taken charge of her physical reaction.

"Can you drive a stick?" I asked, purposely adding the double entendre to my tone but also meaning it. "My Mercedes is a manual." No point in owning a car of that caliber and making it an automatic. Of course, I rarely had an opportunity to drive it. New York City wasn't exactly automobile friendly.

Her nostrils flared. "I'm excellent with my hands and very comfortable around a manual transmission."

"Tease," I replied, using my grip on her to move her backward a step as I stood up. Our torsos met in a heated kiss, my groin touching her lower belly and allowing her to feel my interest. We were wolves, which meant hiding a mutual attraction was impossible. I could smell her arousal just as she could scent mine.

It didn't embarrass me.

Nor did it seem to embarrass her.

She merely stared up at me in direct challenge, her alpha personality shining through.

Part of me wanted to reply by capturing her mouth and nibbling that full lower lip hard enough to draw blood. Domination came naturally to me, and an alpha female would absolutely fight back. I'd have to earn her submission. Any other day, and I'd give up my plans for a chance to bring her to her knees.

Alas, pack responsibilities trumped everything else in my life. It didn't matter that I'd left shortly after my eighteenth birthday. Silver Lake would always be my real home. Twelve years in New York City hadn't changed that.

"I'm going to get dressed now," I said in a low voice. "You're welcome to watch." I dropped my hold from her hips and tugged on my towel, letting it fall to the ground at our feet.

Her eyes danced downward, appreciation clear in her features as her grasp around my wrists tightened even more.

"I'm going to need my hands," I told her after a beat of intense silence.

She swallowed and slowly released me but didn't shy away from me or try to flee from the room. An omega wolf probably would. Maybe even a beta. But not her.

Perhaps fate had chosen the right pairing after all. I'd always preferred obedient women in the bedroom, mostly because I wanted to fuck and then leave. However, Makayla would certainly be a different sort of experience, one I might actually indulge in more than once.

Of course, she would be the only female I could take from this point forward anyway. A realization that made me growl as I stepped around her toward my closet. What the hell was the point in castrating a man after finding his destined mate? I supposed it happened to the female as well, but maybe not to Makayla. Because she wasn't a Bitten wolf.

Not any of the others I knew, either.

*So what are you?* I wondered. I could feel her eyes on my ass as I bent over to pull on a pair of jeans. I turned around to finish the job and grinned while she watched me carefully tuck myself in first. Yeah, I was still hard. And probably would be all day until I convinced her to let me bend her over and take her from behind.

The fated-mate pull was notorious for inducing a healthy amount of lust between wolves when they first met. I just hoped it tapered off after the needs were met. If not, I might seriously have to consider caging her. Because I wasn't a fan of the idea of having to track her down whenever I needed a release.

That would surely piss her off.

Which would lead to even hotter sex. *Angry fucking. Yes.*

An idea for later.

From the glint in her gaze, she'd picked up on my vibes. Perhaps because she sensed the anticipation from my wolf. And I was willing to bet her wolf had similar ideas for me.

It didn't matter if her kind refused to believe in fated mates. That didn't make it any less real.

I slid on a pair of socks and my boots, then grabbed a black sweater—the color matched my mood—and disappeared into my bathroom for a quick minute. Makayla stood by the door of my bedroom when I returned, her arms folded across her chest. That T-shirt of hers was a bit baggy but did little to hide the curves beneath.

Curves I'd felt pressed up against me only moments ago.

Curves I intended to explore with my hands again at some point.

Curves that were mine to keep.

An intriguing concept. I'd explore it more later.

"Ready?" I asked her.

"Waiting for you, Prince Charming," she drawled.

"*Prince Charming*?" I repeated, arching a brow.

"You just wasted ten minutes of my life getting dressed, brushing your teeth, applying deodorant, and doing whatever else just happened in there."

"Combing my hair," I said, completing her list and removing the innuendo from the latter part of her statement. "Had I wanted to jerk off, you would have been waiting for a bit longer than a handful of minutes. I also would have ensured that you could watch." I winked at her and moved around her in the doorway. "Stop staring at my ass, sweetheart. And let's go."

She muttered something unflattering at my back.

*Definitely going to be a challenge.*

I grabbed my keys and wallet and met her at the front door. "After you, *princess*."

She snorted.

I smiled.

*Let the chase begin.*

# CHAPTER 5

## MAKAYLA

FOUR HOURS in the car with Alaric was a really bad idea. The glimmering lights of New York City were still bright in the rearview mirror, and already I couldn't breathe.

His scent overwhelmed me, cloaking my shoulders in a thick blanket of his masculine warmth.

My wolf practically rolled around inside me, belly up, begging him to take me right here in the bucket seat of his sporty little car.

I grabbed the stick shift between us and curled my fingers around it as I inhaled deeply through my mouth.

Didn't help.

That just made me salivate.

*Damn wolf pheromones.*

I'd met some potent alpha types in my day, but Alaric certainly took the attraction to a new level. It probably had something to do with the whole "fated mate" theory.

First of all, no.

Second of all, I couldn't be a fated mate to him because I wasn't from this world.

Third of all, *no*.

I'd consider bedding him—especially after seeing what he had to offer. Because damn, *yes, please*. But mating? Yeah, no, that was a hard pass and never going to happen.

One comment regarding my chosen path would put that whole notion to rest. He'd realize I was incapable of such a connection and move on. Best to just set the record straight now by rejecting the whole concept of us being created for each other.

My purpose was to help those who couldn't help themselves. Anyone who wanted more from me would be strongly disappointed in the outcome.

Packs had their enforcers.

Humans had me.

Hell, this *realm* had me now. Because they weren't strong enough to care for themselves. Hence my reason for being here.

And no man—hot alpha or not—would ever change that.

I glanced at my mirrors again and noticed Alaric watching me. "Yes?" I prompted, not particularly enjoying the sensation of being studied so intently. We hadn't said much to each other since entering the car. He'd just handed me the keys, then I'd followed the signs to exit the garage beneath his condo complex and started the journey north.

"Well, I'm trying to figure out how you know where we're going," he said slowly. "Either you're a mind reader or you're psychic. Which is it?"

I rolled my eyes. "Neither. You mentioned Silver Lake earlier, remember?" It was around the time I offered to drive him. Or maybe right after that. I couldn't recollect the exact sequence but definitely recalled that he'd mentioned Silver Lake. It wasn't the sort of detail I'd soon forget, considering I was from the same pack, but in *my* world, not his.

"And you just happen to know where that is?"

My lips twitched. "As a matter of fact, I do." But I

really didn't want to explain *how* I actually knew that, so I added, "I'm a wolf, Alaric. I know all the packs in this region." A half-truth—I knew all the packs in *my* world. I'd also learned the names of a few in this reality during my first mission in this universe. That'd been an eye-opening experience.

Marc had hand-selected me to help him on the assignment because of my background in human trafficking. Only, I hadn't realized we'd be headed to a new world when he'd recruited me for the case.

I'd been shocked upon our arrival, not only to learn about a brand-new reality but also to meet so many inadequate supernaturals. Such as the vampires in this world and the fact that they could be slayed by a simple stake to the chest. How pathetic could one get?

But then the real adventure had begun as we'd searched through the underworld of crime, desperate to locate Sapphire. We had finally found her in a seedy situation surrounded by vampires and wolves.

Which had been my introduction to the shifters in this reality.

To say I'd been unimpressed would be an understatement.

My jaw ticked as I considered the events of that mission and the reason I'd returned to this realm just a few weeks ago. Sapphire had sent me on another assignment, saying some women needed my help. She had a penchant for fortune-telling, something I'd learned after rescuing her, and I tended to take her premonitions seriously.

However, now I wondered if there'd be an ulterior motive to her plans. It would be just like her to meddle in my affairs. And she would have foreseen the news articles about the Bloodsucker Serial Killer, just like she would have predicted the link to the wolf beside me.

*Oh, you crazy bitch,* I thought as the puzzle pieces came together in my mind. She'd told me the ruby ring was a payment in its own way. I'd thought she meant because it allowed me to travel realms at random.

Now I understood.

*Not happening, Saph. Not ever happening.*

If she were here, she'd just be grinning in that loony way of hers before losing herself to another premonition.

"Something entertaining?" Alaric asked, his gaze still locked on me in the way a hunter eyed his prey.

"Just thinking about a friend of mine," I replied. "She's the reason I'm familiar with packs in this territory." Because it'd been a wolf who had kidnapped her. Fortunately, it hadn't been one from Silver Lake. That would have been awkward.

"And have you been to Silver Lake before?" he pressed.

I considered how to answer that. Technically, yes, but not in this world, so… "No."

"Yet you know where we're going."

"I have a reasonably good sense of direction," I returned. "Are you going to backseat-drive the whole way, Alaric? Because that's going to get old very fast." He wasn't actually trying to correct me at all, but I wanted to change the subject away from how I knew our destination.

Because he was right.

It'd been a slip on my part.

While Silver Lake might be a notable pack name in the region, the directions on how to find it might not be as well known. Or maybe they were and he was just testing me. Either way, I should have asked for directions in the beginning just to avoid all this nonsense. But I'd been so consumed by his scent that I hadn't considered much beyond trying to drive without climbing into his lap and demanding he take me into oblivion.

"Secrets only intrigue me more," Alaric finally said after a beat. "However, I'll let you keep your lies for now. Just know that I don't take kindly to duplicity, so if you try to hurt me or my pack, mate or not, I will kill you."

The serious quality of his words told me he meant them.

"Wouldn't that hurt you almost as much as it would hurt me?" I wondered out loud. The true mates in my world, at least the ones who had fully bonded, often didn't survive when their other half died. Perhaps it didn't work that way for Bitten wolves?

"It would, yes," he replied, his gaze finally leaving my face. "But protecting myself and my pack is worth the pain of losing a mate."

I considered that, my brow furrowing. His statement reminded me of Nathan. He would sacrifice everything for his pack, too. Because he was the Silver Lake Alpha.

Alaric had alpha written all over him, but not in the same way as Nathan.

The former struck me as a lone wolf, while the latter was very much a leader. Nathan would never live in the city, because Silver Lake was his heart. But Alaric's condo confirmed he didn't reside up north. His space was too well lived-in for it to be a temporary home, suggesting he didn't stay with his pack often. Which meant he couldn't be a true alpha.

However, as we drove, I felt his aggression mounting. Like his wolf wanted *out*.

His focus had completely left me and gone to the windows, his vigilance making me uneasy. "Are you expecting something?" I asked. "Or someone?"

He didn't reply, his behavior seeming to be more animalistic than humanlike as he rolled down the window to sniff the air. His palm went to his chest, his fingers massaging the muscle there in a rhythmic caress that nearly distracted me from the road ahead because I pictured him doing that to my breast.

*Goddamn it.*

My thighs clenched, his pheromones hitting me hard in the nostrils and drowning me in lust.

*Definitely. A. Bad. Idea,* I chanted to myself, my lips parting as I forced myself to breathe through my mouth.

"You're tempting my wolf." The low growl in his voice only heated my blood further.

"Trust me, it's not intentional," I managed to reply, my throat dry from his intoxicating aroma. God, no one had ever tempted me like this before. He had to be an alpha. Or at least close to one. Because damn, I actually wanted to get on my knees for him, and that wasn't like me at all.

I was an enforcer by nature. I'd even trained to become one until Nathan had introduced me to his black ops agency. Then my entire world had changed in a matter of years.

I bowed to no one.

Yet a dark part of me wanted to bow for *him*.

*What the hell?*

I tried to shake the sensation by rolling down my window to inhale fresh air.

"I can feel it." Alaric's words came out in a rumble of sound that vibrated through the car. "The turmoil. The pain. The danger."

"From your pack?"

"Yes."

*Shit.* Nathan could do that, too. Well, to an extent. He could speak telepathically to packmates within a certain distance of him. He could also control his wolves, but that wasn't an ability he regularly used.

"Is it your alpha?" I wondered. "Is he calling to you?"

"Something like that," he muttered. "More like my wolf is reacting to a disturbance." He cut me a sideways glance. "Bitten wolves aren't telepathic. We adhere to a hierarchy with an alpha at the top, and we're bonded in a way, but nothing on the mental hive-mind level."

I tried to ignore his knowing stare, but I felt it engraving a hot path along my cheek and my neck. "What?" I demanded after a beat, not liking the way he kept staring at me. The intensity in the car was overwhelming enough without his incessant *looks*.

"Your questions tell me you don't know much about Bitten wolves. And yet, you know where Silver Lake is located. That's very interesting, Makayla. Very interesting indeed."

"It just means I haven't studied your kind. I wouldn't read too much into it."

"Oh, but I am," he drawled. "Did you know we can be killed from things like, say, a knife wound?"

"Most wolves can die from that," I pointed out. "Especially when strategically placed. But yes, I'm aware your kind is more susceptible than others."

"And yet you didn't know about our alpha structure." The taunt in his tone had my grip tightening on the steering wheel. Was he trying to piss me off?

"I didn't say that, did I?" I countered. "I just asked if you could sense your alpha."

"Hmm," he hummed, his body less tense than before. It seemed talking to me had calmed him down. Or perhaps having both windows open helped.

I decided to keep the fresh air flowing as I drove, but the tension licked the air again as I turned off the highway toward Silver Lake.

And it mounted even more with each passing mile.

My stomach churned beneath the weight of Alaric's

growing aggression. "What is it?" I finally asked, my tone breathless. We were maybe thirty minutes out now, and I was ready to pull over and just wish him luck. He could still shift while injured. Then he could run home. Wouldn't be too hard with all the woods around here.

"He's dying," Alaric whispered, the words killing my idea to pull over and instead having me press harder on the gas. "Fuck, I can feel it. He's… his wolf… he's *seeking*." The word came out on a pant, his head falling back against the headrest.

Damn, had he been driving, he would have crashed or stomped on the brakes by now. Knife wound or not, he couldn't seem to move.

"Faster." His voice broke on the word. "Please. Go. Faster."

I didn't hesitate, just did exactly what he asked, putting all my skill and supernatural ability into navigating his sporty little car at highly illegal speeds. Fortunately, it was too late for anyone to be out and too early for cops to be lying in wait.

The path came easily to me, years of driving similar roads in another version of this world paving a trail that wasn't difficult for me to follow.

Until we entered the primary grounds, littered with trees and dotted with homes throughout a sprawling woodsy landscape.

"I need to know what house," I said quietly, although I suspected that I already knew.

So when he gave me the same location of Nathan's main residence, those suspicions were confirmed.

Alaric really was an alpha. Perhaps not *the* alpha of Silver Lake, but the brother of one.

Which meant he'd be the alpha's successor unless he had a strong beta nearby.

*That* was what had Alaric's wolf all up in arms—he could sense his pack's need for him. Their leader was dying, and the animal souls were calling for their heir, begging him to come home, to make everything whole for them.

*I stabbed an alpha,* I realized. *An alpha who thinks I'm his mate.*

The ring on my finger suddenly felt like ten pounds, the reminder of my ability to escape a welcome beacon in my thoughts.

Only, my wolf snarled in response. She wanted to stay.

*We need to go,* I argued.

But as we pulled into the alpha's driveway, I knew I couldn't leave.

*"The silver package has been delivered. They should be dead by morning."*

The sun was kissing the horizon now, the early morning air heavy with mourning.

*"Tyler's been poisoned."*

*Dead by morning.*

Two different conversations, both with related outcomes.

*This isn't a coincidence. It's all related. If I run now, I'll never understand why. And those girls... someone has to save those girls.*

Alaric sat frozen in the passenger seat, his nostrils flaring. I almost reached for him to offer comfort, to say something, anything, to calm him down. But the vibrations growing in his chest kept me at bay.

"I need to go inside." Darkness underlined his tone, his wolf riding just beneath the surface.

"Do you want me to come in with you?" I didn't mean to offer that. I didn't mean to even speak.

But his midnight gaze met mine, the pupils blown wide to engulf his irises. It left me wondering what he looked like in animal form. *Ebony eyes and brown fur to match his hair.* I could almost see it. He'd be big, too.

"He's dying," Alaric whispered. "I can feel it."

I swallowed. That wasn't exactly an answer to my question. But I suspected he was beyond reason at the moment. Grief altered behavior, made some more aggressive and others weaker. Alaric would likely fall in the former. "I'll come in with you," I decided out loud. It just felt right. I'd examine why later.

He nodded as though I'd answered some unspoken question. Then he unbuckled his seat belt and exited the car without another word.

# CHAPTER 6

## ALARIC

MAKAYLA'S PRESENCE calmed my wolf, her gentle energy something I didn't realize I needed until I stepped into my former home.

I'd grown up here with Tyler.

Our father had been the Silver Lake Alpha.

Then he'd passed the property to Tyler once he'd taken over the mantle as leader. It had been a gradual transition with my brother being bitten and turned into a wolf on his eighteenth birthday. He hadn't fully taken over the pack until his twenty-second year. By that point, I'd already left.

I, too, had been turned on my eighteenth birthday. Just two years after Tyler.

Our animals had immediately warred, our desires to dominate passionate and strong. It had been expected since our father had been an alpha as well.

My wolf's innate power, however, hadn't been expected. Tyler being the oldest had meant he should have naturally inherited the mantle, but my inner beast had disagreed wholeheartedly with the birthright. And had we fought one another, I would have won.

So I'd left instead.

Had gone to New York City, found a job with E.V.I.E., and had lived there ever since.

Oh, I visited on occasion. But never for long. It just wasn't my home anymore. It was Tyler's pack now, a point that became clear as everyone moved out of my way with each step I took.

The enforcers—all old acquaintances of mine from my younger years—nodded their respects.

"He's in the master." The statement came from Paul, an old friend of my mine from high school. He'd become a pack enforcer soon after graduating, the position suiting him. But right now, I wasn't interested in reminiscing.

Hell, I never wanted to reminisce.

This wasn't my life anymore.

I glanced at him in brief acknowledgment of his presence, only for him to gesture through the open living area to the corridor beyond it.

Like I didn't know where the main bedroom suite existed in my former residence. *Dick.*

I swallowed a responding growl of annoyance and walked by the lanky, shaggy-haired enforcer without a word.

Hardt, the pack beta, met me outside the doorway of the master bedroom. He dipped his chin in subtle greeting. I ignored him as well, focused on the scene inside.

My parents barely paid me a glance as I walked through the threshold.

Makayla lingered in the hall behind me, her scent an abiding caress to my senses that helped me focus on the scene before me.

*Tyler.*

*Pale.*

*Weak.*

*Dying.*

His eyes were closed, his skin damp with sweat. The pack physician stood beside him with a grim expression. I didn't need to ask to know the verdict. I could see it in the shallow rise and fall of my brother's chest.

The strong alpha I knew resembled a broken skeleton on the bed, his chest exposed and covered in ash-colored lines. *Silver*, I thought, swallowing. *That's how they know he was poisoned.* It was evident in the discoloring of his veins. It went all the way to his arms and down to his wrists.

A machine beeped beside him.

An IV bag hung next to it.

But one look at the bed confirmed there was no coming back from this.

I checked him for signs of injury or a puncture wound and found nothing. "How did he become infected?" I asked, my voice gruff.

Maybe it wasn't the right thing to say.

Maybe I should be focusing on saying goodbye and telling my older brother how much I used to look up to him as a kid.

But I hadn't slept in over forty-eight hours, thanks to the hybrid asshole situation. And all I wanted to do was find out what the hell had happened to Tyler.

"We don't know, but Alpha Warren and Alpha Hendrix have both fallen ill with the same condition." My father's blue eyes lifted to mine, his emotions guarded. I expected nothing less from the man who'd led this pack for thirty years before transitioning the reins to his firstborn. He'd always told us growing up that an alpha's job was to maintain order and unity among the wolves. Emotions played a large part in that leadership, but it had to be regulated. And sometimes, being in charge came at the cost of our own hearts.

We couldn't be seen as weak or crumbling in the face of a broken pack.

"Were they all together today?" I frowned. No, not

today, but… "Yesterday." My brother had phoned me to say he'd be in the city. He'd wanted me to stop by for breakfast at a hotel up in Manhattan. I'd intended to meet up with him.

Alas, the whole hybrid situation had happened, and I'd ended up chained to a chair in the basement of Blood Thirteen. After escaping, I'd spent the morning and afternoon tracking the prick who'd bested me, completely forgetting about meeting up with Tyler.

A decision I very much regretted now. Would I have been able to save him? Or would I have ended up just like him?

"They met for lunch to discuss the disappearance of Gloria Mansfield." My father's tone told me it was a sore subject.

Not surprising. Gloria Mansfield was Alpha Warren's daughter. "I didn't realize she was missing." *Just like Valaria Crimson,* I thought, wincing. I hadn't found her in time, the hybrid and his lackeys having finished her off before I'd had a chance to locate her. He'd made it personal with that gruesome scene, the invitation clear.

*Come out and play, slayer.*

The bastard had even carved my initials into her foot, just to ensure I received the message.

I'd followed him on the twisted offer, and he'd rewarded me at Blood Thirteen by having his minions lock me up with Violet. *"I want to make him watch this time."*

*Demented jackass,* I thought. Part of me had wanted to prolong his death when I'd found him, but I hadn't wanted to risk him going all fire monster on my ass again. So I'd shot him before I could rethink the situation.

"It's not been broadcast," my father replied, referring to Gloria. "But no one has seen her in five days, and it's not like her to just disappear."

No, it wasn't.

But she hadn't been in the hybrid's lair earlier, only Makayla. Had she seen her at some point? It was on the tip of my tongue to ask, but my mother's whimper drew my focus to her.

"Can we do this elsewhere?" she asked softly. "I... I don't want to have this conversation... *here*."

"Right, of course," I agreed, coming forward to kneel beside her at the bed. "Sorry, Mom."

"It's okay," she whispered, leaning into me as I wrapped my arm around her shoulders.

I glanced at my father, noting the concern in his gaze. He could handle a lot, but my mother's grief was not one of those things. Which meant I had to help in his absence.

He couldn't console his mate and the pack all by himself.

That was why he wanted me here.

To live up to my responsibility as an alpha, and not just any alpha, but an alpha destined for this pack.

I'd turned my back on everyone when I'd left Tyler in charge. Because my wolf had been the strongest of the two of us. I should have challenged him. But I couldn't. He was my brother. My flesh and blood. The oldest of the Calder boys. He was supposed to be the stronger one, the one meant to lead, while I moved on with my life and one day found my own pack.

Except I'd never found a pack because my wolf only wanted Silver Lake.

I swallowed, the rightness of being here soured by the wrongness of this situation.

*Silver poisoning.*

*How the hell did you let someone poison you?* I wanted to demand. *You're better than that. You're an observant motherfucker, too. So what the hell? How could you allow this to happen?*

All unfair questions.

What I should really be asking was how *I* had let this happen.

Had I been there, maybe I would have sensed something—*anything*—that could have prevented this. Because clearly it happened during their meeting. Maybe they ingested the poison through a meal or a drink? Or had it been airborne? It definitely hadn't been injected, a fact my eyes had already confirmed, but knowing *three* alphas had been taken down confirmed the gut instinct that it'd been inserted via another method.

Would I have noticed it had I been there?

*Fuck.*

*Fuck!*

I wanted to scream, to rip the damn room to shreds, to demand the physician to do something more useful than just stand there and wait to call the time of death.

This was ludicrous.

Bitten wolves could die as easily as humans, but we healed quickly. My shoulder was proof of that. I hadn't used that arm to hold my mother, but I could at least move my opposite limb now. In a few hours, I'd be able to swing it around, too. And after that, it'd be good as new.

Mostly because of Makayla's nursing.

I found her still lingering in the hallway, her expression blank as she watched me through the open door. Hardt studied her intently, his hazel irises pulsing with interest.

I nearly growled at him.

Wolves could sense mating bonds, and while I might not have scent-marked Makayla yet, our connection would be crystal clear to everyone nearby.

Fortunately, she seemed completely oblivious to the asshole sizing her up. *Maybe ponytails aren't her thing, jackass,* I thought at him, noting his long black hair. *Seriously, what the hell were you thinking?*

Some men could pull off the whole thick-mane-of-hair thing, but not Hardt. He resembled a motorcycle wannabe with his tats and muscular arms. Why my brother had picked him as a beta, I had no idea.

*Totally not worthy.*

My wolf *harumphed* in agreement. Of course, he was focused on Makayla, not the pack hierarchy.

I had to agree with that assessment, too. She deserved a lot better than the likes of Hardt.

Her pretty blue eyes caught mine. Rather than offer comfort, she cringed, then winced, and then shuttered her gaze, making me frown.

*What are you hiding, little wolf?* I nearly asked.

Because guilt practically poured off her in waves, irritating my inner beast.

My jaw clenched, my instincts rioting. *You know something. I can smell it.*

But I couldn't go over there and demand she start talking, because it meant leaving my mother.

*We're talking later*, I told Makayla with my eyes.

She gave a slight nod in agreement, clearly reading the intention from my expression.

I'd meant what I'd said earlier—if I found out she had ill intentions toward me or my pack, I'd kill her. Fuck fate. I could take the pain of living without a mate, because it'd be better than remaining with a duplicitous wolf.

"Alaric." My mother leaned harder into me, her nostrils flaring as she took in the scent of her family. It seemed to calm her momentarily, her shoulders shuddering as she wrapped her own arm around my lower back. "I've missed you."

"I've missed you, too, Mom," I murmured back to her, glancing at my father again.

He just gave me a nod of approval. I supposed that was better than him saying, *Do more.* Which was his usual phrase when we spoke.

He'd never come out and said it, but he was disappointed that I hadn't challenged Tyler for the position of alpha. A pack could only be as strong as its leader, and as the strongest of his sons, it had been my responsibility to take charge.

Only, I hadn't wanted to do that to my brother.

A fact that, he and the others would argue, had made me weak in the end.

And unworthy.

Swallowing, I shoved the feelings aside and focused on my goodbyes. I hadn't seen my brother in over a year. I'd actually been somewhat looking forward to seeing him yesterday, too. Not that I could say that now.

*Damn, man,* I thought, reaching out to draw a thumb down his arm. My shoulder protested the movement, but I fought through the pain. Tyler was worth it. This moment. This final touch.

My chest warmed, stirring a sensation deep inside me that stroked me to my very soul.

It was as though I could feel my brother touching me back, telling me everything was going to be okay, and promising to be there in the afterlife.

Maybe it was in my head.

But I believed with all my heart that he knew I stood beside him now.

*Don't let me down,* he'd say. *Don't let them down.*

*You know I will,* I would reply. *It's what I do.*

*Fuck off, Ric. You can say that bullshit to Dad, but I know the real you. I know why you did it.*

*You don't know anything,* I'd argue. Because that was what I always said. Just as I always smiled afterward. *You really did know.*

*I did,* he would agree. *I really did.*

My throat worked as I tried to hold on to that conversation, to have a real one now, to will him into consciousness to verbally spar with me one last time. This was my brother, my own flesh and blood, my only real link to the pack.

No one else knew me like he did.

It was why I'd left.

The pack would never understand that choice or the heartache that went with it.

*You were meant to lead them first,* I whispered to my brother now. *You should still be leading them now.*

*What can I say, little bro? Fate's a bitch.* It wasn't really him, the words in my mind ones of my own making, but man, they sounded just like him. Because I knew that was exactly what he'd say to me now.

He'd tell me to buck up, shut up, and get the job done.

He'd tell me this was always meant to be my path.

And then he'd tell me, *You'd better not let Hardt take over. He's not a Calder, Ric. He's not you.*

I reached down to grab my brother's hand, giving it a squeeze.

His fingers squeezed back.

So weak and subtle, but there. A passing of the torch. A blessing. His way of saying, *You've got this.*

*And what if I don't?* I wanted to ask him. *What if I don't have this?*

*Then I'll be hovering over your shoulder, cheering you on every step of the way.*

I felt the brush of fur, his wolf nudging mine, all of it

taking place inside my soul and forever ingraining the moment in my memories.

And then it was gone.

*He* was gone.

His last breath kissed the air, and I swore he murmured my name. *Ric*.

He could finally let go because his baby brother had returned home. The new alpha was here. His job was done. And in that final second, I felt his energy pass through mine, blessing the rightful heir.

*Me*.

My mother crumpled into my side, her tears dampening my sweater.

I didn't cry. I remained tall, my hand still wrapped around my brother's fingers, my eyes glued to his face. *Gone. He's gone.*

But I felt him all around me, *in me*, his memory one I wouldn't soon forget. Eighteen years, I had run in his shadow. He'd taught me everything he'd known. He'd groomed me just as my dad had groomed him. We'd taken all the same classes, played all the same sports, and competed with one another every step of the way. It hadn't mattered that I was two years younger; I'd performed on his level and above.

It had only pushed him harder.

Which, in turn, had pushed me harder.

A rivalry born of the best intentions.

A brotherhood I very much missed.

He'd grown into a powerful alpha, his business savvy extraordinary. I had taken my skills elsewhere, but that hadn't made either of us any less proud of the other.

My father might call me weak for not challenging to become the true alpha of this pack.

But my brother had known it was out of respect for my elder.

A familial birthright.

One passing to me now after twelve years of being on my own. I stood before a pack I no longer knew. Beside my parents, who might not even want me here. Before a beta who had challenge written into his expression despite the fact that my brother had literally just died.

If he tested me now, he'd regret it.

I'd destroy him.

There'd be no compassion. I'd put him in the fucking ground.

Because taking me on the day of my brother's passing was a death sentence to anyone who wished to interfere. My wolf growled in agreement, my need to run strong and overpowering my ability to think.

*I can't lead like this*, I realized. *I can't walk out there and offer comfort when all I want to do is rip this damn house apart.*

Someone poisoned my brother.

That someone had to pay.

But I couldn't do that here. I had nothing to go on other than a meeting. And I wouldn't be able to travel back to see it for another few days.

There was a funeral to plan.

A burial ritual I had to attend.

In honor of Tyler's memory. In preparation for consoling the pack. In necessity of taking on a leadership role I'd never wanted.

*I'm alpha now.* The realization slammed into my chest, knocking the wind from my lungs. *I can't do this.* It was never meant to be me.

Only, it was… and I'd turned it down.

And now they all hated me.

Or just didn't know me.

*Goddamn it.*

I needed air.

I needed to fucking breathe.

*I can't do this.* I managed to somehow unlatch my mother and hand her to my father, his blue eyes shrewd and narrowing into disapproving slits.

I just shook my head. I couldn't handle his bullshit right now. It'd been too long since I'd let my wolf out for a run, and if I didn't leave this room right now, I'd shift and rip something apart.

*Tyler's dead.*

*He's fucking dead.*

*Because I wasn't there.*

*Because I put my job before him.*

*Because I put my own pride before the pack.*

No, that wasn't fair.

It wasn't right.

But hell if I could make myself focus now.

I pushed through the house, ignoring everyone and everything in my path, and burst out through the door of the back patio.

Then I took off at a sprint into the woods. *I just need to run and breathe.*

*Run and breathe.*

*Run.*

*And.*

*Breathe.*

# CHAPTER 7

## MAKAYLA

*So, this is awkward,* I thought as I took in the room of grieving wolves.

My heart had broken a little for Alaric, his family, and his pack. Not just because of the loss of his brother, but because of the innate tension flourishing through the small space. Something had clearly happened between Alaric and his pack, something that had alienated him or caused him to feel like an outsider. The discomfort still lingered in the air, making it difficult to swallow.

*No wonder Alaric bolted.*

His emotion had been so raw that I briefly considered waiting until later to approach him, but time wasn't something we had a lot of at the moment. This situation had clusterfuck written all over it. They'd even mentioned that another girl had been taken. *Gloria.* What did the disappearances have to do with the silver poisoning? Clearly something since Vex had received a call about it.

*I really need to talk to Alaric about that call.*

If anything, he'd probably appreciate a distraction.

Besides, I'd known the guy for less than a day, so I didn't feel any guilt about originally keeping the information to myself. However, staying silent going forward would be a real dick move. If that had been my brother lying in that bed, I'd kill anyone—and have every right to—who denied me information that would bring his killer to justice.

Decided, I slipped away to find Alaric. Not that anyone noticed me to begin with; they were all too lost to their grief to pay attention to me.

Alaric's woodsy scent surrounded me as I stepped outside, but I didn't see him. Following my nose, I discovered him pacing in the woods at the back of the property.

His fists clenched at his sides as his body trembled with unadulterated aggression. It whipped across my senses, provoking my wolf. His anger and hostility had mounted over the last several hours, reaching a high point now.

"When was the last time you shifted?" I demanded, recognizing the animal in his pacing. *His inner beast craves freedom.*

Alaric paused and slowly raised his head. His eyes were black, his wolf barely contained, both the man and the animal filled with rage. "Go the hell away, *mate*," he growled, spitting the last word as though it left a dirty taste in his mouth.

"But—"

"Not another word," he bit out. "Unless you want to fight or fuck, go away."

My brows shot up to my hairline. "Excuse me?"

He stalked toward me, his expression akin to an animal hunting its prey. My wolf urged me to run because she knew he would chase. And if his wolf caught her, he would mount her. Which led me to thinking about Alaric taking me like an animal from behind. *Shit!*

As Alaric drew closer, I mentally snapped at my wolf to control herself and held my ground. I'd never been one to back down, yet anxiety danced around the edges of my arousal. *What the hell?* I'd faced bigger, scarier men in my job and had never felt a twinge of uncertainty or fear. *One super-hot alpha looks at me like he's going to eat me for lunch, dinner —and dessert—and I'm freaking out?*

The wicked smile that spread across his face told me he smelled my interest. If he hadn't just watched his brother die, I would've knocked that expression right off his face.

I assumed he would stop prowling forward when I didn't back up in defeat. But he kept advancing, stirring a shiver deep within me. My face heated, partly from the dominant vibes coming off Alaric in waves and partly because I took an involuntary step back.

*Arrrrgh! Don't back down,* I screamed at myself. And yet, I retreated another four steps with Alaric immediately eclipsing all the space I'd put between us. My back hit a tree, halting me midstep as he cornered me against the bark wall behind me.

*Well, shit.*

Alaric pressed into me, his palms settling on the tree trunk on either side of my head to cage me between his arms. I swallowed hard at the glimpse of fury and lust in his intense gaze. The emotions coiled so tightly together that I doubted he knew the difference between them. "You heard me, Makayla."

*Heard what?* I wanted to ask, my mind fracturing beneath the heady scent of man and wolf.

And *why* did it always sound like sex when he said my name? My nipples stiffened, and electricity buzzed over my skin. *What is* wrong *with me?* This alpha caveman bullshit should not make me wet and desperate to take him up on his multiple offers for a ride.

Alaric inhaled, his chuckle dark and not one of amusement but one of a man who knew his prey wanted what he had to offer.

I quivered in response, hating that my body gave me away.

But his did as well, his arousal a heavy weight against my lower abdomen as he leaned into me to ensure I felt every hard inch of him.

"What's it going to be, Makayla?" he asked, his lips grazing mine. "Because I'm not interested in seeing, hearing, or fucking smelling you unless you are here to *console* me like a good, obedient little mate. So either fuck off or kneel and put that sharp tongue of yours to better use."

I almost pointed out that I hadn't spoken much since walking out here, but I couldn't think beyond the pounding of my heart.

His words were abrasive, but my wolf didn't understand anything except his need to dominate. The large, prominent bulge in his jeans pushed into the apex between my thighs, and my inner animal started panting. I fought to keep her intrigue from showing in my own breathing patterns and cleared my throat while silently commanding my wolf to *back off. For the love of all that is holy, he's grieving his brother!* She snarled at my tone, then marched to a dark corner and curled up to pout.

Alaric's body vibrated with unchecked emotion, needing an outlet before he exploded. I had no intention of being the thing he used as an outlet for his grief. A quick, angry fuck sounded hot, but it would only further complicate this situation. Something we definitely didn't need.

A smirk tipped up the corners of my mouth. "Can you see the 'fuck you' in my smile? No? That's because it's not fucking happening, jackass. I just came out here to tell you what I know about the silver poisoning. This shifter Neo—"

In the blink of an eye, I could no longer breathe or speak because Alaric had his hand wrapped around my throat—*the hand of his good arm. Shit.*

His blue irises smoldered with accusation, the aggression coming from Alaric—*the man*—just as much as from his wolf.

"You know something about the poisoning?" he demanded in a deadly voice. "And you are just telling me this now, *why?*"

I tried to respond, but his hold still cut off my flow of oxygen. Clawing at his fingers, my body twisted this way and that, trying to free myself. But he had pressed himself so tightly against me that I could barely move.

Fortunately, he seemed to realize I couldn't talk and loosened his grip just enough to allow me to gulp in a lungful of air. I coughed and sucked in a few more deep breaths before croaking out, "If you stop trying to choke me, I might tell you. But right now…" I paused to inhale, the oxygen burning my raw throat. "You might as well finish the job because if I get free"—another breath—" I'm going to fucking kill you."

He ignored my threat. "Tell me about the silver."

Bitten wolves didn't possess compulsion, which meant that even as an alpha, Alaric couldn't force my will. And yet, both my wolf and I were drawn to his commanding presence. Which really pissed me the hell off.

"Are you a part of this, Makayla?"

"*What?*" Was he fucking high? "Are you seriously asking me that?"

His hand tightened again, not enough to cut off all of my air but enough to make a point. "You weren't exactly trapped in that cell. And you did fucking stab me, after all. Your actions don't exactly scream innocence, *Makayla.*"

"I took you home," I wheezed as he loosened his grip

again, allowing me to speak once more. "Fixed you up. Brought you to your brother so you could say goodbye." Each reminder came out in a rasp of sound, but the point remained. "I *helped* you."

Alaric shook his head as if trying to clear it of clutter. "Something's not right," he muttered. He considered me for a beat before his eyes narrowed to slits. "Are you even my fated mate? Or have you figured out some way to trick me? Did you—"

Not only did I find myself unable to breathe again, but my feet also left the ground as Alaric lifted me up. The expression on his face held so much hate and bitterness that I could smell it tainting his normally intoxicating scent.

Black dots danced in front of my eyes, clouding my vision. *Shit!* I choked and dug my claws into his arms as hypoxia began to crawl toward my brain. My wolf slammed into me repeatedly, trying to keep me from passing out and to force a shift so she could protect us.

"The distraction at Blood Thirteen. Were you part of that ambush, Makayla? Because if you had anything to do with Violet almost being killed—"

I didn't understand why, but his protective tone at the mention of Violet—while accusing his supposed fated mate of trying to kill her—tipped me over the edge I'd been teetering on.

*Enough of this bullshit.*

He still had a weakness I could exploit.

I reached for his damaged shoulder and pressed my thumb into the wound I'd created earlier. Oh, he'd healed some, but not nearly enough, and his wince and resulting growl told me it still hurt like a son of a bitch.

Dick move, yes. But so was choking me.

I pressed harder, provoking him to shift. Taking

advantage of my newfound space, I wiggled my legs out from beneath me and wrapped them around his waist like a vise, catching Alaric by surprise and knocking the wind out of him. Then I partially shifted and swiped a claw up his front, slicing his sweater and skin in the process, drawing blood. His resulting shock allowed me to push his hand away from my throat so I could finally take in air.

Part of me wanted to collapse with relief and just breathe, but I could already sense Alaric beginning to regroup.

I fought the dizziness and sucked in as much oxygen as I could and began fighting my way out of his hold. He tried to loosen my grip around his waist while I struggled to hold on, my thighs clamping even tighter around him. All our grappling tipped us over and took us to the ground. We tussled and wrestled, both of us attempting to dominate the other, but neither of us managed to keep the upper hand for long. His injured shoulder worked in my favor, suggesting he'd be an even fiercer opponent at full health.

I jumped to my feet, and he quickly followed.

Neither of us held back as we fought, and I couldn't help being a little impressed and a whole lot turned on. My wolf basked in the glow of his powerful vibes, loving the way he proved himself to be an alpha in his prime. She believed he could protect us and would be possessive, dominant, and a worthy mate. Which really irritated me. Sometimes I felt like I needed to remind her of her status as an alpha wolf and not a submissive.

Alaric finally took me down and pinned me to the ground, his domineering growl vibrating me to my core. We were both covered in superficial wounds, our breathing hard from being ramped up on adrenaline. I stared into his eyes and saw a reflection of my own emotions.

*Anger.*

*Respect.*

*Desire.*

Except Alaric was also drowning in an ocean of grief.

He lowered his head, his eyes still glued to mine, and covered my mouth with his own.

Lust ripped through me and exploded with the force of a hurricane, knocking the wind right out of me. I knew I shouldn't, but I kissed him back anyway, lost to the high of the moment and the violence erupting between us.

It felt right.

Perfect.

Intense.

And just for a moment, I completely forgot what had provoked our fight. Because all I wanted was to feel. To breathe him in. To lose myself to the flawless moment of *us*.

# CHAPTER 8

## ALARIC

*MINE.*

I blamed my wolf.

There was no other reason I would have kissed Makayla. He was riding me hard after sparring with her.

*Fuck.*

*Bite.*

*Claim.*

*Mine.*

She moaned, opening her mouth and giving me the opportunity to slip my tongue in and taste her. *Damn.* She tasted every bit as delicious as she smelled. If her mouth was this good…

*Temptation personified.*

*Goddamn, I want her. I really want her.*

Fighting with her had been hot as hell. I'd taken all of my anger out on her, and instead of whimpering and begging, she'd hit me back just as hard, refusing to submit. She was all alpha female, and it was sexy as hell. Which meant her submission would be all the more satisfying in the end.

Shit, I'd never been this damn hard before. If she wasn't my fated mate, then whatever pheromones she'd used to trick me were absolutely working.

Makayla wrapped her arms around my neck, throwing herself into our kiss, making it clear that if I wanted to take her, she'd be game.

*So tempting.*

It would definitely alleviate some of the tension suffocating me. Forcing her submission, hearing her beg, fucking her hard until she screamed my name. Yeah, that would relieve *a lot* of stress.

But I held back. Not because she didn't deserve to be dominated—the pretty little she-devil needed a damn good spanking for stabbing me and then using my wound against me. A bratty move, yet also admirable. Because I would have done the same thing.

No, I held back because the timing was shit. And my growing feelings of possession and desire were at odds with my usual relationship preferences. I didn't do possessiveness. I fucked and left. End of discussion.

Oh, but how I wanted to dominate this woman.

Claim her. Make her beg for more. *Yes.*

I took everything out on her, and she didn't cower or hesitate, her tongue battling mine with a ferocity that rivaled my own.

Every lick and nip of her teeth felt like fate reminding me that she'd made Makayla for me. That this woman beneath me was my equal in every fucking way imaginable.

*No. I refuse to accept that. I don't want a damn mate.*

I ripped my mouth from hers and rolled off of her to flop onto my back beside her. My shoulder shot a responding pang down my arm, but I ignored it.

*Jesus fucking Christ. What the hell was that?* I demanded of myself. *What happened to my self-control?*

"Ummm, so... uh," Makayla struggled to find words, then gave up after a few sputters.

Silence descended upon us, and the tension I'd worked out began to creep back in. The aggression had lessened, but the grief and the weight of my responsibilities still threatened to crush me.

"So, yeah, we're even now, right? I stab you… you strangle me… all good?"

Surprised, I barked out a laugh that actually held a glimmer of humor. "No, sweetheart. We'll be even when you get down on your knees and crawl."

Makayla jackknifed up and twisted her torso to glare down at me. Her wild red hair floated around her like fire with the rising sun illuminating it from above. Her blue eyes sparked with irritation, and it made me want to smile. If only because I knew it would piss her off. Angry and riled up looked damn sexy on her.

"I. Don't. Crawl."

The smirk made its way to my lips this time. "We'll see."

She growled, which did nothing to help the hard state of my dick. *Maybe we just need to fuck and get it over with so I can focus on important shit instead of a naked and panting Makayla.* My wolf rumbled in agreement with that plan. He favored any path that ended up with Makayla on her back while I rutted between her thighs.

"So, as I was trying to say earlier, you know, before you almost killed me"—she scowled—"*which makes us even, jackass,* I overheard something about silver while in Vex's cage."

And just like that, the distraction disappeared along with my hard-on. Anger flooded my system once again, and all the secrets I'd sensed in Makayla reawakened my suspicion. "Tell me," I demanded before rolling up into a sitting position to study her features. "And for the record, I warned you what would happen if I found out you were a threat to my family and pack."

"I had nothing to do with the silver poisoning, idiot," she snapped.

"Hmm." I hadn't formed a solid opinion on that yet. "Tell me why I should believe you."

"Don't burn your best bridge to catching your brother's murderer, Alaric."

*Not a bad argument. But I suppose it depends on what information she has for me.*

I nodded and gestured for her to continue. Mostly because I didn't trust myself to respond kindly out loud.

"Okay, so I overheard a call between the hybrid and some other guy about silver packages being delivered. The guy on the phone said they—not sure who, just 'they'— would be dead by morning. I think they meant your, uh…" She trailed off, glancing away, but I followed what she meant to add. *Brother.* She assumed they meant my brother. "Well, Vex sent Neo off to tell the boss," she concluded lamely.

"The boss?"

"Yeah, your expression right now? That's how I felt when I learned he wasn't the jackhole in charge. I followed him to learn more about the trafficking—"

"Trafficking?"

"Interrupt me one more time, and I'll stop talking."

I fought the urge to grin and waved for her to continue again.

"I thought he was the boss because of all the rumors about him and his auctions. But apparently, there's another boss. Which I could have asked him about had you not killed him."

"Had I not killed him, he would have morphed into a

giant, fire-breathing shifter thing, and as I'd already lived through that once, I wasn't keen on doing it again."

She gaped at me. "What?"

*Hmm, shock.* I'd felt the same way when I'd seen the creature in action at Blood Thirteen, which meant she definitely hadn't been involved that night.

My suspicion ebbed a little. She seemed to be telling me the truth, and my gut told me I could believe her.

"It was a real shitshow," I muttered, referring to Blood Thirteen.

Makayla's expression turned pensive as she absorbed the new information.

*It's probably the fire-breathing-shifter thing tripping her up.*

She nodded and shook her head twice. Then finally said, "Well, I'm guessing the silver package is the one delivered to your brother."

"And Alpha Davies as well," my father announced in his deep voice as he stepped around one of the gigantic hickory trees I used to climb with Tyler as kids. "Alpha Hendrix and Alpha Warren have also passed." His blue eyes gleamed with disappointment as he stared down at me. I'd seen that look a hundred times before, but somehow it weighed more heavily on my mind today.

*This isn't the son I raised.*

*Alphas hold the pack together.*

*You can't let them see you like this.*

*You can't be weak.*

The words rang in my ears despite having heard none of them aloud. I didn't want to accept their truth, but I couldn't run away from this life anymore. I had no clue how I would ever live up to Tyler's memory. How I would earn his place and unite my pack.

*Start with solving his murder.* My wolf responded positively to that thought. He didn't understand the words, but he would feel my need for vengeance. I knew he sensed the absence of Tyler's wolf. And like my brother and me, there was love and respect between them, mixed with the innate need of an alpha to dominate and lead.

"Alpha Davies... is a fourth alpha?" Makayla commented, drawing my father and me from our silent conversation. *More like scolding*, I thought bitterly.

He bobbed his head once. "Yes. We just received the call. Tyler"—his voice wobbled the tiniest bit, then he straightened his shoulders and the confident alpha returned—"Hendrix, Warren, and now Davies."

"So someone is definitely targeting alphas, then," Makayla said.

"Yes, it would seem so," my father agreed. He cocked his head to the side and studied her, tension building in the awkward silence.

My father's blue eyes drifted from Makayla to me, and he raised a dark eyebrow. "Are you planning to introduce me to your mate or continue ignoring her and letting her wander into other houses uninvited?"

I bristled at my father's jab. He'd insinuated that Makayla hadn't been welcome in Tyler's home—*my former childhood home*. But I was his brother, and as my mate, that should have automatically made Makayla part of the small group of friends and family.

In addition, I'd wanted her there. And I *hated* the truth of it.

*I don't want a mate.*

*I don't want to need or be needed.*

*I don't want this fucking life that's being forced upon me.*

But despite my desire to reject her, she was my mate, nonetheless, and it infuriated me that my father would make her feel unwelcome. Even if the provocation had really been directed at me.

I sprang to my feet and turned to offer Makayla my good hand—*I'm not* always *an asshole*—but she'd already risen to her full height.

Indicating my father with a jerk of my chin, I stated, "Makayla, meet my father, Hawk Calder. Former alpha of the Silver Lake Pack."

Then I gestured to Makayla. "Dad. This is my, uh, *mate*." My jaw clenched a little too hard on the word. There'd been no way of keeping our destined relationship a secret. We'd just have to deal with the whispers and assumptions for the next couple of days. At least it kept other males from sniffing around her. Killing packmates wouldn't garner me any favors.

My father nodded, his nose rising in a subtle inhale as his eyes roamed over her neck, looking for my mark. When he found no trace of my scent or bite on her, his focus returned to me, and it seemed as if his disappointment had only grown.

"Nice to meet you," Makayla said, seizing my father's focus once more. "I wish it were under better circumstances. But I'm only here to help Alaric take down the bad guys. Then I'm off to do what I do."

My wolf protested at her declaration, growling and pacing in frustration. I agreed with him, but for different reasons. I might not want Makayla as a mate, but nor did I wish to spend my life like a monk.

I cleared my throat. "Makayla isn't a Bitten wolf. She has other priorities." Rather than elaborate on that, I opted to focus on what was important. "I found her locked up in a cage in New York City. She might have some useful information about who did this to Tyler."

Makayla nodded, then told my father what she'd just told me.

He considered her story for a long moment, gave her a

single nod, and then refocused on me. "I need a minute, Ric. *Alone.*"

My jaw ticked, not just at the abrupt—and *rude*—dismissal, but at the knowledge of what he wanted to discuss. *Ascension.* It was needed. The pack would fall apart without an alpha at the helm, but I didn't feel ready to lead them. They weren't mine to guide. Not anymore. However, there was no avoiding the conversation. Whether I accepted or not, we had to discuss it.

I could almost hear Tyler in my ear saying, *Suck it up, bro.*

My gaze slid to Makayla for a beat. Adding a mate to the mix, especially one who kept secrets, would only make my job more difficult.

She had a lot more to tell me. Whether or not she would remained to be seen, but I sensed the mystery in her aura. She'd only told me part of her story. And I hadn't failed to notice her lack of a reason for why she'd been investigating the trafficking.

"Ric?" my father prompted.

"I heard you," I bit out. "But first, I'm taking Makayla to a house she's welcome in—*mine.*"

Without another word or glance at Makayla, I stalked back to the house and around the front to the car. She followed without a word, slipping into the passenger seat and buckling in for the short drive to my two-bedroom cabin. I parked in the driveway, only three blocks away from my brother's house, and stared up at the home I'd never considered to be mine. I owned it, but I rarely stayed it in.

Makayla's scent floated around me, a comforting wave of feminine florals that soothed my wolf.

*Since when do you like perfume?* I demanded, unbuckling my seat belt and stepping out into the spring air. The fresh aroma did nothing to cool my desire for the female exiting the car. Nor did it do anything to dismantle my growing anger over this entire situation.

This mating pull with its mounting attraction was a pain in the ass.

*Distracting and unwelcome.*

I unlocked the front door and stepped inside, expecting it to be a dusty mess. However, it looked as if it had been kept up, or recently cleaned. The smells in the air reminded me of...*home*. At another time, that would have calmed and comforted me. But as I took in the scene before me, I had a feeling it had been my packmates who'd prepared my home for my return. On inspection, I even found the refrigerator stocked with food. They'd gone out of their way to care for someone who'd not been there for them, and it darkened my mood.

The front door shut quietly while I stood in the kitchen brooding over being a shitty packmate and potential alpha. I didn't want to deal with Makayla—my *mate*—so I spun around and marched into the hallway, where I expected to find her awkwardly waiting. Instead, I found her in the living room studying the pictures on the walls and mantel.

Clearing my throat, I caught her attention and jerked my head to the left. "I'll show you where everything is."

I grabbed a towel and an extra toothbrush from a linen closet in the hall, which also appeared to be freshly stocked, and pointed out the bathroom on the way to the guest room. "Your room," I grunted as I tossed the items onto the bed.

Makayla remained oddly silent, but as I felt no desire to talk, I appreciated the reprieve. Our eyes locked for a moment, only broken by my quick glance at the bed behind her. I hardened, and my wolf brushed his fur under my skin, encouraging me to follow through with the ideas running through my head.

Makayla sucked in a quick breath and crossed her arms over her chest, drawing my gaze to her generous breasts. The position put them on display, and her rigid nipples poked into her T-shirt, making my mouth water.

I squeezed my eyes shut and shook my head as though I could toss away all the lustful thoughts and images. "Fuck this shit," I muttered as I turned to leave.

"Oh, wait. Coffee?" she asked, her voice soft and coaxing.

I glanced over my shoulder, frowning darkly, but gave her a sharp nod and led her to the kitchen. There had to be a coffee maker somewhere. I opened two cupboards before spying one beside a myriad of other cooking utensils —were all of these new?—and set it on the counter for her.

"Thank you." Her lips tipped up into a small smile.

"I need to see my father. I don't know when I'll be back."

Makayla considered me for a minute, making me start to wonder if she planned to bolt as soon as I left. *Those cuffs are looking better and better, baby.*

"I'll be here when you get back," she finally replied, as though she had to think about it.

I didn't know if I believed her, but I didn't have the energy to push it. Instead, I simply gave her a curt nod and left to find my father.

# CHAPTER 9

## MAKAYLA

I SIGHED in absolute bliss as the first sip of hot coffee slid down my throat. It felt like an eternity since I'd indulged in one of my few true vices.

After another sip and a happy moan, I carried the mug into Alaric's living room and went back to snooping. There was a sprinkling of photos and mementos on the walls and the fireplace mantel, but I didn't find anything where he looked older than a teenager.

He clearly didn't come home often, and I had noticed his subtle surprise at entering and finding the cabin prepared for his arrival. It only added to the perception of his disassociation with his pack. But they obviously cared about him because someone had prepared his cabin for his arrival. My pack would have done the same thing for me, except I didn't own a cabin back home.

The thought of home reminded me that I hadn't checked in with Nathan or the shifter council since I decided to investigate Valaria Crimson's death. My index finger brushed over the enchanted ruby, and I considered using it to head back right now, despite my promise to be here when Alaric returned.

*Hmm, had it really been a promise, though?* I wondered. *Would he even care if I disappeared?*

His muttered curse before he'd left pretty much summed up my own feelings about this electricity between us. I'd never before experienced the pull I felt with him. It drew me to him like a magnet, something that seriously annoyed me.

Never mind my hussy wolf, who wanted to just roll over and beg him for a thorough lay. Her reaction to Alaric worried me a little. She'd never been so keen on a man. Attracted, sure. But with Alaric, she actually fought for control as though she wanted to break free and give in to the desire between us. It was too soon. Too fast. *Too much.*

*Go ahead and pout,* I told her. *It's. Not. Happening.*

Hmm, maybe I should leave. It would certainly be easier if I skipped town—or the universe, if I wanted to be technical—and forgot all about Alaric and his ridiculously good looks, his alpha vibes that ruined a girl's panties, and his mouth that was made for sin.

*Jackass,* I thought as I squeezed my thighs together.

However, I had to weigh the mate bullshit against my mission. I couldn't leave those girls. And I'd become invested in finding out what the hell the silver poisoning had to do with the trafficking cases.

*They need me.*

*Alaric needs me.*

*For now.*

The last drop of my beverage disappeared, and I stared morosely at my empty cup. I wanted more, but I hadn't been to bed in… a day? Maybe two?

Although, the likelihood—even without the coffee—that I would fall asleep seemed slim.

I wandered to a window and surveyed the familiar landscape. Everything here was the same and yet different. *How different?*

My wolf whined, and I thought about how long it had

been since I'd shifted. Probably a week or so. The city wasn't the best place to let my inner animal loose. And whenever I went home, which wasn't often, my wolf had the freedom to run and play as much as she wanted. Which explained the similar sense of belonging I'd felt upon arriving.

While our Silver Lake resided in another realm, this place still felt like home. And my wolf wanted the freedom I typically gave her when surrounded by trees and our pack.

*We could both use a good run, huh?* Maybe I could burn off some of the raw hunger eating at me and have some fucking control over myself the next time I saw Alaric.

Leaving my clothes in the guest room, I left the cabin and immediately shifted before trotting to the nearest copse of trees. I decided to explore for a while, see what differences there were in the two realities of Silver Lake, before going for a swim.

I loved the city, but sometimes I really missed the lake. It was home.

# CHAPTER 10

## ALARIC

"I DON'T THINK it's a coincidence that you found your mate the same week as your brother's death," my father said quietly from his seat beside the fire in his den.

It had taken me nearly two hours to find him here.

After leaving Makayla at my house, I'd wandered on foot back to Tyler's home, expecting my parents to still be there. But they'd left shortly after the pack coroner had arrived to handle my brother's remains.

A morbid part of me had forced myself to stand there and watch the process of removing him from the house, like I needed to witness every minute in order to believe this was really happening. Several other packmates had joined me in silence, their distress a palpable wave to my senses, one my wolf had ached to console.

But I didn't know how.

Did I touch them? Talk to them? Offer words of wisdom?

All I wanted was to go for a run, to hide in the woods, and never return.

However, alphas didn't cower. So I'd opened my arms and hugged them. Or maybe they'd hugged me. I couldn't really say, only that it had felt right to accept the strength of the pack and offer my own in return.

It only lasted a few minutes. Yet I could smell their wolves on me now as I stood inside my father's upgraded den. He and my mother resided in the house next to Tyler's, a home they'd built during my youth because they'd known our family home would one day belong to the new pack alpha.

The windows lining the back of his proverbial cave overlooked the same woods as his den-like office back at the other house. However, the deck outside was bigger.

He sat by the fireplace, the chair beside him empty and waiting for me.

I considered his opening statement regarding Makayla and our mating not being a coincidence. It wasn't exactly a greeting, but I preferred it over his usual disappointment.

"It wasn't just the same week, but the same day," I clarified as I took the seat beside him, a small coffee table the only item between us. He'd already poured two glasses of scotch from his minibar across the room. My glass lacked ice, just the way I preferred it.

"I found her right before you called me earlier," I continued as I picked up the tumbler. "She stabbed me when you told me about Tyler."

My shoulder still ached. Although, I'd forgotten about the pain while sparring with Makayla. And it hadn't just been the physical agony, either. But everything. For a blissful moment, she'd given me peace.

Which unnerved me more than I wanted to admit.

My father's lips curled into genuine amusement. "Is that why you favored one arm during your little wrestling match outside?"

"I should have known you were watching," I muttered before taking a long gulp of the fiery liquid. It was just what I needed to take the edge off.

"I suppose you'll tell me the injury is why she won," he added, ignoring my reply.

"She didn't win."

He grunted. "She had you by the balls, son. At least own it."

"I seem to recall pinning her." I set my glass down. "Which means I won."

"Except you kissed her afterward, thereby giving her the win." He grinned to lessen the insult. "It's all right. Your mother gave me quite the chase, too. She got all the way to Ohio before I *pinned* her down."

A snort came from the doorway. "You mean until I finally let you catch me." My mother's long, dark hair hung over one shoulder, her slender arms folded as she arched a brow at my father. "And why did I let you catch me, hmm?"

"Because you wanted my heart, of course."

"Of course," she deadpanned.

I just shook my head. I knew their story from years of hearing it repeated in my youth.

My father had used his computer skills to locate her whereabouts, then he'd ordered flower deliveries from every florist within a ten-mile radius to send her lilies—her favorite flower—all day, every day, *everywhere* she went.

She'd finally given up the chase when she'd arrived at a new hotel to find her room already flooded with fresh flowers. It had been clear that he knew her patterns and locations and that he wasn't going to stop inundating her with gifts until she agreed to heel.

"I do love those earrings," my father said, eyeing the rubies on her ears. Another story I knew all about—he'd given her those the day she'd let him catch her.

"My stalker gave them to me."

"Yeah?"

"Yes." She pushed away from the door. She appeared almost normal despite today's trauma, but the light red rims of her eyes underlined her deep-seated pain. She wouldn't let the pack see her cry. She probably wouldn't even let me. Mostly because she wanted to be strong for everyone else. The only one she'd allow to see her true agony was my father.

Which explained why they'd returned here before the coroner had finished.

She'd needed a moment.

My father likely had as well.

Just as I'd needed one, too. *While Makayla watched.* She'd accepted my pain and had allowed me to essentially take out my frustrations on her. *Just like a mate.*

I swallowed, pushing the thoughts away.

Except I could feel my father offer solace to my mother now and vice versa. They were both hurting *together*. Grieving in their own way and helping bolster the other through their mating bond.

Emotions weren't a weakness. They were a strength. And alphas knew better than anyone the importance of harnessing that strength to better support the more vulnerable members of the pack.

Transitions of power were never easy, especially under these circumstances.

Which was precisely why my father hadn't even waited an hour before demanding I come see him.

He wanted to talk about my ascension.

And all this small talk about mates was just his way of breaking the ice.

The only reason I allowed it was because of my mom. She needed this far more than my father or I did. She needed a discussion of normalcy to distract herself from the agony ripping her apart inside.

"I don't recommend wooing by stalking, Alaric." My mother's advice came with a soft yet slightly chastising glance at my dad. He merely smiled, no sign of regret in his expression.

"I think I'll be okay." Because I didn't intend to *woo* anyone. Makayla might be my mate, but there would be no wooing between us.

My mother gave me a knowing smile. "Playing hard to get?"

"Not playing at all," I drawled.

"Hmm," she hummed, a habit I most certainly picked up from her. She always made that noise when she didn't believe something, just like I did.

"Don't do that."

"Don't do what?" she asked, feigning innocence.

"Makayla doesn't want a mate, and neither do I."

"Hmm," she repeated.

I glowered at her. "Seriously. Don't."

Her green eyes glittered in response. Tyler used to give me a similar look when amused, his forest-green irises the same shade as our mother's. He'd had her thick, dark hair, too. As did I. But my eyes were the same shade as my father's, just like my ebony fur rivaled his, while Tyler and my mom had brown coats.

"I give him a week," she said conversationally, glancing at my father. "He'll be on his knees, begging, by the end of it."

I huffed a laugh. "Not a chance in…" I cleared my throat. Cursing in front of my mother would be in bad form. She might be an alpha female surrounded by wolves all day, but I was her son. And while I might not see her often, a certain amount of respect was always due to one in her position. "It's not going to happen," I rephrased.

"Why am I having déjà vu?" she asked, looking upward

and tapping her elven chin. "Oh, right." She gave my father a knowing look. "Looks like he'll be chasing her after all. Like father, like son." She blew us a kiss, then turned to leave with a genuine smile on her face.

It might have been at my expense, but I didn't begrudge her the reaction. Mostly because I knew it distracted her, if just for the moment.

The same mirth shone in my father's expression, putting me a little at ease. I picked up my drink to take another sip as he shook his head. "You're so fucked."

I choked on the liquid, his curse so unlike him. "*Dad.*"

"Just calling it like I see it, son," he replied, lifting his glass to click it against mine. "She stabbed you, huh?"

My mood soured. "In the fucking shoulder."

He chuckled and shook his head. "Well, this pack can use a strong female. What kind of wolf is she, anyway?"

"Not one I recognize," I muttered. "And she won't tell me."

"Interesting," he replied. "I'd say Lycan, but she's too pretty. And she's not feral enough to be Totemic."

"Lycans can be pretty." Not that I'd really met any. I shook my head. "Yeah, I don't know what she is. As I said, we met this morning."

He nodded. "Well, whatever she is, something tells me a few enforcers are going to have their hearts broken by her."

I rolled my eyes. "No one will have any hearts broken because she's not theirs."

"So she's yours?" he countered, the taunt clear in his tone.

My jaw ticked. "I'm not having this conversation."

"We're absolutely having this conversation," he countered, some of his mirth dying behind a mask of seriousness.

*And here comes the alpha,* I thought, downing the rest of my drink for some much-needed liquid courage. I might be an alpha, too, but if anyone around here could put me on my ass, it was my dad.

"I shouldn't have implied that she wasn't welcome at Tyler's home," my father said suddenly, shocking the hell out of me. "I was hurting. Hell, I *am* hurting. And my anger over the situation was misdirected. I'll make an apology to her directly as well. She's obviously welcome here. Just like you."

"Am I?" I asked, meaning it.

"Of course you are, Alaric. This is your pack."

"But is it?" I pressed. He started to open his mouth, but I lifted my hand. "No, please, hear me out, Dad. I haven't lived here in over a decade. I left to allow Tyler to lead. I barely know these people now. Yeah, I grew up with a lot of them, but I'm not the boy I was at eighteen."

"No, you're a man at thirty," he countered. "A man who belongs here with his pack."

"Do you think the others agree with that?" I wasn't blind. I'd felt their wariness, had seen some of their uncertain looks, had experienced the awkwardness of those hugs outside. "Whenever I've come back, I've been forced to run alone. I'm too alpha for the enforcers. Too lone wolf for the pack in general. How am I supposed to lead?"

"Oh, Alaric. You were born to lead this pack."

"Yeah?" I arched a brow. "Then why was I born second?"

"Because you needed the extra push to succeed," he replied without missing a beat. "Fate intended for you to challenge your brother, but you walked away instead. And now…" He trailed off, his gaze going to the fire. "And now she's forcing your hand."

"Are you saying Tyler *died* because I didn't take up the

mantle of alpha?" I demanded, furious by the insinuation in his statement. "Because I decided to let my brother lead rather than *destroy* him?"

"You wouldn't have destroyed him," my father muttered, ignoring my other comment entirely.

Because he believed fate had done this to right a wrong. *My* wrong.

My fingers curled into fists, shooting a spasm up my arm to my shoulder. But fuck if I could feel it. Not over the rage boiling inside me. "I left for the betterment of the pack," I said through my teeth.

"You left because you didn't want to take down your idol," he corrected, flashing me a look that was all wolf. "Tyler was a worthy alpha. But that doesn't detract from the fact that you are stronger, faster, and more appropriate for Silver Lake."

*More appropriate*, I repeated to myself, growling through the words. There was nothing appropriate about being pit against one's flesh and blood for a position we'd both been trained for.

"Why haven't you found another pack?" my father asked suddenly, his eyebrow arching. "You're an alpha, son. It's your natural inclination to find other wolves to mentor. Yet you haven't been drawn to any of the surrounding packs. Why?"

"Because I was too busy making a life for myself with E.V.I.E."

He laughed without humor. "Bullshit. You didn't find another pack because none of them called to you like Silver Lake."

My jaw hurt from clenching my teeth so hard. Rather than reply, I just glared at the fire.

He wasn't wrong.

But he wasn't right either.

I hadn't wanted another pack. Too much responsibility. *Too much pain.*

Leaving Silver Lake had been the hardest mission of my life. I'd done it for all the right reasons, but that didn't mean it'd felt good.

Leaving had made me both strong and weak. Strong because of how difficult it had been. Weak because... I should have fought my brother for the right to be alpha.

But how could I hurt the man I'd considered my best friend all my life?

How could I challenge the one I'd looked up to for guidance and training?

He'd been bitten first, his alpha nature awe-inspiring. I'd never expected to be so much like him. I'd never anticipated being *stronger*.

I ran my fingers through my hair and blew out a breath. "I can't ascend until I know what happened to him," I blurted out. "It won't be right. I need to find his killer, Dad. I need to *avenge* him." Hell, I needed to avenge them all. "Someone is targeting alphas. Which means I could be next. I'm not even going to discuss ascending until I fix this problem. And even then, I'm not promising anything."

My father's wolf stared at me, the alpha in him unappeased by my unspoken rejection. "You'll do what's right for the pack, as an alpha should."

"What's right for the pack is finding out who is targeting alphas, and taking him down," I countered.

His nostrils flared, his animal snarling at me through his darkened gaze. "And who will console the pack while you're off playing slayer, Alaric?"

"Do you really think they can be consoled with their alpha's murder unsolved?" I ached a brow. "Wouldn't bringing the killer to justice serve almost as a right of initiation back into the pack?" I leaned toward him. "They don't even want me, Dad. I'm not one of them. I'm an outsider. And before you say it, yeah, I only have myself to blame, and I own that. But if I'm going to stand any chance at winning their respect, then I need to do this *my* way. Not yours."

I wasn't sure where the words came from, but they felt right.

And from the look on my father's face, they'd also been the right ones to say.

"I'm not promising anything," I quickly repeated, aware that my statement made it sound as though I'd already made up my mind to ascend. But this wasn't about my place as alpha so much as honoring my brother's memory. While also appeasing the pack, providing them closure, and ensuring none of the others could be hurt, too.

All right, so maybe it was about proving my worth on some twisted level. But that wasn't why I had to do this.

"Discovering who did this will protect us all," I whispered. "They're targeting alphas, Dad. Alphas like you and Mom. Alphas like me." I couldn't just stay here and assume my leadership role. I had to ensure everyone out there was safe first.

Everyone including myself.

My father studied me for a long moment, the alpha notorious for thinking through every possible angle before delivering a verdict. Not that his verdict would necessarily apply here. I'd already made up my mind, and he had to see that in my expression.

I was just as alpha as he was. Just as stubborn, too.

"You know I'm right," I added, my voice low.

"Not necessarily right," he replied, his tone rivaling

mine. "But an alpha needs to trust his instincts, and I trust yours."

My heart stuttered with his words, the praise in them so unlike any I'd received from him in years.

*I trust yours.*

"You'll need to remain for the funeral," he added. "And I suggest you consider putting in your notice at E.V.I.E."

My mood plummeted.

That last statement sealed my fate, or at least the one he intended for me. Because he didn't see me refusing the alpha mantle. He saw me solving this case and returning to my rightful place.

Which meant he'd ignored half of what I'd said and had only chosen to hear what he'd wanted to hear.

Typical.

"I'll stay for the funeral," I replied, ignoring the latter half of his statement. Because hell if I could promise to follow through with that. "Anything else?"

"We'll need to review the pack records," he said. "But that can wait until you're ready to accept your role."

"Right." I couldn't decide if I wanted to punch him or hug him. The former because the old man clearly wasn't hearing me. And the latter because I craved the comfort.

Which only irritated me more.

I hadn't lived the lone-wolf life for over a decade just to succumb so easily.

I didn't need him or his soothing touch. I just needed my wolf.

Fuck, I needed to *run*.

With a nod and a muttered "Thanks for the drink," I left.

If he had any more to say to me, it could wait.

My animal desired freedom.

And I had every intention of giving it to him.

I shifted before the last of my clothes hit the ground, my paws already beating over the earth and taking me straight into the trees. I no longer felt a damn thing. Not the pain ripping down my arm from my injury. Not the agony my father stirred inside me with his words. Not the torment I felt from my brother's untimely death. Nor the anger of his brutal murder.

Just air.

Forest.

Rain.

*And female.*

My nose twitched, my wolf hungry for that delicate scent.

*Where are you, Makayla?* I wondered, picking up the subtle traces of her perfume. *Where did you run off to, little wolf?*

I took off along her fragrant path, my mother's words taunting me every step of the way.

*"Looks like he'll be chasing her after all."*

*Just for a harmless run, Mom,* I thought at her, thankful she couldn't actually hear me.

However, I knew all I'd hear in return was her tinkling laugh followed by a, *Didn't even last an hour, let alone a week.*

# CHAPTER 11

## MAKAYLA

*FREEDOM.*

*Fresh air.*

*Familiar scents.*

My wolf frolicked through the forest and along the banks of the lake, melting all my stress away. This place felt like home, yet brand new at the same time. A conundrum that enthralled me, encouraging me to explore every corner of the Silver Lake Pack lands.

I didn't think about anything, just let my wolf's instincts drive me. Eventually, I slowed to a more leisurely pace and basked in the warmth of the sun's rays filtering in between the bare branches from high above.

*Beautiful*, I thought, almost purring with happiness.

Voices floated to my ears, drawing me toward a group of shifters in human form lounging around the lake. I remained hidden in the forest, not wanting to be seen.

Considering what the pack was going through, I doubted they'd be receptive to an outsider joining them right now. Not that I really wanted to talk to them either. I preferred my solitude. However, Alaric's name from their lips had me pausing to shamelessly eavesdrop.

"Paul."

"Yeah?"

"Do you think Hardt will challenge Alaric?" a woman asked.

*Hardt?*

Quietly, I prowled to the edge of the tree line and peeked through to see a couple—one man and one woman—sitting on a blanket, lounging in the sun.

"Maybe." The man, who I assumed was Paul, appeared thoughtful. "I mean, Hardt's always been here for the pack. And Alaric... left."

She nodded slowly, then asked, "Didn't you two used to be close?"

He ran his fingers through his thick black hair and lifted his eyes to the sky while he contemplated. "Yeah, in high school. But he barely talks to me now when he visits, so I guess we weren't that close. Honestly, I'm surprised he didn't find another pack. Why is he even here?"

*Maybe because his brother died, asshat?* I swallowed a huff of annoyance and turned away to continue my meandering, no longer interested in what these two had to say. *And how about saying, Thanks for coming, Alaric. Welcome home.*

Exiting a copse of trees, I realized I'd ventured into someone's yard, so I scampered back into the foliage. But I stopped again at the mention of Alaric's name. Pivoting back, I spotted two men standing at a grill with another handful of people sitting in deck chairs nearby. Funny thing about shifter communities—a wolf wanders by and people barely notice.

"Do you want to follow Alaric as alpha?" one of the men—a tall, muscular blond, like a Viking—queried in a haughty tone.

The other man—shorter, but no less built and a cute, freckled ginger—sighed and shifted his weight from foot to foot. "He hasn't been around much in the last few years, but Alpha Tyler trusted him."

Viking grunted and flipped the meat on the grill. "Maybe, but does that make him alpha material? I mean, what does he know about being an alpha?"

Ginger scowled, and I nodded in agreement even though they couldn't see me. "He grew up here. And you know Alpha Hawk taught them both until they were bitten and Tyler took over."

Viking shook his head, his chin lifting to a stubborn angle. "Do you really want to follow a leader who was so jealous of his brother that he had a tantrum and took off when he didn't earn the spot as alpha?"

Ginger looked unsure again as he ran a hand through his pretty hair. "We don't really know—"

"That's my point! We don't know Alaric. Do any of us really know him?" He directed the last question to the group, who had been sitting quietly, listening to their exchange.

Eventually, everyone shook their heads.

Having heard enough of their nonsense, I trotted off. I felt a little offended on Alaric's behalf. I barely knew the man, and I could already tell he was born to lead—to be an alpha. And underneath the grief and anger, I'd sensed that he'd missed his home. I didn't know the story of why he'd taken off and hadn't often returned, but I would've bet my favorite knife that he had a damn good reason.

"What if he doesn't want the job?"

Another set of voices interrupted my alone time, and I sighed.

"Hardt will probably take it. He's beta."

I didn't stay to hear more of their conversation, but the question percolated in my mind. *Does Alaric want to be the Silver Lake Pack Alpha?*

As his supposed mate, I personally rebelled against the idea of being tied down. I also had no desire to inherit the responsibilities that came with being in charge of a pack. I loved my job, and too many people needed me.

Alaric seemed to be in a similar situation—working for E.V.I.E., fighting the bad guys, living the life of a lone wolf. Would he give it all up?

*Good thing neither of us wants anything to do with this fated-mate bullshit,* I thought. My wolf snarled, and I rolled my eyes. She had fallen for it hook, line, and sinker.

I wandered for a little longer until a strange sensation skittered down my spine.

*Alaric.*

How I sensed his presence, I didn't know.

But I *felt* him approaching, just like I caught his brooding, aggressive mood.

I inhaled deeply, his woodsy scent enthralling my wolf.

*There.*

I glanced over my shoulder as a wolf with glistening black fur stepped through the underbrush, his body twice the size of mine. *Definitely an alpha.*

My wolf perked up, her intrigue piqued by the display of power and impressive strength. *One step,* I thought. *All he needs to do is take one more step, and my wolf will roll over in a flirtatious display of submission.*

Which would thoroughly embarrass us both.

Or at least me.

*Not. Now,* I commanded her. She might be the one people saw, but I was still in charge. Well, I should be, anyway. But she certainly wasn't making it easy.

Which explained her wolfy little grin—both a taunt at my thoughts and a statement out loud.

*Mine,* she was saying. *That wolf is mine. And I want to play.*

I wanted to bang my head against a wall. *Have some dignity! Act like an alpha, for fuck's sake!* I shouted at her.

Alaric narrowed his all-black eyes at me, the human blue completely eclipsed by that midnight color. His big head cocked to the side, and he studied my wolf curiously.

My animal didn't care what I wanted, and since she was in the driver's seat at the moment, I sidled up to him and leaned close, inhaling deeply because he just smelled so damn good. Blue flashed in his eyes, and heat blasted through me at the desire and possession I glimpsed in both the black and blue irises.

Blood thundered in my ears, my heart raced, and my body throbbed with need. If I didn't get the hell out of here, our wolves were going to fuck, and I had no idea how that would affect this whole *mate* business.

Lifting my ears, I glanced at the path in front of me, then back at Alaric. He hesitated for a beat, then began to trot in the direction I'd indicated. We ran for a while, enjoying the companionable silence between us.

My wolf wanted to flirt and encourage him to chase, but I held tight to my resolve. Our animals were simple creatures, their needs uncomplicated. However, their emotions were also powerful and wild. They had an innate desire to dominate, and to be dominated, to go hard and fast, and to possess each other in every way because they saw no need to hold back.

If I ran, he would chase. I knew these woods like the back of my hand, and I was fast, so he likely wouldn't catch me. But it seemed better not to tempt fate since she'd already fucked up our lives. My wolf disagreed adamantly, her desire to play nearly overriding my ability to think.

*I need a distraction. Something familiar.*

I slowed to a walk and changed course, deciding to search out my secret spot, hoping it existed in this reality. It was secluded and peaceful, a perfect place to think and just *be*. Perhaps sharing it with Alaric would be a bit of an olive branch. Or at least help him lose some of the weight pulling him down.

When I neared the watering hole, I broke through the trees and ran to the water, dropping my head to take a drink of the cool liquid. I felt, more than heard, Alaric join me—something that shouldn't have been possible. Only mates who had completed the second stage could sense each other like this in my realm. The sensory bond grew with each stage and could eventually result in telepathy between the mated pair.

I tried to clear my mind and enjoy the stillness and beauty around me, but my head wouldn't stay empty. *Maybe I just need to stand on my own two feet.*

After taking a few steps back, energy hummed through the air as I engaged my shift. Alaric watched me through midnight eyes until I'd completed the transformation.

Then his blue irises began to bleed into the black as his beautiful fur coat disappeared and he righted himself on two legs within what was only seconds. That alone proclaimed him as an alpha—his ability to transition so quickly without even a flinch—but as he stood to his full height and folded his arms across his broad chest, his dominant persona lashed at my senses like a razor-sharp whip.

He was hot as hell.

All hard, toned, masculine *alpha*.

Naked.

Proud.

Fucking ripped and beautiful and well-endowed, too.

Definitely a prime specimen of a man.

My wolf purred in agreement.

*Tramp.*

My heart pounded in anticipation.

And my thighs clenched with an ache only he could satisfy.

*Yeah, shifting was a stupid, stupid idea, Makayla.*

A slow, wicked smile tugged at the edges of Alaric's full lips. "What's wrong, Makayla?" he asked, arching a brow. "Did you swallow your tongue?"

*Yes.* "No."

I swallowed hard, wishing really damn hard that I wasn't naked. His wolf senses would allow him to scent my arousal, just as he could see every goose bump on my skin, my beaded nipples, and maybe even... My tongue darted out to check, and I almost sighed in relief. *No drool.*

Alaric's gaze glittered as he blatantly explored my body. He opened his mouth to speak, and I had no doubt that whatever he said next would turn me on even more.

We needed to focus on something else. "How did the meeting with your dad go?" I blurted out.

Wrong. Question.

His amusement died beneath a wave of palpable tension. Without a word, he walked into the water and sank under the surface, emerging half a second later with water sluicing down his perfectly sculpted body, his arms bulging as he pushed his hair back from his face.

*Shit. Shit. Shit.*

Sexy, hot, *wet*, naked man.

What had I been thinking? Oh, right. I'd lost my damn mind to chiseled abs, a sexy V, and, good grief, how could anyone have an ass that perfect?! I shut that train of thought down before I jumped on for a ride.

*Wait, why can't we fuck?*

*I can't remember.*

*There's a reason. Right?*

*Yeah, it's time for me to go. Byyyyye.*

I started to back up and Alaric turned, his eyes narrowing, causing me to freeze midstep.

"Don't." He uttered the word tightly, his jaw clenched, and his blue orbs flickered with an internal fire. "Don't or I'll chase you."

# CHAPTER 12

## MAKAYLA

ADRENALINE SHOT THROUGH MY VEINS.

*Run. Chase. Play.*

My stomach clenched at the thought. But something in Alaric's tone gave me pause. Maybe it was the growl underlining his words. Or perhaps it was the warning glimmer in his gaze.

Either way, it caused my back to stiffen as I arched a challenging brow. "Then I hope you're fast. It'll make it all the more satisfying when you can't catch me."

Alaric's eyes darkened as he watched me with an unblinking stare.

Unease trickled through my veins.

"Trust me, sweetheart. I'll catch you. And I can't promise to behave when I do." The growl in his voice told me his wolf was just under the surface, waiting for an excuse to come back out to play and *dominate.*

My confidence in my ability to outrun him slowly waned with each passing second. *Okay. Maybe I should... obey. But in my own way.*

I scoffed as I made my way to the water, making it clear this wasn't an act of submission so much as a show of respect. Yes, that was what I would choose to believe.

He grunted in appeasement and relaxed, his gaze lifting to the sky.

Spring in New York could be chilly, but as shifters, we ran hot, and with the sun shining down on us, the lake felt refreshing on my fevered skin. *A whole different kind of hot.*

We lounged in silence, again finding it comfortable and easy rather than awkward.

I waded into slightly deeper water and floated on my back, thinking about our next moves.

"My father expects me to take over. To give up my job. To give up my life. And come back to manage this pack. To lead them as their alpha." His words were quiet and... *tired.* Like he just couldn't keep them in anymore, and for whatever reason, he chose me to open up to. Probably because he felt safe confiding in me—a notable outsider.

Also maybe because there was no one else in the pack for him to talk to. At least, that'd been my assessment after roaming the grounds for hours.

The whispers and conversations I'd overheard on my run floated back to me, each one confirming a solitary thought. *They don't know him.*

And people always feared what they didn't know.

*He must feel so alone.*

Except, I also sensed the kindred spirit in him. The lone wolf, just like I had in myself. Which made it easy for me to relate, at least on some level.

"I know what that's like, to be expected to do something and not do it," I admitted, drawing his interest. "As a kid, I always wanted to be an enforcer. I trained for it. But my alpha, Nathan, saw more potential for me and offered me the chance to earn a place in his black ops agency."

"You turned it down?"

I let my feet drop to the soft floor of the lake and shook

my head. "No. I went into his training program. But my family was pissed. We're close, and they hated the idea of my being gone and unreachable for however long in who knows where."

"They wanted you to continue on the path to being an enforcer," he translated.

"Yes. They wanted me to stay home. To be a part of the pack. To protect the pack." I shifted my focus from the trees to him, deciding that I wanted him to understand my choice. "My packmates weren't the ones who needed me. They have other enforcers. And I thought I would be one of them, but my true calling revealed itself to me while I was training with Nathan's agency."

"True calling?" he repeated, arching a brow.

My lips tipped into a crooked smile. "Freelance."

"Meaning?"

"I take assignments to help those who can't help themselves." I tried to find a better way to phrase it, to make him understand my passion. "Shifters have packs. We're supernatural. We heal quickly." I looked pointedly at his shoulder. "But humans are fragile. Actually, I'd argue that everyone in this realm is fragile." The last was muttered under my breath, and the flare in his pupils told me he'd caught it.

Clearing my throat, I clarified: "Shortly after I started training with my alpha's agency, he took me on a mission. It was supposed to be a learning exercise, but it taught me more than any other experience of my life."

"What was the mission?"

"A trafficking case, and it involved one of the girls at my school. Her father was one of the men in charge of the operation. He was this rich, handsome, typical businessman, with a charming smile and indulging wit. Yet behind closed doors, he beat her and her mother and

helped transport innocent *young* girls. Like, ten years old."
My fists clenched just thinking about it. "And I had no
idea. I'd missed all the signs. I realized then that my
purpose was never to overlook anyone or anything ever
again."

"That's why you were interested in the hybrid."

I nodded. "I saw the news about Valaria Crimson and
started asking around. When I heard the rumors about
trafficking, I just knew I had to take this case."

"And which black ops agency is it that you work for?"
he asked, fully invested in our conversation now.

Probably because I'd finally given him a little glimpse
into the real me.

"As I said, I'm not actually with his agency now. I'm
more freelance." A vague response, but true. I also didn't
see the point in giving him a name. He wouldn't recognize
it. So I settled on another truth instead. "My alpha had a
fit at first, but he quickly came around to my way of
thinking. I can be persuasive when I set my mind to it." I
snickered as I thought about how I'd hounded him until
he'd finally given up on being mad. "However, Marc had
to work a lot harder to gain back Nathan's good graces,
since he'd been the one to tap me for the freelance work."

"Marc?" Alaric's eyes narrowed and jealousy colored
his tone. My wolf reacted positively to his possession and
filled me with the desire to bite him and show him whom I
belonged to. A rash reaction, one I shoved back with a
vengeance.

"My mentor, Jean-Marc de la Croix. Marc for short." I
watched him carefully, curious if the name rang a bell to
him. But his responding nod gave nothing away. Then his
attention seemed to drift, going somewhere else and
darkening his mood once more.

I debated how much to tell him, but something pushed

me—or, more like pulled me to him and urged me—to give him the knowledge that I truly understood some of his pain. I wanted to lighten his load. And I also wanted him to know me a little. Maybe because I'd just spent the better part of my day living through what would clearly become intimate history for him. It only seemed fair for me to give him a little piece of me in return.

"I don't go home much either," I confessed. *Too busy gallivanting around worlds I don't belong in, like this one.*

Alaric glanced at me for a moment, and I spotted the guilt lurking in his blue orbs.

"My parents don't really know the extent of what I do —my mother would flip the hell out—and every time I go home, they put pressure on me to return." I ran my fingers through my hair and sighed. "I love my pack. But I don't want to be tied down like that."

He met my gaze and held it, assessing me with an inquisitive expression. "Why?"

I shrugged. "Free spirit, I guess."

He continued to study me, but he seemed a bit less moody. I sank into the water until it reached my neck, and peered upward. The rays of the sun streaked across the sky, and I followed their path to the sparkling water. This spot of Silver Lake spoke to my soul, and some part of me felt happy that it was just as beautiful in this realm. Perhaps Alaric would think of me whenever he happened upon it. For some reason, that thought appealed to me. The idea of Alaric forgetting my existence felt wrong.

"What kind of wolf are you?" he asked bluntly. "And what did you mean about everyone being fragile in *this realm?*"

Yeah, I should have known he wouldn't let that slide. It wasn't an intentional slip, yet it'd felt right to say. *So maybe I should give him the truth. If he freaked out, I could just jump the realm with my ring.*

I continued to stare off into the distance, unsure of how to begin. "You wouldn't believe me if I told you," I responded honestly.

"Try me."

"I'm from Silver Lake, but in a different world."

Silence.

Shaking my head, I turned to face him with an "I told you so" look that I punctuated out loud by saying, "I told you that you wouldn't believe me."

"Actually, I do," he replied, shocking me. "My E.V.I.E. partner recently left this reality for another one. Not sure what exactly happened because my boss didn't give me all the details, but she disappeared with some royal vamp."

"Royal vamp?"

"Cassius."

*Dimitri's cousin?* My eyebrows shot upward. "You're sure that's his name?"

"Yep. The night before I saved you—"

I scoffed and started to protest, but his mouth curved up slightly and I realized he was messing with me. So I rolled my eyes and kept quiet.

"Violet and I went to Blood Thirteen to investigate a lead on the Bloodsucker Serial Killer, but it turned out to be a vampire nest. 'By invitation only' made a lot more sense once we realized they were waiting to kill a bunch of humans." Alaric's expression filled with anger. "Anyway, they locked the doors and shut out the lights, and mayhem descended in the form of sharp objects and screams."

"Whoa," I breathed.

"Yeah. Violet and I fought back—I had some UV bombs, and we both had our stakes—but the hybrid subdued us with some kind of chemical. We woke up tied to chairs in silver chains." Alaric tunneled his fingers through his hair and blew out a harsh breath before returning his hands to the water. "Next thing I knew, Cassius showed up out of fucking nowhere with Luci— Violet's hellhound. He freed Violet, but the jackass left me there."

I was a little shocked at that. *Cassius is a dick, but not the devil.*

"Well, he loosened my chains enough for me to escape from them myself. But he's still not winning any awards, as far as I'm concerned."

*Ahhh. Yes. Dick, not devil.* I did wonder sometimes, though...

"By the time I managed to free myself, he and Violet were long gone."

My hands swished around in the water as I contemplated Alaric's story. "Huh. That makes sense," I concluded.

"It does?"

"Yeah, Cassius is from my universe." I held my hand out to Alaric, palm down, and wiggled my index finger to show him my ring. "A witch gave me this ruby. She made a similar one for Cassius. He probably took Violet back to our world." Although, I wasn't sure why. Was she the long-lost slayer he once loved? *Kseniya*, if memory served right. Maybe she'd changed her name to Violet in this realm?

Alaric moved closer and took my hand. I ignored the tingling sensation on my skin wherever he touched.

"How does this explain things?" he asked.

"You know the portal near E.V.I.E?"

"Of course."

"This ring opens up one like that, but it gives me the ability to travel back and forth through the realms."

He inspected the ring, turning my hand this way and

that. "That's incredible." He sounded fascinated, but then a growl rumbled in his chest and his pupils went solid black for a few seconds, alerting me that his wolf adamantly disagreed with that assessment.

When Alaric's blue irises returned, his eyebrows furrowed and his mouth pressed into a straight line, clearly irritated. Although, it didn't seem to be directed at me, and the moment quickly passed.

Alaric released my hand, and my wolf whined at the loss of physical connection with him.

"So if you had that, how did you end up in a cage?"

I grinned. "I let Vex catch me. It seemed like the best way to acquire some answers, you know, by playing the victim. He gave me a bit with that phone call about the silver poisoning, and I'd intended to find out more, but…"

I trailed off and waved a hand at him.

"Then I happened," he muttered. "Okay, yeah. I guess I shouldn't have killed him."

I gave him a small smile. "It was hasty."

"It was," he agreed. "I'd been focused on what I knew he could do, and I had no idea that he'd…" His throat worked, his emotions spiking to the surface.

*I had no idea that he'd poisoned my brother*, was likely what he'd meant to say.

All I could do was nod. "I know."

Determination hardened his features, chasing away his guilt. "I have to find out who is behind this."

I closed the distance between us and put my hand on his forearm, giving it a comforting squeeze. "We will," I promised him. It was such a natural reaction. A phrase I hadn't really meant to say but couldn't take back.

Because we would find out who did this.

There was no alternative now. I wanted to know more about the trafficking ring. He needed answers regarding the silver poisoning. It made sense for two lone wolves to work together to discover those explanations, and whatever links existed between them, and take down those responsible.

I told him that without words, squeezing his forearm once more.

Electricity hummed between us.

We were so close, the heat radiating from his body bathing me in warmth. My thoughts clenched, butterflies erupted in my stomach, and my pulse accelerated.

Alaric's dark blue eyes blazed with fire as his gaze dropped to my lips before lowering to my breasts and traveling back up again.

We'd been lounging beneath the water, but we were both standing now, and the depth hit just above his hips. That put every sinuous, chiseled, wet muscle on display, including the sexy V carved into his abs and framing his hips. A thin trail of hair bisected the middle, leading to…

I swallowed hard, unable to stop myself from following that sensuous path to his prominent erection.

The clear water did nothing to hide it.

Just as it did nothing to hide me.

Because we were both naked.

And very, *very* alone.

# CHAPTER 13

## ALARIC

*BAD FUCKING IDEA.*

I knew I shouldn't.

I knew what would happen if I did.

But my instincts had me swaying closer, my wolf growling in approval.

I couldn't take my eyes off her lips. Shit, I couldn't take my eyes off of *her*. Those pert tits, rosy peaks, flat stomach, bare mound. Maybe I'd been wrong about fate, because damn if this woman wasn't made for me. I cupped the swell of her hips and brought her flush against me before lowering my head and pressing my mouth to hers.

*Really bad fucking idea.*

Her body rubbed against mine, my cock kissing her pussy, her taut nipples scraping over my chest, and goddamn, she tasted so good. I deepened the kiss, pushing my tongue into her mouth and devouring her as if she were my last meal.

Makayla moaned, and my wolf roared to the surface, his impulse overpowering my self-control.

*Bite.*

*Mark.*

*Claim.*

I bit down on her lip—*hard*—and growled as her blood

hit my tongue. My animal *demanded* more. But my mind rioted, reason struggling to fight my wolf's possession and ground me once more.

*I can't.*

*I shouldn't.*

My muscles locked down.

My heart fucking stopped.

I was so hungry for her, starving for more than just a kiss. I needed to feel her body writhing beneath mine, to hear the sound of my name falling from her lips as she fell apart.

*No,* I told myself, pulling away, my need for control overriding my physical instincts. *No.*

"I shouldn't have done that." I forced the admission through my teeth and backed up several steps.

Makayla's tongue darted out to clean her lips of the remaining droplets. "No, you shouldn't have," she agreed.

I didn't have any words for her, so I nodded and waded out of the water, quickly shifting and taking off. It was a dick move, leaving her to find her own way home. But I needed some space before my wolf pushed me hard enough that I gave in and did more than kiss her.

It would've been so easy.

Palm her ass, lift her up, and slide right inside her tight, wet heat. She was my fated mate, the only woman I would ever desire again. *Shit.* Why shouldn't I indulge?

Stupid question, and I knew the answer, but that didn't stop me from considering it. Or fantasizing about it.

Letting Makayla leave wouldn't be easy. Losing one's fated mate could be devastating to a shifter. And the closer we grew to each other, the more difficult it would be. Even without our emotions involved, having sex would risk the plan.

*Yeah, fucking is a very bad idea.*

Except, with each step I took away from her, I wondered *why* I couldn't just keep her.

She wanted me.

I wanted her.

Why not just... *mate?*

I shook my head, trying to clear it. I barely knew the woman. And on top of that, she wasn't even from here.

*Damn it.*

How would this even work? Further, was she even my destiny? How could my fated mate be from another realm? Maybe another version of her existed in *my* world. A more appropriate choice. More submissive. Willing.

Well, Makayla was willing.

And did I really want a more submissive mate?

My earlier episode suggested I couldn't handle a docile mate. I needed someone strong... like Makayla.

*To hell with this.* I didn't want to think about her. I didn't want to think about life. I didn't want to think at all.

My paws pounded over the earth as I skimmed the boundary of the pack, searching for any and all threats, my wolf's natural inclination being to *protect.* It didn't matter that these wolves weren't mine. I would forever want to serve them in some way.

This used to be my home.

*It could be again, too,* a softer part of me thought.

I shoved the voice away, locking it up with the others inside my mind.

And just ran.

I ran until I couldn't breathe.

I ran until I ached.

I ran until I couldn't do anything more.

And then I turned back to my cabin, the moon shining brightly overhead. My stomach growled with hunger, and my limbs screamed at me for overuse, but my animal spirit purred with contentment.

*At least one of us is happy,* I thought glumly as I shifted back into human form on my porch.

Makayla's scent lingered by the door, suggesting she was already home.

*Home,* I repeated to myself. *Not home.*

With a growl, I grabbed the door handle, ready to stalk inside.

Only to freeze as someone called my name from the street.

*Hardt.*

*Ah, hell.* I did not want to deal with his bullshit right now. He could only want to talk for one reason. And it rivaled the one my father had earlier.

I wasn't stupid. I knew the whole pack wanted to know if I intended to ascend. But I didn't have an answer yet, nor would I have one anytime soon.

"Alaric," he said again, like I hadn't heard him the first time.

"Hardt," I returned, very aware that he'd said my name twice without addressing me as *Alpha*. That shouldn't have bothered me since I wasn't sure if I wanted the job or not, but somehow… with him… it bothered me a whole hell of a lot. "How can I help you?"

"I'm hoping you have a few minutes to chat."

*I don't,* I nearly replied. Instead, I pushed open my door and said, "After you." Because I didn't quite trust him at my back.

It was just an instinct.

Probably because I rarely trusted anyone at my back.

Once inside, I left him in the foyer to go grab a pair of jeans and a long-sleeved cotton shirt. Hardt had made himself at home in my kitchen when I returned, his hands all over my fridge as he searched for something.

When he pulled out two beers, I cautiously accepted one, then stared at him as I popped off the tab. "How've you been?" I didn't actually care, but it seemed like the right thing to ask.

"Good," he replied. "Well, minus… everything."

"You mean my brother being murdered?" I arched a brow. "Yeah, that sucks." Dick thing to say, but I wasn't in the mood for small talk right now.

He didn't flinch, but his brow did come down. "Look—"

"Alaric?"

My body stiffened—*all* of my body—at the sound of Makayla's husky voice. The way she said my name reminded me of hot, sweaty sex. She joined us in the kitchen, and I nearly swallowed my tongue.

*That towel… needs… to drop,* I thought, eyeing the too-small fabric wrapped tightly around her long, lithe frame. She had her arms folded across her chest, accentuating her full breasts and providing a sinful display of creamy flesh.

Hardt released a low sound, almost like a growl.

And I found myself wanting to march into my living room to wrap Makayla up in a blanket. Shifters were usually pretty cavalier about nudity, but something about him seeing her in this state had all my hackles rising.

Which smacked of jealousy, and that irritated the hell out of me.

"What do you need, Makayla?" The question came out in a harsh tone, my wolf striving for dominance as I attempted to force him to heel. *Not. Now.*

Her eyes narrowed, but she smiled—a smile I imagined would shrivel a lesser man's balls. "I don't have any clothes."

*Oh, right.* I set my beer on the counter and stalked past her without another look, going straight to my room. After searching through my things for something small enough to fit her, I finally found a T-shirt and a pair of sweatpants that were too feminine to have been mine at any point, which probably meant they belonged to a girl I'd slept with on those rare occasions when I'd come home. For a brief moment, I wondered if that would bother Makayla, then chastised myself for caring at all.

Clothes in hand, I retraced my steps to find that Makayla had stolen my beer. She'd also ventured from the kitchen into the living room. Hardt must have followed her because now he stood near a window. He was smiling and his eyes were undressing her—not exactly difficult in her skimpy attire—and possession welled up inside me.

I hated Hardt for ogling her.

I hated myself for being jealous.

And I hated Makayla for being so damn gorgeous.

To her credit, she looked uncomfortable, which should probably have made me less of an asshole. But I was agitated and feeling hostile. And since I couldn't show weakness by attacking Hardt, Makayla became my target.

I reclaimed my beer and set it on the table. Then I slapped the clothes against her stomach, gripped her elbow, and walked her into the hallway.

"You should cover up the goods, or we might get the wrong idea and you'll find yourself being double-teamed," I drawled. Then I raised an eyebrow suggestively. "Unless you're into that kind of thing, then by all means, baby, drop the towel."

Makayla rolled her eyes and marched past me. "In your dreams, *mate*," she tossed over her shoulder. I snagged her arm before she went too far and maneuvered us around until I had her pressed up against the wall. I

117

shackled her wrists with my hands and held them above her head, letting the clothes and towel pool at our feet.

"Oh, I'm sure I'll dream of you tonight. But it won't be about sharing you. It'll be about chaining you to my bed and using your body like my own personal playground." I placed my lips at her ear and ground my erection into her naked mound. "And you know what I'm going to do, Makayla? I'm going to make you climax over and over until you beg me to stop. Or maybe I'll push you to the edge, only to drag you back down, then do it again and again until you beg me to let you come. Either way, you'll beg, baby. You'll crawl, too."

Makayla scoffed, but it came out breathy, almost like a moan. "Not happ—"

"Are you sure, sweetheart? Because I'm willing to bet you're fucking drenched right now."

She sank her teeth into her bottom lip, drawing my gaze to the freshly healed skin. My wolf growled in disapproval, eager to bite her again and ensure the claim lasted this time.

Then she shook her head, denying her arousal.

I smirked, fully aware of the lie. "If you're not dripping for my cock, then you won't have any need to get yourself off, will you?"

Her jaw hardened, her teeth digging deeper into the pink flesh. "Nope," she managed to croak.

I shrugged and released her. "Okay."

With murder in her pretty blue eyes, she bent down and gathered up the fallen clothes, giving me an exemplary view of her spectacular ass. She straightened and walked toward her room.

"Makayla," I called after her. Tensing, she stopped but didn't turn around. "Just remember, I'll smell the heady scent of your orgasm and hear the moans you make when climaxing. And I'll know it's *my* tongue, *my* fingers, *my cock* that you're wishing was pumping between those silky thighs."

Makayla walked stiffly into the guest room and slammed the door so hard it rattled the windows. Satisfied that her night would be as miserable as mine, I returned to the living area to find Hardt making himself at home on my sofa.

"Just making sure she knew where to find everything," I explained coolly as I picked up my beer.

"Right." He leaned back in a display of cocky nonchalance, the neck of his bottle clasped loosely between two fingers. I'd never cared for this guy in high school. And I really didn't care for him now.

*How was this guy Tyler's beta?*

"I just stopped by to see if you need anything. You haven't been around for a while, so it may take some time for you to get reacquainted with the pack."

*Hmm, really? Because it sounds like you're trying to make a statement about my prolonged absences, Hardt,* I thought, nodding along.

"As you know, it's the job of leadership to ensure all pack members feel welcome and at home. So I'm just doing my job."

"Your job?" I repeated. "As beta?"

"Well, technically, I'm acting alpha at the moment, what with your brother's death and all."

"Yeah?" I took a sip of my beer while holding his gaze, daring him not to look away. "I could have sworn that honor fell to my father, *Alpha* Hawk, right?"

"As Tyler's beta, he frequently left me in charge when out of range for a meeting, like the one he just took in New York City."

"I see." *That doesn't make you alpha, buddy,* I thought, and

I allowed him to see that knowledge in my gaze now. *I definitely won't be bowing to you. Ever.*

I didn't break our stare, just continued to test his mettle, wondering how long he could play this dominance game.

A beat passed.

Then two.

"I'm just here to help, man," he said, his gaze finally leaving mine. "The pack can use more of what they know right now, and I've spent the last decade maintaining the order under Tyler's direction. I'm a good resource, is all. So I just wanted you to know that I'm here. To help, I mean."

*Uh-huh.* I took another drink, then set my beer to the side once more. "Well, I appreciate the offer, Hardt," I told him, not giving anything away while ensuring he knew I saw right through his bullshit.

He wanted the pack.

Fine.

Maybe I'd let him have it.

Or maybe he'd piss me off enough to ensure I fought for it.

Time would tell. If I chose to stay, he didn't stand a chance. And the way his gaze had flickered away from mine confirmed he knew it, too.

"So thanks for stopping by," I added with a lazy smile, not so subtly kicking him out. *Wants to help, my ass.*

Fortunately, he showed some intelligence and chose to let me escort him out.

"Seriously, let me know if you need anything."

"I absolutely will," I replied, forcing a grin. "Have a good night, Hardt." *And maybe find a cliff to jump off of while you're at it.*

He started down the sidewalk, and a final thought occurred to me. "Oh, and, Hardt?"

His hazel eyes glowed in the moonlight as he glanced over his shoulder, his long hair twisting with the wind. "Yeah?"

"The next time I catch you checking out my mate, I'll castrate you with my teeth." This time my smile was genuine. "You feel me?" I didn't wait to hear his reply, just shut the door and turned around to find Makayla standing behind me with an arched brow.

# CHAPTER 14

## ALARIC

MAKAYLA PLACED her hands on her hips, the sweatpants a near-perfect fit. However, now that we were alone, I sort of preferred the towel. "Your mate?"

I lifted a shoulder. "Doesn't mean I'm going to do anything about it, but yeah, Makayla, *you're my mate.*" Something we'd already established.

"And that means I can't be with another guy in your pack?"

"His interest in you has nothing to do with you and everything to do with pissing me off." I didn't mean for that to sound like a hit to her ego, so I quickly clarified with, "It's a direct insult to ogle you the way that he did, and he knows it. And he's done it twice now."

She frowned. "Twice?"

"First at Tyler's house, and again in *my* house."

Her eyebrows lifted. "Oh."

"Yeah." I ran a hand over my face and shook my head. "Sorry. I'm not trying to take this all out on you. It's just…"

"A lot?" she suggested, leaning against my foyer wall.

"Yeah. Yeah, it's a lot." I glanced around her at my kitchen. "And I'm starving."

"Me, too," she admitted, her eyes running over me.

I arched a brow.

She swallowed. "I didn't mean it like that."

"Sure you didn't." I prowled toward her and nipped the air in front of her lips. "But I wasn't kidding. I need food." Then I could think about sex. Maybe. Actually, probably not. Definitely not.

*Shit. Just... focus on one thing at a time.*

Makayla followed me into the kitchen, a question lurking in her pretty eyes.

"What do you want to ask me?" I wondered out loud as I started going through my fridge.

"I'm just..." She trailed off as she took over one of the stools beside my counter bar. There were two, but seated on the dining room side, allowing the chef in the kitchen to see the dining and living area beyond. *An open floor plan,* my mother would call it. *For entertaining.*

*Because I liked entertaining people.* I nearly rolled my eyes at the thought.

"Do you think someone like Hardt would be a good alpha to your pack?" Makayla finally asked, the words coming out in a rush almost as though she'd had to talk herself into voicing them.

I snorted. "Absolutely fucking not." I didn't even need to think about the answer. It was the most obvious one to voice. "Why, do you?"

"I... actually, no."

I looked over the door of the fridge to find her frowning. My brow furrowed in response. "Did he say something to you?" I'd only left them alone for a minute, but he'd clearly followed her into the living area. And the jackass had been grinning when I'd returned.

"Not exactly. Well, yes. I mean, no. I mean..." She shook her head, a growl leaving her mouth that had me fighting the urge to grin.

It was the first time I'd seen her at a loss for words, and I found the reveal a bit charming. It made her more human. Or just, more accurately, relatable.

"He wanted to know if the two of us would be staying. I figured he meant the two of us"—she pointed a finger back and forth between us—"so I told him no and that I will be going home."

And that killed my amusement.

*I will be going home.*

Of course she would be, but the way she said it with certainty had me wondering what the hell I would do when she left. Unless she wasn't my true fated mate. Maybe the jumping between realms had somehow crossed our fates?

"He was—well, very pleased," she continued. "And I realize now that he wasn't asking about us as a couple so much as asking about *you*."

"Because he wants to be alpha."

"Yeah."

I shut the fridge, having let half the cold air out already without really paying attention to the contents.

"There's a casserole in there," Makayla said, gesturing to the closed door. "If you're looking for something easy, I mean. Someone dropped it off earlier with instructions on how to heat it." Her lips pinched. "Savannah, I think?"

"Tyler's girlfriend." Or I assumed that was what he'd called her. They weren't mates, just... *close*. "My mom probably made it for Savannah, but she would want me to have it to make sure I ate something." I shook my head, my smile sad. "She's always looking out for everyone except for herself." I made a mental note to visit her tomorrow. She was probably one of the few packmates I still somewhat knew because of her ties to my brother.

"She was his girlfriend, not his mate?"

I nodded. "Yeah. Neither of them had been duped by

fate yet." I winked at her to soften the insult. "They chose each other."

"What would have happened if fate *duped* them later?" A familiar twinge of humor danced in her eyes as she repeated my playful word.

"They would have broken up." Which I would have sucked for them. Thankfully, I didn't have that problem now since I'd opted not to date exclusively with anyone. My job hadn't really allowed for intense relationships.

"Just like that?" Makayla asked as she pushed off the stool to join me in the kitchen.

I watched as she opened the fridge to pull out the casserole, apparently deciding that she needed to take charge. I didn't argue, especially when she bent to place it in the oven. The woman was fine even in a pair of sweats and a T-shirt.

"For a Bitten wolf, a man can't *perform* for anyone other than his mate," I said, addressing her question regarding Tyler and Savannah and what would have happened if one of them had found their destined mate. "So, they wouldn't have had a choice."

Makayla stilled with her ass in the air, making me want to tap her with my palm.

I knew it was my reveal that gave her pause—the fact that I'd just admitted she'd be the only one capable of satisfying me ever again—but I enjoyed her reaction too much to really think through what it all meant.

Locking her up in a cage was becoming more and more appealing.

She gathered her thoughts after another handful of seconds, then straightened to fuss with the oven. She had a little instruction card clenched in her fist when she finally turned to face me. "So you'll never be able to…?"

"Fuck another woman?" I finished for her. "Nope." It came out a lot calmer than I felt. Maybe because I was too exhausted and hungry to focus on it right now.

Or maybe because it was just life.

"What about a man?"

I blinked at her. "What?"

"You said you can't fuck another woman, so what about a man?"

I chuckled. "I can't perform sexually with anyone except you, Makayla," I rephrased. "Assuming you're my true fated mate." I considered her for a moment. "You're not from my world. Maybe there's another version of you running around this realm." I arched a brow and smirked. "A more docile, subservient you."

She snorted. "Not fucking likely."

I waggled my brows. "That could be fun. Two of you in my bed."

"You couldn't handle even one of me in your bed, let alone two," she shot back.

"Oh?" I cornered her in the kitchen, pressing her up against the counter by the oven. "You sure about that, *mate*?"

Her humor disappeared behind a wave of heat, her pupils dilating with interest. I brushed my lips against hers, tasting and teasing, and testing her resolve.

She responded with a light brush of her own.

Then a firmer kiss, one underlined in *want*.

I gripped her hip, holding her to me as I returned the embrace, my tongue dancing along the seam of her mouth, seeking entry. She parted for me like a good little wolf and allowed me to explore her with open curiosity.

This was different from before.

Less urgent.

Almost… *sweeter*.

126

A subtle exploration, a coaxing, a softening in resolves.

"Alaric," she whispered.

"Makayla," I returned, inhaling her addictive scent.

She swallowed, her eyes closed as she relaxed into me. We didn't push boundaries or demand more, just held on to one another, our wolves providing unspoken comfort as we remained locked in an intimate position.

It felt like seconds passed when the oven beeped to announce it was up to temperature. Then Makayla released me and stepped away. I allowed it because I needed the space. I needed my control. Shit, I needed my damn brain.

She'd just… obliterated me with a subtle touch.

My walls all tumbled down at her feet, leaving me open and vulnerable in a way that I didn't understand. I quickly worked to restore them, but somehow I knew she'd left herself a backdoor entrance. She'd be able to destroy me again with another little flick of her tongue.

And that scared the shit out of me.

"It's been a really long day," I said, my voice gruff. "After we eat, we need to sleep."

"Yeah." She cleared her throat. "Yeah."

"Good," I replied, unsure of what I actually meant by that. It just sounded right, so I paired it with a nod.

Then I prepared the table.

Waited for the food to finish.

And ate with Makayla in silence.

By the end of our meal, my shoulders were no longer lined with tension and I was starting to feel like myself again. Which made it easy to say good night to Makayla without issuing an invitation for something more. She muttered a similar response. Then we locked ourselves inside our respective bedrooms.

And didn't speak for the rest of the night.

# CHAPTER 15

## MAKAYLA

*WHERE AM I?* I wondered as I stared at the pale ceiling above me.

My nose twitched, the scent of trees and man overwhelming my senses.

The memories of yesterday, or maybe two days ago at this point, all assaulted me at once.

I palmed my eyes, groaning as my limbs protested any and all movement. Probably because I hadn't slept in... well, I couldn't remember the last time I'd experienced such a thorough night's rest. Lowering one hand, I peeked at the windows, noting the late afternoon sun.

Yeah, I'd totally slept for at least twelve hours.

And now all I wanted to do was sleep more.

*Coffee,* I decided, rolling onto my side. *Coffee is good. Coffee is God. Coffee is life. Yes, coffee.*

I tumbled off the mattress onto my bare feet. The sweatpants Alaric had given me were at the foot of the bed. I left them there in favor of just wearing his T-shirt. It smelled like him. Unlike the pants, which smelled like another woman.

I didn't want to know.

Because I wasn't supposed to care.

*And coffee is all that matters anyway,* I decided, stalking out into the hallway while tugging the T-shirt down over my thighs. It covered my ass. It'd do just fine.

I yawned, then finger-combed my hair, fully aware that I probably resembled hell turned over. *Good thing I don't care, right?* I reminded myself. Again.

I'd decided last night that not caring was the best medicine for this lust brewing between me and Alaric.

If we fucked, who cared?

If we didn't fuck? Also didn't care.

*Care. Care. Care. Yep. Going to repeat that alllll day. Wait, don't care. Two words. Damn it.*

With a shake of my head, I continued forward, only to pause as Alaric said, "She's not from our world but from a different realm."

My brow furrowed. *Excuse me?*

Just whom did he deem acceptable to share that secret with? I mean, sure, I hadn't expressly stated not to broadcast my status as an out-of-realm visitor, but as my supposed mate, he should know that information was highly confidential.

"She has a ring from a witch," he continued, causing the hairs along the back of my neck to rise. "That's how she comes and goes."

With a growl in my throat, I stomped forward, ready to give him—and his unsuspecting company—a piece of my mind, only to freeze as I realized said company was Alaric's father.

*Oh.*

*Ohhhh.*

Yeah, okay. I could see why he, uh, felt it was okay to share my secret.

I'd have done the same with my alpha.

Clearing my throat, I tugged at the T-shirt flirting with my thighs and tried to force a smile. "Hi." *Lame-ass greeting, but whatever.* "I just want some coffee." And then a shower, and a shovel, and a grave, and then I'd just make myself right at home.

Alaric stood in his kitchen with his father at the stools on the bar side of the counter. His dad looked at me with interest, noting my bare legs, then glanced questioningly at his son.

"As I said, she's not from here," Alaric continued.

*Do women in this universe never walk around half-naked? Just curious...*

"I see," his father replied, staring between us. Then he arched a brow at his son. "Well, don't just stand there. Get the woman a coffee."

I bit my lip to keep from smiling. *My savior.*

Alaric grunted and went to work preparing me a mug.

However, Alpha Hawk faced me, his expression serious. "Makayla," he said, his tone sending a smattering of goose bumps down my arms. *Absolutely an alpha*, I thought.

"Alpha Hawk," I returned.

His lips twitched. "Not according to my son. He says Hardt's the new acting alpha."

Alaric grunted again.

"You're alpha to me," I clarified. "I won't be using the same designation for *Beta* Hardt."

Hawk grinned. "Oh, I think you'll fit in here just fine, Makayla."

I merely smiled, not committing to a damn thing. *Because I still don't care, right?*

Alaric set a mug on the counter for me. "Any cream or sugar?"

"None," I replied. I needed it black and heavenly today. Or this afternoon. Or was it early evening? I glanced out the windows of his living room and frowned. *Maybe early evening, then.* Rather than overanalyze it, I walked over to the counter, prepared to take my coffee and leave.

But Hawk had other plans for me.

"I'm sorry for what I said to you yesterday," he said, his tone solemn. "I shouldn't have implied that you weren't welcome in Tyler's house. There's no excuse for it. You're Alaric's fated mate, which makes you pack, even if you're from another realm."

I swallowed. *Operation Do Not Care is failing. I repeat, Operation Do Not Care is failing.*

I tried to smile, to accept his apology and move on, but one look at the grieving alpha had me parking my butt on the stool beside him with a demure nod. "It's okay. Yesterday was... stressful for all of us." I crossed my legs and did my best to keep the shirt covering all my intimate bits. *Really should have worn the sweatpants, Makayla. Jealousy is green, not naked.*

Hawk looked meaningfully at his son. "Ric, why don't you run home and get some clothes from your mom? She's about the same size as Makayla, so it'll be a good fit."

Alaric stared at him for a long moment, then sighed. "All right."

I glanced between them, somewhat amused by the subtle alpha dominance undertones of their little exchange. Alaric wanted to refuse, probably because his father had issued it like a command. But he wouldn't because he clearly respected and deferred to the older alpha.

And yet, I sensed that his wolf would win in a fight.

Had it been this way between Alaric and Tyler, too? An obvious victor, yet Alaric had always submitted out of respect and love for his family?

"I'll be back," Alaric said, walking toward the door in a pair of jeans and nothing else.

I admired his ass on the way. Because I could. Because I wanted to. Because those jeans were tight and practically molded to his backside. And because… *mmm.*

I distracted myself with some coffee but noticed Hawk's amused glance. He'd totally caught me ogling his son. If he expected an apology, he'd be waiting for a while. Besides, he was a big part of the reason for Alaric's looks. He'd clearly given his son the sculpted cheekbones, pretty blue eyes, and chiseled jaw structure. The fitted sweater and jeans suggested they shared a similar physique, too. His hair was a bit lighter than Alaric's darker strands, but overall, they very much resembled each other.

*Like father, like son.*

Something that became increasingly evident as Hawk studied me with a shrewdness that rivaled Alaric's.

"I'm going to need more coffee before the questions start," I said, moving off the stool to top up my mug.

Hawk chuckled. "About the realms? Nah. I don't have any questions. Although, I'm sure Nathan is worried about his missing packmate."

I froze with my hand on the handle of the coffee maker. *Alaric must have told him about my job,* I realized, relaxing a fraction. "Uh, Nathan's used to me wandering off."

"Sounds like me with Alaric," Hawk replied, watching me as I poured more steaming liquid into my mug. I turned toward him and topped him up as well, then returned to my stool. "Although, E.V.I.E. is a bit different from KBO Consulting."

Okay, *that* detail was something I hadn't told Alaric. I looked sharply at Hawk. "How do you know that?"

Rather than answer me, he pushed a set of files toward me. "I brought this over for Alaric to review. It's some details on the poisoning cases from the other packs. I assume you'll be working together on this?"

I studied his features. They gave nothing away. And the look in his eyes told me he wouldn't tell me anything, either.

My jaw ticked.

He just took a long sip of his coffee, saying nothing and everything at the same time.

This was no ordinary alpha. But I should have anticipated that with him being Alaric's father.

*How does he know about KBO?* I wondered, unable to stop myself from replaying his statement on repeat in my mind.

"Do you know Nathan?" I demanded. Nathan knew about the alternate realms, but he'd never mentioned knowing the Silver Lake Alpha.

"Let's just say we share a mutual friend." He slid the folders closer. "I've already skimmed a lot of the details. Nothing jumped out at me as important, but maybe you'll notice something I didn't. There are some surveillance images of the lunch, too. I suggest you and Alaric review all of it for clues that the others may have missed." He finished his coffee and stood to stretch. "Alaric said you were taken by the hybrid and overheard a conversation. Anything else important that I should know?"

I wanted to ask him the same damn thing, but I knew better than to engage an alpha in a game of wits. He'd win purely because he designed the rules, not me.

Rather than try, I considered Vex and his conversation. Then I frowned, recalling something I'd tried to tell Alaric yesterday and failed to because of his aggression outburst. "The hybrid, Vex, sent a shifter to deliver information to the boss. The shifter's name was Neo. Bitten breed. Short, scrawny little thing for a wolf, but definitely a wolf nonetheless. Sound familiar?"

Hawk frowned. "No, but I'll put out a search for all Neos in the region, see what photos I can gather for you to review."

I nodded. "He'll be easily recognizable."

"Good." He tapped the files. "This is sensitive content. Alaric's strong; however, he may need a moment to process it." His blue eyes held mine. "Don't go easy on him, Makayla. But don't go hard on him either."

A chill graced my spine. "Alpha Hawk…"

"I know you're going to tell me that your kind don't do fated mates and that you're going back to your home realm," he said softly, his expression knowing. "But I think fate works in mysterious ways."

He stood, then leaned against the counter beside me, his sapphire eyes reminding me so much of Alaric's.

"Two lone wolves," he mused. "Both forced into a situation where they have to work together, doing what they do best—tracking down assholes who deserve punishment. That's not a coincidence, Makayla. Nor is it a coincidence that Alaric's here now. He was always meant to lead this pack. I only wish it hadn't required me to lose a son for my other one to finally realize his destiny."

I swallowed, unsure of what to say to that.

"But as I said, fate works in mysterious ways." His smile was sad. "Guide him, Makayla. You're here for a reason, too. Together you'll figure this out." He pushed away from the counter, heading toward the hallway, then paused to say, "And I'll have Jude tell Nathan you're safe. If you were my wolf, I'd be worried."

*Jude? As in the head of E.V.I.E. Jude?* I wondered.

But Hawk was already on his way out, leaving me to throw wordless questions at his back.

I looked down at my ring, debating using it to flash home to demand some of those answers from Nathan.

However, if I did that, he wouldn't just let me turn around and head back.

And now wasn't the time to leave Alaric alone.

He needed my help with this case.

I looked at the files, somewhat mollified by the distraction, and flipped the page. *Let's see what you know.*

# CHAPTER 16

## MAKAYLA

BY THE TIME ALARIC RETURNED, I'd already read through all the files.

And the answer as to what they knew? Nothing. Absolutely nothing.

I glared at the documents, offended by how little they told me. "All these reports tell me is the alphas died by silver poisoning that they'd likely imbibed. A guess based on the fact that the enforcers who'd accompanied them to the city were all fine—and none of them had attended the main lunch meal. Which means they know jack all about anything. And the supposed surveillance? It's just a few photos, Alaric. How the hell am I supposed to find anything useful in photos?"

Alaric grunted and set a bag down beside me. "That's why I have Jude sending me over visual footage from the restaurant and the hotel. I want to see everyone that walked in and out of that place in a seventy-two-hour period. I also want to talk to Paul since he was the enforcer who'd accompanied my brother to the meeting."

I nodded. "Good. You should have Jude pull street footage as well."

"He's on that, too." Alaric sounded tired. "We'll have everything in a few hours. He's shipping me a tablet since I left all my toys at home." He braced his forearms on the counter beside me, his head falling forward on a sigh I felt all the way to my soul.

I frowned at his defeated pose, then sniffed the air around him. A subtle perfume wafted off his bare skin, the scent decidedly female.

And not from his mother.

I wasn't sure how I knew that, maybe because the fragrance smelled *young* or *too fruity* to be matronly.

"Did you take a side trip on the way back?" I asked conversationally as I looked at the bag near the bottom of my stool. "Decide I needed another woman's clothes rather than your mother's?"

He looked at me sideways, his dark hair falling into his blue eyes. "Careful, Makayla. You almost sound jealous."

"I'm not." *I totally am and I hate it.*

"You are," he countered, his lips curling slightly. Then he sighed, his expression falling once more. "Savannah was with my mom and hugged me. She's... struggling."

"It's only been a day," I pointed out. "Wounds like death don't heal overnight."

"True. But not all of us have the ability to just grieve." His sapphire irises flared. "I can't... I don't know how to embrace them, Makayla. All I know how to do is avenge him. But the pack needs *more*." He lifted off his elbows to grip the marble counter, his forearms flexing as he tightened his hold. "Hardt was outside hugging them all. Giving them the affection they apparently need. And that's just not me."

"That doesn't make you a bad alpha," I pointed out softly. "There's a time for emotional bonding, and there's a time for protection. Your pack might be hurting right now, Alaric, but what they need more than anything at the moment is to feel safe. And you're doing that by finding Tyler's killer."

Some of his tension ebbed as he looked at me. "I don't feel like I'm doing enough. I mean, hell, I took a nap instead of hunting the bastard down."

"You *slept* because you'll be worthless if you don't take time to rest," I countered. "What was the first thing you did this morning?"

"Called Jude about the surveillance."

"Exactly."

He arched a brow. "Exactly what?"

"You didn't think about doing that last night because you were hungry and exhausted and hurting. But you slept and woke up with a clear mind and immediately knew what to do." I pointed at the files on the table. "I'm guessing you knew these would be useless before your father even handed them over."

I had no idea what Hawk thought would hurt Alaric in here. Except for maybe the images of the vacant chair next to Tyler at lunch—he'd clearly saved it for someone, and I could only assume that someone was Alaric.

"I wouldn't say 'useless,'" Alaric muttered. "Just... not as thorough as E.V.I.E." He opened the closest file, his gaze skimming the image of his brother at the table. His lips thinned, but he said nothing, moving through each item with a shake of his head. "Autopsies are against pack practice. So I'm not surprised that all these notes are superficial. I could tell by looking at Tyler yesterday that he'd ingested or inhaled the silver."

He shut the folder and went back to squeezing the marble, his head falling once more.

"I was supposed to meet my brother the other day, but the hybrid jacked up my plans with the whole Blood Thirteen incident." A growl rattled his chest, the agonized sound coming from the depths of his heart, but he swallowed it and stood up. "I don't know if I could have stopped it, and there's nothing I can do about that now except find out who did this."

That was how I'd felt after the incident in high school with the whole trafficking issue. I could either beat myself up over it or find a way to make it right.

We couldn't bring Tyler back.

But we could bring his killer to justice.

"I need to shower," he said. "Then I want to eat."

"Do you want me to make something?" I suggested, pushing away from the counter. He'd given me coffee. It only seemed fair to return the favor with food. "Maybe breakfast?"

"Breakfast for dinner," he mused. "All right." He started toward his room, then turned, his gaze locking with mine. "Thank you for being here, Makayla."

I smiled and nodded, not sure what to say.

It felt right.

So I stayed and made scrambled eggs.

Alaric showered and came back in another pair of jeans, his hair towel-dried and dripping water down his defined torso. I pretended not to notice and focused on the food instead. But his knowing gaze told me he'd caught my interest.

Could he blame me? The man was gorgeous and alpha and just *wolfish*.

I didn't try to talk while we ate, choosing companionable silence instead. Afterward, he cleaned up while I showered, and by the time I returned, Alaric's E.V.I.E. tablet had arrived. There were actually two, so he handed me one and led me to the living area, where we reviewed surveillance footage and other documents all night.

By morning, we had all our victims printed and lined up on the wall in chronological order. It was a mix of women and alpha shifters, all with no correlation.

I squinted at them, unable to make heads or tails of their links. "I mean, Valaria was a wolf. Same with Gloria. But these other girls were all human."

Alaric grunted in agreement. "And Gloria is still missing."

"Because the hybrid is dead?" I suggested.

He considered that and shook his head. "Honestly, I don't have a damn clue." He scrubbed a hand over his face and sighed. "I either need more coffee or some sleep."

"Sleep," I voted. Because my brain was a mess of details that I couldn't sort.

Alaric nodded. "Nap."

"At least four hours."

"Done," he agreed with a yawn.

It wasn't until I lay down that a new strand of connections started to form in my mind. One linked to the trafficking case I'd worked on with Marc a few years ago. The one where I'd met Sapphire.

I frowned as I chased the thoughts through my mind, puzzling them all together.

*Four alphas.*

*Hendrix. Warren. Calder. Davies.*

*Weiser Pack.*

*Elk Neck Pack.*

*Silver Lake Pack.*

*Beaver Creek Pack.*

They were the alphas who'd helped bring justice to the two assholes in charge of Sapphire's trafficking ring. "Fuck," I muttered, sitting up. "*Fuck.*" How the hell had I missed that obvious link?

I rolled right back out of bed and walked into the

living room to start looking at all the locations again.

Valaria Crimson had been from the Elk Neck Pack. As a famous heiress, she'd been considered a prized jewel from that clan of wolves. She'd been the fated mate of one of the wolves higher up in the pack. I didn't know the whole story, just that they considered her and her connections valuable. As far as making a statement went, attacking her certainly achieved it.

And then there was Gloria Mansfield, Alpha Hendrix's daughter. She was mated to a beta within the Weiser Pack, hence her different last name. Her whereabouts were unknown, and his pack would be consumed with the funeral preparations now, in addition to trying to find her.

So that left Silver Lake and Beaver Creek as two areas mourning the loss of their alphas, but with no missing packmate. *Yet.*

My instincts prickled, the hairs dancing along my arms.

I had to wake up Alaric and tell him the links. This couldn't be a coincidence. Girls missing, alphas targeted— it all connected back to the trafficking ring Marc and I had helped take down three years ago.

*Except…* I frowned. *Except everyone involved was caught and killed.*

The alphas of those four packs had been in charge of punishing the wolves behind the kidnappings and the murders. So had someone picked the mantle back up to continue the auctioning circuit?

I glared at the images, something not quite clicking.

*Why are the vampires involved? Why a hybrid?*

I palmed the back of my neck and blew out a breath. "I'm missing something."

"You're supposed to be sleeping," a deep voice drawled.

"So are you," I returned, not bothering to look away

141

from the board. At least I didn't have to wake up Alaric now, as he was already here. "Roughly three years ago, I took a trafficking case in this realm. One of the witches from my world had been taken by some supernats from this universe." I lifted my hand. "The same witch who gave me this."

"How the hell did they take her from your world?"

I grunted. "Great fucking question." One we'd never fully answered. "Sapphire—the witch—called it fate. She's a bit of a seer, so she knew she was going to be taken." I glanced at him, which was a mistake because he stood in the living area in just a pair of black boxers, and he looked damn good, too. I cleared my throat and focused on my story. "She sent Marc instructions on how to find her. And she told him to recruit me."

It'd been fairly straightforward. Marc and Nathan already knew each other, making the connection easy to facilitate. As I'd finished my degrees by then, and had numerous cases under my belt, I wasn't exactly new to the field. And trafficking had become my specialty at that point.

"So he showed up at KBO, hired me for the case, and used the ring she'd gifted him to take us both to this world." I paused and twisted my lips to the side. "The rings aren't easy to create. They require a lot of magic, and slayer blood. Somehow, Sapphire has managed to make them, though. Because I have one. Marc has one. Cassius, too. But it's not common, despite how it seems. And we never found out *how* she was taken. I've actually wondered if she jumped realms to be captured on purpose."

Because it would be just like Sapphire to sacrifice herself for the greater good. However, I had no idea why she'd involve herself in another world's affairs, unless it had a bigger endgame.

*Like the one I'm standing in now,* I thought, looking at the images again and narrowing my gaze.

"What's KBO?" Alaric asked, distracting me.

"Nathan's company." Which reminded me... "Something your father apparently knows."

"What?"

"Yeah, he knew about KBO *and* my alpha."

"What? How?"

"I'm guessing from Jude because he said he was going to have Jude pass a message on to my alpha that I'm alive and safe."

Alaric blinked. "Jude, as in my boss?"

"Unless you know another Jude, I'm assuming he's the one."

"Do you know Jude?" Alaric asked.

"Not directly, but I think Marc went to him for information during the mission I just mentioned." Which reminded me that Nathan was the one who had mentioned Jude and E.V.I.E. before we'd left, meaning he absolutely had a link there. I repeated that out loud to Alaric, then added, "Anyway, we needed a list of all the shifter packs because we knew Sapphire was taken by a wolf."

He settled onto the couch, his muscles rippling with the movement. He patted the cushion beside him, and I sat, too, both of us facing the wall of photos and case details.

"Sapphire's the reason I'm back in this realm," I continued. "She sent me here on an unrelated case, but I'm starting to think it was all a setup, that I'm here because of this." I pointed at the wall. "It's related to her somehow. And it makes sense because all the alphas who were attacked? Those were the ones who delivered justice to the wolves involved in the case three years ago."

"I remember this," he replied. "You're talking about the ring run by the vamps."

"Yeah, but they had help from some wolves, too. That's how they acquired the more *durable* assets." I shuddered with the adjective, hating what it implied. But it'd been the term used during the case. "They'd trafficked wolves of all kinds, humans, and even a few other vamps."

He nodded. "Right. E.V.I.E. handled some of the later cleanup. But it wasn't my case."

"Probably because Jude let Marc and me run the show." Not that we'd given him much choice. We'd used him as a consultant more than anything. "We killed several of the vamps in charge, as well as a few shifters. But the alpha council in this region handled Alpha Bortex."

"McKenzie Pack," Alaric replied, looking at me. "I knew he was forced to retire, but I didn't know this was why."

"His involvement was something that came out when the shifters were questioned afterward." I lifted a bare leg to tuck under me. "They were the bodyguards for the girls. And a few were in charge of *recruitment*, too."

*Recruitment* being a fancy way of saying *kidnapping*.

"We found out later that he issued the majority of the commands to the wolves involved. At that point, the case was pretty firmly out of our hands. We were only here to save Sapphire, and the girls, which was done. The alphas in this region were in charge of Alpha Bortex's punishment, as well as those of the other wolves involved."

This realm didn't have a council like the one in my universe. The packs of this world had more of an unspoken alliance where they met when needed but otherwise maintained order within their own territories. In this case, the alphas throughout the region had met and delivered a verdict.

"All I know is he died in the end," I concluded.

Alaric nodded. "I remember that, too. But I never asked why. I've… avoided pack affairs."

Because he didn't want to be an alpha. I understood that.

"Now I'm wishing I'd been more involved," he muttered. "Instead, I just helped take down the vamp nests after that whole thing fell apart."

"Still an important job." Marc and I had handled those in charge, but maybe we'd missed one somewhere. I stared at the wall again and shook my head. "This has to be related, Alaric. They're taking girls and restarting the trafficking ring—or I assume that's what's happening—and they're targeting the alphas that punished Bortex."

"And you think your witch friend ensured you'd be here to help," he added.

My lips twitched. "If you met Sapphire, you'd agree with my guess. She's a conniving little witch." I looked at him. "I'm willing to bet she saw our fates crossing and decided to throw me in your path, too."

His blue eyes sparkled. "I'll have to thank her later for castrating me."

Ah, yes, that little reveal about his inability to *perform* for other women. "Maybe that, uh, will fix itself, when I leave the realm?" I winced as I said it and quickly searched for something else to say to change the subject. Only, all the hairs along my arms began to dance, drawing my gaze to the window.

Something felt… *off*.

Alaric tensed beside me, clearly picking up on the electrical charge in the air.

His hand settled on mine, the action protective.

Then a scream rent the air, sending us both to our feet and through the front door.

To find a dead body lying in the grass.

# Chapter 17

## Alaric

"WHAT THE...?!" I shouted as I vaulted off the porch and ran to the mutilated body lying on my front lawn.

Petite frame.

Tangled, long strands of hair.

Blood.

*So. Much. Blood.*

My wolf growled in fury, the utter savagery of the scene calling to all my instincts to *protect*.

But it was too late.

The girl was very dead.

I knelt beside her slain form to check for a pulse anyway, the habit coming naturally. Black-and-blue marks littered her pale skin, making me wince as I rolled her to her back.

With a broken nose, split lips, and blackened eyes, it would be difficult to determine her identity. Her lack of belongings and clothes only made it more difficult.

But she was definitely a wolf.

I could smell it on her skin. *Bitten.*

Not one of mine, though. Not from Silver Lake.

*Fuck. Who the hell would do something like this?*

Makayla dropped down on the girl's other side and began

examining her in a clinical manner. Perhaps I should have expected that reaction after all I'd learned about her, yet it still surprised me that she seemed so desensitized to the scene before her. I recognized it because it echoed my own reaction to the situation. We'd seen too much for this to do anything more than fuel our need to capture and kill the culprit.

A crowd began gathering nearby as I scrutinized the body and the area surrounding the victim, searching for anything that could be of potential use.

"She hasn't been dead long," Makayla murmured.

I nodded in agreement. "Maybe five or six hours. Still enough time for whoever did this to be long gone."

My wolf snarled, urging me to let him free so he could hunt the murderer down. *Not yet.*

"Unless they are from around here," she said, voicing a possibility I didn't want to consider. Her lips curled down, her nose twitching. "Do you smell that? It's…" She sniffed, her eyes narrowing.

I inhaled with her, searching for whatever she'd caught with her senses. *Blood. Bitten wolf.* I frowned. *Two. There are* two *Bitten wolf scents. Sort of.* "A shifter." *Maybe a mate? A friend?*

"Except, it's tainted." She studied the victim, then shook her head. "Something's familiar. Like I've smelled it before. However, it also kind of reminds me of Vex."

"He's dead." But I caught the subtle hint of smoke in the air, too. "Another hybrid?"

"Perhaps." She didn't sound convinced. "I don't know. Maybe it's a scent from that bar." She shook her head, then continued her perusal, checking the girl's neck for a claiming mark, and froze. "Alaric," she whispered, her blue irises flaring as she caught my gaze, then gestured down to the female's throat.

I followed her line of sight to find what she wanted to show me without bringing anyone else's attention to it.

"*Fuck*," I seethed through clenched teeth when I spotted the bruising on her inner thighs. It pointed to the very likely possibility that she had been raped. Which seemed like a hell of a coincidence considering that a big part of our investigation included a sex trafficking ring.

I swallowed the bile in my throat, then continued examining the scene with my shifter-given senses.

A variety of scents marked the poor girl, some of them shifter and familiar. That made me frown. I sniffed again, noting the scents of my own wolves on the girl. *Because she's in our lands?* I wondered, inhaling again and catching the rusty old stench that could only be related to one species.

*Vampires.*

*Why the hell does she smell like a vampire?*

Makayla scowled, likely arriving at the same conclusion. I could almost taste her confusion and anger, which... was strange. I shook off the bizarre sensation to refocus on—

Another scream rent the air, turning my attention toward a hysterical Savannah. Hardt immediately pulled her into his arms, his low voice hushing her as he consoled her.

My eyes narrowed as several other packmates gravitated toward him for strength, like he was some damn beacon of light in this morning of darkness. Even the damn sun seemed to illuminate him from above. *What the fresh hell is this bullshit?*

"It's all right, Savannah," he cooed in what should have been a soothing tone but came off as patronizing. "Tell them. They need to know." His tone held a note of authority.

I almost snorted.

It sounded like a damn mouse trying to mimic a lion.

I cleared my throat, my instincts driving me to take charge and speak. "What is it, Savannah?" I infused just a slight alpha rumble into my voice, the sound meant to call for attention while also offering a soothing undertone of protection to it.

Hardt's expression told me he didn't appreciate me inserting myself into the conversation.

I let him see just how much I cared about his opinion with a quick look. *Fuck. Off.*

"Th-that's Kristen Whiting. She was staying with me. When she didn't come back to my house after her run"— she broke off as a fresh bout of tears cascaded down her cheeks—"I-I thought sh-she left to go home. She's from the McKenzie Pack." The last part came out on a whisper, her slender shoulders curling in defeat.

*Well, at least that explains why I smell my pack on the girl,* I thought, somewhat relieved but also devastated for Savannah.

"McKenzie?" Makayla repeated, her lips curving downward into a frown. Her blue eyes were pensive when they met mine. "Alpha Bortex," she whispered low enough that only I heard her. "This blows my theory to hell."

I nodded in agreement. If people from Bortex's pack were also being targeted, it was highly unlikely that someone among them was seeking revenge by poisoning the alphas and taking the girls. Which left us back at square fucking one. "Shit."

The smell of vampire hit my nose again, and I moved over to finish inspecting Kristen's neck. It took a little searching because of all of the bruising and swelling, but eventually I found what I was looking for—two small punctures just to the left of a major artery. That explained why her skin appeared ashen. However, the bite marks were smaller than normal.

My fingers flexed, my instinct to grab a stake hitting me square in the gut.

*A vampire was on* my *land. Around* my *pack. Unacceptable.*

My wolf snarled and snapped, ready to tear them limb from limb.

*I need to hunt these leeches down and put them in the ground.*

Makayla leaned close, her floral scent replacing the vampire stink, and before I could stop myself, I inhaled deeply. Her natural perfume softened my anger and pain. Or perhaps it was just her nearness that caused me to relax.

"Where's the nearest vampire coven?" Makayla asked.

"About fifty miles away," I replied, my mind already forming a strategy for a search patrol. *We'll head west, then—*

"No one in our pack would do something like this," someone said loudly, drawing me from my thoughts.

"I agree. It has to be a setup," Hardt stated confidently as he placed a consoling hand on the shoulder of the woman who'd spoken. A few more people made comments, but they were all directed toward Hardt. They were looking to him for leadership and comfort and solace.

Emotional support—something that didn't come naturally to me. Especially after leaving my home and family. Working for E.V.I.E. meant I couldn't afford the distraction of *feelings*. That was how a slayer got himself killed.

Being methodical, following the investigation, and taking down the bad guys—that was what I knew.

Vengeance and justice, too.

Finding the asshole who did this and protecting my

pack was how I could help them. The fact that the situation appeared to be orchestrated by vampires, well... *Now we're in my element. I can do what I do best.*

Still, it irritated the shit out of me to see the way the pack gravitated toward Hardt as if he were the man in charge around here. If they didn't want to see me as their alpha, they should at least have been looking to Alpha Hawk for leadership.

"Ric."

*Think of the man and he appears,* I thought on a sigh as the crowd parted for his entry.

*And here we go.* He would chastise me over my handling of the situation and then take over. Just like when I was a kid.

*In five, four, three, two...*

He stopped in front of me, his gaze on the gruesome scene.

I cleared my throat and gave him a quick summary of my findings. He might not approve of my choices, but I could at least play the role of good slayer.

"Someone left me a sick present," I muttered. "Looks like a vampire's doing. Has the pack had any issues with leeches lately?" I had to ask, but in my gut, I knew it wasn't related to the pack at all. This body had been strategically placed on *my* lawn. This had to be related to the silver-poisoning case. Maybe someone didn't approve of me taking out the hybrid and his bloodsucking buddy.

Or maybe it was related to one of the many cases in my past.

I'd certainly pissed off a lot of vampires in my time.

My father thought for a moment. "Nothing beyond the normal turf wars. You know how the vamps are about the boundary lines."

"Yeah." But the nearest one was a little over fifty miles

out, which meant they'd come pretty far into our territory before dropping off the bloody gift.

"Alaric?" Makayla had crouched down by Kristen's foot and was staring intently at the sole.

Dread descended like a thick blanket, déjà vu slamming into me.

"*Alaric,*" one of the E.V.I.E. technicians had said just a week ago from a similar position on a different victim.

*On Valaria Crimson.*

I fought the urge to vomit as I stepped around Kristen's body to join Makayla.

One glance was all I needed to confirm the similarity.

*AVC*

My initials. Burned into the flesh of the victim.

*Fuck.*

The same three letters had been carved into Valaria's heel, likely by a knife. But this one resembled a brand.

*Sick bastards,* I thought, my nostrils flaring as I stole a deep, calming breath.

*The vamps are taunting me.*

*Bloody invitations.*

*Sick pricks.*

"What—" Makayla started.

But I shook my head and gave her a pointed look. "Later," I said under my breath, the word for her ears only. We weren't going to discuss this on my lawn, with a dead body, in front of my packmates.

She closed her mouth and bobbed her head once.

I jumped to my feet, my hands clenching at my sides as my gaze swept over the group that had accumulated. Alpha or not, I owed it to Tyler to fix this. Hell, I owed it to my dad, too. I owed it to the whole damn pack.

Someone had poisoned my brother.

Then a vamp felt confident enough to drop a body in my yard.

I couldn't stand for that. Not now. Not ever.

"I'm going to find out who did this," I said, my voice low and underlined with promise. "And I'm going to make them fucking pay."

"And how are you going to do that?" Hardt demanded. "You probably brought this to us with all your E.V.I.E. bullshit."

"All my *E.V.I.E. bullshit* is how I'm going to fix this," I retorted, not missing a beat. "All my *E.V.I.E. bullshit* is how I'm going to find out who killed my brother—the alpha of Silver Lake—and deliver justice."

He snorted, his disbelief palpable.

A few others conveyed expressions of dubiousness, but more of them appeared relieved.

The pack didn't doubt my ability to fix this problem. However, some of them exuded skepticism over what came next.

I hadn't accepted the alpha mantle. I hadn't promised protection. I hadn't guaranteed them a damn thing other than vengeance.

How could I protect Silver Lake if I rejected the role as alpha and returned to my previous life? Was that my choice? I wasn't sure. But if I did go that route, it would sever my tie to the pack completely. I would truly be a lone wolf.

*A castrated lone wolf.* My inner animal seemed to push that thought at me, but I ignored him. That was the least of my worries, but it didn't make it any less true.

*Focus,* I thought. *Focus on the here and now and take charge. For Tyler.*

I spotted two Silver Lake enforcers in the crowd and called them forward. "Paul. Timothy. Do a perimeter run and see if you can pick up a trail for the vamp smell," I ordered.

They glanced in Hardt's direction, and I growled. Their heads snapped back to me, and my expression had them muttering, "Will do" and "Got it." Then they took off for the woods, stripping along the way.

I gritted my teeth at the very idea of what I had to do next. *With all the clenching and grinding these days, I'm going to end up toothless as well as ball-less.*

It took me a second to force the words from my mouth. "Hardt, I need you to take Kristen's body to the coroner and make arrangements with her family to come and pick her up." I hated asking him for anything, but as the pack beta, it would be expected that he be issued an important task.

He looked like he wanted to argue, and my wolf snarled, ready for a fight. However, to both our disappointments, he nodded and gave Savannah one last hug before approaching the body. Makayla ran inside and returned with a blanket for him to wrap Kristen in. I had no idea where she'd found it. Probably in one of the linen closets. Regardless, it was a thoughtful gesture.

"Thanks," I said to her.

She responded with a small smile.

Hardt didn't acknowledge her, his gaze on Kristen.

Then he picked up his head and met my gaze directly. "So you're just going to run off and play hero and leave your lost, grieving pack members without someone to give them comfort and reassurance?"

"I don't remember saying that at all," I replied.

His eyes narrowed. "You're focused on solving the crime and avenging your brother, not giving the pack what they really need."

I arched a brow. "Yeah? And what's that?"

"*Heart*," he said through his teeth, and I couldn't help but wonder if he meant his name or the organ.

"Sometimes it's not about having heart," my father interjected before I had a chance to reply. "Sometimes, an alpha needs to be logical and take charge so he can handle the threat while his people grieve in peace."

Hardt said nothing.

My father stepped forward to clap him on the shoulder, his expression stern yet somehow full of understanding as well. "The pack needs more than emotional succor right now, Beta Hardt. They need protection. It's a decision only an alpha truly understands, so let's leave the leading to my son, yeah?"

# CHAPTER 18

## MAKAYLA

*DAAAAMN! Maybe I should call the fire department because someone just got BURNED.*

It was an immature and ill-timed thought, but I couldn't help it. Whether Alpha Hawk had intended it to be or not, that had been some class A passive-aggressive insulting.

Unfortunately, my amusement was short-lived because Hardt's expression turned sour and his eyes filled with bitter contempt. His gaze took in all three of us, but his animosity lingered longer on me. Because I'd gotten him a blanket? Or was it something else?

Alaric snarled low in warning, his wolf flashing in his gaze.

I understood the feeling because the more Hardt glared at me, the more I wanted to shift and teach the motherfucker how to properly bow to an alpha.

However, the sound of Alaric's increased rumble had Hardt smoothing his expression. He bent to secure the blanket around Kristen, then stood with her in his arms and returned to the small gathering. Alaric's jaw clenched as Hardt showered the crowd with gentle words and alpha-like promises. The beta was really toeing a line, one that would hurt like hell if he made one wrong step. Because I had no doubt Alaric would kick his ass on principle alone.

Hardt took his leave with several pack members trailing after him like lost puppies.

A few looked to Alaric first, and he lifted his chin in response, dismissing them with the kindness of a true alpha.

Savannah surprisingly lingered, her sad hazel eyes flickering to Alaric and then to Hawk and back again. She stumbled forward a little, her movements awkward and broken.

Alaric reached for her. "Come here," he whispered, opening his arms for a hug.

She practically dove at him.

A low rumbling echoed in my chest.

*Cut it out,* I thought at my wolf.

Then Savannah pressed her nose into Alaric's bare chest, and my wolf full-on growled.

*Back the hell off,* I snapped at her—my wolf, not Savannah. *He is not ours.*

Alaric met my gaze over the girl's head, his blue eyes sparkling with mirth.

*Seriously. He chooses now as a good time to be amused?* I narrowed my eyes at him. *You're lucky I don't have another knife,* I thought at him. Not that he could hear me.

His lips twitched, and I suppressed the desire to give him a high five. In the face. With my fist.

When Savannah's gaze darted to mine, my wolf threw herself against me, trying to get out. It must have shown in my eyes because the girl jumped away from Alaric like he was on fire. Her gaze darted back and forth between me and Alaric a couple of times before she mumbled, "Um… sorry."

I sighed. "It's fine. Pay no attention to the wolf behind the curtain. She's confused."

Alaric coughed to hide a laugh. At least, I assumed that was the cause of his strangled sound.

"Don't make me stab you again."

Now his lips twisted into a full-on grin. "I believe it's my turn to play with a knife, sweetheart." Then he looked down at Savannah again, noting the fresh tears in her gaze. "Oh, Savi," he whispered, holding open his arms once more.

"It's... it's not... you," she stammered. "I just... I miss him. And she—*Kristen*—was here for me. And now she's dead, too. Everyone's dying around me." She started to shake, and he pulled her against his chest once again.

His gaze met mine over her head, all humor gone from his eyes. "Why don't you head inside with my dad and bring him up to speed on what we've found so far. I'll just be a minute."

My first instinct was to growl and tell him *he* should go inside while *I'd* be just a minute. *But since I'm not jealous, it would be weird.*

"Sure." My response came out a little strangled, what with my wolf digging her claws into me as if it would keep me from taking her inside. *Is there an off button in there somewhere?*

Summoning all of my strength, I forced myself to pivot and put one foot in front of the other until I entered the cabin. I made a beeline for the coffee maker and started brewing a new pot. It'd been a long night, and I suspected an even longer sleepless day would follow.

Hawk whistled from the living area, his focus on the murder board. "Wow. Looks like you two have been busy."

"As a consequence of sleeping all day yesterday, we worked through the night," I responded, though I was only half listening because my ears were straining to hear something from outside. *Ugh! Focus, Makayla!*

I trudged across the room to where Hawk stood scrutinizing our photos and files. He reviewed everything in silence for several minutes before arching a brow at me. "Well?" he prompted. "I assume this has all led to some sort of theory?"

"Yeah, initially, but—"

The door opened and Alaric entered, his face drawn and his shoulders slumped.

Hawk shifted his focus, his stance protective. "Is Savannah all right?"

Alaric shook his head as he joined us in the living room, coming to stand between me and his father. "She's falling apart, Dad. First Tyler, and now Kristen? Apparently, they were best friends. But I'm guessing you knew that already."

"Yeah, I did," Hawk replied.

"This is so messed up," Alaric breathed. "She's all alone."

"No family?" I asked, feeling guilty for how I overreacted outside. *Damn wolf.* Of course, she was perfectly content now with Alaric beside me, his scent woodsy and intoxicating and entirely lacking Savannah's floral perfume.

"Her parents died just after she finished high school, and like her, they had no siblings," Hawk said, responding to my inquiry about her family. "Everly and I took her under our wing, and that's how she and Tyler became close."

"Mom came by to get her while I was outside," Alaric said. "I think they were going to go for a run."

Hawk nodded. "Good. Your mother will know how to

help her. Now, why don't you two show me what you've come up with?"

"Coffee first," I breathed when I heard the machine ding, alerting me that it had finally finished brewing.

I grabbed a steaming mug for each of us and handed them out. Then we went over all the links and photos, and I told Hawk what happened three years ago with Sapphire. I also explained the theory I'd come up with and how the new development—a victim from the McKenzie Pack—had caused me to discard it.

By the time we were done, I could see the pride in Hawk's eyes as he observed me and Alaric. He was impressed by our findings but also wary of what it all meant.

"You think another hybrid dropped Kristen's remains on your lawn?" Hawk asked, his gaze on Alaric.

"I'm not sure. The ashy scent reminded me of the hybrid I killed the other day."

*And it reminded me of something else,* I thought, frowning to myself. *But what?* I couldn't pinpoint it. The memory was there and gone in a flash, tainted by the odd underlying addition of smoke. As Vex had been my one and only experience with a hybrid, I didn't have any other suspects for my list. So I just shook my head, unable to add anything else of use.

"All right, so it seems we have someone creating hybrids. A trafficking ring. Murdered wolves. And missing girls." Hawk recapped it all while scratching his chin, then he dove into a string of potential theories that left all three of us staring at the murder board afterward in an attempt to figure out our next lead.

"Well, at least we have Neo," I said after a beat.

"Neo? Who the fuck is Neo?" Alaric growled.

"The wolf Vex sent to tell the boss about the delivered

silver packages," I replied, my gaze still on the board. "Have you found anything on him yet?"

"How the hell would I have found anything on him?" he demanded. "This is the first I'm hearing about him."

I glanced at him. "Okay, first, that question was for Hawk. Second, I tried to tell you about him when you went all…" I trailed off and made a gesture of an explosion. "And then you were all"—I growled and crossed my arms over my chest—"and focused on the boss after I mentioned Neo the second time."

Hawk chuckled.

Alaric's frown deepened. Clearly, he did not share his father's amusement.

"So you probably didn't hear it over all your snarling," I added as though he hadn't already caught on to my jibe.

"Cute," he drawled.

"Aren't I, though?" I winked, then focused on his dad. "Any leads on Neo?"

"Not yet, but I only sent out the request after we spoke yesterday. It'll take a bit to gather the packs' files, especially with everything else going on."

I nodded. "Okay." I drained the rest of my second cup of coffee and set it on a nearby table. My attention went back to the board, my body thrumming with caffeine. Tapping my jaw, I studied the documents. "I feel like I'm missing something, and it's driving me crazy."

We'd added a new section to the board while talking to Hawk—a spot for things that seemed to point to experiments. Like the silver packages, which we assumed had been manufactured somehow, and the hybrid, because how the hell had he been made? Hawk had had no suggestions. He'd been pretty alarmed to learn about the fire-breathing capability, as had I.

*Still think he's some sort of dragon breed,* I thought, narrowing my gaze at the experiment part of the wall.

"Okay, we have a hybrid, maybe two, and silver tools… so some sort of lab?"

The Ferris wheel of facts in my head suddenly slowed, and one by one, they jumped off the ride and grouped together.

*Hybrid.*

*Silver tools.*

*Lab—or a warehouse…*

"A warehouse!" I exclaimed as I spun around to face the men. "A warehouse on Grand Street."

"What about a warehouse?" Alaric asked, clearly confused by my outburst.

"After Vex's phone call about the silver, he specifically mentioned a warehouse on Grand to Neo."

Alaric frowned. "Well, that's an interesting detail." He checked the time, then glanced out the windows. After a beat, he looked at his father. "I can't leave to check it out."

A gleam entered Hawk's gaze. "Why not?"

"Because it doesn't feel right." He palmed the back of his neck and blew out a harsh breath. "I… I feel… *needed.*"

His dad nodded. "That's your wolf talking."

"I know." He flinched. "He won't let me go even if I want to."

"Because the alpha in you senses a threat *close to home.* Listen to those instincts, son. They'll guide you."

Alaric sighed. "Then who is going to check out the warehouse?"

"E.V.I.E." The idea just sort of tumbled from my mouth without thought, but it made complete sense. Although, I supposed offering to go would make even more sense.

However, I sort of understood Alaric's comment about

not being able to leave. My wolf felt similarly, something I'd have to investigate more later. Maybe she just missed Silver Lake?

I shook off the sensation and focused on Alaric. "Maybe Jude can send someone to check it out?"

Alaric already had his tablet in hand, pulling up a text screen to shoot a message. "On it."

He finished typing, then looked at me and his dad. "How soon until the files on Neo are rea—"

His question was interrupted by a ringing. I half expected it to be Jude, only the sound came from Hawk's phone, not Alaric's.

Hawk pulled the mobile from his pocket, answering, "Calder."

"Sir, Beta Mavi from Elk Neck Pack called into our main line. He wants to talk to you," a male voice said, his deep voice easily carrying to my wolf ears.

"Beta Mavi?" Hawk frowned. "What happened to Beta Byers?"

"I think that's why he's calling, sir," the man replied.

Hawk's shoulders squared, his sharp gaze cutting to his son as he said, "Thanks, Rick. You can put him through."

Alaric braced his legs, his stance rivaling his father's protective posture. I smiled a little inside at the sight, noting how similar Alaric was to his dad. I'd noticed it outside earlier, and I'd glimpsed it during a few other interactions, but now with the way they held themselves in the same stance, using the same tone while speaking, I realized just how identical they were.

Alaric was definitely born an alpha, destined to lead.

However, my musing ended when a deep voice said, "Alpha Calder, sorry to meet like this, but we have five more sick wolves. All silver poisoning and fresh." There was a pause as the male cleared his throat. "We think it's linked to Alpha Warren's funeral."

"Why?" Hawk asked, his body vibrating with anger.

Alaric appeared the same, tension lining his limbs and tightening his jaw.

"Because the funeral was last night and our leadership all fell ill within hours of the ceremony," Beta Mavi replied, his tone gruff. "We... we think the ritual cup was somehow laced with silver."

I wasn't familiar with Bitten pack burials but suspected that part of the tradition was reserved for those in power positions. Which explained Hawk's confusion about Beta Byers.

"It's... it's why I'm acting beta," he added, confirming my assumption.

"Inform the others," Hawk told him, the alpha clear in his voice.

"Yes, sir," Beta Mavi replied.

"I'll organize a council meeting as well," Hawk concluded. "Be sure to attend."

"Of course, sir."

"As well as your acting alpha," Hawk added. "Assuming you have one?"

"Not yet, sir." Beta Mavi sounded uncertain. "I... I would be next in line."

"Then call yourself Alpha Mavi," Hawk said, his tone underlined in command. "If someone wants to challenge you later, so be it. But own the position, son. It's how you maintain order within your pack."

"Y-yes, sir," *Alpha* Mavi replied, not sounding at all certain or in charge. He cleared his throat. "Thank you, sir."

"You're welcome." Hawk ended the call, then he looked at his son.

"Spiking the ceremonial cup would have to be an inside job," Alaric said, not missing a beat. "Which means Elk Neck is compromised."

"And Gloria is still missing," Hawk added, emotion darkening his voice. "First someone enters our boundaries and attacks a wolf under our protection—because Kristen was under our jurisdiction while visiting—and now someone has attacked a burial rite."

Alaric's chest rumbled, his wolf agitated. "We need to confer with the other packs. Find out who else was attacked." He glanced down and then up again. "And I should also reach out to McKenzie Pack about Kristen."

A very alpha-like thing to say, but Alaric didn't seem to notice.

His father did, though. I caught the glint in his blue eyes, the pride eclipsing his frustration for just a fraction of a second before his shoulders fell on a sigh. "We can't properly honor Tyler's life under these circumstances. Not when I can't trust the unspoken laws of engagement to be upheld for a funeral."

"Yes, whoever is doing this lacks any and all honor," Alaric agreed, as did I.

Because who the hell attacked mourning wolves during a funeral? *A monster,* I thought. *A fucking monster.*

Hawk swallowed, his expression shadowed as he softly admitted, "I don't know what to do. I can't not bury my son. But I can't risk the pack either."

My heart broke for him, not only because he had to voice that confession, but also because he was right. They couldn't host a funeral under these circumstances. And they also couldn't just leave Tyler's body in a state of unrest. It went against the natural order for wolves. We mourned our dead as a pack. That was the same across both realms.

"We'll bury him tonight," Alaric decided, taking charge. "Just family. Give him the moment he deserves, then avenge him by bringing this asshole to justice." He stalked over to his father and grabbed his shoulders. "And when this is all said and done, we'll give him a proper ceremony."

His father met and held his gaze. Then he pulled his son into a hug that would crush a smaller wolf.

Warmth spread through me, Alaric's actions speaking volumes about his future. He'd been slowly changing, taking the mantle without even registering it, because it came naturally.

*Hawk's right,* I thought as the two men continued to embrace one another. *Alaric's absolutely meant for this. He just needs to realize it for himself.*

# CHAPTER 19

## ALARIC

I PRESSED my palm to Tyler's gravesite, my eyes closing as I whispered a mental goodbye to the man who would always be my idol.

*Run free, brother,* I said to him. *Until we meet again.*

Time seemed to stand still around me.

The air froze, allowing me this brief second of grief.

I took it.

I swallowed it.

I embodied it and allowed it to settle in my soul.

This was the sort of moment I would always remember. The moment I would avenge. The moment that would shape my future.

Not because of my alpha legacy.

But because of Tyler's legacy.

*I'll kill them all,* I promised silently. *You will rest easy, brother. I vow it.*

My father's warmth seeped into my side as he murmured a blessing out loud, praising Tyler for his life and the sacrifices he made for the pack. They were old words meant for a traditional ceremony, but only five of us were here to observe it.

Me and my parents.

Makayla and Savannah.

It was oddly fitting. A small ceremony of family. And yet, I barely knew Makayla. However, when my father had shown up in his all-black suit, I'd automatically grabbed her hand to take her with me.

I refused to consider why. I refused to think about it all. Tyler had my focus, my heart, my mind, my grief.

I swallowed, my fingers curling into the free dirt. We'd buried him ourselves using shovels. An old-fashioned method, but an oddly calming one. The task had consumed my mind, allowing me to thrive in the present with my brother and family. *And Makayla.*

She stood just behind me, her floral perfume a welcome scent on the incoming evening breeze. I was no longer frozen. Time no longer stood still. Life revived around me.

My father had stopped speaking, all of us saying our own form of goodbye. I couldn't even remember when I'd crouched or how long I'd been squatting. My legs ached, my hands were filthy with dirt, and yet my heart beat a little steadier now.

I'd said my goodbyes.

I'd made my vows.

And now it was time to carry out those promises. To seek vengeance. *To kill.*

Except I needed rest before I could properly take on those tasks. I'd meant to sleep earlier, but the events of this morning had bled into the afternoon and evening. And now here we were, close to midnight, standing over a freshly covered grave with nothing but the moon as our witness.

I stood and wiped the dirt from my hands on my black pants, then I faced my father.

Alpha Hawk Calder.

A true leader.

He lifted an arm for a hug, and I stepped into his embrace like I used to when I was young. For just a breath, I allowed myself to feel vulnerable, to be the kid from my youth and accept my father's affection.

And then I returned it, my wolf brushing his beneath our skin, giving him the reassurance he needed.

*I'm here.*

*We're going to fix this.*

*We'll avenge Tyler together.*

My dad clapped me on the back, his signal that he felt my words more than understood them, and then he released me to pull my mother into a hug.

Savannah stood beside her, looking lost.

I almost stepped toward her, but Makayla took my mother's place and wrapped a comforting arm around Savannah. They didn't know each other. However, it didn't matter. Makayla's alpha pheromones provided a blanket of peace and comfort that instinctually soothed Savannah's wolf, allowing the two women to bond.

*This is why,* I thought. *This is why I grabbed her hand.*

She belonged here.

In this moment.

With us.

*Family.*

Her bright blue eyes met mine, a current of understanding falling between us. Even if we chose not to continue into the future together, I would forever know that fate had delivered her to me at precisely the right moment.

A gust of wind caressed my cheek, my brother's presence all around us, his spirit blessing this precious second.

There and gone in the space of a blink.

"Goodbye, Tyler," my mother whispered. "We'll see each other again."

"We will," my father agreed, kissing the top of her head.

Savannah sniffled, her gaze on Tyler's gravesite. "Fate might not have called him mine, but I did."

"Then that makes him yours," Makayla replied quietly. "Always."

"Yes." Savannah looked at her. "Thank you."

"Anytime," Makayla replied, giving her another squeeze.

Savannah cleared her throat and took a step away. "I actually think I'm going to… run back." She swallowed. "I feel like being alone with my wolf, just for a bit."

"Are you sure you don't want company?" my mother asked.

"I'd be happy to run with you," I interjected, innately disturbed by the prospect of leaving Savannah to mourn on her own.

But she shook her head. "No, no. I really… I just need to do this… by myself. For a little while." She winced. "I… I need to grieve. With my wolf."

Makayla moved to my side, her hand finding mine and giving it a squeeze. My hackles immediately smoothed— hackles I hadn't even realized were raised. But the notion of just leaving a packmate to hurt… *alone*… unsettled my wolf.

"Please," Savannah pressed, the word soft, a packmate seeking permission from those she saw as alpha. "I need this."

"Of course, Savi," I told her, using the nickname I knew she preferred. "But if you need one of us, don't be afraid to seek us out, okay?"

She nodded, her lips curling into a watery smile. "I

know. You all have been... the family I needed. Thank you." She took another step away, then turned for the woods and disappeared behind a tree. A moment later, her brown fur poked into view, her eyes gleaming yellow beneath the moonlight.

And then she bolted into the underbrush.

My mother bit her lip, uncertainty etched into her features. "I feel like I should go with her, Hawk."

"Sometimes it's best to let them fly a little," my father whispered to her. "She'll come back when she's ready." His blue eyes met mine, the message not lost on me. "They always do."

My usual gut reaction of annoyance didn't appear.

Instead, I felt resigned. Like I'd been running from something all my life and had finally decided to just start walking.

Not away from my destiny necessarily, but around it.

A trail of what-ifs sprawled out before me, the choices vast and intimidating.

I shook my head, exhausted and not wanting to ponder that mess right now. It resembled a maze of torment that all led to the same end.

Makayla gave my palm another squeeze, drawing my attention to her beautiful face. *You okay?* she seemed to be asking.

I nodded, then brushed a kiss against her forehead, thanking her for being with me tonight. It felt so natural, my lips against her skin, that I lingered for half a beat before pulling back.

Approval radiated from my mother as she melted into my father's side.

Then the four of us made the long walk back to the pack.

We could have driven, but this experience was about

reflection and honoring Tyler's existence. With every step, I thought of a new memory. Some of them, I shared out loud with Makayla, just because it seemed right to tell her about my brother.

She laughed a few times, entertained by our antics.

My mother joined her, too, adding her own commentary about the trouble we used to cause together.

It was uplifting in a lot of ways, our mutual reminiscence refreshing. "I can't believe you know about that," I said, a laugh in my voice. "God, Tyler and I were sure we'd kept that secret from you."

My mom scoffed. "Please, there's not a damn thing you two did that I don't know about."

"Her ears are even better than mine," my dad added, winking at me. "But she's right. You two were not nearly as stealthy as you thought you were."

I chuckled, shaking my head. Tyler and I had done some stupid shit as teenagers, like setting off that firework by the old shed. "You two weren't even home," I recalled.

"Doesn't mean we were deaf, boy," my dad retorted. "That firecracker nearly blitzed my damn hearing."

"Oh, come on. It wasn't *that* loud." *It totally was.* Tyler and I had immediately regretted setting it off, and proceeded to destroy all the others.

"You two weren't wolves yet," my mother pointed out. "So of course it wasn't loud. *To you.*"

Well, she had a point there. I couldn't even imagine what it would sound like now.

"This sounds like something my brother would have done, only with a toy gun or something," Makayla said. "He went into the military at eighteen, mostly because he wanted to make a difference in the world. But I think it was also his penchant for loud noises and the potential to blow shit up."

"Is your brother older or younger?" I wondered out loud, aware that I barely knew anything about her family.

"Older. I was only eight when he left for the military." She smiled. "Pretty sure that's what motivated me to join enforcer training. I wanted to be like him. Or I thought I did, anyway. Then my skill set evolved, and I realized my true calling."

"And what's that?" my mother asked.

"Helping those who can't help themselves," she replied, smiling. "I went freelance, not wanting to be tied down to my alpha's company, and here I am."

"Fate put you exactly where she wanted you," my dad agreed, giving her a knowing grin.

Makayla just shook her head, but amusement shone in her expression. "I think Sapphire had something to do with it," she admitted.

"The witch?" my dad asked.

"Yep." Her lips popped on the *p*.

My dad gave my mom a brief summary of Sapphire being the witch Makayla had saved, and then added the bit about the witch's penchant for fortune-telling.

"Hmm," my mom hummed, doing that thing she loved to do. *And passed on as a family trait.*

"Don't," I warned her.

She merely smiled. "I did give you a week, didn't I?" She looked at my dad. "I get to pick our next vacation spot when I win."

"Win?" Makayla repeated.

"My parents are betting on us," I muttered, shaking my head again. "I say we leave them now and let them go find something else to place wagers on."

"I didn't bet against you," my dad was saying. "So you can't exactly win."

"I can," my mother argued. "And I will."

I bit my lip to keep from laughing, then tugged on Makayla's hand. "We'll let you two continue that conversation without us," I said, already walking in the direction of my house. "See you tomorrow, Dad."

"Five o'clock," he called back to me.

"I know." I'd been there when he'd made all the arrangements with the other alphas to meet tomorrow. Just as he'd been there for my conversation with the McKenzie Pack Alpha. That'd been... difficult. Yet I'd somehow found the right words to say.

Just like I had tonight with my parents.

*Maybe I'll figure this shit out, Ty,* I thought with a glance upward.

I pictured my brother's face and imagined what he would say back to me right now. *Of course you will, bro,* he'd say. *But first, you need to go seduce that pretty wolf.*

My lips twitched. It was like I could really hear him in my head. Probably because we'd spent many years glued to each other's hips.

"What's that look about?" Makayla asked, a smile in her voice.

"Tyler." Which probably didn't surprise her since we'd just spent all night talking about him. "I was thinking about what he'd say to me right now." I looked at her, studied her gorgeous, perfect face, and grinned. "He had no filter."

She leaned into me as we walked, her presence a balm I didn't realize I needed. "What would he say to you right now?"

I allowed my eyes to roam over her long-sleeved black dress. My mother had brought it for her to wear, as well as a pair of black sneakers. Wolves didn't really do heels. Not practical. And we liked to walk. A lot. But I imagined

Makayla would look good in a pair of stilettos. They'd accent her calves nicely.

"You look rather famished, Alaric," she said, a false note of concern in her voice. "Maybe you should have eaten earlier. Wouldn't want you to pass out from starvation."

My lips curled as a laugh taunted my chest.

*This girl.*

*This fucking girl.*

She knew exactly what to say to lighten my mood. And I sort of adored that about her. Hell, I loved a lot about her. The way she'd helped me with everything tonight. This week, even. How she'd essentially become my rock. The life-beat in my heart.

It all scared the shit out of me.

But fuck if I could be bothered to run right now.

I wanted more.

I needed her to give me more of that life, to ground me in this harsh world, to provide me with the anchor I required to remain docked in the present. "Will you tell me more about yourself?" I asked as we entered my house. "More about who you are, Makayla? I don't even know your last name."

And I found I wanted to know everything about her.

Every single beautiful detail.

"Laurier," she said, locking my front door behind us. "Makayla Laurier."

"No middle name?"

"Oh, I didn't realize we were going to get that personal." She gave me a sultry look as she started backward, her hand still clasped in mind. "You sure you want to talk? You still look hungry."

"Are you offering me something, Makayla No-Middle-Name Laurier?"

"Makayla Mae Laurier," she corrected. "But if you call me Makayla Mae, I'll stab you again."

I laughed outright. "That sounds like a challenge, sweetheart."

"I thought we decided I wasn't the sweet type?"

"Well, now, actually, if I recall, you asked me if you looked sweet to me." I ran my eyes over her again, grinning, as she kicked off her shoes. "And the answer is yes, delectable, even." I released her hand to grab her hip, yanking her to me. "So I'll give you a choice."

"A choice?" She smiled. "I like choices."

"I know you do, *mate*," I replied. "So I'll give you one."

"I'm listening."

"Good." I wrapped my arm around her, my opposite hand going to her thick, red hair. "We can talk all night, and you can regale me with stories of your childhood, similar to the ones I just shared tonight."

"Or," she prompted.

"*Or*…" I drew the word out, my voice dropping to a seductive murmur. "You can let me spread those creamy thighs and allow me to find out if you're as sweet as you smell." I walked her slowly backward toward the bedrooms. "Either way, it's happening in my bed. Talking or tasting. The activity choice is yours. The location decision is mine."

Her nostrils flared. "And if I just want to talk?"

"Then I'll listen to everything you have to say," I promised, guiding her expertly into my room and nudging the door closed with my boot. I drew my teeth across her bottom lip, loving the way she quivered in response. Her eyes practically burned into mine as I whispered, "What'll it be, mate?"

# CHAPTER 20

## MAKAYLA

*SEX. Definitely sex.*

Except that hadn't been one of his choices. Not quite. *Tasting*, he'd said. *To see if I'm as sweet as I smell.* Just the thought of his sensual words sent a shiver down my spine.

Because yes. Yes, I wanted that. Right now. With him.

And he'd given me the choice.

It was like he knew me without knowing me. A conundrum I didn't quite understand, one I chose to ignore now. We'd been sniffing around each other for the last few days, our attraction clearly mutual. Yeah, there was the whole fated-mates thing, but that didn't mean I couldn't sleep with him. Hell, if anything, it meant I *should* fuck him. A lot. Like over and over again until this whole burning sensation between us ebbed.

If that was even possible.

"Makayla," he murmured, his grip tightening in my hair. "You're not speaking. Should I infer that to mean you've chosen the other option?"

I licked my lips, his mouth a scant inch from mine. "Well, there is at least one thing you should know about me first." I trailed my fingers up the middle of his black dress shirt. He'd left it open at the collar, allowing a teasing glimpse of flesh to show.

*I want to lick him right there,* I thought, drawing back to study the dip in his clavicle bone. *Then I want to lick a path down his body and trail that light dusting of hair to the prize below.*

My stomach clenched with the image in my head, his body a treat I wanted to sample every inch of. "If you're going to taste me, then I want to taste you, too." I met his sapphire eyes, his irises illuminated by the moonlight streaming in through his window.

A vibration rumbled beneath my fingers, his wolf responding favorably to my words. "I want to go first."

My thighs clenched, his growl underlining those five words. It wasn't a request but a demand. A promise. A sealing of fate.

"Yes." There wasn't anything else to say. I could talk all night about myself just to try to avoid this, but why? What was the point? We both wanted each other. We were adults. "Yes," I repeated.

His lips curled into a feral grin. "Yes what?"

"*This.*" What the hell did he need? A map? Because if that was the case, we had a problem. I expected experience. I wanted him to take me to the damn moon with his tongue. Right. Fucking. Now.

"Oh, no, Makayla." His touch slid from my hair, his palm wrapping around my nape. "I want you to say it. Talking or tasting."

"Well, you seem to be in the mood for talking." Which was a giant waste of time.

"I'm absolutely not in the mood for talking, sweetheart." His arm tightened against my lower back, pulling me impossibly closer. "And I think we both know that." He rocked into me to punctuate his point, and I nearly swallowed my tongue.

*Because dear God, yes. Thick. Pulsing. Hot.*

I swallowed. "Alaric." It came out on a whine, my wolf

taking over my voice and shredding all sense of dignity within me.

"Say it."

*Damn man.* I arched into him, my fingers curling into his shirt and yanking downward to rip through the buttons of his fabric. He wanted words. I wanted actions. But hell if I was too proud not to play his little game.

He wanted me to say it?

I'd fucking say it.

"Taste me, Alaric." I grabbed hold of his belt, my nails sharpening as I tugged at the leather. "Or I'm going to find another wolf who will."

He growled in response to that, his arm turning to cement around me. "Not fucking happening."

"Then you had better damn well happen," I told him. "And you'd better be fucking phenomenal, too."

Arrogance darkened his expression. "Oh, Makayla." He released my back to catch my wrist, his opposite hand granite against my neck. "I'm better than phenomenal." He guided me backward until my legs brushed the mattress. "Don't move."

I didn't understand why he'd said that until the blade appeared in his hand. One minute, he was holding my wrist, and the next... "Alaric..."

"Shh," he whispered, drawing the knife down the middle of my chest. Not harshly, or even enough to threaten, but just the feel of his dagger had goose bumps pebbling down my arms.

*He must have had that in his pocket,* I thought, dizzy as he reached my belly button. *A prepared alpha. An armed wolf. A protective man.*

God, why was that such a turn-on?

My limbs turned to jelly just knowing he'd been armed all night, ready for anything.

And now…

Now he was drawing the blade along my thigh, to the hem of the dress and back up beneath the fabric. My thighs tingled as he softly traced my skin. So tender and sure, with no hint of hesitation. But up, up… *there*.

I froze, his name tickling my tongue.

He hushed me again, his gaze holding mine, studying my reaction to his ministrations below.

Not quite against my bare skin, just tracing the edge of my lacy panties up to my hip, where he deftly slid beneath the string to slice it right off.

A jolt went straight to my core, my body reacting to the intimacy of that act.

But he was moving again, and I stood transfixed by his actions, both terrified and excited by what he intended to do next.

The cool metal met my opposite hip as he severed the thin strap of my underwear. My legs trembled as he caught the lace with his blade and drew it out from between my thighs.

*Goddamn.*

I'd never let someone play with a weapon in bed before. Maybe a little clawing, but nothing like this.

He removed the knife from my skirts and lifted it upward between us, drawing my focus to the black lace twisted around the blade. Then my lips parted as he licked the damp part of the fabric.

A rumble sounded in his chest, and dear God, I almost combusted at the sight of his wolf overtaking his irises. Approval emanated from him in palpable waves, his hunger striking me in the gut.

"Fucking delicious, Makayla." His tone was the kind that usually accompanied a demand to strip or to kneel.

But he said neither of those things. Instead, he set his knife on the nightstand and grabbed my hips.

My dress disappeared in the next second, his hands having reached up to grab the straps and rip it down the middle.

"Now," he said softly, his gaze falling to my bra, "we're almost even." He bent to nibble my neck, his teeth skimming my pulse as he pushed me back onto the bed.

"Almost even?" I breathed, my chest heaving as he shifted me upward to the pillows.

"Mmm," he hummed, settling over me and licking a path downward to my breasts. "Knife play." He latched onto my nipple through the fabric, biting down and sucking at the same time.

I bowed off the mattress, my heart a rapid thundering sound in my ears.

"I prefer my method," he said against my lacy bra. "So much more sensual than stabbing." He bit down on the fleshy part of my breast, his teeth breaking the skin as he marked me with his teeth.

"Alaric," I hissed.

He laved the wound with his tongue, his chuckle all masculine arrogance. "Biting is also more sensual." He licked me again. "But now I made you really bleed."

I growled.

He chuckled again.

Then my bra disappeared, and he made it up to me by worshipping me with his mouth. *Christ, his tongue*, I thought, delirious as he traced my taut peaks and destroyed me again with his teeth. No more blood, just harsh tugs accompanied by soothing licks, to the point where I was ready to just float on up to heaven without the orgasm attached because he was just *that good* with his mouth.

Hell, I wouldn't be surprised if he made me come like this.

Because every single euphoric button I possessed was pressed in the span of minutes with his skilled mouth.

Only, he was nowhere near done.

Electricity shot up my spine as he began to descend, his blue eyes capturing mine as he kissed a path all the way down the center of my body.

He settled between my sprawled thighs, my center weeping in warm welcome, only to pause as he caught sight of my hip. The wolf marking practically gleamed in the moonlight, a beacon that somehow made me feel more exposed. And yet, it'd always been there. A literal birthmark that I'd carried all my life.

"All wolves of my kind have one," I told him, reading the question in his gaze.

"It's beautiful," he murmured, bending to trace the reddish-brown brand with his tongue. Heat curled in my lower abdomen in response, his intimate touch setting my blood on fire. "You're beautiful," he added, his voice low and darkly erotic against my inherited tattoo. "And you taste very fucking sweet." He nipped my hip bone before drawing his mouth to the heart of me, his lips wasting no time in sealing around my clit and sending me into a wave of euphoric convulsions.

Not an orgasm.

Not yet.

But damn close.

And unlike anything I'd ever experienced.

His name left my mouth on a prayer I couldn't hold back, his skill one that deserved my praise and so much more. He'd promised to deliver, and damn, did he deliver.

I felt devoured, revered, and utterly annihilated by his tongue, his teeth, his lips, his mouth. Stroking. Sucking.

Licking. Nibbling. All in a sequence that defied meaning. He added his fingers, too, his touch a searing brand inside me that sent me tumbling closer to the edge. Ready to fall. Ready to explode.

"Alaric," I whispered, begging him with my voice.

*I don't beg.*

*I don't crawl.*

But in that moment, I was willing to do whatever he damn well wanted so long as he allowed me a few seconds of dark oblivion.

And he knew it, too.

I could see it in his eyes as he stared up at me from between my thighs, the pride a palpable force that only made me burn hotter for him. This arrogant alpha *knew* he was good. The best, even. And he loved that I now knew it, too.

Damn, we hadn't even fucked yet, and I was ready to just lie down and supplicate.

He didn't force me to admit it. He didn't make me crawl or do any of these things. Just knowing he'd won was enough to push him forward, to clamp down on my sensitive bud and shoot me right into the stars.

I screamed. I panted. I shook. I went blind. The pleasure burned inside me, rippling through my limbs, claiming me from within and drowning me in a cloud of rapture that left me replete and oddly restless beneath him.

It wasn't enough.

It wasn't nearly enough.

And yet, I'd completely shattered for him.

But it wasn't his mouth that I craved now. I… I wanted *him*. "Fuck me," I demanded, not allowing myself a moment to even think about it. "God, Alaric, I need you to fuck me." I was in agony without him inside me, his presence one I required to breathe, to survive.

That orgasm had awakened my beast, her instincts rioting through me and commanding his wolf to complete us. To fuck us. To *please* us.

"You want my cock, baby?" he asked, his lips wet and suddenly against mine. "I thought you wanted to taste me." He dipped his tongue into my mouth, allowing me to indulge in my own flavor. *Musky. Feminine. Sweet.* God, he was right. But that didn't matter. What I needed, craved, and *required* was what mattered most.

"Fuck me," I repeated, arching into him and finding him as naked as me.

He'd kicked off his shoes and pants.

I didn't know when.

I didn't care when.

I just... oh God, he was so damn hard. "Inside me," I demanded. "Now, Alaric. Fuck me now." It wasn't a full moon, so I couldn't get pregnant. I couldn't contract diseases from him or anyone. Therefore, no protection was needed. Only him. "*Now*," I repeated, my nails turning into claws as I scratched down his back. My legs went around his hips, my soaking heat kissing his impressive arousal.

He growled.

I growled back.

There were two alphas in this bed, and I'd issued a demand. He would fuck me, and he would fuck me now. I sank my teeth into his lip, drawing blood, then went to his neck to do the same. If he wouldn't give me what I wanted, then I'd—

He slammed into me, eliciting a guttural sound from my throat. It vibrated through us to the bed and the walls, the pleasure of the moment eclipsing all rational thought and engulfing us in a sensual fog.

I licked the wound on his neck, then bit him again to

spur him on, needing this, needing him, needing everything he could give me.

He responded in kind, his beast taking over to drive the pace and drowning us in his savage energy.

*Hot.*

*Rapturous.*

*Heaven.*

Or maybe it was hell. It borderline hurt, our movements harsh and underlined in alpha strength. God, I'd never experienced anything like Alaric and his power. All that pent-up dominance resulted in a ferocity that stole my breath. But I took every thrust, accepting every nip and bite, and returned his fierce attention with bites of my own.

Alpha on alpha.

Man on woman.

Wolf on wolf.

It was an intimate dance underlined in deep, dark emotions. Alaric's pain from the loss of his brother. His frustrations over the pack and the expectations laid out before him. His anger over the situation with the hybrid. And the utter bliss he found in my presence, a soothing mechanism he hadn't realized he needed.

All those thoughts seemed to burst through me, his feelings touching mine as I unleashed my own back onto him.

My desire to solve this case.

My need to help others.

My innate loneliness over never finding the right place within my pack—an emotion I hadn't really ever noticed before, but one I felt now. Something from my childhood. A misplaced feeling I'd long buried after choosing my path. Why it chose now to surface, I didn't know.

And I was too lost to the rapturous dance with Alaric to consider it more.

He took us to new heights, introducing me to a euphoric world unlike any other.

His bite slayed me. His touch burned me. His cock branded me.

Every beautiful stroke sent me climbing that much higher, until my insides couldn't take it anymore and I burst wide open for the world to hear and see.

*So. Much. Heat.*

*So. Much. Pleasure.*

Dear Almighty, the passion—it was the most intense of my life, forever altering my understanding of sex. Alaric followed me into oblivion with a shout, his wolf growling in his chest and sending me tumbling into a third climax, my inner walls squeezing Alaric's cock as though to hold him there for the rest of my damn existence.

And we were only in missionary position.

Jesus, what could he do when driving into me from behind?

Up against a wall?

Over the counter?

All the ideas floated through my mind at once, some of them darker than any I'd ever envisioned for myself, and yet oddly right. I could almost sense Alaric doing the same, his brain already considering which way to take me next.

*Again,* I swore I heard him say. *We are doing that again.*

I huffed a laugh, my mouth finding his to lose us both to a kiss underlined in promise.

Because yeah, we were totally doing that again.

And probably a third time for good measure.

And then a fourth because why not?

Sleep was for the weak.

"We're not weak," Alaric said, somehow reading my mind.

I smiled. "Prove it."

He nibbled my lower lip, then pressed his mouth to my ear. "Get on all fours and I will."

# CHAPTER 21

## MAKAYLA

*Mmm. Damn, I feel awesome.*

My body felt used and abused. Satisfied and content. The events of last night replayed in my mind, and a slow smile spread across my face. My wolf purred in agreement.

A warm, strong body was curled around me, and I sighed as I snuggled deeper into his embrace.

*This feels so good. Oh, yes, I could absolutely get used to this.* Something about that thought gave me pause, clearing the sleepy fog from my mind.

I froze.

*No. It feels too good.*

*Shit.* I tried to squirm away, but Alaric's arms tightened around me. His hardness pressed against my ass, making me tingle with the memories of how he'd felt moving inside me.

On my back.

On my knees.

Against the headboard.

*Oh God, even on the dresser.*

We'd practically fucked across every inch of his bedroom.

My damn thighs were probably bruised. And yet my wolf radiated contentment, thoroughly pleased.

If I were being honest with myself, I'd agree to also being *thoroughly pleased*. He'd absolutely lived up to—and beautifully surpassed—all expectations.

"Good morning," he rumbled softly.

"Mm-hmm," I hummed.

"That's my line, sweetheart." His voice sent shivers down my spine. As did his impressive length searing my backside.

*Fuck it,* I thought. What could it hurt to indulge? Because, damn, last night had been dirty and decadent all rolled into a series of phenomenal sex.

I wiggled around to face him, and his mouth curled up into a sleepy smile in response.

I took in his beautiful face, strong neck, broad shoulders, and sculpted chest. "Do you think…?" My voice trailed off as a mark on Alaric's pec captured my focus.

*What in the…?*

*Oh!* I jackknifed up in bed, unable to look away from the reddish-brown tattoo-like brand of a wolf marring his skin.

That had definitely *not* been there last night.

"*Fuck,*" I breathed.

"Give me a minute, sweetheart. I'm still waking—"

"That's impossible," I interrupted. "We haven't—we didn't—we're not. This is wrong." My voice rose higher and higher until I was all but squeaking. I scrambled to my feet, standing over Alaric like some kind of giant, glaring down at him.

He sat up, his expression suggesting he thought I'd lost my mind.

How I wished he were right.

I reached down to touch him, just in case.

And nope. Definitely real. Definitely branded. Definitely *my* wolf.

He didn't seem to notice, his gaze turning concerned as I began to pace, all the while glaring at his tattoo and willing it to go away.

Could he not feel it?

Was I imagining it?

*Maybe… Maybe…*

Alaric grasped my hand to stop my movements. "Makayla, what the hell is wrong with you?"

I pointed a trembling finger at his pec. "*That.*"

His gaze dropped to the wolf tattoo. "What the hell?" He released me to poke at it, his expression more curious than anything. "Huh." After poking it again, his eyes drifted to my hip. "You have—"

"Yes," I groaned as I sank back down to the mattress.

He shrugged as if I'd just informed him that it was Tuesday when he thought it was Monday. "Never been into tats, but whatever."

"You don't understand. This is… this means… it doesn't work… and it's impossible. We can't be—we can't!"

Alaric simply stared at me. "That made no sense. But I'm going to take it as a compliment that you've forgotten how to properly speak English." He caught my wrist and yanked me into his lap, his smile wicked. "Let's see if I can make you lose your voice next."

I shoved him away and rolled off the bed and onto my feet again. "No, no. No more touching. No more *this.* No more *mating*," I declared, holding out my hand like a stop sign.

Alaric flopped back onto the pillows with his hands behind his head. "A bit late for that, sweetheart."

I sputtered for a second, then glared at him and began to pace once more. He merely grinned, which, of course, made my wolf do cartwheels inside me. I tugged on my hair to keep myself from wrapping my hands around Alaric's neck and throttling him. Or strangling myself. I couldn't decide what I wanted to do more.

*This is bad. This is so bad.*

"It's fine," Alaric said as he peeled back the covers and moved to the edge of the bed.

He had his talk with the alphas today. And—I glanced at a clock on his nightstand—since we'd slept all of the morning away, he was running out of time to prepare. His father wanted him to attend as the Silver Lake Alpha, a task Alaric had accepted without argument. He hadn't yet commented on the future of that role, and I suspected he wouldn't for some time. Still, the position looked good on him.

However, I wasn't done flipping the fuck out!

I scrambled onto the mattress and up to his side, grasping his biceps to keep him from standing until we figured this shit out. "How are you not more freaked out, Alaric?"

He shrugged. "I grew up understanding the concept of fated mates. The moment we met, I knew you were my future. Doesn't mean this has to be a thing, Mak. We like each other. Let's just leave it at that for now."

"For *now*? I don't think you understand the gravity of this situation, Alaric. *We're mates.*"

He palmed my cheek and brought our faces close together. "I'm aware, sweetheart. But feel free to keep fighting it. It's kind of hot." His blue eyes were dark with desire, and he covered my mouth with his own.

I almost gave in, but I was terrified that if we continued, it might deepen the bond. Who the hell knew what would happen then? There was no rule book for crossed fates!

"You don't understand," I said, pulling away. "This isn't how it works for my kind. That mark should only show up after completing the first and second stages. And... and... it's darkening, too. *Shit.*" I pressed my palm to his chest again. "This wasn't here last night. Right? Like, you've never had a birthmark here?"

He arched a brow. "The thing about birthmarks is that you're born with them. They don't come and go."

"I know that, Alaric."

He grinned. "Then the answer is no, sweetheart. I didn't have a wolf on my chest until this morning."

"Ugh, that's not what I mean." Seriously, how was he not upset about this? "Did you have a birthmark here at any point?"

He must have heard the seriousness in my tone because his expression turned pensive. "No, Makayla. It's always been smooth skin. No mark."

"Then maybe it's temporary."

Now he rolled his eyes. "Fated mates are not temporary."

"My kind doesn't do fated mates!" I said for the thousandth time. "We have five stages. They are specific and have to be followed for that"—I pointed at the *darkening* brand on his pec—"to happen."

His hand slid from my cheek to the back of my neck. "Rules don't seem to apply here, sweetheart." He kissed me again, his calmness seeping in through our *bond*. Which meant he could feel my anxiety, too. Yet he countered it with a sweep of his tongue across my mouth, demanding I open for him.

I clamped down my jaw instead. *No.*

He growled and nipped my lower lip in response. "You run, I chase. And, baby, that just turns me on more."

My wolf spun in a dizzying circle inside me, liking the sound of that.

*No*, I repeated.

I shoved him away again, and he allowed me to flee with a laugh, clearly unbothered. He stood from the bed, momentarily distracting me with his tight, sexy ass. Then he disappeared into the bathroom, and the fog of lust dissipated.

I dropped my face into my hands and groaned. *It's not supposed to happen like this.*

"Like what?"

I froze for a second, then my head popped up and I stared at the bathroom door in disbelief. "I didn't say that... no. No! No, no, no! You can't be in my head!"

*Totally in your head, sweetheart.*

This wasn't right. I shouldn't have heard him in my head. "Impossible. Impossible. This is impossible!"

*You know, Bitten mates don't usually have telepathy.*

A growl of frustration escaped me, and I mentally snapped, *I'm not talking to you.*

*Hmm, well, if you're not talking to me, could you speak to yourself a little more quietly? You're giving me a headache.*

I grabbed a pillow from the bed and screamed into it, only to hear him laughing in my head.

The next thing I knew, the pillow was torn from my hands and Alaric stood directly in front of me in all his naked glory. I tried really hard not to think about dirty things and how turned on I was at the sight of him, but his devilish grin told me I'd epically failed.

He captured my hand and tugged me off the bed and into the bathroom, filled with steam from the running shower. "If those are the kinds of thoughts you are having about me, this telepathy thing might not be so bad," he said with a grin, and he pushed me into the hot spray.

*Or I could stab you again,* I thought darkly.

He tsked. "Hmm, now, I thought we covered proper knife play last night." He grabbed a bar of soap from a nook on the wall and began láthering his hands. "Or do you need another lesson?"

# CHAPTER 22

## ALARIC

MAKAYLA SPUTTERED BENEATH THE WATER, her thoughts vacillating between want and denial.

*Yes, please.*

*No. Not happening.*

*But last night—*

*Cannot. Be. Repeated.*

My lips twitched. "You let me know when you've worked all that out, sweetheart."

She glared in response, the water dampening her beautiful red hair to a ruby shade that matched her ring. I set the soap aside, then ran my hands over my body as a taunt. Her pretty eyes followed the path of my touch, her pupils dilating with a desire her mind adamantly fought.

*No. We can't be mates. We just can't. I don't want a mate!*

"Why?" I asked her, picking up the soap again to lather a few more suds into my palms for my legs. "Why are you so against having a mate?" I knew why I had never craved one, but we hadn't discussed her reasoning before. Just that she didn't want one.

Her lips tugged down. "It's... it's not that I'm against you..."

"That's not what I asked," I replied, bending to draw

my hands along my calves and thighs. "I want to know why you don't want a mate. Not me, just a mate."

I stood to find her nibbling on her lip, her pensive gaze matching the thoughts in her mind. She ran her fingers through her hair, then shifted when she heard me thinking about the water. *This telepathy stuff is really useful,* I noted.

She snorted in response.

"Can you imagine what it'll feel like when I make you come?" I asked conversationally. "I'll be able to *hear* your pleasure. Just thinking about it makes me so damn hard." Her gaze dropped to my erection, her nostrils flaring.

"You're trying to distract me."

"I'm trying to point out that there are benefits to this arrangement, Mak," I replied, turning to rinse the soap from my front. I could feel her eyes on my ass.

*Like granite...* Her muttered words had my lips twitching. But I didn't interrupt her perusal by replying. Instead, I waited. Because I could hear her thinking through her reply to my question about mates. She wanted to explain it right, and I was more than willing to wait.

It wasn't until I had the shampoo in my hand that she finally said, "It's not that I'm anti-mating. I'm just... I've spent the last decade discovering my place in the world. And I'm not ready to give that up for a mate."

Her words gave me pause, the shampoo bottle frozen in my palm. "You think your mate would make you choose between him and your job?"

"Wouldn't you?" she asked, making it personal rather than theoretical. "You're an alpha, Alaric. If you decide to take over this pack, I'm obligated to them just as much as you are."

It was on the tip of my tongue to dismiss that statement, yet I couldn't find a voice for my words. Because it felt wrong to say something like, *It's a moot point anyway.*

*I'm not taking over.* I wasn't sure I believed that. And so I couldn't claim it out loud.

*"Listen to those instincts, son. They'll guide you."*

My father's statement replayed through my mind as Makayla blew out a breath.

"I'm not from here," she blurted out, speaking her thoughts aloud rather than keeping them secluded to her head. "You weren't even born with the mark, Alaric. Like this all has to be some sort of mistake. An eligible true mate in my world is born with the mark of their animal, regardless of their origin."

"Is that why you asked me about birthmarks?"

"Yes." She grabbed the shampoo from me and squirted a healthy amount into her hand. "Between the different worlds and your alpha status, I don't know how this could work, Alaric." She held out the bottle for me to take back from her. "I won't give up who I am. I've worked too hard. I love what I do. And I refuse to be tied down."

I considered that for a moment, then admired the view as she lathered the shampoo into her hair. Then I followed suit and switched positions with her when she mentally asked for the water. When she finished rinsing, I took over the showerhead again and did the same. Then I leaned against the wall while she started soaping up her gorgeous body.

"I became a slayer because I've always enjoyed adventure and the thrill of the chase," I said. "It also placated my more aggressive instincts and gave me a purpose. I protect people because it's a natural inclination." My blood heated as a soapy droplet trailed over her stiff nipple, taunting the rosy peak and glistening in the low lighting of the bathroom.

I cleared my throat before returning my gaze to hers.

"At no point would I ever expect you to give up what

you love for me, Makayla. I understand the desire to be a lone wolf more than most, and I would never expect you to just stop doing your job because we're mates." It felt important to say that to her because it was true. I'd never even considered tying her down.

Okay, no, that wasn't true.

"I'll admit I've fantasized about locking you in a cage to use to my heart's content, but that's purely to feed my sexual beast," I said, aware she could probably hear it in my mind, so I might as well get that out there right now. "But part of the fun of that imagery is knowing you'd fight like a hellcat and make the sex so much hotter as a result."

"I would kill you." The serious quality in her tone just made me grin.

"And the battle would be erotic as fuck," I drawled.

"Until you died."

"Hmm," I hummed, taking a step toward her. She didn't move, which placed my hard dick right against her soapy belly. "Or you'd end up panting beneath me."

"Only from the exertion of stabbing you."

I chuckled, amused. Then I leaned in to draw my nose along her cheek, my lips going to her ear. "The pull between us is mutual, Mak." I pressed my mouth to her thundering pulse, stirring a shiver from her. "It's magnetic and electric and hot as hell. And while I might not have wanted a mate, I'm not going to belittle what exists between us, sweetheart. Last night was the best sex of my life, and I fully intend to repeat it."

"Then you've not listened to anything I've said."

"On the contrary, baby, I've heard every word." I nipped her neck, then stood to my full height to recapture her gaze. "You don't want a mate who will tie you down and demand you quit. Well, good news. I'm not that kind of mate. You want to keep working freelance, go for it. I'm not going to hold you back."

It'd go against every part of me to do such a thing.

Except for in the bedroom. That might be fun.

But in the real world? In life? Hell no.

"However, I would like to know more about your job." I stepped backward to dampen my hair again, then plucked the conditioner off the shelf.

"More about my freelance life?" she asked, sounding surprised.

"Yeah, like how it all works. You mentioned training with your alpha's company... uh, KBO?"

"KBO Consulting."

I ran my fingers through my thick strands, coating my hair with the moisturizer. "Yeah, that. You worked there before Marc recruited you for the gig here, and then you went freelance, right?"

She nodded, a note of pride touching her expression.

"So, what does that mean? You go back and forth between realms, looking for jobs?" I understood what "freelance" meant, just not how it worked for her.

She retrieved the conditioner and mimicked my movements, then said, "Well, Marc shared my contact details with several of his clients back in our home realm. I have a soft spot for taking on trafficking cases, as I've mentioned, so I get a lot of missing person files. Usually girls. But I've also been trying to establish myself in your world. That's not been as easy, considering I'm not from here. However, Sapphire kept sending me leads. Including the one that brought me here most recently."

*Which I now know was a total setup,* she added in her head. *Thanks, Saph.*

I didn't comment on her mental note since it wasn't meant for me. Instead, I focused on what she'd said out loud. "Why have you wanted to establish yourself here?" I asked before dipping backward to let the shower pour down over my head. Wolf-ear perks allowed me to hear her just fine, even over the rushing water sound.

"Honestly? Because your realm needs me more than my own does. Your supernats are… less robust."

I snorted. "What makes you say that?"

"Well, for starters, you kill vamps with stakes. Ours don't die that easily. Ours are also much faster and stronger, can compel, and have a whole slew of upgraded traits."

*Huh. Does that apply to Cassius?* I wondered.

*Yep,* she replied without missing a beat.

Not that I'd been asking her, but it was good to know.

*He's a royal, too. Part of the Vampire Dynasty bloodline. His cousin, Dimitri, is the former king. He was dethroned. It's a whole thing.*

*Interesting,* I replied, finishing with the water and switching spots with her so she could rinse. "Okay, but wouldn't that make it easier for humans to survive here, then?"

"Around vampires? Yeah, I guess. But it's more… your humans are just as dark and dangerous as ours… and I have a stronger skill set to help handle those issues?" She voiced it like a suggestion, but I followed what she meant.

"You think the supernaturals of this realm are too weak to properly protect them." I tried not to be offended by that. *Tried and failed.*

"I just acknowledge that I'm stronger, and you all could use my brand of assistance," she rephrased.

"Uh-huh." I caught her hip as she finished washing her hair and backed her up against the wall. "You think I'm weaker than you?"

"Well, you're mortal."

"Mortality just means I value life more," I argued. "And I still heal quickly."

"Not as fast as me."

"Yeah?" I bent to bite her neck, breaking the skin and laving the wound. She hissed with pain, then grabbed my shoulder and dug her claws into my skin.

"What the hell?" she demanded.

I grinned against her throat. "Just testing your healing, *mate*."

She growled.

I growled back. Then I kissed her cheek. "So you're immortal, then?" That would certainly pose an interesting challenge for our *connection*. It was a revelation that should probably bother me a bit more, but all I could think was, *That makes her indestructible.* And that thought strongly appealed to my wolf.

"I stopped aging, or will stop, sometime in my twenties," she said. "It's not an exact science. But yeah, I'll stay this way… and I'm hard to kill."

"Well then, that just makes it even easier to accept your job," I admitted. "Not that I needed the extra reasoning. You can clearly take care of yourself. Knowing you're more unbreakable just adds another layer of security to it."

She met and held my gaze, her blue eyes searching. "You really don't care that I take jobs that put my life on the line every day?"

"You just claimed to be immortal."

"Yeah, but I can still die."

I studied her. "Are you trying to convince me to lock you up, Makayla? Or do you want to be free? I'm confused."

"I'm just… I'm surprised you're so open to the idea of me working."

"Why wouldn't I be?" I countered. "I work for E.V.I.E.

for a reason. I've taken numerous cases that endangered my well-being. Case in point, the hybrid. So I'd be a hypocrite to keep you from your passion, especially when I'm also passionate about your kind of work." I cupped her cheek and pressed my lips to hers. "I'm not going to chain you down, Mak. Not unless you beg me to while naked, of course." A man had his standards, after all.

Her lips twitched, the first sign of true humor touching her face. "I'll never beg for that."

"Never say never," I teased, kissing her again before drawing back, my tone falling serious once more. "Let's not overreact to this, okay? I understand it's a lot to accept, especially with the whole realms thing. But I'm not going to go all beast on you and start making demands. As I've said, I never wanted a mate. However, last night certainly proved there are benefits to it, and I'll very happily indulge in those benefits again."

# CHAPTER 23

## MAKAYLA

VERACITY RADIATED FROM ALARIC, his conviction palpable.

He meant it.

If I wanted to continue working, he wouldn't stop me. And while he'd joked about caging me and chaining me up, I knew he hadn't really meant it—outside the bedroom, anyway. He wouldn't force me to stay here with him. He wouldn't force me to do anything. Because on some level, he understood my need to continue helping people. Probably because of his work as a slayer. Or maybe it was just his lone wolf relating to mine.

Regardless, his words set a part of me free.

The dread I felt this morning melted away, disappearing down the drain with the water from the shower, leaving me breathless and light.

*One day at a time,* I decided. *We'll take this one day at a time.* He might be mine. Or he might not be really mine. The realms made it tricky and definitely provided an obstacle for us to overcome.

However, for the moment, I'd accept what this was, indulge in the sensations between us, and not worry about what it all meant.

*For just today.*

*Tomorrow, I'll… I'll just see what happens.*

I lifted onto my toes to kiss him, showing him my gratitude with my mouth. He indulged me in long, sensuous strokes with his tongue, his cock a brand against my lower belly. But he didn't try to push us any further. He just returned my embrace, his mouth holding a whisper of promises. Vows. A subtle display of the future to come.

*Mine*, his touch hummed.

However, he didn't force it.

He just enjoyed our connection, choosing to live in the moment rather than demand either of us accept our destiny.

And I found I liked that approach.

It gave us cause to revel in the sensations without overthinking them.

We remained in each other's arms until the water started to cool, merely kissing and touching and holding one another. It was intimate and warm and exactly what I needed. By the end, I felt so at peace that I nearly forgot what lay ahead of us.

*The alpha meeting.*

Alaric would represent Silver Lake as the temporary alpha, and his father would attend as well. I'd probably spend the time continuing to review all the files.

"Okay, so there's one thing I don't understand," Alaric said as we wrapped ourselves up in two oversized towels.

"Only one thing?"

He grunted. "Well, several. But specifically, I'm wondering how payments work. Like, do you only accept cash? And is our cash good in your realm?"

"Ah." I followed him into his bedroom, where he started going through the drawers for clothes. I'd have to go down the hall to find some that fit me. "So, when Marc and I originally popped into this world, he helped me establish an identity. It just made things easier. I actually have a bank account here, a name, even an address." I frowned. "Assuming my landlord received my rent money."

"In New York City?" he guessed.

"Yep. I have a place in the same building here as I do back home. Both are rentals since I don't like to put down roots."

He nodded. "I'd be the same way in your position. I only bought my condo in the city because of working for E.V.I.E. It made sense."

I also suspected he'd done that to have an excuse to remain close to his pack, but I didn't voice that assumption out loud. Mostly because I suspected he'd probably deny it, and I preferred not to ruin our bonding moment. He probably heard it floating around my head anyway.

*Damn link.*

He cleared his throat, giving me a look. "None of that."

"I didn't say anything."

"Uh-huh." He pulled on a pair of jeans, leaving me a little disappointed. I rather enjoyed admiring his gorgeous, naked body. "Okay, so you have an account here. And that's how you're paid? Like, by clients in this realm?"

I shook my head. "No. Not exactly. I… take my payment via other means."

"Elaborate." He phrased it as a demand, but I caught the curiosity in his gaze, so I decided to let it slide.

"Well, sometimes there's a finder's fee related to the victims, and in that case, yeah I receive direct payment. Other times, I take some of the excess cash lying around before I turn over the scene to the authorities." I shrugged. "I usually donate a lot of that back to shelters, though. Or I give it to the girls. But there's never a lack of wealth in these situations. And I don't require a lot to live on."

"So you're like a common-day Robin Hood."

"Yeah, with claws," I deadpanned.

He grinned. "I like it. But I think I'm still going to require Jude to pay me directly. It's much easier to manage."

I laughed. "Where do you think he gets his funding?"

He considered that. "Probably via similar means to you, or from private benefactors." Then his gaze lifted upward, his expression turning thoughtful. "You know, I wonder if my father is one of those benefactors. That would explain how they know each other." His focus returned to me. "Assuming that's the whole connection with your alpha, and him knowing about KBO, and all that."

"It's a good guess."

He nodded, then sighed. "Well, whatever the connection, my dad won't just straight up define it for me. He'll want me to discover it for myself. Just like he thinks I'll magically take over the alpha mantle on my own." He flinched with the words, his expression darkening.

I studied him, curious. "Why don't you want to be an alpha? Because of your job?" Seemed fair to ask that since he'd wanted to know about my desires regarding a mate.

He fell silent as he disappeared into his closet. When he returned, he had on a tight gray shirt, and his hair looked freshly combed by his fingers.

"Yes. And no." He led me to the door, then started down the hallway toward the guest room, clearly guiding me along so I could get dressed, too.

Once we were inside, he continued, "I became a slayer because I wanted a physical outlet, and killing vampires definitely provided that. It's not easy turning eighteen, becoming a wolf, and realizing you can't lead the life you anticipated. Yes, I could have stayed and taken over as alpha, but where would that have put Tyler?"

"Could you not coexist?" I wondered out loud, unsure of how the hierarchy worked here.

"Maybe. Maybe not. I wasn't willing to find out. So I left instead."

I pulled on a pair of borrowed jeans and a T-shirt, noting how his mom was pretty close to my size. Then I finger-combed my hair into a similar style to Alaric's and met his gaze. "And now?" I asked.

"And now... I feel like... I feel like maybe Tyler would still be alive had I not run away twelve years ago." The words were soft, his expression even softer. He winced upon saying them, as though he hadn't expected to utter them out loud. "I feel like I made a mistake, Makayla."

The confession hung between us, the air stilted with tension and sorrow.

I considered how to reply, a thousand statements filtering through my mind at once and not a single one sounding adequate enough. So I finally settled on the only truth I could give him.

"The thing about mistakes," I started, swallowing. "Some mistakes might have consequences we can't undo, but we can always find ways to say we're sorry. Ways to fix those wrongs. Ways to make it up to those we hurt. Everyone makes mistakes in life, but it's how we right those mistakes that truly defines us."

That was a realization that had struck me when I was eighteen.

I'd missed the obvious.

People had been hurt because I hadn't seen through a charade.

And so I spent my life righting that wrong.

Just as Alaric could spend his life fixing his mistakes, too.

"Denying the mantle because you respected your brother

isn't a fault, Alaric," I added. "You saw him as worthy. And so you gave him a chance to lead. What happened to him might have happened with or without your decision. Hell, it could have been you who died. But the fact of the matter is, you're still here. And I'm guessing Tyler wouldn't trust anyone more than he'd trust you to avenge him."

It was a wild statement, one that came from a part of me I didn't fully understand, but I felt the truth of it as it left my lips.

*Alaric is worthy.*

*He's a good alpha.*

*And he will solve this.*

He had determination written all over him. I'd witnessed it several times over the last few days. I'd also seen it when he'd taken down Vex. He didn't beat around the bush or play alpha games. He *was* an alpha. A strong wolf with a strong will. "You're going to find out who did this, and you're going to make them pay."

Because I recognized the same drive in him that I had in myself.

And one look into his eyes told me his soul understood mine just as mine understood his.

It should've frightened me, sent me running for the hills, but all I could do was reach for his hand to give it a squeeze. "I'm going to help you, too."

He stared at me as I stared at him.

Then he leaned forward to press his lips to mine, not in a hungry caress but in an emotional one. Too brief and quick. Too soft and tender. Yet perfect and right and exactly what we both needed. "Thank you, Makayla," he whispered, pulling away. "Thank you."

I swallowed and nodded, then cleared my throat. We needed a distraction. Something other than standing in a bedroom with all this heat and emotions simmering between us. We had work to do, and none of it would get done if we continued down this path.

He seemed to agree because he cleared his throat. "We, uh, should go make some coffee."

"Yes," I agreed, nodding eagerly. "Coffee."

*Coffee. Coffee fixes everything.*

I went straight to the kitchen, only then realizing that we had company. "Oh!" I gasped, spotting Hawk at the counter with a mug already in his hand.

"Morning," he drawled, glancing at the clock. "Or should I say 'afternoon'?"

"We were up late," Alaric said, joining me in the kitchen.

Hawk's gaze went to the bite mark on my neck, then he arched a brow at his son.

Alaric merely shrugged in response.

My cheeks burned as I mentally chastised myself to focus.

*Breathe,* Alaric suggested into my mind, his hand gently brushing the back of my arm. The amusement in his mental tone didn't help my flustered state. Nor did the fact that I'd never been flustered before I met this stubborn, broken, sexy alpha.

Hawk's lips twitched and I mentally groaned.

Alaric chuckled in reply.

Rather than acknowledge him, I chose to pour the rest of the coffee into two mugs and promptly began brewing a second pot. Because I was going to need it.

Alaric kissed me on the temple as he took his mug, then he joined his dad at the kitchen counter. "I assume you're here with something interesting?"

"I have Neo files," his dad informed us.

*Thank you,* I thought, glancing upward at the holy whatever above. *Thank you for the distraction we all need.*

Because this whole mating thing… yeah, I didn't… yep.

*He's mortal,* I muttered to myself. *Like… is this even possible?*

*Seems to be,* he replied, reminding me that he could hear my thoughts.

*Stop.*

*Not my fault you're yelling at me, sweetheart.*

*I'm not talking to you.*

*Right, you're just talking about me.*

I growled at him, belatedly realizing it was out loud.

Hawk's brows furrowed in response, but Alaric merely grinned and said, "She just needs more coffee."

Not a lie. I really did. I needed the life-reviving fluid to be able to process what all this meant. I practically downed my first cup, the liquid hot and scalding the back of my throat. But I didn't care.

Alaric poured me a second just after the pot finished brewing.

And something about that made me want to purr, roll over, and beg him to take me again.

I ignored the impulse.

At least until he mentally whispered, *You know I can smell how much you want me, right?*

*Doesn't mean it's going to happen again.*

*We'll see, sweetheart.*

*Hmm,* he hummed, and the sound sent goose bumps down my arms.

Did he have to be so damn sexy? And something told me he would only get better with age.

Which reminded me of what I'd been thinking about before Alaric had interrupted my thoughts.

*Immortality. He's not immortal. Fuck me sideways…*

*Happy to, baby.*

*Shh.* I threw a glare in his direction as he settled at the counter on the other side of his dad.

*Does this mean I'm stuck with him for life?* I wondered, still thinking about the immortality problem. Like, what happened when he died?

*Ouch. That was harsh.* Alaric's mental tone held a wealth of amusement.

Mine did not. *Cut it out.*

I didn't find it the least bit funny that he could die tomorrow. He was going to grow old.

*And holy shitballs. Will I be fucking a grandpa wolf someday?* My gaze floated to Hawk, and I couldn't help thinking, *At least he'll look like his dad.*

*I heard that.*

*Stop!* I growled again.

And Hawk cleared his throat. "Yeah, so, as I said… Neo files?" he prompted, gesturing at the documents on the counter.

*Distraction,* I remembered. *Yes. Distractions are good.* "Show me," I said, giving him my undivided attention. And not at all thinking about how Alaric would look like him in a few decades. *Sexy daddy wolf.*

# CHAPTER 24

## ALARIC

MAKAYLA FOUND NEO RIGHT AWAY. One look at his photo, and I understood why. "He's a scrawny little guy," I said, eyeing his details. "Only five foot five?"

"I know," Makayla replied. "I wasn't surprised at all to learn he was the gofer of the organization."

I grinned, amused. Then I stuck his details on our board. I'd totally need to repaint this wall when we were done, but whatever. We needed the space, and the blank white area functioned as a much more vast surface than a standard corkboard.

"All right. So he's from Elk Neck Pack." I palmed the back of my neck and blew out a breath. "Well, that explains the silver poisoning at Alpha Warren's funeral."

"I just sent a text to the Elk Neck Beta," my father said, sliding his phone back into his pocket. "Hopefully, he can track the scrawny shit down."

Makayla nodded, her brow pinched. "That'll be a good lead. However, I'm still trying to figure out how the McKenzie Pack fits in to all this. It's like a road map to my first case in this realm, except the McKenzie Pack Alpha— Landon, right?"

I nodded. "Yeah, he took over for Alpha Bortex."

"Right. Okay, so then technically, I suppose, that pack

was involved in that ring several years ago. Except Bortex had been the leader. So I originally thought that maybe someone wanted revenge on those who punished him for his involvement in all that. But now, with Kristen's death, and her being from McKenzie Pack, it doesn't fit. And the whole invitation thing for you, specifically, completely demolishes my theory, too. You had nothing to do with that incident. So why issue you an invitation to come out and play?"

I growled low in my throat, the scene shooting through my mind and overlapping with that of Valaria Crimson. "They want me to come back to the city."

"Yes, but why?" Makayla pressed, her attention on the board. "Is it a trap? Or is it a way to distract you from something else?" She tapped her jaw. "In my experience, it's never a good idea to follow the predator's path. I prefer to create my own."

"Do the unexpected, go at it from another angle," my father agreed with a nod.

"It feels like a trap, but if I don't go and someone else is hurt..." I exhaled harshly as my eyes rose to the ceiling.

"Jude can handle what's happening in the city," he said.

"I think the real answers are here," Makayla added.

A knock on the door interrupted our conversation. I shared a glance with my dad, then walked over to answer it, the smell on the other side unfamiliar.

"Mister Calder?" a short man with a dusting of light brown hair asked as I opened the door.

"Which one?" I demanded, not in the mood to play another twisted game.

"Uh." Shorty checked his documents. "Alaric Calder. It's a package from Jude Reyes."

"Ah, boss. Gifts," I drawled. "Should have started with

that." I signed for the package, then left the little guy on the porch to find his way back to his vehicle.

I opened the thick envelope as I returned to the living area. "I always knew he liked me," I said, grinning at what I found inside.

Surveillance from the city.

Reports of attacks on senior vamps.

And much, much more. I whistled. "Looks like E.V.I.E.'s been busy."

"Indeed," my father agreed.

We spent the rest of the afternoon reviewing everything, and by the time we were done, our murder board had doubled in size.

All three of us stood back and surveyed the wall. "Shit," I mumbled, overwhelmed by the sheer volume of information. There were answers here. I knew it in my bones, but we had to make sense of the chaos.

Makayla crossed her arms over her breasts and traced her mouth while humming thoughtfully. Then she scratched her chin and said, "It's as if someone is trying to provoke a turf war by removing all the leadership." She reviewed a few more items before blowing out a frustrated breath and stepping back. "But I don't get how this is related to trafficking."

"Maybe it's a smoke screen." As the words left my mouth, I realized how true they were. "It's a fucking smoke screen." I stalked up to the board and pointed out the cluster of vampire covens who'd lost their leadership over the last week. "While everyone is scrambling, trying to determine who is in charge, the trafficking ring is flourishing in the background. The girls are going missing because no one is there to protect them, and no one is noticing they're gone until it's too late because—"

"Because they're all too busy trying to figure out their

new hierarchies and also trying to determine who killed their leaders," Makayla finished for me, her eyebrows hitting her hairline.

"Shit," we breathed at the same time.

"Shit," I repeated. "I need to take a head count. And we need to warn the other packs."

IT HAD TAKEN three hours to complete a head count of Silver Lake. Having everyone home and on pack lands had helped us complete the census in an orderly fashion.

But we were missing one wolf.

*Savi.*

"She's not at her cabin," my mother said, her voice thick with tears and her hands wringing in front of her. "No one has heard from her since before the… before last night." She swallowed. "She went running alone. We should have… I should have…" She trailed off, her expression falling.

"It's not your fault, Everly. She wanted to be alone, and we respected those wishes," my father said.

I couldn't speak.

Because I didn't trust what I had to say.

I wanted to explode.

Because I should have insisted on accompanying her. She was a broken wolf, mourning the love of her life, and she'd needed my alpha strength to protect her.

And now…

My stomach clenched, my wolf pacing wildly inside me, unfurled by the concept of a missing wolf. An innocent. A sweet girl. *Savi.*

Not wanting to lose it in front of my mother, I stalked out of my cabin and into the woods. "*Fuck*!" I roared.

I paced between two trees, my blood flowing hot with liquid lava, ready to erupt. My insides reached a boiling point half a breath later, and I shouted again as I sent my fist flying into one of the trees, spraying bark in every direction.

I'd been so damn lost in my grief and caught up in Makayla that I hadn't done what an alpha should have. I hadn't protected a vulnerable member of my pack, and now she was God knew where, probably suffering like the other girls.

*Tyler, fuck, I'm so sorry, brother.* I'd already let him down when I missed our lunch, and now this...

A twig snapped and I spun around, ready to fight, ready to fucking *kill*.

Makayla leaned against another tree, observing me with an unreadable expression. I expected to find wariness, anger, pity, anything but the nothingness on her face. Perhaps she understood me better than I realized. An emotional reaction from her—or anyone—would have sent me over the edge. It was the other reason I'd walked away from my mother. I couldn't handle her guilt because it was my responsibility to care for Savannah, not my mother's.

"Not now," I snarled at Makayla and resumed pacing.

"I think you owe that poor, unsuspecting tree an apology."

"I said *not now*."

"You don't want to be consoled?" Her tone held no indication of condescension, but I felt it in her mind.

I stopped and whipped around to glare at her. "Is that what you came out here for, Makayla? You want me to give you a fast, hard fuck?" I narrowed my eyes. "Or did you come out here to pick a fight? Because, baby, in the mood I'm in, fighting will only turn me on, and you're going to find yourself fucked either way."

Makayla rolled her eyes and pushed off of the tree. "The pity train just derailed at the corner of Suck It Up and Move On. This isn't going to help Savannah, so stop throwing a tantrum, and let's figure this out like the alphas we are."

I froze, my jaw hanging open, while all the blood in my body rushed straight to my cock. It was sexy as hell when she went all alpha female on me.

Her eyes dropped to my groin before returning to my face, and a smile slowly curved her lips. She'd been goading me, knowing it would turn me on and get me out of my head.

"You in the market for a spanking, sweetheart?"

She blinked innocently and scoffed. "I'd like to see you try."

*Challenge accepted.*

*It wasn't a challenge, asshole.*

Amusement overtook my mounting aggression, causing my lips to twitch. Makayla did all that for me. She'd calmed me and my wolf in the process, allowing me to clear my mind and think logically.

I held out my hand, and she closed the distance between us, tucking herself under my arm instead. "Thanks," I mumbled as I inhaled her floral scent and let it chase away the last of my anger.

"Anyti—um, sure."

Her hesitation wasn't lost on me, and neither was her chanting of, *One day at a time,* in her head. But I pretended not to hear and kissed the top of her head. "I need to go meet with the alphas soon."

We'd postponed the meeting as a result of the search—every pack had completed their own head count—and now we were set to meet in the virtual conference room at nine o'clock sharp tonight. Most of the alphas attending were all like me—temporary leaders taking over in the time of crisis.

Makayla nodded, and we walked around to the front of my house in contemplative silence.

Savannah still weighed heavily on my heart, but Makayla had helped me clear away some of the fog of my rage, allowing me to focus on finding Savi and killing the assholes responsible for all this pain and suffering.

Once we were back inside, I called Hardt and told him to gather all of our enforcers and come to the cabin as soon as possible. While we waited for them, Makayla, my father, and I worked on a plan for patrols. We split the pack land into four quadrants and broke the days into segments for patrols and perimeter checks.

Hardt and the enforcers shuffled in ten minutes later, and I gave them the rundown and handed out assignments. Paul and Steve were on quadrant three. Timothy and Gregory took the fourth zone.

"You've got your thing this evening," Makayla piped up as we were making assignments, pointing to quadrant one. "I'll take a patrol shift tonight."

"I'll take one tonight as well," Hardt announced, gesturing at section two.

I didn't like the idea of him being out there with Makayla, but I had no doubt that if I voiced that opinion, Makayla would try to kick my ass. And as hot as it would be, I didn't relish the idea of her stabbing me again. Besides, they'd be in entirely separate areas anyway. So I shoved down my irrational jealousy, told my wolf to knock off the growling, and simply nodded.

Makayla headed out, ready to get to work. Enforcer Enrique followed her, and I gave him a pointed look, telling him with my eyes that he'd better protect her. He acknowledged me with a nod. They wouldn't run together, but he'd be nearby if there were any issues.

Hardt tapped Enforcer Reggie as his partner for patrol, and all eight wolves departed from my home in their animal forms.

Leaving me to prepare for my meeting with the alphas, which was in about thirty minutes.

I gathered the files and materials I needed, then headed toward Tyler's house. He had all the telecommunications equipment that was required for this, plus a much nicer office area. And it seemed fitting to be in the Silver Lake Alpha's house while I addressed other leaders of the Northeast Bitten wolf packs.

Some of Makayla's thoughts drifted into my mind along the way.

*Good grief, I should have grabbed a coffee before leaving. Nothing is better than coffee.* A pause. *Well, Alaric is definitely better than coffee.*

I tried to keep my presence from being known but lost the battle and laughed.

*Out of my head, Calder.*

*Don't fantasize about me so loudly.*

*Ugh! I'm not talking to you.*

I shook my head with another chuckle and did as she asked. I focused on the meeting ahead so I wouldn't listen in on her thoughts. Appealing as the idea might be.

Just before nine, my father and I gathered in Tyler's office. I sat in the executive chair behind the large oak desk, feeling an odd mix of reactions. I'd never wanted to take Tyler's place as alpha, yet sitting here seemed to confirm that I had no choice in the matter, which left me feeling a bit awkward and unsure.

However, then a series of memories assaulted me, ones of me playing with my brother in this room while our father worked on pack business. And later of me visiting Tyler here and being so damn proud of the alpha he'd become.

*This was always meant to be your place, Ric. Stop living in the past and fucking own it.*

I could feel Makayla's presence on the periphery of my mind and knew she'd picked up my thoughts about Tyler and the words I'd imagined him saying. But she remained silent, and when the first alpha appeared on the big screen plastered to the wall of the office, I pushed everything else away and focused on the task at hand.

# CHAPTER 25

## ALARIC

"NEO'S DEAD." The Elk Neck Beta flinched as he said it, his gaze lowering in a subtle display of apology before returning to the camera. He cleared his throat. "From the scene, it's obvious someone hunted him down and slaughtered him."

My jaw clenched.

All the alphas and betas had assembled in their various offices, their stances solemn and tones quiet. Many of them had looked to me to kick off the conversation, so I'd started with the obvious question: Have you found Neo yet?

And, well, they'd found him.

Dead.

*What the hell?*

I wanted to rage and demand he tell me how the hell his team had let that happen—how the fuck they'd managed to let our best lead die—but my father stepped in, giving me a moment to collect myself.

"Word obviously got around when we sent the information to all of the packs," he said from his chair beside me. He'd pulled over one of the two from a table in the corner, sharing the executive desk with me and facing the camera and screen against the wall. "Don't blame yourself, Beta Mavi. I'm sure you did what you needed to do. However, I recommend that all of us evaluate who had access to that information and assess if they could have warned someone with ties to Neo."

I nodded in agreement and took a few slow, deep breaths, then I moved on to other topics.

We each shared what we knew, which wasn't much, with the other packs. I told them some of the information we'd gathered from Jude's files and explained a few theories Makayla and I had come up with along the way, as well as the fact that I'd been specifically singled out by the initials carved into the victims' feet.

"We decided that I'm needed here, and Makayla pointed out that if I go to the city, I'll be playing by their set of rules," I added, feeling oddly hollow without her nearby.

*She really should be here*, I thought, noting all the males on the screen. Not a single female in sight. *What is this sexist bullshit?*

Makayla's agreement brushed my mind, causing me to bite back a smile. *I thought you weren't talking to me, baby?*

She started humming in response, and the smile broke free, curving up my lips.

"Alaric."

The sound of someone saying my name pulled me back into the meeting. I glanced at my father, who'd been the one to grab my attention, and cleared my throat. "Sorry."

I'd never heard of Bitten mates acquiring telepathic links, so this development would take some getting used to. Same with the mark on my chest. Although, I kind of liked the reddish-brown wolf tattooed into my flesh.

I probably shouldn't since it just tied me down more, but I couldn't really argue destiny's choice here. Sure, fate had essentially castrated me, but now that I'd tasted Makayla, I understood why. The woman had effectively ruined me for all other females, because no one would ever come close to comparing to what we'd experienced last night. I was absolutely determined to have her beneath me again just as soon as I figured all this shit out.

*Which would work a hell of a lot faster if I focus on the conversation at hand, and not my dick,* I thought, forcing my attention back to the meeting.

Beta Mavi was providing a report on the Elk Neck Pack count, just as all the others had. "No one is missing," he concluded. "And we've enforced a strict curfew and lockdown."

"Good," my father said, his tone conveying full alpha authority. "Unfortunately, Silver Lake wasn't as fortunate. We're missing one of our own, Tyler's former consort —Savannah."

*Consort* was a fancy term for a non-mate lover. Not all that uncommon for an alpha because not all of us found our mates.

A few low murmurs came through the speakers. None of the others had been impacted yet, but Savi's disappearance suggested they could be at any moment.

"We've enacted security protocols," I began, only to be interrupted by a knock at the office door.

I shared a look with my father, who merely called out, "Come in."

And in waltzed my boss.

Jude Reyes.

Director of Eliminate Vampiric Influences Everywhere.

"What the hell?" I muttered under my breath.

As usual, he was impeccably dressed in a perfectly fitted suit and Italian loafers. Not a strand of his dark hair was out of place, and his Van Dyke–style beard was close-cropped and tidy. The only things about his appearance that kept him from looking like an airbrushed model on a magazine cover were the wrinkles on his forehead and around his lips from pursing them when he was stressed.

Violet often described him as deceptively debonair. I called him ruthless, but fair… to a degree. He might've looked the part of a gentleman, but he had worked his way up the ranks in E.V.I.E., and he was as deadly as the rest of us.

As he approached the desk, he greeted each alpha by name, cluing me in that he knew more about shifter life than he'd let on. Particularly, because most of those alphas were brand new or temporary. Yet he knew every single one of their identities, which implied that he understood the pack hierarchies and who would be next in line to lead.

"Alpha Alaric," he greeted me last, pulling up a chair to join my father and me at the desk. Then he bowed his head in subtle reverence as though I'd already ascended. Which explained why he hadn't called me Successor Alaric or Heir Alaric, but Alpha Alaric.

It sounded weird coming from him. However, I didn't correct him. He was still my boss, right?

He turned to my father, and they shook hands. "It's been a while since we spoke in person."

"Twelve years, give or take," my father responded. "Still playing chess?"

Jude smiled, an expression I'd rarely seen on his face, so it stunned me for a minute. "Frequently, but as for the opponent I suspect you are referring to, we started a new game recently. One of my slayers mated a wolf in his pack."

My head popped up at that. "What? Who? In a Bitten pack?" I knew just about every slayer who worked for

E.V.I.E., and I hadn't heard a word about another fated mate among our ranks. Although, very few of them knew I was a wolf. So maybe they hadn't thought to tell me.

"Rowan Sokolov," my boss replied.

"Violet's best friend?" I asked, picturing the little pixie slayer with long, silvery lavender hair.

My boss arched a knowing brow. "Yes. She's mated to one of Nathan's wolves."

*Nathan?* I blinked.

His expression and tone strongly suggested that he meant Makayla's Alpha Nathan. Which confirmed that Jude was how my father knew about KBO. But, of course, I couldn't ask for clarification with the horde of other pack alphas and heirs watching. As it was, we'd completely derailed from the topic at hand and had ventured into unrelated territory.

*My Nathan?* Makayla's voice piped up, clearly having overheard my thoughts.

I growled in my mind, just barely managing to keep the sound inward. *No, not* your *Nathan, Makayla.*

*Chill, dude. Or don't, because it's kinda hot. But save it for later.*

I chuckled, but I was still lost to the revelation Jude had just confirmed with a few choice words.

*Twelve years,* I marveled. When I first started at E.V.I.E. Because of course my father had had something to do with that. *Is there anyone I know who isn't living a double life?*

*I prefer to think of it as my best life,* a soft voice replied.

I mentally snorted. *Baby, after last night, I think we both know our best life is when we're fucking.*

*One-track mind,* she mumbled. *I'm going back to not talking to you.* Then I sensed her mind drift somewhere else.

I refocused on the meeting. Jude clearly did the same, because he addressed me and asked, "Have all the packs done a head count?"

I nodded. "Gloria is still missing, and one of my pack is now, too. Savannah. Tyler's consort. No other reported wolf-related disappearances."

Jude's wrinkles deepened as he pursed his lips. "The vampires have taken to counting their nests as well. So far, they've reported three names of missing female vamps. With the leaders being picked off, the city is a mess of chaos, at least in the underworld."

"That's to be expected," the alpha of the Montauk Pack said, his tone annoyingly smug for someone who had yet to be impacted by these events. He was only here since his pack existed in the Northeast. But they were notorious for looking out for themselves and themselves alone. "The leeches don't have a clue how to handle hierarchy."

Well, I couldn't argue with that claim. Vamp nests were notably unorganized, making them easy to pick off.

Jude continued as if the alpha hadn't spoken and gave us a rundown of a few non-Bitten wolf clans who were also missing girls. Bringing the total to eleven. And we had no way of knowing how many more human females had been taken—too many missing person cases to link them all.

The number eleven reverberated inside me. It might as well have been a thousand. It didn't matter how many had been taken; I would be equally as angry and determined to kill the twisted bastards holding them hostage.

Jude smoothed a hand over his beard. "I put feelers out to some contacts, and I've assigned a few slayers to search for information on any upcoming auctions. They've already gathered a few potential leads."

He shared them, but to my disappointment, none of them were familiar to me. I wondered if Makayla had knowledge about any of them and again thought about how she should've been here for this.

"Send me copies of the files," I requested of Jude. "I'll have Makayla review them."

"Why?" the newly ascended alpha of the Weiser Pack inquired. The curiosity in his voice told me it was an innocent question more than an accusatory or derogatory one. As the only other alpha here missing a wolf, I decided he deserved a thorough response.

"Makayla's my mate," I started, ensuring the respect was given where due. *Say something bad about my woman and you won't like my reply*, I added with my eyes. "She specializes in trafficking cases and has experience locating missing persons. She also helped expose Alpha Bortex's involvement in that incident a few years ago. So she's very familiar with all the players on the board and how cases like this usually work."

That seemed to impress the Weiser Pack Alpha because he nodded in approval.

*Good boy*, I thought. Had he given me any other response, I might have reached through the screen and throttled him.

As it was, I still wanted to punch the alpha from Montauk. He looked bored out of his mind, making me wonder why the hell he'd even chosen to show up. *Go back to your pansy pack*, I wanted to say to him.

But Jude distracted me with a nod. "She'll likely have good insight into some of this information. You should bring her to the meeting next time."

A few of the leaders—primarily the older alphas—scoffed at the idea.

However, the young alpha heir of the Beaver Creek Pack said, "I'd like to meet her."

"Me, too," Beta Mavi added.

A few others nodded in agreement, then the alpha of

the Shokan Pack—another area of wolves untouched by all this—yawned and asked, "What's next?"

It'd been a long day, and we were running into the later hours of the night.

"We need to try to get into one of the auctions," I stated.

"If it's at all possible to secure an invitation to one, I have the connections to do it. So leave that to me," Jude said.

I agreed, and no one else questioned him. After a few more minutes of strategic discussion, I thanked everyone for attending and ended the meeting.

Jude air-dropped the files to my tablet, then turned to my father. "I believe I'm long overdue for that scotch."

My dad smirked. "Everly will love seeing you, too. She prepped the guest room for you as well."

"You knew he was coming?" I asked, looking at my dad. "And you didn't tell me?"

"You didn't ask," he replied.

"I was a little busy doing a head count." And reacting to news of Savi going missing.

Jude clapped me on the shoulder. "Alpha looks good on you." He glanced at my dad. "I'm taking credit for some of that since you dumped him on me when he was eighteen and barely an adult."

My father grunted. "*Dumped* is a harsh word. More like I encouraged you to find him when he ran off."

My jaw ticked as I read between the lines. "You recruited me because of my dad."

"Well, that and your alpha wolf status," he replied. "I knew you'd make a fine slayer, and you surpassed all my expectations, Ric. You're exceptional."

"He really is," my father agreed, making me decidedly uncomfortable.

"And you know Makayla's alpha," I said, wanting to switch the topic away from me. "Which is how my dad knew about KBO."

"Yeah, about that." Jude cleared his throat. "I have a message from Nathan regarding the future of your balls if you so much as harm Makayla, or upset her, or something. I should've written it down. Her brother was involved, too. I don't quite know. Just, don't piss her off. I don't want a bunch of angry alpha-like wolves entering our realm just to hunt your ass down, all right?"

I snorted. "Don't worry about me, boss." *Apparently, my balls have been threatened by your alpha and your brother,* I drawled to Makayla. *Someone should inform them that you handle my family jewels just fine on your own.*

A laugh sounded from her, but nothing else. She appeared to be consumed by her patrol duties, which should be coming to an end in about an hour.

That gave me enough time to drop everything at my cabin and join her.

"I'm going to go find Mak and bring her up to speed," I told my dad and Jude.

"Come by for breakfast in the morning," my dad said as I started to walk away. "We need to talk more about the future, son."

My hackles didn't rise like they would have a week ago. Instead, all I felt was a subtle pounding in my heart and the piquing interest of my wolf. We still had a case to solve, but he was right to want to secure the leadership of Silver Lake. The wolves couldn't properly thrive without an alpha.

"Okay," I said with a nod. "I'll see you in the morning."

On the walk back to my cabin, I searched for

Makayla's mind again and immediately felt calm seep into my bones. I waited, but she didn't say anything.

*Still ignoring me, sweetness?* I asked.

I felt her amusement even though she remained silent. And somehow, through our link, I sensed her starting to run. Not in fear. Not for exercise. But to play.

With a shake of my head, I laughed. *Keep running, baby. Only makes me want to catch you more.*

# CHAPTER 26

## MAKAYLA

I GRINNED at Alaric's taunt and gave up my silent treatment to tease him back. *Catch me if you can, Alpha.*

*Yeah, I'm going to need you to call me that the next time I'm inside you.*

I shivered at the promise in his tone. My wolf completely agreed with his idea and tried to turn around and head on back to his house, ready to give Alaric whatever he wanted. I righted our course, refusing her antics. *Look, sometimes we have to make him chase us,* I chastised her. *It makes being caught that much sweeter.*

*I don't plan on being sweet when I get my hands on you.*

*Neither do I,* I warned devilishly.

*Maybe we should let our animals run the show for a little bit,* he suggested. *My wolf is craving a playdate with his mate.*

I felt him shift into animal form, his energy a warm caress against my mind. Then I caught his thoughts as he entered the woods.

We were definitely linked on an intimate level, a realization that sent a shiver down my spine.

Part of me thought it was hot.

The other part remained uncertain.

We were in uncharted waters with all this mating stuff.

The connection could disappear when I left the realm… or not.

What if letting Alaric's wolf mount mine cemented us together even more? I didn't want to cause Alaric pain if I left. Nor had I come to terms with the idea of being mated to a mortal.

*Put it all out of your mind, Makayla,* I lectured myself. *One day at a time, remember?*

*That's right, baby. Just focus on what I'm going to do to you when I catch you.* Alaric's comment was smug but also low and sexy and rumbling through my body as though he were right next to me.

*I have no idea what you're talking about, Alpha,* I said, my tone demure. His responding growl had me grinning and adding, *I might need a detailed reminder.*

*Oh, sweetheart. I promise to be very thorough so that by the time I'm done, you'll never forget a second.*

I giggled. Fucking giggled! Like a damn schoolgirl. But I couldn't help it. And shit, I was so turned on that it made it hard not to simply flop to the ground and wait for him to ravish me.

*Maybe—*

I paused and skidded to a halt as a familiar scent reached my nose. My head swung in the direction it had come from, my enhanced night vision making it easy for me to survey my surroundings. *I smell something…* I silently followed the fragrant trail, like a hunter stalking its prey.

*Probably the sweet smell of your pussy, baby. I can't wait to taste you again.*

*I'm serious, Alaric. It's unusual, but I know it from somewhere. It's almost…*

I trailed off, stopping in my tracks and sucking in a quick breath, hoping my instincts were wrong.

*Ash.*

*Bar basement.*

*Hybrid.*

*Same odor.*

*Similar to the one on Kristen's body, too.*

All the details assaulted me at once, my hackles rising. *Shit.*

*Makayla? What's wrong? Are you all right?*

*Hybrids. I smell hybrids.*

*What? Where are you? Where's Enrique?*

I glanced around, assessing my surroundings. I couldn't see the predators, but I knew they were there.

*About a mile east of my spot by the lake. Near the border of Silver Lake territory. Not sure where Enrique is. We separated as soon as we arrived.* I hadn't thought much of it because I usually worked alone. But now…

Branches rustled on my right, and I whipped around to see a large gray-and-brown wolf lumbering through the underbrush, his yellow eyes fixated on me. A human followed him. At least, he *looked* human.

*There's a big wolf here that I don't recognize. Brown and gray fur. And his snout is bent at a weird angle. Hmm, I wonder if any other part of him is bent.*

Alaric remained silent, but I sensed through our connection that he was not amused.

*The other man with him resembles a human… but also doesn't. Explain.*

*He doesn't smell entirely human. Like there's something's off about him. He's the source of the ashy scent. You know, like the hybrid. A, uh, Vex Junior, I guess?* Seemed like a good name for him. He even had the same dark hair and bulky build to him.

*Fuck! I'm coming. Don't engage unless you have to, Makayla. Wait for me to back you up.*

*A bit too late for that since they're both staring right at me.*

*Damn it!*

I would have apologized, except it wasn't really my fault these two jackholes stepped into my path. Besides, it'd been my job to patrol the area for tonight, so... I'd do my job.

Bendy growled at me, low and menacing, as he slowly approached.

*Aww, Bendy wants to be friends*, I drawled, then growled right back at him. *It's not nice to snarl at new friends, dude.*

Electricity ran through my fur, causing it to stand on end as I adjusted my stance.

Bendy snapped his jaw in response.

*Yeah, I can do that, too, bud*, I thought, then yawned dramatically at his antics. *Boring. Next.* However, even as I thought it, I felt a hint of unease, my usual sarcasm doing little to calm my nerves.

*How did they even get here?* I wondered, glancing around. We weren't that far into the territory boundaries, but to be this ballsy... I swallowed. *Alaric...*

*I'm coming*, he vowed.

Vex Junior skulked off to the side, apparently leaving us wolves to work things out. Bendy took a bold step forward, and I moved back—an instinctual reaction to the confidence pouring off the wolf before me.

He wasn't *that* big. But the fact that he seemed so confident in his ability to take me down caused all my hairs to stand on end. Either he was underestimating me as a female, or I'd missed something obvious. Both guesses left me feeling uneasy.

*I don't think he's going to wait for you*, I said as Bendy prowled forward. *Alaric...*

*Almost there!*

Bendy lunged and I darted to the right, Alaric's snarl loud in my head as he sensed my rising panic. Vex Junior had circled around behind me while I'd been focused on Bendy, and I was officially trapped between them. *Shit.*

*Makayla!*

Alaric's words were lost as something sharp dug into my shoulder.

A dart.

From a third presence in the woods.

Someone hidden from my view while I'd been focused on Bendy and Vex Junior.

*Oh, hell… rookie… mistake*, I thought, my mind fogging over. *Fuck.* My knees gave out, the drug hitting my system far too quickly. *Not good. Not fucking good. I…*

My wolf whined.

Or maybe I did.

I couldn't hear well over Alaric growling in my head. And my heart beating. *Thump. Thump. Thump.*

Someone laughed. The third form barely blinking in my vision. There and gone and covered in dots.

I attempted to shake it off, to regain control and focus my eyes. But black swirls distorted the scene before me, blanketing me in a world of full night. No stars. No light. Not a thing.

Blissful silence descended.

And then… *nothing*.

# CHAPTER 27

## ALARIC

*MAKAYLA!* I shouted her name as my paws pounded over the earth, my ears twitching for anything and everything around me.

But only the sounds of the night met my senses.

I spun around, tracking her scent, my heart in my fucking throat. *Where are you?* I demanded. *Why can't I feel you?* It was like she'd been cut off.

Or maybe knocked out.

*Shit, you'd better not be dead.* We'd just met. *If I lost her… No.* I refused to follow that strand of thought. *Not fucking happening.*

Someone had taken her.

She'd called one of them "Bendy" because of his crooked snout. He had brown and gray fur. That didn't help me much. Neither did his scent. I tracked it with my nose, unfamiliar with the owner. Definitely a Bitten wolf, but not one of mine.

I picked up the trace of his friend, the smoky undertones reminding me of the hybrid. Which was why she'd called him "Vex Junior." It seemed my mate had a penchant for nicknames. *I wonder what she called me when we met?*

A question I'd ask when I found her.

Because I *would* find her. And I'd kill those who dared to take her from me.

*Come on, Mak, talk to me.*

Nothing.

*Fuck!* I howled, my wolf in agony over losing his mate. He could feel her life force, but it wasn't enough. She wasn't safe. Gone. *Missing.*

The realization crippled my ability to focus, my entire world standing still as I reacted to a loss unlike any I'd ever experienced. Tyler's death had gutted me. But losing Makayla—it shredded apart my fucking soul.

How had someone I'd just met begun to mean so much to me?

*This is fate,* I realized. *This is what fate does. How fate works. Why we know our mate upon sight.* It was like our souls had been bonded in a previous life and had finally found each other again.

Only to be ripped apart.

*Destroyed.*

She'd only been in my head a day, and already I missed her.

*How the hell will I survive if she actually leaves?*

A concern for another day.

Right now, I needed to find her and annihilate those who dared to touch her. I also needed to trust in her own strength. *She'll survive this. She'll find a way to contact me. Together, we will fix this.*

I stole a deep breath, my chest aching from lack of oxygen because I'd forgotten to breathe. *Think, Calder. Think. You're smarter than this. You're stronger than this. Locating people is what you do. You're a damn wolf. An alpha. Cut the shit and find your girl.*

My brother's voice was loud in my head, his spirit heavy against mine.

He wasn't really talking to me. I knew that. Yet, it was exactly what he'd say to me now. Or maybe it was just what I would say to myself.

Regardless, it worked.

I put my snout to the ground and tracked Makayla's scent to a set of tire tracks in the dirt. I growled at the sight. Not only had someone taken my mate, but they'd also driven onto *my* land, during her patrol. Those patrol routes were brand new. No one knew about them except the inner circle. So how the hell did they—

A presence at my back had a snarl building in my throat.

*Hardt.*

Of course.

*That son of a...*

I turned on him without a second thought, pinning his wolf to the ground on a rumble of sound that came from my heart and soul. His yellow eyes immediately went to the side in a show of submission, his body entirely still beneath mine. Not fighting. Not attacking. Not doing anything at all.

He didn't whine.

He didn't growl.

He didn't make a damn sound, just remained utterly still with my jaws exceptionally close to this throat.

*What the fuck is wrong with you?* I wondered. *What are you doing here? Did you help them take her? Are you the fucking mole?* Part of me knew these were unfounded questions based on an emotional reaction to Makayla's disappearance. But his presence here was suspicious considering his patrol had been on the opposite side of the—

"Alaric." The deep voice came from the forest.

*Dad?* I slowly lifted my gaze from Hardt to my father. He stood with his hands out in front of him, buck naked.

*He must have run here in wolf form.* I cocked my head, confused. *How did you—*

The leaves shuffled as more wolves approached behind him, their auras all prickling through my conscious. More were on their way in animal form—a fact I felt more than knew.

I blinked, startled.

*What are they all doing here?* I slowly released Hardt, my mind swimming with questions and foreign words. *Why can I sense them all?*

I swore a few of them *replied*.

I heard them in my head, their concerns poking at my psyche and demanding they be heard.

*What the hell is going on?* I'd experienced emotional connections with my pack before, but nothing on this level. It resembled a web of unspoken thoughts, their auras painting my vision in bright colors and telling me exactly who joined me in this quadrant of the pack land.

I recognized them all. Every name. Every set of eyes. Every *step*.

My heart skipped a beat while my wolf took it all in stride, entirely at ease with the development. Like he'd expected it all along.

It seemed to soothe him, too. All my pent-up fury melted away, leaving me eerily calm, like their presence had helped me focus. *Makayla's gone. I need to find her. I can't do that if I'm panicking.*

My fur smoothed, my breathing returned to normal, and I took another step away from the wolf on the ground, releasing Hardt entirely from my violent—and incredibly irrational—reaction. Did I still dislike him? Yes. But he hadn't deserved to feel my teeth at his throat.

Hardt began to shift back into human form but remained on the ground. He immediately put his hands up like my dad. "I heard your call, Alpha. That's why I'm here. It's why we're all here."

*My call?* I shook my head, trying to clear it. *What call? Do you mean my howl? And did you just call me "Alpha"?*

He couldn't hear me, of course. Yet I swore a flicker flashed through his eyes, almost as though he'd *felt* my questions.

*Impossible.*

Bitten wolves didn't have a hive mind.

"Where's Makayla?" my father asked, stepping out of the woods, his posture exuding dominance. And yet, I sensed his subtle submission toward me. It was a bizarre acknowledgment that hummed along the fringes of my awareness but wasn't outwardly displayed.

I shoved the sensation aside and called upon my human form, shifting back to two legs in a handful of seconds. The energy shimmered along my skin, taking me to my full height as I crossed my arms and locked gazes with my father.

"A hybrid and a wolf entered our lands and took her," I declared, not bothering to explain how I came to know those details.

I hadn't told anyone about our telepathic link yet, mostly because I didn't want to grow attached to something that might change. However, right now, I was exceptionally thankful for that connection to Makayla. I could feel her life force thriving with mine, confirming she was alive despite her inability to speak.

"Where's Enrique?" I demanded, scanning the wolves in attendance.

No one answered.

"He's supposed to be on patrol out here with Makayla," I added on a low growl. "Find him. *Now.*"

Paul and Steve immediately took off at my command, searching for their missing colleague.

The others all exchanged a look, then Hardt knelt beside the set of tire tracks that I'd found, his expression thoughtful. "Definitely truck size, based on the treads. Want me to follow and see where these lead?" he offered in a calm voice, his gaze not meeting mine.

A show of submission.

Reverence.

Deferring to the one he considered alpha.

*What the hell changed over the last day to earn that response from him?* I dismissed the thought and instead nodded. It was a smart request, one worthy of a beta's focus. "Yes. Report back what you find."

He dipped his chin respectfully and shifted back into wolf form to take off through the woods.

Then two enforcers stepped forward, heads bowed. "Would you like us to do a thorough perimeter sweep, Alpha?"

I studied them, surprised by the address. *Just like Hardt. Interesting.* "Yes," I said. "Take Colton with you, too." I gestured to the third enforcer present, who had remained in wolf form near the trees. "Jinx, I want you to stay here."

He was the fourth enforcer on-site, standing behind a large trunk and completely out of sight. Yet somehow I knew he was there, and it had nothing to do with my nose. He stepped out to acknowledge me with a subtle nod, his stance also reverent.

Had my agonized howl forced the entire pack into submission?

"What else?" my father asked, his expression expectant. "Where do you want the rest of us?"

I cleared my throat, thinking on my feet. "Jude's still here, right?" I didn't know why I asked because I sensed him on the property, too. An aura that didn't quite fit yet wasn't a threat. *Something's happening to me. Something… bizarre.*

"He's with Everly."

I nodded. Because… again… I already knew that. I swore I could even hear her thinking about Jude and whatever he was saying to her. I shook my head again, this sensation insane, but not entirely unwelcome either.

Still, I needed to focus.

"All right. I want everyone back at the main camp. No wandering. No night runs. No leaving the central roads unless otherwise directed." I met the gaze of each wolf nearby. ."Make sure everyone knows." It felt like a compulsion of sorts, like my command served as more than just words. I also swore my words traveled through the pack psyche, telling them all to congregate in the safety zone.

*So damn weird.*

"I need toys," I continued, pushing the thoughts out of my mind. "Toys from Jude. Surveillance. All of it. There are security cameras on all the main roads near Silver Lake. That vehicle will be caught on one of those feeds, and we'll track it." Once we had that, I could use technology to pinpoint Makayla's location until she woke up.

Pride colored my father's expression. "Good. Anything else?"

I considered him for a moment, then decided to hell with it. I needed all the help I could get, and for that, I couldn't hold myself back. Every detail was crucial, even ones that were hard to believe or potentially temporary.

"Yeah." I cleared my throat again. "Makayla and I seem to have established a telepathic link via our mating.

Once she wakes up, I'll need to focus on whatever she has to say. So I need you to stay close and take charge when that happens." It would leave me temporarily weak because I'd give her my complete attention, just as a mate should.

"Of course," he agreed, not commenting on the telepathy. "Let's get back to Jude."

I nodded.

Shifted.

And ran back to his house.

All the while chanting, *Wake up, Mak. Wake. Up.*

# CHAPTER 28

## ALARIC

*Mak?*

I waited.

Silence.

I sighed, irritated, and checked my watch. Only thirty minutes had passed, but that didn't make me any less stressed about this situation.

My father stood right beside me, the murder board splayed out over the conference room wall of my brother's house. It'd only taken a few minutes for everything to be moved because several pack members had helped.

Their display of solidarity had calmed me a bit, as it somehow allowed me to share my burden. Just a little. Like a unit. And it also bolstered the assurance that we would work together to find her.

It was strange accepting that resolve after so many years of working alone, but it felt right to let them help me. To operate as a team. To be a real pack.

My father reached out to squeeze my shoulder, somehow sensing my unease over Makayla's continued silence. "We're going to get her back, son."

Hardt nodded, his back to me as he dragged several sets of surveillance videos up onto one of the screens. "I'm scanning all potential routes out of our territory and using heat censors to check truck occupants. I have six I'm watching so far." He pointed to them. "They're all within appropriate range with at least three heat signatures inside. Two of them have someone in the back as well."

"And I'm searching for ownership details on all those trucks," Jude added, sitting beside the beta and watching images fly across the screen.

"You mean while someone at headquarters scans auto records?" I rephrased for him, aware that although he wasn't inept when it came to technology, he wasn't a hacker.

"Same thing," he replied, arms folded, expression serious as he continued "supervising." Our region had been updated with thermal equipment, which would hopefully help him identify a body in a truck bed.

I started pacing, calling for Makayla every few seconds and flinching when she didn't reply.

At least I could feel her life source thriving in our bond.

"Alpha?" a deep voice asked from the doorway.

I glanced at the young wolf, realizing immediately that he was talking to me. Everyone had been calling me *Alpha* since returning to the house. And I didn't have the energy to correct it. Nor did I really want to at this point.

"Yeah, Rick?" I asked. He was about ten years my junior, but I remembered him from my childhood because we shared a similar name. And he'd always been the helpful sort. A good kid. Loved his books. Now he ran the phone lines for the pack.

"Alpha Landon is on the line requesting to talk to you," he said. "He called right after the meeting, but you were already gone. And I haven't had a good moment to tell you to call him back." He swallowed. "Sorry. I-I should have told you—"

"It's all right," I interjected. "You can put him through to the conference line."

"Of course, sir," Rick replied, bowing his head.

He practically ran from the room, causing me to glance at my father. "I swear I'm not that threatening." Although, I felt fucking threatening right now. If Makayla didn't wake up soon, I was going to lose my shit.

Hardt snorted, clearly poking fun at my statement.

Even my father smirked.

Glad they could find amusement in this situation.

The phone's ringing cut off whatever he would have said, and I picked it up with a casual, "Alpha Alaric." Since everyone else was calling me that, I might as well own it.

My father's grin widened.

I ignored him in favor of the wolf on the other line.

"I'm sorry to phone so late," Alpha Landon said by way of greeting. "But I found something while preparing for Kristen's burial."

I frowned. "Something on the body?"

"No. Something about her connections to former members of my pack," he replied. "Kristen was Kevin Gamington's daughter. That might not mean a lot to you, but he was one of the enforcers who helped track down Bortex after the trafficking ring was busted a few years ago. Actually, he was *the* enforcer to catch him after he tried to flee." Alpha Landon cleared his throat. "Kevin also has a son. And, well, his son is missing."

My blood went cold. "Do you think he was taken?" Because that would stir up the murder board.

He hesitated. "No. I… I think he might be involved."

My eyebrows lifted. "Why?"

"Because he didn't return for the mandatory head count. He also hasn't been by to pay his respects to Kristen, which I found strange."

"That could still mean he was taken," I pointed out. Although, he didn't fit the victim profile at all. "Would he have known about our hunt for Neo?" I wondered out loud.

"He's an enforcer, like his father. So yes. He had access to the information."

"You think he might be the mole who leaked the information about our search for Neo."

"It's a suspicion, yes. Since he's not been around, he wouldn't know that you found Neo in Elk Neck."

"But it wouldn't matter if he knew we were looking for a Neo," I translated.

"Right."

I nodded, wincing. Then another thought occurred to me. "What does he look like in wolf form?"

"Uh, brown and gray fur," he replied. "On the larger size and built like your typical enforcer."

That fit Makayla's initial description, at least in terms of bulk and coat color. And there was one other thing I recalled... "What about his snout? Is it bent a little?"

Landon remained quiet for a beat, his silence giving away his answer before he said, "Uh, yeah. He broke his nose before being bitten. It's never been quite straight."

*Damn.* "He matches the description of a wolf who crossed into my territory tonight."

"As in visiting?" he asked. "Because he went—"

"Alpha Alaric," Paul interrupted, running into the room, his body covered in blood. I nearly dropped the phone at the sight of him. Then Steve entered behind him with a dead Enrique in his arms.

"Fuck," I breathed. "I have to go." I instinctively handed the phone to my father, who finished the conversation for me while I focused on the slain enforcer. "Tell me everything."

# CHAPTER 29

## MAKAYLA

I woke with a jolt, my head hitting whatever I was propped up against hard.

*Ouch! Son of a bitch!*

Another bump jolted me across the cold metal bed beneath me, my fur replaced by bare skin. *What the hell? Where am I?* Wind teased my flesh, leaving a cold kiss behind that elicited a shiver to my very soul. I tried to open my eyes but couldn't, my head still fogged by whatever the fuck had happened.

I recognized the sound of a truck rumbling around me. Felt each and every rock as the tires rolled over the rough terrain.

But I had no idea where or how I'd ended up here. My wolf felt just as sluggish inside me, her disorientation leaving me confused.

*Mak?* The deep voice pierced my mind, the familiarity a calming caress to my senses. An incredibly different reaction from the first time I'd heard him in my thoughts. Now all I felt was eternally grateful. My wolf even perked up her ears a little upon sensing him in my head.

*Mak?* he repeated.

*I'm… I'm here… somewhere.* I grimaced. *Where am I? What happened?*

*You were taken.* A growl underlined his tone, his frustration palpable.

*Taken?* I repeated, frowning. *What? When?*

Except the memory slithered into focus as I uttered that last word. *Oh. Oh, hell.*

The three men in the forest.

Bendy. Vex Junior. The unknown third blob.

The dart.

*They drugged me,* I realized, a fresh wave of annoyance slapping my senses. *Those jackholes drugged me. Goddamn it!* I hadn't properly evaluated my surroundings, giving them the upper hand.

Aches spasmed through my limbs as my immortality fought the substance inside me. *How long have I been out?* I asked.

*About an hour,* Alaric said.

I groaned under my breath. As a shifter, I possessed an accelerated metabolism that burned through alcohol and drugs at a much faster rate than a human. And probably quicker than the shifters in this realm, too. But an hour was still a long time.

Normally, when I allowed myself to be taken, I was awake within twenty to thirty minutes.

So whatever they'd hit me with had been a more impactful dose than my usual.

I frowned. Wouldn't that make this amount almost lethal for a mortal? Or was this their typical means for subduing a supernatural?

Hmm, but Vex hadn't hit me with this strong a dose. Perhaps because he hadn't had enough on hand at the time?

*Makayla?* Alaric prompted.

*Sorry, still trying to wake up,* I said, meaning it. *Want me to portal back to you?* I asked. *Or let them take me to their lair?*

*Portal back*, he replied without missing a beat. *We have some leads to follow. We can find these assholes via another way that doesn't require putting you in jeopardy.*

*I'm never really in jeopardy*, I started, my snarky side coming out to play.

Except that snarkiness came to an abrupt halt as I went to stroke my ring. *It's gone*, I thought, my eyes flying open as a zing of alarm shot down my spine. *Fuck! Fuckity fuck!* I tried to pull my hands around to search them, but they were cuffed behind me.

However, a few cursory strokes of my fingers confirmed my greatest fear.

*My ring is gone!* I shouted in my head, panic rising in my throat. *It's spelled to transition with me, Alaric. Which means they took it.* That couldn't be good. That meant... that implied... that they *knew* about the ring. It also explained my heavy drug dose.

I relayed all that to Alaric, goose bumps riddling my limbs and tightening the skin across my chest. *Deep breaths*, I coached myself, missing whatever Alaric said back to me. Because I was too busy trying to rein in my mounting panic. *I've been in worse situations. I can handle this. I've got this. I'm okay.*

*Tell me what you see*, Alaric demanded. *Tell me what you feel. What's around you. Focus and help me find you, Makayla.*

His words grounded me, gave me something useful to do.

*Backup*, I thought. *I have backup.*

*You have more than just backup. You have me*, he snapped. *Now help me find you.* The repeated demand helped me steal another deep breath.

*Okay*, I whispered, allowing him to pull me into a sense of calm that I desperately needed.

Losing my shit helped no one except for my captors.

I wasn't some damn damsel. I knew how to take charge and fix situations like this. So they had my ring. I'd just find a way to get it back.

Taking a deep breath, I surveyed everything around me.

*I'm in a truck bed. It's rough terrain,* I said as another bump rattled me against the metal floor. *It's dark and I'm lying down in the back, so I can't see much. There are tall trees all around me. Exceptionally green, so there's a water source.*

I paused to engage my other senses.

*I can hear the frogs and flipping fish.*

I sniffed the air.

*It smells mossy. Like a swamp… or wetlands, maybe? There are a lot of songbirds, too, and I think…*

I inhaled deeply, closing my eyes to allow my senses to formulate a scene in my mind.

*Balsam fir trees,* I sighed, reveling in the woodsy fragrance. *They only grow a few places at home, but I don't know the area in this realm.*

*Passing the details on to Hardt. He's monitoring a bunch of trucks all over the Northeast.*

*Good.* Although, the whole thing made me feel a bit useless.

I knew every acre for miles and miles in my home realm. However, while this Silver Lake was very much like where I'd grown up, not all of the surrounding areas were the same. There were developments that were grasslands in my world. Different town names. And other small things that made it nearly impossible for me to pinpoint my exact location.

*We've been on the same straight path since I woke up,* I added, realizing we hadn't deviated much.

*That's helpful, too. Keep talking to me.*

I agreed and relayed the rest of our movements to him.

At one point, the truck slowed and made a sharp right turn, then drove for another five minutes before coming to stop.

*Be careful, Mak,* Alaric whispered as if he were right next to me.

*Always.* My ears perked as the doors up front opened. *I think they're coming.*

Not wanting to lose my advantage, I forced every muscle to relax and evened out my breathing to feign sleep.

The back of the truck bed dropped open with a clang.

I began to count between inhales and exhales, needing to remain absolutely calm and quiet. These weren't humans but supernaturals with enhanced senses.

Thankfully, they seemed rather confident in the dosage they'd given me. Because they didn't bother checking me for signs of consciousness.

Rough hands threw me over a bulky shoulder as though I were a rag doll. From the stench, it appeared to be Vex Junior. I really wanted to know what made the hybrid types smell like the inside of a cigar.

The muscular giant grunted and stomped over the ground. I swiftly changed his name to *Hulk Junior* in my head as he kicked something hard, bouncing me on his shoulder without a care. His actions very much embodied the phrase, *Hulk smash!*

*Yeah, well, Makayla stab!* I thought darkly back at him. *There is definitely a stake headed your way, dude.*

*Focus, Makayla,* Alaric said softly. *Is that bent-snout wolf with you?*

*I can't look around to confirm that, but I hear two sets of footsteps ahead of me,* I replied. *One of them is probably Bendy.*

*I think his real name is Robert Gamington. He's Kristen's brother.*

My heart skipped a beat. *Her brother?*

*Yeah. Alpha Landon from McKenzie Pack called. He said he's missing an enforcer, Robert, and he suspects that's the reason Neo was killed.*

*Because Robert would have had access to the information.*

*Yeah.*

*Shit.*

*Yeah,* he repeated.

HJ—Hulk Junior abbreviated—pivoted beneath me, knocking me back into my surroundings with a flourish. My eyes fluttered open on instinct, and I caught the edge of my scenery. Just trees and plants. I relayed that to Alaric, then closed my eyes again as a door opened up ahead.

"Take her down," a cultured voice said. "I'll call the boss man with the good news."

HJ grunted, stepping through the threshold.

*It's a cabin,* I clarified, trying to see as much as I could before he turned. *Doesn't appear to be all that…* I trailed off as HJ stomped down a set of stairs. *Didn't look big upstairs, but we're heading down toward a basement now. At least two stories down.*

*Searching all known properties matching your area description now.* That statement held an ounce of frustration, one I understood because I'd be flipping the fuck out if it were him who'd been taken. He wanted to be able to help, and I hadn't given him much to act on. But there wasn't much I could do about that given the circumstances.

When we reached the bottom of the steep staircase, and I peeked around again.

*Concrete walls, floor, and ceiling, all with water stains. We're in a big room, but there are hallways to the left and right.*

"Put her in the first cell," the cultured voice called down the stairs. "It's empty."

*Empty cell? What are the others filled with?*

*What about cells?* Alaric asked.

*They're putting me in the first one because it's empty,* I explained. *I'm guessing that means there are other girls here.*

*Savannah?* he asked, hopeful.

*I don't know yet.*

Hulk Junior turned to the left.

I shut my eyes, uncertain of where the third captor had gone.

It took years of training to keep myself from crying out in pain and cursing a blue streak when HJ tossed me onto the cold, hard floor. My shoulder took the brunt of it, my arms twisting at an awkward angle behind me because of the cuffs.

*Makayla?*

*I'm fine,* I gritted out. *Just becoming acquainted with my new cell.*

HJ shuffled away, and the cell door slammed shut with a haunting squeak before the lock clicked into place. Then the giant's stomps faded down the hall.

I waited a beat, listening intently.

Chains clinked nearby, suggesting the presence of other captives.

A wheeze in the distance tickled my ear.

And the soft thuds of feet heading upward.

Nothing else. No one breathing nearby. No whirring sounds of technology. Just me and my own heartbeat.

I slitted my eyes to confirm what my ears had already told me. *I'm alone.*

Alaric's relief was palpable. *Can you free yourself?*

*Yeah, but it's going to take me a minute to handle my cuffs.* Because they were behind my back and my arm still smarted from the rough treatment. Not to mention the residual effects of the drugs.

Whatever they'd dosed me with was seriously potent.

But I had this.

Just needed to squirm a little.

I bit my lip to keep from crying out as I righted my arms behind me. It hurt like a son of bitch, shooting pain up my limbs as I situated myself into a position I could work with.

A countdown started naturally in my head. By the seventy-two-second marker, I found the release on my shackles. Traffickers always invested in cheap shit, especially when handling girls. It certainly came in useful in these types of situations.

With a little twist, I slipped the metal from my wrists and set them quietly on the floor before stretching out my abused body. Then I slowly rose to my feet and tested my balance. *A little sore, but I'm okay,* I told Alaric, sensing his concern.

I cleared my throat and focused on my surroundings once more, feeling more at home with every cataloged detail.

*Same stunning décor in my cell. Water-stained concrete, more water-stained concrete. Except there are chains screwed into the walls. Silver, from the looks of them. Same with the bars. As far as dungeons go, this certainly ranks higher than the one you found me in back at the bar. It's more like...* I trailed off as memories tumbled through my thoughts.

Sapphire.

The dusky dungeon we'd been trapped in.

The cold concrete.

The *wet* air.

I shivered. *Could this be the same place?* No, that'd been closer to New York City. It would have taken us longer to reach that point.

*What's outside the bars?* Alaric prompted, pulling me back to him once more.

I slowly tiptoed to the cell door, uncertain about what —or who—waited in the corridor.

*It's a long hallway lined with bars. There are windows at the very top, way over my head, like, two stories up. And they're too high for me to climb up there to look around. They look blacked out, too. At least from here.* I studied the lock on my door. *Give me a minute and I'll look in the cells.*

I snatched the silver bracelets from the ground, braced for the pain this time, and broke off the single strand of one cuff.

It wasn't an ideal tool, but it would do the trick.

Silver bars took me a few seconds longer than regular bars because I preferred not to let my skin touch the metal—a skill that had to be perfected when the lock was on the outside of the door. Fortunately, I had a lot of experience with similar challenges.

*I haven't heard anything since Hulk Junior left me in my cage,* I said while I fussed with the lock. *Other than some clanking of metal, which I assume is coming from the other captives.*

*Don't take risks.* Alaric's low warning wrapped around me in a commanding caress, the alpha in him attempting to protect his mate from afar. It made me shiver, something that nearly caused me to touch the silver bars, but I corrected myself in the last second and heard the subtle *pop* of the lock.

I pulled the door toward me as slowly as possible, hoping to avoid any noise, but the hinges protested just before I had the opening wide enough for me to slip through. I winced and paused, holding my position and listening for any indication that someone had heard. I made a mental note to start carrying a tiny bottle of metal lubricant.

Glancing down at my nude body, I sighed. *Yeah, never*

*mind.* I couldn't even keep my damn ring, let alone a bag of supplies.

Fortunately, no one came running. I also didn't hear the sound of voices, so I let out the breath I hadn't realized I'd been holding and slipped out of the cell.

*I'm in the corridor now,* I said, taking a step toward the exit, when the rattling sound echoed behind me. I winced. Part of me wanted to dart up the stairs and take my chances with the bad guys up there. Or slip into the night. Escape. Find Alaric. Return.

But a stronger part of me refused to leave anyone behind. Savannah might be down here, too.

Biting the side of my cheek, I started exploring, searching my surroundings to determine who else was here and also to potentially find another way out.

The cells were filthy. Some of them were bloody and holding the stench of death. Others had girls chained up in a drugged state, their eyes vacant to the world.

My heart broke upon seeing them, but I'd spent years hardening myself to the morbid scene. Feeling bad for them didn't help them. They needed to be freed, and to do that, I had to keep going.

So I did, peeking in each cell while looking for anything that could be useful. *I think there are only one set of stairs*, I said, almost to the end of the first corridor. *And all that's left in these cells are battered women. Mostly human.*

I shivered as I reached the last cell and found the source of the wheezing I'd heard from my cell. My stomach churned at the sight of a small girl curled into another female's lap, her breathing labored as she fought off the chill of the cement beneath her.

*Dying,* I thought, my heart clenching. *She's dying.*

*Who?* Alaric asked.

*A girl,* I whispered, turning away from the sight. The

girls hadn't noticed me. None of them had. They were too drugged to even care.

I crept back down the hallway toward the main area, my heart pounding each step of the way. *Those assholes are going to pay, Alaric*, I seethed.

He huffed in agreement.

I started toward the stairs, only to be distracted by the clanging of metal echoing down the other corridor. My instincts warred again, curiosity battling with my need to run.

But a soft cry pierced my ears, followed by a scent that had my nose twitching with familiarity. *Savannah*, I thought, following that thread to the corridor. It was lined with larger cells and medical equipment. I searched for any tools I could use, like a scalpel or a saw, only to be caught off guard by a whisper.

"How could you?"

The words were so soft, almost nonexistent.

"How could you?"

A feminine voice. Agonized. Heartbroken.

"How could you?"

I followed the sound, drawn to it, needing to know more.

"How could you?"

A soft cry followed, the delirious tone breaking on a scream.

I ran toward her, all the way down the hall, and found Savannah at the end, strapped to a table as a machine pumped something into her veins. *What the fuck?* I thought, looking around, confused by the scene unfolding before me. *I have to help her!*

She continued to mumble those three words, her eyes rolling into the back of her head as she trembled violently.

*What's happening?* Alaric demanded.

I tried to tell him, my thoughts coming in rapid succession, the words flying through my mind in uncharacteristic chaos. But I felt the silver in the air. The wrongness. The pain!

"Savannah," I whispered, trying to figure out where to begin in helping her escape. The clamps were solid silver without a key in sight.

"Looking for these?" a deep voice drawled from behind me.

I swung around, my body perking up for a fight.

Only to be slammed in the face with a boulder-sized fist. *Fuck!* Stars blinded my vision, setting me back a few paces. Then another hit to my stomach sent me to my knees.

*Makayla!* Alaric roared in my head.

But I was too dizzy to reply.

The world faded.

Blinked in and out.

Then the familiar burn of silver pierced my senses, and suddenly, I jolted back to life on a chair. I had no recollection of how I'd landed in one, or who had put me there, but my ankles and wrists were bound in a similar way to Savannah's.

And when I looked up, it was into a pair of muddy brown eyes set in a mutilated face that would haunt my nightmares for years to come.

"Hello, Makayla," he greeted, his voice underlined with an eagerness that made my blood run cold. "Welcome to hell."

# CHAPTER 30

## MAKAYLA

*WHAT'S HAPPENING?* Alaric demanded.

*I was caught,* I muttered, stating the obvious. Then I gave him a brief rundown of events as my mind began to clear, followed by a quick description of the disfigured guy in front of me.

*Brown and gray hair, kind of like the wolf from earlier. But his nose is more than bent. His face is downright grotesque. Did Alpha Landon say if Robert is disfigured?*

*Yeah, he mentioned a broken nose, but nothing about other disfigurements. Are you okay?*

*Been better,* I answered honestly. *Pretty sure they set me up to fail. Like a trap.* It was the only reason I could give for why they'd let me wander around before stopping me.

Or maybe I'd actually escaped. Temporarily.

Perhaps they'd expected me to go up, which would explain why they'd all been out of the basement.

Regardless, I was officially fucked now. *They've clamped me to a chair. I don't know if I can wiggle my way out of these cuffs.* They were tight and suffocating and burned like hell.

*We have a lead on your location because of your description of the firs and swamp,* he said. *And Hardt tracked the truck to a country road that leads to a cabin.*

I wanted to be relieved. But the familiar guy was

looming far too close to my face for that. My nostrils flared as I tried to determine this guy's wolf type. I jolted as the subtle fragrance of smoke taunted my nose in return. *Oh, shit. Hybrid.*

And yet, there was also something familiar about his scent.

I inhaled again.

*Kristen.*

*Shit.* This was the scent I'd picked up on at Kristen's crime scene. Faint, but present. And just like before, there was something oddly recognizable about it. I couldn't place the familiarity, but I swore I'd smelled this guy before. Except the underlying aroma of ash and copper pennies distorted the fragrance. *Who are you?* I wondered, eyeing him suspiciously. *Why do I know you?* How *do I know you?*

I felt more than heard Alaric's shock. *Another hybrid?*

*Yeah, I'm looking at two right now. Hulk Junior and… the familiar guy.* These rats were suddenly crawling out of the gutters all over the place. *The latter is the one I smelled on Kristen.*

*Fuck.*

*My thoughts exactly.*

HJ stomped into the cell with a tray that he set off to the side, and behind him, a vamp entered in an all-black suit. Was this the boss? Or the familiar guy?

I looked between them, trying to discern who was in charge here.

They both had an air of authority.

Although, the vamp had a douche-like air around him, too. He reminded me of decorations on a cake. *Like a cuntcake*, I decided.

But the other guy… he… was not pretty or clean-cut. All mass and strength and danger.

I shivered as the familiar one came to stand in front

of me, his hands clasped behind his back and his legs braced shoulder-width apart. His appearance was fairly benign until he suddenly smiled. A shiver ran through my body. Never in my life had I been this close to pure evil.

*This…* I thought, swallowing. *Yeah, this is the boss.* I could see it in the way his shrewd gaze ran over me, like he was trying to size me up and decide what nefarious thing to do to me next.

A chill swept down my spine.

This had been my goal all along. But without my ring… *Fuck.*

*Which one is the boss?* Alaric asked, his words helping to ground me in the present and keep me from feeling the despair clawing at my insides. Something about this guy just screamed *wrongness. Warning. Lethal.*

I swallowed again and whispered back, *The familiar one is the leader. The guy with the scent I recognize and can't place. The hybrid.*

"You know, you cost us quite a bit three years ago," the familiar one drawled. "Then you disappeared without a trace. I didn't understand it. At least not until you explained it to Alaric."

*What?* How could he even know that? And three years ago? *Shit, this is all related.* Just like I'd originally thought. I conveyed it quickly to Alaric, and he grunted in agreement. *Where did I tell you about my ring?*

*The lake,* he replied almost immediately.

The memory of that day came back to me. We'd been swimming…

*Someone… heard me. Someone followed me. Does Silver Lake have a mole?* I wondered.

Alaric's reply was lost as the familiar hybrid grinned again, his expression so dark that I found myself unable to think beyond my impending dread. Power poured off this man, his beast dangerously close to the surface.

*How do I know you?* I wanted to demand. I'd seen this man before. Felt him. *Smelled* him. And yet, his face escaped all my memories. *How?*

"You can't place it, can you?" He cocked his head a little to the side, reminding me of a curious dog. Only, on him, it was creepy as hell. Because I wanted no part of this creature's interest. "Well, after you and your friend came in and dismantled my boss's operation, I was taken by the alpha council to be tried. They subjected me to death. And so I died. Only, I came back." He waved a hand over his body. "Like this. As a hybrid."

He crouched in front of me, his muddy gaze radiating fury, the pupils dancing with black flames.

"I didn't realize the sacrifice I would make to my appearance to survive. I suppose I have you to thank for that, don't I?"

I blinked at him. "I…" I trailed off, frowning. "Bortex?"

It was a guess.

A suggestion.

An… impossibility.

And yet, I'd recognized his scent. I knew him, even while I didn't. Was this why? Because Bortex, former alpha of McKenzie Pack, stood in front of me?

A memory of the Bortex I knew slithered through my mind—an image of the alpha wolf standing in the dungeon taunting a female shifter, his broad shoulders bulging and his dark head tipped backward on a vile laugh.

Shit, he looked *nothing* like that alpha wolf now.

*However…* I squinted my eyes, taking in the broken structure of his face, the ashy streaks of his hair, and the disfigured lines of his jaw.

He was like a much more contorted version of Bendy.

"Yeah, I'm reasonably certain that I didn't have a damn thing to do with that becoming your face," I said. I'd never punched the guy. The vamps had been my focus that day, as well as freeing the girls. The wolves involved had been taken by their own packs.

"Oh, but you did, Makayla," he countered, that twisted grin back in his features and in his voice. "You're the reason I was caught and tried. And therefore the reason I was executed. Being reborn as a hybrid was the only way for me to survive, and *you* led me to that situation."

Well, that was certainly a warped way to look at it. "You chose to traffic girls."

"And you chose to interfere."

"I'm not going to apologize for doing my job," I drawled, some of my confidence returning now that I knew *whom* I faced. I relayed the reveal to Alaric and noticed his lack of surprise. Like he'd already come to this conclusion somehow before this point.

"Oh, you'll apologize soon. In fact, I think you'll be begging me by the end. But first, I need to make you a little more pliable. Can't have you breaking out again." He grinned. "Even if I do get a thrill from watching you work."

A tremble traveled through my limbs, his gaze too knowing. Too intelligent. Like he knew far more about me than he was letting on.

I was still missing something important.

A link that I couldn't quite see but sensed that it existed.

I needed more information. A better explanation.

"If you were watching me that day at the lake, why didn't you take me then?" I asked, thinking out loud and following my instincts. "Why wait until now?" Because he clearly hadn't realized who I was when Vex had first taken me. *Except...* "Vex said he thought you were keeping me for yourself. You've known who I was from the beginning." Which brought me back to, *why now?*

"Yes, but not *what* you are," he drawled. "At least not until you explained all those details to Alaric. And as to why I didn't take you that day, it's because I wasn't the one who overheard your conversation. Titanium did. Well, he and another of my men. And they knew better than to try to take you in front of Alaric."

"Titanium?" I repeated. *And who was with him?*

Bendy grunted from the hallway.

"Seriously?" I looked at the crooked-nosed shifter. "Your name is Titanium? Not Robert?" It was a taunt. One I really shouldn't have released but couldn't help saying. Sarcasm was my friend, my rock, and I could *really* use that rock right about now.

Bendy—I refused to call him Titanium—bared his teeth to me.

Rather than respond to his idiocy, I refocused on the boss man. "You sent the little guy to spy on me?" He wasn't physically small. Just clearly lower on the totem pole.

"Actually, I sent him to deliver a package to Hawk. But he was stopped by the damn beta. His information-gathering on you was a consolation prize used to convince me to spare his life."

I arched a brow. "Beta Hardt stopped him?" And he didn't report that to Alaric or Hawk?

"He asked Titanium why he was in the territory, which he smoothly lied about and said he was there with Kristen, a known friend of Tyler's consort."

"Couldn't jeopardize the other contact," Titanium inserted.

"Precisely right," Bortex murmured. "However, unfortunately, Kristen found out about that claim later, and I think you know what happened from there."

Titanium captured her. *His own sister. Jackass.*

And then...

"You bled her and left her on Alaric's yard with an invite in hopes of drawing him back to the city." That explained the small pinpoints on her neck. His fangs must not be a normal vampire size. I could make all sorts of jokes about length here... but I refrained.

"Yes, I bled her after realizing she wouldn't be useful to our operation. But a friend left her in the yard. Not me."

*A friend? What friend?* "And the initials in her foot?" I prompted, wanting to milk him for all the information he had to give. If I was going to be in this situation, I might as well make good use of it. And he was far more forthcoming than Vex had been.

He grinned. "I branded her skin to invite your mate out to play."

"Why?"

He merely smiled. "Doesn't matter, does it? You're here now. Chained to a chair. Ready to play." He snapped his fingers for one of his minions.

Apparently, interrogation time was over. Which was unfortunate because I wanted to know who the "other contact" was, this mysterious friend who had placed Kristen's body on Alaric's yard. I suspected it was one and the same.

And why didn't Hardt report Titanium's presence to Alaric or Hawk?

I started to tell Alaric the details of my interrogation with Bortex when the rattling of instruments caught my attention. Vampire Cuntcake stood next to the tray HJ had dropped off, preparing a syringe of some kind.

*Drugging me again? Are they timing this shit or something? What were you saying about Hardt?* Alaric demanded. *He found Robert in the territory. Did he tell you or—*

My thought cut off as Vampire Cuntcake stepped toward me, holding up the needle filled with a cloudy gray liquid. "Now, normally, I would have you drink this, but I'm fairly certain you're not in the mood to swallow."

*Uh, Alaric…* A shiver started up my spine.

"So this will have to do," Vampire Cuntcake continued, tapping the syringe. "You know, I don't normally stoop to the level of menial jobs. But going into that alpha meeting as a caterer to deliver the silver solution was worth it to stir such chaos. It blinded them all to our real plans. It's still blinding them."

*Silver solution? Vex's phone call… This is the asshole who poisoned Tyler. Shit!*

Alaric growled in my mind, his mounting anger palpable and temporarily blinding me. *Who?*

*Vampire Cuntcake,* I replied. *Pretty-boy vamp with the needle in his hand.* Which would normally serve as my indicator to end this rather informative interrogation. But I didn't have my escape mechanism.

*Shit. We have a lead, Makayla. We're coming. I promise.*

The liquid in the syringe shimmered in the light for a second, and my eyes widened. *You'd better hurry,* I said, my heart skipping a beat. *Because he's about to pump me full of silver.* And I had no idea how much my body could take.

*What?!* Alaric lost all vestiges of his calmness, his wolf rioting inside his mind and making mine whine in response.

*Deep breaths,* I coached myself. *Just…* I started to struggle with the cuffs around my wrists, but these weren't the kind that easily unlatched. They were solid. Hard. And *burned.*

"I'm very curious to see how your body reacts to this. You're not immune to silver, I assume?" Vampire Cuntcake asked conversationally.

"Stop dicking around, Todd, and do it," Bortex demanded.

*Todd?* I repeated in my head, still fussing with the cuffs. They were so tight that I could barely move. *Vamp's name is Todd, Al—*

The bloodsucking son of a bitch stuck the needle into my arm before I could finish my thought, shooting the liquid straight into my vein and momentarily blinding me to the world.

Alaric raged in my head, but I could barely hear him over the rushing sound in my ears.

I couldn't hold it in. My head fell back, and a bloodcurdling scream ripped from my chest. My body shook, my limbs trembling beneath the onslaught.

Liquid silver.

In my veins.

Going straight to my heart.

*Oh. Fuck.* There was no stopping this, no cure that I knew of, no… way… to… survive.

A tear trickled down my cheek, the weakness stirring a laugh from my captor. Or captors. I couldn't really tell, their reaction swimming around me in a wave of distortion.

*Makayla!*

I blinked, uncertain of whether that voice belonged to me or Alaric.

*I… I don't know… what to do,* I thought, my usual flavor of wit… gone. My breath stunted. My mind… fracturing.

Was my heart even still beating?

Someone patted my cheek that I barely felt beyond

everything else. "I'm sure you'll be much more docile in just a few minutes."

My veins burned, eliciting a whimper from my throat. Or maybe another scream. I… I couldn't hear. No, wait, I could, but it was all just so loud. So intense. So… cold? No, hot. No, cold. Oh God…

My kind were susceptible to silver, but it took a hell of a lot to kill us. However, a concentrated dose directly to the vein… *Will I be able to survive this?*

Alaric shouted something in my head.

*Shh…* I needed to focus. To think. To… to… something.

*Don't you dare leave me, Makayla!*

What? I didn't understand. Leave whom? Alaric? Why would I leave? I tried to open my eyes, to study my surroundings, to remember what I'd been doing with my fingers.

But everything was shutting down.

Except for a link. A subtle connection. A rope tethering me to another. *Alaric.*

His presence soothed me in a manner I didn't really understand. I'd never wanted a mate. But Alaric… I… I liked Alaric. His scent. His wolf. His touch. His comfort. I could feel him all around me, caressing me with his essence, kissing my spirit with his own, and anchoring me here.

I tugged on him.

Reveled in his protection. His strength. His power.

So much energy. So much heat.

His mortality didn't matter. Not to me. *Right?* Right. I… I wanted more time, though. Sixty years would be a gift. Much better than days.

*Days.*

*Days.*

*Days.*

Wow, I was dizzy. The whole room spun, my vision a swirl of darkness prickled with light. Alaric. Yes. Yes, my Alaric.

I sensed him in my head, my heart, my soul, his presence swathing me in a possessive cloak. His growl rumbled through me. His fury palpable. His concern tugging at my tear ducts.

*Don't be sad,* I told him. *I'm floating.*

*Floating.*

*Floating.*

*Floating.*

Yeah, hmm, flying was not recommended. It made me feel woozy. Broken. A bit... dehydrated? No. I wasn't making sense. Nothing made sense.

Except Alaric.

*True mate.*

He bore my mark. I felt it thriving on him, that sexy little wolf pulsing on his chest as I mentally stroked it with my fingers. *Mine. My mate. My Alaric.*

*Yours,* I heard him whisper back. *Yours.*

Alaric's voice bolstered me a little, but it was fleeting.

He asked something about cuffs.

I flew around in my mind, humming to myself, trying to seek reason. *Metal. Unfasten. I know how to do that.* My brother, Asher, had taught me. Nathan, too. And Marc.

*Easy-peasy.*

*Except no.*

*Nope.*

*Clamps burn.* But not as much as my veins. They were on fire. Flaming me from the inside. *Alaric,* I breathed. *Alaric?*

*I'm here.* His deep tones were accompanied by a whisper

of strength, resembling a mental hand. I grabbed on, yanking him into me, needing more.

*True mate.*

*Mine.*

*Mine.*

*Mine.*

A laugh echoed off the walls, reminding me that I wasn't alone. *No, no, not ready…*

"Impressive, Makayla." A cold stroke against my too-hot cheek. "Truly impressive. If you survive this, you'll be the perfect test subject for some other experiments we're planning. I don't think we'll try demon blood with you, though." He ran a finger over my lips, and I gagged. "You don't want to breathe fire, right?"

The world tilted on its axis once more, the chair dipping and moving. A roller coaster ride. Not recommended. *Downward slope… not… nope. Ugh.*

"I told you she wasn't special," one of them said. The… the cakey one, maybe. "She's going to die like all the rest."

*Not. Going. To. Die.*

*No, you're not,* Alaric agreed, his voice strong in my mind. *Keep leaning on me, baby. Take it all.*

My brow furrowed, but a voice interrupted my ability to focus.

"Hmm, maybe you aren't as strong as we thought." He sounded disappointed.

*I'm a badass,* I slurred in my thoughts.

*You are,* Alaric agreed, tugging at my psyche.

"Might as well," someone said, sounding resigned. "At least he'll be here soon."

"Then the real trial can begin," the other agreed.

*Trial?* I repeated. *Trial… test… trial… thread…*

*something...* I almost had it, almost connected all the moving dots in my mind, when he stuck me again.

Another prick.

More fire.

Bright light.

*Oh, fuck...*

Chaos.

Words mingling. Voices, too. Alaric. Me. Them. Everyone.

Sounds. Growls. Screams.

*Walking... walking... walking... to the bright, pretty... light.*

All the while hoping I'd find Alaric on the other side. Waiting.

# CHAPTER 31

## ALARIC

MY HEART FUCKING STOPPED.

Halted.

Broke.

Crumbled into dust.

Proverbially taking me to my knees on an exhale that nearly killed me. Except I felt Makayla there, hanging on by a thread, her psyche a blink on my radar, her strength crushed to a tiny point that throbbed with *need*.

The need to survive.

The need to breathe.

The need to *thrive*.

I shoved every part of me into her, my soul screaming in agony as I followed a path I didn't understand, yanking my mate from a place I'd never known existed, and weaving my essence through hers in a way that shouldn't be possible.

It just… happened.

My wolf reacted.

And I didn't fight him.

I let him guide me into this darkness, marrying my soul to hers in a manner that defied all time and space. *Makayla*, I pleaded, my spirit infusing hers with life, all inside my mind.

I vaguely understood that I sat in the passenger seat of my father's truck.

I vaguely heard the voices around me.

I vaguely felt my pack's concern.

Just as I vaguely sensed their responding strength, pouring into me, *through* me, to the life force that needed it most.

To Makayla. My mate. My other half. The lighter part of my soul. Tainted with silver. Dying. Screaming in mental agony. And yet absorbing the energy my pack had to offer. Taking what *I* had to give her.

All my strength. All my breaths. All my blood, my being, my very fucking core, gifted to *her*, begging her to pull through. To return to me. To walk away from the bliss of death and back into my life. My world. Our future.

Fate put us together for a reason. I understood that now, could see the paths intertwined, the reason Makayla and I had always been meant for one another.

Two alpha wolves. Strong. Independent. Yet so much more impactful together. Makayla grounded me, made me realize my place in this world, focused my power, and encouraged me to lead. Not by telling me what to do. Not by even knowing what I should do. Just by existing and putting me in the situation I was meant to be in through destiny alone.

Driving me to be the alpha I needed to be, not just for her, but for my pack. For *me*.

She brightened my future.

She gave me a reason to feel.

She forced me to be a better wolf.

Perhaps not all at once, but that was our intended path to walk together.

Just as I would support her own endeavors, be alpha enough to understand and know when she needed her space, and not drown her beneath a sea of orders and commands. She was meant to fly, to help others, to be the voice for victims too weak to help themselves.

And I was meant to stand beside her, help her, bolster her, and give her my strength in times like this. To be her rock, her foundation, her *power*.

I bolstered her now, breathing life into her veins, giving her the energy she craved in order to *fight*.

Because together, we were unstoppable.

Together, we could defeat death.

Together, we were meant to *lead*.

She would provide me with the emotional backbone I required to be right for my pack, just as I'd give her my physical strength when she found herself in a situation of need.

*Give and take.*

*Live and learn.*

*Inhale and exhale.*

It was like an out-of-body experience, one that floored my mind but felt too right to fight. Our wolves were dancing, frolicking, engaging in this bond that our souls had cemented. She was forever mine. I was forever hers. No realms would change that. She could run, but I'd always chase.

I hadn't wanted a mate.

Because I hadn't understood the purpose of one until right now, in this moment, as I felt our spirits intertwine. She was the reason I'd felt empty all my life, the reason I'd left Silver Lake, the reason I'd been in New York City at the right time, in the right place, to *find her*.

Had I fought my brother and claimed my throne twelve years ago, I might have missed this link. I might have missed *her*.

Everything in my life had happened for a reason.

My fleeing to the city, taking a job with E.V.I.E., being invited out to play by psychotic hybrids with a penchant for destroying pretty girls.

All of it had put me in Makayla's path, ensuring I would one day meet my other half. Become whole again. Fly free and love and live and have a real heart. *Her* heart.

But I gave her all of mine now, my wolf pouring every ounce of my being into hers and fortifying her for the journey ahead.

*Wake up, Makayla,* I told her. *Wake up. Fight. Live.*

Silence.

I didn't panic.

I waited.

I inhaled.

I exhaled.

I allowed my pack to continue bolstering my reserves, allowed myself to feel their collective concern, and reveled in the realization that they saw me as theirs. Their alpha. Their leader. Their *wolf.*

I belonged to Silver Lake. I'd *always* belonged to Silver Lake. I was just lost before, searching for my purpose, looking for *her.* My Makayla. My soul. The beat to my heart.

*Come back to me,* I encouraged her softly. *I know you're there. I feel you running, but, baby, I'm going to chase you to the end of time and space and drag you back by your pretty hair.*

I swore I heard a growl.

I merely smiled in response.

*You want to play; we'll play. But I don't play fair, baby. My wolf is fierce and protective, and you're trying to die on me, and that's just unacceptable. Now fucking fight like the badass I know you are and breathe. Fucking breathe, Makayla.*

The truck ramped over a bump, momentarily drawing

me to my surroundings. My father drove. Hardt was in the back spouting off directions. He and Jude had found Makayla based on her scenery descriptions. There was only one swampy area with balsam fir trees within a one-hundred-mile radius of Silver Lake.

Two cars followed.

All armed with wolves and military-grade weapons, courtesy of Jude's connections.

Sometimes it paid to have a boss with strong government ties. He had a lot of favors to call in, and he'd used one for us.

*You'd better be alive and ready to fight when I get there, baby,* I said to Makayla. *We're only twenty minutes out at most.* Because we'd turned off onto the back roads some time ago, which meant we were on her trail now. I could almost smell her on the wind.

I closed my eyes again, feeling her life force feeding from mine, and relaxed as I continued to blast her with my strength. Those bastards had pumped her veins with silver, and I had no doubt it would have killed her if she were a Bitten wolf like me.

However, I sensed her immortality lingering between us, bolstering her, and replenishing itself through me and my pack.

I didn't quite understand this hive-mind-like sensation happening between me and my wolves, but I embraced it. I accepted them. Because I didn't have time to fight it. And I needed their strength, their vigor, their support, to save my mate. So I welcomed their essence into my mind. And I *claimed* Makayla.

*Mine,* I thought at her. *Mine forever.*

*Mine,* she echoed on a mumble.

I stilled. *Makayla?*

277

She hummed something incoherent in response, her yawn palpable in my mind.

My fingers dug into the jeans along my thighs. *Makayla. Talk to me.*

*Napping,* she muttered.

*No time for napping, baby. I need you to wake up and kill.*

*Kill?* she repeated, sounding interested in that.

Part of me wondered if she preferred killing over fucking, but I didn't want to waste time by asking. *Yeah, Bortex.*

*Bortex?* She yawned again. *Already dead.*

*No, Mak. He's alive. And he pumped you full of silver.*

*Silver?* The word came out a little clearer. *Something... there's... Alaric... something... dots?*

*What about dots, sweetheart?*

*Connection. Link. Hmm.* She sounded high. *Trials. Trials coming.*

*Makayla, you're not making sense.*

*Burns,* she whispered back, a palpable shudder traversing our bond. *Everything burns.*

*I know, baby,* I said, sensing her agony. *Push the pain to me, and take what you need to revive your strength.*

*That's not... that's not possible.*

*It is, Makayla,* I insisted. *I'm already pushing energy to you. Don't you feel it?*

She fell silent again. Then she started mumbling about *dots* again. *Puzzle pieces. Piece together. Dots. Trials. Friend. Lake. Titanium. Knew me. Knew... about my ring. Ready for me. Grabbed me.*

*Alaric!*

Her shout splintered across my mind, only for me to realize it wasn't her but my father.

Flashbangs erupted around us.

Followed by an electric wave of current that temporarily blinded me.

And in the next moment, we were surrounded.

*Shit!* It was an ambush. A trap. And from the looks of it, we were severely outnumbered.

# CHAPTER 32

## ALARIC

*Two alphas.*
*One beta.*
*Four enforcers.*
*And the director of E.V.I.E.*

I quickly analyzed our situation, calculating our next move. We were surrounded by at least twelve assailants. That was an estimate based on the trajectory and number of flashbangs erupting around us. I couldn't actually see or hear a damn thing.

Another blast went off to my right, making my ears ring.

I flinched.

Better than gunfire, but still painful as fuck to a shifter's senses.

*They're trying to distract us,* I realized as another set went off shortly after the first. *Or incapacitate us.* Assailants didn't use flashbangs for any other purpose. If these assholes wanted us dead, they would have started with guns.

*Alaric?* Makayla whispered, her voice dreamy and fading in my mind.

*Damn it.* Her soft tones were accompanied by a hum of burning life, her inner flame near its end. I growled, the dual hit of the attack and her hanging on by a thread setting me distinctly on edge.

*Take what you need,* I commanded, shoving vitality to her through the little pinpoint in our connection. *Take it, Makayla.*

I needed her to focus on using our link for recovery so I could properly concentrate on my situation.

These assholes were attacking *my* pack. *My* men. And they had *my* mate.

I clenched my jaw, my mind working in overdrive as I assessed my options. Makayla whimpered, her wolf releasing a low whine that had me snarling in response.

We did not have fucking time for this.

*Stop. Fighting. Me,* I demanded. I possessed an antidote in the form of life energy, and she needed to accept it—*and me*—right fucking now.

I didn't wait for her acceptance. This wasn't up for debate. I couldn't divide my attention between her and my wolves. And by some stroke of fate, I had the ability to help her.

So I did.

I shoved all my vitality into her with a blast of power that knocked down every mental wall between us. No more hiding. No more calling this connection between us impossible. No more denying destiny.

We were linked for a reason.

And it was time we used that link for our joint survival.

The flashbangs continued to erupt around me, the sound deafening. But I put all my focus and effort into Makayla, forcing her to acknowledge and indulge in our bond.

This wasn't how mates worked for my kind.

But I felt in my bones how it worked for *hers.* And I fully embraced it, *demanding* she accept it and survive.

Her mental gasp traveled to my mind, her shock a palpable electric wave that jolted my chest. Then a typhoon of emotions and comprehension followed, her soul opening to mine and finally acknowledging what I'd known from the beginning.

*We're mates*, she marveled, her voice holding a hint of deliriousness. *True mates.*

She'd said that earlier, but I picked up on the understanding in those two words now. Not only did she feel it, she *believed* it, and that revelation unraveled a cyclone of insanity.

My pulse raced, my breathing erratic, my awareness slipping.

Chaos unfolded inside me, the sensations and thoughts and varying strengths a whirlwind of confusion slashing at my mental faculties. The world fractured around me beneath a web of *voices* that penetrated my concentration, each word assaulting my ability to process logical thought.

*What's happening?* I wondered, dazed from the onslaught.

Makayla's hum of life cascaded over all of it, her heart beating in time with mine as our souls rejoiced in a matrimony deeper than any explicable bond.

My blood heated, my chest warm with the knowledge that not only had I found my other half but she was also alive and starting to thrive again. I felt her contented sigh all the way to the depths of my core, could hear her quickening pulse, her mind locking irrevocably with mine.

But there were others.

*So. Many. Others.*

I cursed, blind and deaf from my surroundings and positively crippled inside my mind.

It all happened in the blink of an eye, my world crashing and rebuilding in a breath.

I sensed everyone. My wolves. My pack. My own father. And still, above them all, *my mate*. Like a net of connections, each life strand tied to me and Makayla—as their bonded alpha pair.

My palms met my eyes, a single word roaring through my mind as I attempted to sort through the disorder. *Quiet!*

I needed to be able to think. To focus. To fucking survive. And I couldn't do that with all this mayhem unraveling in my damn head.

Everything went still.

No, not everything. *Everyone*.

All my wolves.

All their minds.

Silenced beneath my command.

I rubbed my forehead, confused as hell. Then my father whispered my name. Not out loud, but via some invisible connection. I looked at him, or tried to, anyway, but the flashes of light continued to erupt around us. Not gunfire. Not a war zone. Just constant bombs meant to keep us paralyzed in the car.

*Holding us captive*, I realized dizzily. *They're disabling our senses to keep us here.*

*Yes*, my father agreed.

I hadn't realized I was talking to him, but it felt right. Easy. Like I should have always had this ability to speak to him telepathically. However, it'd only manifested in me today. Right now. Tonight.

Because of Makayla.

I tried to ask her to explain, but she wasn't quite ready yet, her soul still healing. But I felt her strengthening with every breath.

*Almost there*, I thought at her. *You're almost there.*

She absorbed strength from me in response, depleting my reserves in an instant. Only for my pack to re-bolster my power in the next second, their psyches all miraculously connected to mine.

It was impossible, and yet, exactly what I required to survive. A sense of rightness settled over me as I explored the links once more, the voices softer now, like everyone had heard my demand to quiet their minds and were doing their best to listen.

Or maybe I'd thrown up a barrier.

I didn't know how any of this worked, but part of me instinctively understood the hive mind—a part of me that was heavily tied to Makayla. Like she'd been brought here to help me in this moment, to ensure I knew how to take over the mantle as alpha of Silver Lake.

Her soul brushed mine, a soft kiss of reassurance, and I responded with another charge of vitality through our wide-open link.

My pack immediately balanced me, shooting an electric boost through my veins.

I inhaled deeply, reveling in the sensation. It helped me see and hear beyond the bombs going off around me. It revitalized my senses. Gave me a mental map to follow that overrode my reality.

Everything softened, my eyes falling closed as I focused on my new senses, seeking out the minds of the wolves closest to me. We were in three different cars, all encircled by assailants and their unending flashbangs.

But no gunfire.

No death.

Except... as I tentatively reached out to the psyches of my four enforcers on-site, I found a severed link.

*How?* I demanded, frowning. *Where?*

The web inside me expanded, showcasing a myriad of invisible strands tied to each life under my rule.

*Steve*, I realized, stroking the frayed end of his connection. His mind was quiet. Gone. *Dead*.

Yet another set of thoughts were very much alive nearby, the panicked undertones catching my focus and pulling me to the essence in question. *Paul*.

*Ah, fuck. What's happening? Why do I feel so weird? Focus, idiot. Keep the gun on Jude. He might have a knife. A hidden weapon. Boss wants him alive.*

A low rumble echoed inside me, my wolf furious by the hint of disloyalty lurking inside Paul's mind.

The male went silent, but I felt his fear.

*Oh, fuck,* he whispered to himself, his thoughts reigniting with a flourish of alarm.

He'd killed Steve.

But that wasn't all.

I anchored myself in his psyche, ripping out his thoughts and diving into the source of his betrayal. He tried to mask his guilt, running through each memory that he wanted to hide in a poor attempt to lock them away. But I heard everything. Every fucking statement he'd made, in every fucking situation.

*Makayla is Alaric's mate. She's not from here. She has gifts. Unique ones. I overheard them talking about her ring at the lake. She can portal and switch realms.*

*Kristen's body. Placed on Alaric's lawn. Message received.*

*Makayla's taking quadrant one. I'll distract the others.*

*Alaric's mentally linked to her. She's telling him everything. Yeah, you can test it when you grab the E.V.I.E. director.*

The sequence ended with the memory of killing Steve.

All the pieces came together in succession, bolstered by his thoughts. Paul was working with Bortex. He'd passed along intimate details regarding Makayla's origin and then provided her location to be taken. And he'd engaged in a conversation right before we'd left tonight, informing Bortex of my mental connection to Makayla.

This had all been a trap, one Paul had helped orchestrate.

To capture Jude.

That was the reason the men hadn't started killing yet. They were waiting for permission, and for something else. Some sort of trial. Something involving me.

I rolled my neck, my anger mounting with each passing second.

Makayla breathed into my mind, her pain bolstering my resolve.

Bortex and his men had taken my mate and shot her full of silver. All for some sort of fucked-up experiment, the details of which weren't located within Paul's mind. That was fine. I'd find out more my own way.

These bastards were attacking my wolves. They had Savannah. And now they wanted Jude. While the E.V.I.E. director might not be my charge, he was still my boss and friend.

And their worst offense—they'd hurt Makayla.

My wolf snarled inside, taking over my instincts.

Fuck the flashbangs.

Fuck the outnumbering odds.

And fuck Paul.

I took the gun from my holster in one hand and opened the door with the other. These assholes wanted to play? We'd damn well play.

Paul had given away a key secret within his mind— these military jokers were under orders not to kill, which gave me a clear and obvious advantage.

Because I had no problem pulling the trigger.

A few of them shouted when I rolled out of the car, their trajectory of attack shifting to me.

More flashes and loud noises sounded, but I sprinted right into the fray, taking one of the men out with my fucking fist to his throat.

He went down, his helmet rolling off his head.

I grabbed it, securing it over my head, then put a bullet between his eyes.

*Humans.*

*They're fucking humans.*

I sent those messages to my wolves, pissed off all over again. Bortex was using soldier types to attack a bunch of well-trained wolves.

That explained why they were more immune to the flashbangs.

But it also made them exceptionally easy targets. I assumed they all had on armored vests, just like me, which left their necks as the only viable place to put a bullet. And now that I had on a helmet, I could hear again.

See, not so much. This thing had night vision enabled —something I didn't need as a shifter—and it was distorted to a human-grade sight.

I ducked behind a massive tree, listened for the sources of the flash grenades, and focused on their footsteps over leaves and grass and the scrape of boots against rocks. It helped me paint a visual of our surroundings, locating each assailant by sound alone.

I was wrong.

There were only eight of them. Seven now that I'd taken one down. And according to Paul's thoughts—which I remained tapped into—these men were supposed to distract us with flashbangs as they surrounded the automobiles to detain us.

They'd almost succeeded.

Now their footsteps told me they were scattering,

searching for me while also trying to continue distracting the vehicles.

I'd divided their focus.

*What now, Paul?* I asked him, my voice darkened by a hint of violence. *Are you waiting for Bortex to save you?*

I didn't understand how the whole hive-mind thing worked, but I caught his responding growl, just as I heard several of my wolves whining at the fury pouring off their alpha, and most importantly, I still felt Makayla. She'd almost returned to awareness, her thoughts syncing with mine.

*Betrayed.*

*Trap.*

*Trial.*

She was no longer muttering about dots but piecing together the events in my head with everything she'd learned through her interrogation earlier.

I took out two approaching men, their trajectory given away by their heavy stomps, and then I rolled behind another thick cluster of bushes. The flashes stopped, the men shifting the proverbial spotlight to me—the real threat.

A few of them cocked their weapons.

I grinned. *Decided it's okay to kill now?* I mused.

Paul's terror radiated outward, the sensation stoking my inner ire.

*Yeah, you should be scared,* I told him. *I'm going to fucking destroy you.*

The spike of his fear confirmed that he heard every word I said to him. However, the coward refused to reply. Not that I needed him to say a damn word. I could read every thought in his mind.

*Start counting,* I taunted. *Three down. Six to go. Because yeah, I absolutely include you in that list, Paul.*

The forest fell silent around me as the last of the flashbangs died.

*About damn time.*

This was the kind of moment I'd prepared all my life for—I could see again, hear every breath and sound for several yards in every direction, and I could *taste* my impending victory in the air.

I concentrated on another approaching set of footsteps, taking aim, and then paused upon sensing Paul's resolve.

He wanted to use Jude as a shield.

*Control him*, I heard Makayla breathe, her mind opening up to mine to explain how alpha links worked for her kind. It was a crash course that I absorbed directly from her experiences. I took in as much of it as I could with the few seconds I had to spare and swallowed as the facts unfolded in my head.

The hive mind encompassed all my wolves, granting me access to their thoughts. Their life sources were formally tied to mine as their pack alpha. And that attachment allowed me a strand of control.

Not as a puppet master, but as a commander.

The lead wolf.

The one in charge.

The alpha of Silver Lake. *His alpha.*

*Drop it,* I demanded, blasting Paul with a wave of dominant energy that had his much weaker mind bending beneath my will. *Now.* The human part of him tried to fight it, his thoughts shouting out in the negative.

But his wolf… his wolf was *mine*.

And his wolf bowed.

His strand frayed a fraction of a section later, his mind telling me that Jude had just sliced a blade across Paul's throat. I didn't see it so much as feel it, and I sent out a warning blast to my wolves not to mourn the loss of his traitorous life.

My father responded in kind, his mind rolling right alongside mine as the approaching soldier finally reached my hiding place. I ripped the helmet off my head and fired a bullet into his throat. He went down with a gurgle, and the others all ran toward me, some of them reaching for flashbangs to toss.

But I was faster, stronger, and far more prepared.

I squeezed my trigger, taking out two more men before pulling up behind another tree just out of sight of the remaining two.

Their footsteps were uncertain, their breaths coming in pants.

A bullet cracked from the forest. *Hardt.*

A second one followed. *Dad.*

Leaving us in the clear, having taken down all eight soldiers and our traitor.

I pulled away from the tree, pride blossoming in my chest, as a pulse of energy whipped through the woods, bringing me to my knees. My cheek met the dirt, my eyes frozen in an open position while my mind tried to comprehend what the hell had just happened.

Another wave cascaded around us soon after.

"What the hell?" Jude's voice carried through the clearing, his tone strong and entirely unfazed.

Electricity zipped through my veins, the static leaving me paralyzed on the ground.

*Some sort of weapon,* my father wheezed into my mind.

*The fuck is that?* Hardt gasped.

Timothy and Gregory were in a similar state of shock, their bodies equally still.

Only Jude appeared to be moving around. He had his fingers to my father's neck, sensing for his heartbeat. I felt his touch as though it were on my own skin, but it was my father's senses, not mine.

Then a slow clap echoed through the trees, a burning scent following.

*Run,* I wanted to tell Jude. *Run!*

*He won't run,* my father replied.

And sure enough, the bastard merely stood, his expression blank as he waited.

Bortex stepped into view, his boots a few feet from my head. "Well now, that truly was impressive, Alaric."

He finally stopped clapping, his grotesque appearance rivaling the description Makayla had provided me with earlier. She muttered something unintelligible back at me about a beauty contest.

"I expected a bit more weakness, what with Makayla's silver situation and all," Bortex continued. "But you took down all eight of my men in just a handful of minutes." He crouched before me. "They were my best, too. All hyped up on Lycan blood."

I tried to snort.

But whatever electric pulse he'd sent through me had left me a drooling mess at his literal feet.

The bastard ran a finger over my cheek, then flicked my jaw as he considered me thoughtfully. "You know, I wonder what a new team could accomplish under the influence of your essence instead." He canted his head. "Let's find out, shall we?"

# CHAPTER 33

## MAKAYLA

*WHAT A WEIRD DREAM.*

It started with being injected with silver and ended with Alaric going into full alpha mode in my mind. My wolf purred at the memory, pleased with his behavior.

I almost shook my head in disgust, when a prickle to my conscious held me still.

*Wait…*

The skin around my wrist *burned*. My mind also felt a bit sluggish, my thoughts not fully connecting. But it was right there. A hint of truth. Reality. The facts of what had happened.

*Taken.*

*Poisoned.*

*Trap.*

*Betrayed.*

The sequence of events slammed into me beneath angry blows from a consciousness that mingled with mine. *Alaric.*

He growled in response, his wolf highly agitated.

I nearly blinked, but again that prickle held me captive. Some part of me aware that I shouldn't move. *No, not me. You. What are you doing?*

*Keeping you safe,* Alaric snarled. *Don't let them know you're awake.*

My lips threatened to curl down, but that wave of dominance forced me to remain unmoving.

Normally, it would piss me off to be controlled in such a way. But in this moment, I rather appreciated it. Because I needed his presence to mask my physical reactions to my waking state.

Confusion, frustration, and *pain* rippled through me. It was enough to make me want to gasp, but I swallowed it. No, I didn't even do that. I just... exhaled. Softly. As though lost to slumber while those around me waited.

I sensed them now.

A hybrid and a shifter.

*Where are you?* I asked Alaric.

*In a room near yours,* he replied, his tone irritated. *Bortex used some sort of sonar tech to disable me and the others. Bastard tossed me on a table and clamped me with silver. He has me watching a screen, waiting for you to wake up so he can start his trial.*

Again my lips threatened to curl down, but this time I stopped them before his compulsion kicked in. I desperately grasped for my last real memory, then realized... it was all *real.* I hadn't been dreaming, just lost to a delirious state of recovery while his strength and our connection saved me from certain death.

*Shit,* I breathed in my mind. *Shit. Shit. Shit.*

I sorted through everything we'd exchanged, all the information he'd provided along the way.

Paul was a traitor. Bortex wanted Jude and had set all this in motion as a trap. Then, upon learning about my unique mental connection to Alaric, he had decided to test how deep our link went by poisoning me and sending his best men out to take all of them down at some predetermined rendezvous point.

*How did you find me?* I wondered.

*Hardt. He tracked the fir trees and swamp, then Jude did a search on the local properties.*

Some of that sounded familiar, like he'd mentioned it before. *Paul didn't help at all?*

*No. Had no idea he was involved until he killed Steve.*

Yeah, I had a memory of that, too. *You went all, like, Hulk smash on the soldiers.* That was the part of my dream I'd enjoyed, listening to him kick ass.

But now he was caught.

And everyone was waiting for me to wake up.

To start a new trial.

*Where's everyone else?* I asked, but even as I thought it, I felt the answer.

Because I was just as connected to Alaric's pack as I was to him.

*Oh.*

Our mating link had granted me access to the hive mind via him. Or maybe… it was the other way around. Regardless, I was firmly embedded in his pack now. I couldn't even sense Nathan or my home realm.

My heart skipped a beat, my breath threatening to halt in my lungs.

But Alaric's dominance took over, forcing me to relax.

I could fight him. I might even win. However, I allowed his compulsion, needing him to ground me before I lost my ever-loving shit. Never in my wildest imagination could I have come up with this possibility. But now that it stood before me, I had no choice but to accept it.

He was my true mate.

The other half of my soul.

I'd… accepted it before. But not quite.

Not until he'd plowed down all my walls and forced me to acknowledge his spirit as mine.

I couldn't even hate him for it. Because he'd done it with the best intentions, saving my life, and now... now I was still strapped to a chair with him in another room, and wasting precious time overthinking a connection I never had a choice in ignoring.

Walking away from him now would kill us both.

I had no idea how we'd progressed this far in such a small amount of time, but fighting it would only hurt us both.

And I very much wanted to survive this situation.

I also wanted to kill Bortex and the vamp who had spiked my blood with silver.

My resolve settled, my mind focusing on the task at hand, and I felt more than heard Alaric's approval.

*Good to have you back, Mak,* he said. *Now, how the hell are we getting out of this mess?*

*Are you still disabled?* I asked.

*Not exactly.* His mental voice wavered just enough for me to sense his depleting energy.

*Oh, hell...* He'd been focusing the last vestiges of his strength on holding me still... while a machine fucking bled him. *Alaric!*

*Priorities, sweetheart,* he whispered. *The pack's bolstering me, something Bortex realized when my father passed out in the other room.* Some of his ire traveled through those words.

*How long was I out of it?*

*Long enough,* he muttered. *But you're fully restored now, and that's what matters. Now help me figure out a way to survive.*

I didn't reply right away, my mind processing the location of the others first. Everyone was still alive and in this wing, including Savannah. She appeared to be the most damaged, her mental waves altered by whatever the machines were doing to her.

But Hawk, Hardt, Timothy, and Gregory were all unconscious.

*They willingly gave me their energy first so I wouldn't absorb any from you,* Alaric explained before I could ask how I'd been protected from his need.

*Where's Jude?*

*In my room,* he growled. *They're trying to torture information about E.V.I.E. out of him while making me watch. So far, he's refused to speak, which is only making Bortex's man get more creative. He started with fists. Now he's crushing fingers.*

*Wolf, hybrid, or vampire?* I asked, trying to focus on information and not the image of what was happening to Jude.

*Vamp in a suit.*

*Cuntcake,* I guessed. *Goes by Todd.*

*Yeah,* he agreed.

*Then Bendy and HJ must be in my cell.* Or at least nearby. Because I could smell them. *We need a distraction so I can free myself from these cuffs.* I couldn't exactly break my thumbs and wiggle myself free while they watched. It'd give away my conscious state.

*Not sure I can do that,* he admitted, his tone holding a note of lethargy. *Bortex is too close.*

*Have you notified the pack to send reinforcements?* I asked.

*Yeah... but I have my strongest men here. I told Rick to reach out to E.V.I.E. for backup.*

*And?* I prompted.

*And they're on their way, but it's a four-hour drive. It only took Bortex thirty minutes to knock out my wolves on-site. I can feel them falling back at main camp now, Mak. I... I can't keep... pulling their energy.*

His hesitation pierced my heart.

Because I understood.

It was him… or them. And an alpha would always choose his pack's safety over his own.

*Shit,* I thought, my mind whirring as I fought for an escape route. We definitely needed a distraction, but how could we create one if we were both strapped to chairs? *Bortex is waiting to see how long it takes for you to start siphoning energy from me, isn't he?*

*Yes, I think so.*

*Then maybe we need to give him what he wants?* I suggested. *It'll distract him from torturing Jude and maybe prolong our stay long enough for reinforcements to arrive?*

*I'm not fucking taking energy from you after I just brought you back,* he snapped.

If I hadn't been trying to remain utterly still, I would have rolled my eyes. *I didn't mean for you to actually do it. I know how to play the part of a damsel, Alaric. I can put on one hell of a show and really draw it out.*

*That might encourage him to torture me more, just to test the impact on you,* he replied.

*True. But I can take…* I trailed off as a tapping sound started, the echo one that seemed to make everyone still in the room.

Even Alaric fell silent, his mind assessing.

The rhythmic tick continued in the same pattern.

I focused on it, repeating it in my mind.

*Single tap. Single tap. Single tap. Single tap. Single tap. Pause.*

*Long tap. Long tap. Pause. Single tap. Single tap. Pause. Long tap. Single tap.*

*Long tap. Long tap. Pause.*

*Long tap. Single tap. Single tap. Single tap.*

*Single. Single. Single. Single. Single.*

*Long. Long.*

*Single. Single.*

*Long. Single.*

*Long. Long.*

*Long. Single. Single. Single.*

*Five minutes,* I translated, recognizing the Morse code on its third round. *Nathan's here.*

*What?* Alaric had recognized the Morse code as well, translating it in time with me. *I don't get the last set. MB?*

*Madam Bishop. My old code name from my KBO days. Nathan is obsessed with chess. He gives all his agents code names based on pieces and locations of those pieces. I'm Madam Bishop because I have a tendency to shift diagonally in a case.* It was his way of calling me unpredictable and also lent to a joke about distance when I'd told him I wanted to go freelance and cross realms. *He's here, Alaric.* I had no idea how, but I felt it within my bones that my alpha had come to help me.

*Bortex hears it,* Alaric said. *He just asked Todd to go check it out.*

*Distraction it is,* I decided, releasing a scream as I pretended to wake up. *Gotta give them five minutes.*

*I sure as fuck hope you're right,* Alaric replied as he released a bellow of his own.

*Me, too,* I thought. *Me, too.*

# CHAPTER 34

## ALARIC

"ALREADY?" Bortex mused. "That's a shame. I really thought it would take hours for your entire pack to fall, but maybe they need to be closer." He walked forward to play with the machine pulling blood from both of my arms and considered it for a long moment.

The vamp stood just behind him, forgetting all about having to go check on the tapping as Makayla released another bloodcurdling scream—a sound I never wanted to hear from her ever again.

Bortex nodded in approval at whatever he saw on the monitors, or maybe at her agonized yell—I wasn't sure.

Regardless, we had them thoroughly distracted now.

No, not just distracted... *amused*.

"I'm going to fucking kill you," I seethed, not needing to try at all to feign my pain. My veins were on fucking fire from his messed-up contraption. And Jude didn't look much better. The vamp had been torturing him with some sort of bone crusher, taking out each digit one at a time. He only had his pinky left intact.

But Jude proved to be a badass to his core, the male not once screaming. He just stared ahead, his expression mostly resolved despite the bruises blemishing his jaw.

However, now, he glanced at me, his eyes conveying some sort of unspoken message.

*I think Jude knows Nathan is here, too*, I told Makayla.

His dark eyes flicked to Bortex. "You owe me a suit," he said, then spat some blood out of his mouth. The vamp had hit him a few times to warm him up.

The hybrid blinked at him. "Excuse me?"

"When this is done, I want a new suit," Jude informed him.

Bortex huffed a laugh. "When this is done?"

"Yeah," Jude replied, rolling his head around and cracking his neck. "This suit isn't cheap. And your idiot torturer ruined it." He looked down at his sleeves. "Unacceptable."

Leave it to Jude to care more about his suit than his bodily harm. The man's pain tolerance was admirable. It made me wonder what supernatural substances he took to bolster his reserves, because he certainly wasn't reacting like a human. Bortex wanted details on E.V.I.E.'s technology and access to the company's servers. Jude hadn't so much as flinched in response. He hadn't spoken until now either.

And yet that shock wave hadn't taken him out earlier.

Interesting.

*Ow, son of a bitch!* Makayla shouted in my mind.

*What? What happened?* I demanded, my pulse skipping several beats faster.

*Breaking thumbs*, she gritted out. *Fuck a duck.*

*Breaking... thumbs?*

*Cuffs*, she reminded me. *Figure I have them distracted... ow... with my screaming fit...* She paused, her hiss of pain another sound I never wanted to hear from her again. *Which consequently also allows me to mask... the agony... of... this.*

Another curse followed as she broke her other thumb.

I started to ask if she was all right when Todd clocked Jude across the face. The E.V.I.E. director tongued his teeth, then spat another mouthful of blood at the vamp. "Have at it, leech."

*Yeah, Jude definitely knows Nathan's here.* I had no idea how, but it was clear in the way he challenged the vampire now with his gaze.

"I'm never giving you anything useful." He sounded so nonchalant and carefree. "Might as well make a snack of me."

A commotion sounded up above, causing both Bortex and the vamp to spin toward the door. "What the fuck was that?" the vamp demanded.

Jude looked at him. "Backup."

Bortex growled, his nostrils flaring as the scent of shifters followed.

"How the hell did they get past the alarms?" the vamp asked, his haughty tone filled with disbelief.

I suspected Nathan had something to do with that. Or maybe Jude. There were things he'd clearly not told me about tonight—including whatever backup plan had been engaged. Because none of the wolves upstairs were mine.

Jude never played a game without being ten steps ahead, and he proved that now with a mere glance. He wasn't smiling so much as waiting. Expectantly.

A disturbance sounded from the other room, followed by Makayla's snarl in my mind.

She cursed in my mind, her pain spiking along our bond. Then she naturally pulled strength from me, leaving me wilted on the table, the pumping of my veins too much coupled with her need for energy.

My pack pushed more to me, but I closed them off, not wanting to incapacitate anyone else.

And then a series of explosions came from down the hall.

*I'm almost free*, Makayla panted into my head. *But they know. And fuck, HJ has one hell of a punch.* She sounded dizzy yet focused. *I'm going to stab him. Just as soon as I can feel my damn thum—*

*Makayla!* I shouted as something loud rattled the table beneath me.

*Are you fucking kidding me?!* Makayla snapped.

And then her mental voice shut off.

I shouted her name, my vision coming and going as the stench of sulfur and flames grew beside me. *Bortex. Shifting. Hybrid.* I tried to tell her, my reserves depleting as my wolf withered inside me. I needed more energy. More life. But my pack... I couldn't... I couldn't take any more from...

*Alaric!* Makayla's voice flourished through my mind, slapping across my consciousness and yanking me back into the present.

Bortex had gone all beastly hybrid beside me, his head ducked at the ceiling above. I glanced at him. "Seriously. One ugly... fuck..." I thought out loud, swallowing.

He turned his beady eyes on me, flames billowing from his mouth before he charged through the door to deal with the chaos in the hallway.

Makayla blasted me with energy, her anger a snarl in my mind. *Don't be a stubborn asshole!*

*What?*

She didn't explain, just shoved more power into me from her own connection to the pack.

Ah, hell, I hadn't thought of that. *Makayla...*

*Don't you dare*, she snapped.

Smoke and fire arced down the corridor.

Chaos broke out.

Men in black armor poured through with high-tech

military-grade rifles and a whole slew of toys that I would have drooled over in another reality. But right now, I could barely keep my eyes open.

My wrists were suddenly free.

The machine stopped.

And Makayla slammed me with another pulse of pack life, drawing my focus to her. Standing over me. Her blue eyes wild with fury. Then her mouth came down over mine, her lips hard and urgent, her tongue mastering mine.

My world spun, part of me wondering if I'd somehow gone to heaven. Then she bit down hard enough to draw me into the present.

Ash littered the air.

Gun powder residue, too.

I just blinked, dumbfounded and confused.

Then a roar came from the hallway. *Bortex.* Followed by a shock wave that had Makayla—who had seemingly appeared out of nowhere—falling onto me, incapacitated by the weapon.

Jude cursed.

But a round of bullets graced the air, followed by ferocious growls.

The momentary paralysis lifted.

I blinked at Makayla.

She slowly rolled off me, her movements pained from the residual shock of whatever the fuck that weapon was. I followed her just as slowly, as a wave of fire billowed down the corridor outside the door.

Jude snorted, a stake in his hand as he watched the inferno blaze from the doorway.

The ground shook a second later, the flames dying.

Then he whistled low and said, "Here." He tossed the stake to someone in the hall. "Drive that through the fucker's heart."

Makayla and I ambled forward just in time to see a male dressed in all black shove the stake into Bortex's chest. "That's two kills you've taken from me tonight, Marc," Makayla said, sounding supremely pissed off.

The guy on the floor glanced over his shoulder. "Try moving faster next time, then, rookie."

She growled. "Not a rookie."

"Totally a rookie," another voice said, causing her head to whip down the hall.

"Asher?" she asked, her tone riddled with shock.

The man in question pulled a helmet off his head, his thick brown hair a static mess of strands as his piercing blue eyes landed on Makayla. "You didn't think I'd let Nathan have all the fun, did you?"

Another male grunted in response as he removed his head armor. His aura and tall, muscular stature boasted power.

*Alpha*, my wolf immediately recognized, a low growl forming in my chest. I didn't release it, aware that he wasn't here to challenge me, but that didn't stop my inner animal from pacing in annoyance at having another dominant male so close to my mate.

"You must be Nathan," I guessed.

His silver eyes met mine, his wolf staring right at me. "And you must be Alaric." He shook out his mane of long, blond-brown hair before shifting his focus to Jude. "I gave you that amulet for Makayla. Not for your own personal use."

"Yeah." Jude ran his fingers through his dark strands, then palmed the back of his neck. "I didn't get a chance to hand it over before she was taken. Figured I'd test out the beacon—you know, make sure it worked and all that."

"Right," Nathan replied, the single word radiating alpha energy and aggression.

Several other men in black entered the hallway, all of them in helmets—which I guessed were what had blocked the men from succumbing to the shock wave. Although, these newcomers smelled like humans, not wolves. When they all focused on Jude, I realized they were his personnel. But not... slayers. It had me arching a brow at him.

"There are a lot of layers to E.V.I.E., Alaric. Pity you won't be hanging around to learn about them all." He focused on his men. "Report."

They provided a summary of the events on the grounds, the dismantling of mines and alarms outside, and the casualty number.

Twelve dead.

All of them Bortex's men.

That brought the total up to twenty with the eight from earlier, twenty-one if I included Paul.

Plus Bortex, the vamp, and the two who were in the cell with Makayla.

"Did any get away?" I asked, considering the facility and the need for multiple personnel to run it.

"No," one of the men replied. "All men accounted for."

"There'll be more," Makayla inserted. "This is only a branch of the operation."

"But a main one," Jude said, eyeing her. "Similar to the cell you took down for Sapphire."

"Yeah, but apparently all the leadership wasn't wiped out appropriately," she returned, glancing pointedly at Bortex.

"Won't happen again," Jude assured her. "Because I'll be handling it instead of the packs." He gave me a look that dared me to argue.

I considered it for all of a second, then nodded. "Have

at it, boss." If I was going to trust anyone to dismantle this mess, it was Jude Reyes.

His lips parted to say something as a shimmer in the corner had us all turning toward a portal forming at the end of the wall.

Nathan, Asher, and Marc all aimed their rifles at the swirling magic.

Then Marc cursed as a blue-haired pixie of a female skipped out into the hallway. "Ah, fuck. What the hell do you want, Sapphire?" the man demanded, his tone holding a touch of exasperation.

The female blinked at him, her gaze narrowing slightly. "Hmm, I didn't time that quite right. Your helmet should be off, not on." She glanced at her wrist as though checking for a watch. "Well. I'm here anyway. Now, where's the ring?"

# CHAPTER 35

## MAKAYLA

"You totally set me up," I accused, folding my arms.

Sapphire blinked her bright blue eyes at me. "Hmm?"

"You heard me."

"Did I?" She returned her focus to the ring in her hand —one Marc had found on Bortex's corpse moments after her arrival. He'd removed his helmet, mostly because Sapphire had told him to twice, then he'd checked the hybrid's pockets and all but threw the ruby-stoned ring at her.

She'd caught it and blown a kiss at him in response.

He'd rolled his eyes and muttered something about her sanity before stalking off toward Savannah's cell. My brother had gone with him, as had Alaric.

Nathan and Jude had secured the other rooms, including helping Hawk, Hardt, and the two remaining enforcers wake up. And now they were all focused on the human cages in the other hallway, leaving me alone with a distracted blue-haired witch.

She held the ring up to the light, examining every crevice, then hummed happily. "Thanks for keeping this safe, Mak."

"Keeping it safe?" I repeated.

She slipped a chain from her neck and threaded an end

through the ring before reattaching the necklace at her nape. Then she thumbed the bright blue sapphire amulet situated at her breastbone. The ruby ring glistened beside it, the magic seeming to spark to life.

I half expected her to create a portal and jump through it, but instead her dazzling gaze lifted to mine, the blue irises displaying a clarity I rarely saw on her.

"Your new portal stone has some…" Her head bobbed back and forth as she considered how to continue. "Unique qualities," she finally finished. "It still allows you to move between realms. But it also does some other things."

"My new portal stone?" I asked, looking at her amulet.

Her fingers brushed the precious sapphire and smiled. "Oh, yes. It's a ruby, too. Just like the ring. I thought it would be quite pleasant for you to match the family jewels."

I stared at her. "You're not making any sense." Which was pretty par for the course with Sapphire.

"Earrings," she murmured, her expression brightening. "Protection and all. But the earrings don't portal. They just glimmer with love. So much love, Makayla." She grabbed my hand. "Oh, I'm so pleased for you!"

"I have no idea what you're talking about," I admitted.

She sighed in response, low and dramatic. "Always have to spell it out." Then her eyes widened, her lips curling into an excited grin. "Oh! Spell it out. Get it?"

I just continued to stare at her, aware that she would find her point eventually if I didn't give in to her insanity antics.

She giggled.

Then sighed again before saying, "Fine, fine. The amulet is my real gift to you for saving me all those years ago. The ring was just temporary, and I need it back now. It's a Romanov heirloom and the key to finding the famous

Queen of Slayers." She brushed her finger over her lips. "But, shh, that's a secret for now. Maybe we'll invite you out to play. Maybe we won't."

Her eyes took on her usual faraway gleam.

"The future is murky," she whispered. "Depends on choices. So many choices."

She shook her head as though to clear it, the witch rarely remaining in the present for long.

"Anyway, the new amulet—which I believe Nathan has just retrieved from Jude in the other room—is the one you seek." She glanced down the hallway toward the main room. "It has all the same properties, and new ones. Did I mention the new ones?" Her blue eyes danced over me. "When did you find clothes?"

I huffed a laugh at her abrupt subject change. "Marc brought them for me." A pair of jeans and a tank top, plus a pair of socks and sneakers.

"Jean-Marc," Sapphire mused, her expression twisting into one of pure amusement. "Sexy man, that Jean-Marc. Bit of a dick, though."

"You're just as fucking charming as ever," Marc returned as he stepped into the hallway. As a vampire— and a French royal one at that—he had excellent hearing. Something Sapphire obviously knew.

Their "relationship" seemed to span multiple decades, or maybe even centuries, something Marc had failed to mention when he'd recruited me to help retrieve her from this realm all those years ago. He'd just called her a nuisance of a witch with a penchant for fortune-telling. I'd later realized that she'd reached out to him for a reason— she trusted him. To an extent, anyway.

They weren't dating.

Actually, it was rather clear that they didn't even like each other at all.

But she helped him with cases, and he returned the favor by occasionally saving her ass when needed.

I didn't know all the particulars because I didn't ask.

"It looks like Savannah's going to be okay," Marc told me, ignoring Sapphire.

"Very okay," the witch chirped. "So very, very okay. More than okay. Purrfect really." She gave him a bedazzling smile as he turned to glare at her. "Wolves should learn to purr, don't you think?" she asked him.

"Why are you even here?" he demanded.

"For this," she said, gesturing to the ring at her chest. "Obviously." She gave me a look like I should agree with her, then she shrugged. "I also wanted closure. This whole mess is finally coming to an end. Assuming you check the hard drive over…" She trailed off, considering the rooms. "Well, it's around here somewhere. All the other locations. Research files. Everything to content your pretty little head." She reached out to pat him on said head, and he growled at her.

"Fuck off, Saph."

Her lips twitched in response. "You love me."

"I absolutely don't."

I left them to their bickering while I focused on Savannah. She was awake now, but her mental presence felt a bit murky. Probably because I hadn't fully explored this new hive mind yet. I used to only be able to connect to Nathan as the alpha, and now I *was* the alpha as Alaric's bonded mate. It was still rather alarming to even experience and feel, but the rightness of it made it easier for me to accept.

*Alaric is mine. My true mate. My alpha.*

*Damn straight I am*, he replied without missing a beat.

*Is this how it's going to go? With you always lurking in my head?* I wondered, heading toward him.

*Not my fault you're practically shouting your possession, sweetheart,* he returned as I entered the room. His blue eyes glittered with promise, but his expression held a somber note to it.

Savannah was still on the table, her cuffs unfastened and the machine pulled free, but she didn't appear fully lucid yet. She kept muttering something about a mate and flinching every time she sniffed.

"Do we know what they were pumping her full of?" I asked softly, grimacing as Savannah curled into a ball on the metal bed.

"Some sort of cocktail of various shifter blood laced with silver," my brother said, his focus on a computer screen near the pumping machine. "It seems like they've been testing different toxins on a variety of shifters. Savannah was tolerating it better than the last female subject."

"Valaria," Alaric clarified. "Her record is among the electronic files. There was one on Kristen, too. But Kristen's was much shorter."

"They declared her demeanor inappropriate for testing," my brother added in a low growl. "But Valaria withstood a few hours of treatment before they deemed her unviable." His jaw clenched as his blue eyes met mine. "These are some sick motherfuckers. And you let yourself be captured by them?"

"Well, only initially," I said. "When I had my ring. Then they…" I trailed off, my brother's thunderous expression telling me not to continue that statement.

"Then they kidnapped you from Alaric's lands," Nathan finished for me. "Yeah, we're aware." His presence was hot at my back as he met and held my mate's gaze, their animal pheromones mounting in the small space.

"We had a traitor in the pack," Alaric replied evenly. "A traitor that has been sufficiently dealt with."

Nathan said nothing.

I reached out to open my connection to him, to tell him to cut it out. Then I remembered my link to him no longer existed. Because of my ties to Alaric. "Shit." I whirled around to face him. "I can't feel you anymore. Like at all."

His focus remained on Alaric for another beat, his expression unmoving. Then he slowly looked down at me. "Because you're no longer one of my wolves."

I winced. "Nathan——"

"You found your true-mate match," he continued, cutting me off. "To the new alpha of Silver Lake, in this realm. And it seems your mating has provided him with some unique abilities." He shifted his attention to Alaric again. "Right?"

"Telepathic links underlined in energy," my mate replied.

"Not just energy." Nathan studied him. "Immortality. Your entire pack is linked to it now." He folded his arms, his expression pensive. "I'm betting your children will be naturally born shifter wolves, too. No more need for biting."

"You're saying Alaric is immortal? Like me?" I asked, hope sparking inside me. That'd been an outstanding issue... one I wasn't sure how to address.

"Not just Alaric. The entire pack." His silver irises flicked to me. "Can't you feel it, Makayla? As mate to the alpha, you're just as connected to them as he is. The life source is infinite, isn't it?"

I wasn't sure I'd describe it as *infinite*, but I definitely felt it pulsing through me. "It's... deep?"

"With no end in sight." He gave me a small grin.

"That's the immortal pull of energy. It can end, but it takes a lot. As I believe you've both found to be true through this experience, yes?" Darkness kissed his features, his eyes narrowing. "Don't ever put yourself in a situation like this again, or I'll kill you myself."

Alaric growled.

Nathan growled back.

I rolled my eyes. "It's not like I did this for fun," I muttered.

The two alphas squared off, eliciting a small whimper from Savannah that immediately had the males toning it down several notches. She released another soft sound as my brother laid a palm on her shoulder. Alaric moved forward, his mental vibes telling me he was going into protective mode, only he paused midstep, his eyes widening.

Savannah's connection to our pack flickered again, her mental state seeming to blink in and out of focus. Alaric's gaze lifted to me, a question in his eyes.

But Nathan responded before I could say anything. "Well, that's interesting." He took a step forward to stand by my brother, their gazes on the girl. "I can sense her in my web." His silver eyes lifted to Alaric. "Do you feel her trying to leave?"

"I don't know enough about the hive mind to explain it, but she's…"

"Blinking in and out," I finished for him. "Fading and reappearing."

Nathan nodded slowly. "Like she's shifting packs."

"Why?" Alaric asked. "Because of the toxin?"

"Maybe," Nathan said, his attention back on the girl. "Or maybe it's something else entirely."

*A mating bond,* I thought, glancing between him and my brother. *Maybe?*

Alaric ran a hand over his face, his thoughts confirming he'd heard me but didn't know what to say.

"How about you let us clean up here," Nathan offered, his demeanor a little less aggressive now. "We can work with Jude to take down the other cells, give you and your pack a bit of a recovery break. And we'll... touch base on Savannah's state."

I felt Alaric's wolf bristle in agitation, not wanting to bend to the other alpha.

*He has the resources to take care of her and mend her back to health,* I quickly pointed out. *And he's not going to hurt her.*

I could also sense her agreeing to this path in the web, her psyche searching for a new beginning, a way to start over. And something about my brother and Nathan had her gravitating toward them.

Maybe it was all in my head.

Maybe I read the strands wrong.

But I felt the rightness of the decision in my gut.

Jude entered before Alaric could reply, his features carved into lines of annoyance. "I can't figure out how that shock wave gadget worked."

Nathan snorted. "Toy too big for you to handle?"

Jude just looked at him. "Play any chess lately?"

My former alpha's amusement died. "I seem to be missing an entire set. With the exception of a single piece."

"Oh?" Jude arched a brow. "Shame, that." He glanced at me, then held out an amulet. "This is from your brother, by the way. I had intended to give it to you after the meeting, but you were out on patrol. Which was why I'd stayed. And then shit hit the fan." He shrugged. "Anyway." He dangled the necklace for me to take, the ruby on it matching my ring.

I took it from him and studied the amulet. "This is what Sapphire was talking about."

"Yeah, she made it with a few tweaks," Nathan said. "One of them is an activation key that'll tell us if you're in trouble, which is what Jude decided to test."

"Technically, Makayla was in trouble," Jude pointed out.

"I totally had it handled," I lied, earning me a snort from someone behind me.

*Marc.*

He stepped into the shrinking space and eyed the others. "The crazy witch just disappeared. Something about Dimitri's waning patience."

That earned a real grin from Nathan. "He finally going to take back his kingdom?"

"Fuck if I know," Marc muttered. As a *Monarchie du Sang*, a fancy term for the French royal vampires of my realm, he tended to stay out of the Russian Vampire Dynasty drama. He rolled his neck. "All right, we have a lot of cleanup to do. Jude's men have already moved the other humans out and handed them over to mortal law enforcement. Hardt and Hawk are with the other wolf down the hall, and—"

"Gloria?" I asked, hopeful.

He nodded. "Yeah. They've already notified her pack, and her wolves are on the way. She was just unconscious, not yet experimented on. Her file said they were waiting on her mate's capture. The sick fucks intended to test their mating bonds."

My stomach soured at the thought, aware of what that implied. It made me want to kill them all over again. But Marc had taken care of HJ and Bortex, and my brother had taken out Bendy. I guessed that Jude had handled Cuntcake, which I allowed since he'd been tortured by him. Which reminded me... "You healed very fast," I told the E.V.I.E. director, glancing at his hands.

He took in my working thumbs and smiled. "As did you."

"Yeah, but I'm a wolf. I should heal fast." And having the pack tied to my psyche certainly helped with that, too.

"Hmm" was all he said before sharing a long, knowing look with Nathan. "Well, I think we can start wrapping up here. We have several other sites to hit, according to the drives my men are going through."

"Do those drives confirm his goals?" I wondered out loud.

Jude studied me for a minute, his arms folding in a similar manner to Nathan's. "The auctions were a smoke screen for the experimentation. They took girls, tested their blood for viability, then sold the ones they couldn't use. It helped give them a profit to continue their science projects, which involved super-soldier technology that E.V.I.E. is confiscating."

"Confiscating," Nathan repeated. "How fortuitous for you."

"Nothing about this situation is fortuitous," Jude shot back. "But I will be figuring out that shock wave tech, just like I'll be taking one of your helmets that miraculously protected you from it." The statement was pointed and resulted in a smirk from Nathan.

"I make it a habit to prepare appropriately for my opponents," he drawled in response.

"I know," Jude replied, a measure of respect in his tone. "Which is why I'm borrowing your helmet."

Nathan didn't argue, but he did appear amused.

"Super soldiers," Alaric repeated, bringing the conversation back to Bortex's apparent goals. "Was that what he considered those humans to be out in the woods?"

Jude unfolded his arms and slipped his hands into the

pockets of his dress pants. "It appears so, yes. They were under orders not to kill."

"Yes, I know. They wanted to take you alive for questioning." A note of suspicion underlined my mate's tone.

"Fascinating how it all worked out, isn't it?" Jude asked, a dare lurking in his question. "They try to kidnap me for questioning, yet I end up with all their tech. Almost like fate put me in the right place at the right time. Similar to you and Makayla ending up in the city together. Just imagine what life would have been like had you chosen to follow your alpha path a decade ago? You might not have ever met. And your pack would still be plain old Bitten wolves, too."

His statement reminded me a bit of Sapphire and her proclivity for altering destinies.

She'd deliberately set me on Alaric's path.

But it was our decisions in life that had truly crossed our fates, placing me in the right place... at the right time... just like Jude had said.

And because of my ties to Alaric, his pack was stronger, *immortal*, and forever enhanced. I'd finally accomplished what I'd originally intended to do—I'd helped those who were weaker than me, by literally giving them my strength and improving their chances for survival.

I almost smiled.

Fate could be twisted and fucked up.

But in the end, it always served a purpose.

And I'd finally served mine.

# CHAPTER 36

## ALARIC

AN ONSLAUGHT of voices prickled my mind, growing louder as we entered Silver Lake Pack boundaries.

Those voices reached a crescendo when we pulled into the narrow driveway in front of my cabin.

I took in the crowd, my heart in my throat. "How do I…?" I trailed off, uncertain of how to phrase my question. I should have spent more time with Nathan this morning. He could have told me how to handle the hive mind.

Or he would have told me to buck up and figure it out on my own.

Our wolves hadn't exactly liked each other. He'd radiated alpha energy, something my inner beast had read as a direct challenge.

Maybe it had been.

Maybe it hadn't been.

I hadn't stuck around long enough to find out, choosing instead to respect the male who had protected and mentored my mate for most of her life. We'd ended on a cordial shaking of hands, a threat lingering in the air.

If I hurt Makayla, he'd hurt me.

That was fine because I had no intention of ever harming my mate. Besides, she'd have my balls in a vise long before he could arrive to help.

She snorted beside me, clearly having read my mind.

"Stop peeking in my thoughts," I admonished playfully.

"Stop talking so loudly," she tossed back, using a variant of my words from earlier.

"You two are going to make things interesting around here," my father said from the back seat. This was his truck, but he'd let me drive. "As to how to handle your pack, let your wolf guide you."

"I was talking about the thought situation," I informed him. Even though, yeah, there was that bit to consider, too. With a sigh, I closed my eyes and tried to find an off switch somewhere inside the hive mind. I'd been able to quiet them all earlier with a command, but that seemed cruel to do now. They were all just curious to understand the changes, their admiration and awe shining brightly through each of their invisible cords.

Makayla reached over to rest her hand on mine. "Nathan once said it took him a while to master the privacy screens, but there are ways to manage it all down to a low hum." She grimaced as she said it, her own mind trying to process it all with mine. "But yeah, this is going to take some work."

I nodded in agreement. "Well, time to face the masses."

Only a coward would stay in the car and hide.

And I wasn't a coward.

I opened the door and stepped out of the truck. Everyone seemed to quiet around me, their gazes all on the one they considered their alpha. *Me.* There wasn't even a hint of distrust or question regarding my ability to lead, their minds all open and eager and *thankful.*

It was a heady mix that left me a bit dizzy, but my wolf took it in stride. He'd accepted the role of alpha long before I had. And some of that arrogance helped me stand tall now.

Because I was an alpha.

*Their* alpha.

I might not have been able to accept that a decade ago, but I couldn't bring myself to regret that decision. Had I not chosen to work for E.V.I.E., I might have missed my chance to meet Makayla.

Together, we made the pack stronger. Fiercer. *Immortal.* What a total mindfuck that was to accept, but I couldn't complain. It strengthened my wolves. Strengthened our bonds. Made us a tighter unit.

I embraced that knowledge, pleased with the outcome.

The road was bumpy with a lot of hurdles I would have preferred to avoid, but here I stood… exactly where I was meant to stand.

"Thank you for keeping me and Makayla alive last night," I said to them all, aware that they would have felt my absorption of their energy through the freshly established pack link. "There's a lot to explain about what's happening to Silver Lake. I don't understand it all. But we'll learn together."

"And I'll help explain as well. You know, since these changes are coming from me." Makayla's palm met my lower back as she moved to my side, her show of solidarity bringing smiles to my pack members. It was an action that meant more than words. She intended to stand by me. Forever.

I felt her resolve radiating through our bond, her decision made hours ago after realizing our fates were always meant to intertwine.

This was her pack now, too.

Several pack members hummed their agreements.

Then my mother stepped forward, her pride a palpable

energy that wrapped me in a hug long before her arms encircled my neck. I returned her embrace, her happy thoughts bringing tears to my eyes.

*I really need to figure out how to turn this off,* I said to Makayla, my tone gruff. Because, hell, that was an emotional punch I did not need.

*We'll figure it out,* she whispered back to me. *Together.*

*Together,* I agreed. We hadn't spoken about the future yet. We just sort of knew where we were headed without the conversation. However, I suspected we'd still engage in it, as there were a few unresolved items between us on that front.

Particularly the one surrounding her job, which I would not be taking from her.

"Welcome home, Alpha," my mother whispered into my ear before kissing my cheek. My father placed his hand on my shoulder, giving it a squeeze, then pulled my mother into his arms to guide her back into the crowd.

Everyone around us rumbled a similar sentiment, all welcoming me home... as *alpha.*

The word reverberated through their minds and out their mouths, the revered hum singing to my soul.

It wasn't the first time I'd been called by the title, but it meant so much more coming from my mother and my pack as a unit. "Thank you," I responded quietly.

"And welcome home, Alpha Makayla," my mother added softly, her lips curling.

Several members of the crowd echoed the comment, causing Makayla to melt a little into my side. Her resulting smile lit up her entire face, her acceptance a radiant light inside her that basked all of us in a warm glow of approval.

"Thank you," she said, repeating my sentiment, but in her own way. Then she stepped forward to embrace my mother, the two alpha females hugging and setting the pack even more at ease just as the other two trucks pulled up in front of my house.

Everyone turned to face the newcomers, a hint of unease lining some of their shoulders as Hardt jumped out of the driver's seat.

Timothy and Gregory hopped out of the other truck, flanking him as he approached me.

Makayla took a step away from my mother, her stance protective.

*It's okay,* I told her, already reading Hardt's intentions. It wasn't done on purpose. I just… had no idea how to block him out yet. A quirk that had worked in the man's favor earlier because I'd felt his shock over Paul's betrayal, and his subsequent anger at himself as a result.

Hardt had known Robert and Paul were friends after training to become enforcers together, so he should have pieced together that there might have been a link between them in regard to the Bortex case. Of course, he hadn't realized Robert had been there with a special "package" for my father—a package that the computer records on-site had indicated contained silver.

Another fact that made me wish Bortex had suffered more.

But I didn't hold the incident against Hardt.

While I agreed that he should have caught on to the link between Robert and Paul, I didn't blame him for not telling me about Robert's appearance on our lands. He'd handled it as a beta should. And it hadn't been a noticeable breach that really required alpha involvement.

However, I'd sensed his internal vow to never keep details—no matter how trivial—from me again. That was apology enough.

Hardt stepped forward, his eyes holding mine for a

beat while everyone around us held their breaths. Then he went to one knee, his head bowed as he said, "Alpha."

A collective gasp went through the crowd, followed by a round of relieved sighs as he glanced up at me from the ground with a grin on his face.

"It's about time you came home," he added.

I huffed a laugh and shook my head. "I had to find my mate."

"And we're all very glad that you did," he replied.

I held out my hand to help him up. Not that he needed it. The gesture just served as an assurance to the pack that we were comfortable working together.

More than comfortable, really.

He'd been the first to give me energy when I'd needed it, bolstering me while I'd fought Bortex's machine.

Hardt stood, his height nearly bringing his eyes to mine. But he flicked his eyes away again in a show of reverence. I pulled him in for a hug, thanking him with my actions for having my back out there.

Then I stepped back and looked at him. *Really* looked at him.

He'd demonstrated loyalty to me last night and again this morning even while he'd still questioned my ability to lead. However, I realized now *why* he'd questioned me. Why he'd pushed me. Why he'd infuriated me.

It had never been about disrespect.

It had been about protecting his wolves. The pack came first for him. Just as it should.

"I see why my brother picked you as his second," I told him softly. "You're loyal to the pack. Protective. Exactly what they need. And while we might not always see eye to eye, I don't want a second who will just roll over and take it. I want a second who will push me onto the right path, even if it means facing my wrath." I held out my hand again. "Thank you, Beta Hardt. For everything you've done for me and the pack."

Shock washed over Hardt's features, and I locked eyes with him again, giving him a glimpse of my trust in him. He straightened, his chin dipping in acknowledgment and acceptance of his role. His thoughts confirmed what his body already told me, but he gifted me another subtle display of submission by shifting his gaze downward. Then he gave Makayla a similar show of respect by bowing to her before returning to stand with our pack.

This seemed to trigger a ritual, one I'd never been around to witness but suspected had been done for my brother after I'd left all those years ago.

One by one, each of my packmates came forward to acknowledge me as their alpha. Some bowed. Some hugged me. Some kissed me on the cheek. Their gratitude and acceptance enhanced the sensation of belonging, welcoming me home and confirming there was nowhere else they would rather have me be.

My father stood last among them, his expression giving nothing away.

Silence fell over the crowd, everyone dying to know what their former alpha thought of the ascension.

He stepped forward, his stride sure, his movements powerful. He didn't pull me into a hug; he yanked me into one, his arms fierce around my back as he held me hard and long against him. "You've become the man I knew you could be. I'm proud of you, son. And I know Tyler is, too."

Such quiet words.

But passionate, nonetheless.

My heart stuttered, my breath failing me. I wasn't sure how to respond. Alphas were meant to be strong, to balance the emotions of the weak. However, the sensations brewing inside him poured through the hive mind, bathing me in every ounce of his pride and happiness at seeing me finally take the mantle he'd always considered mine.

He practically shoved his thoughts at me, wrapping me up in his feelings and squeezing the life from my lungs.

Then he pulled away with a glimmer in his eyes, and the sensation ended abruptly, my father shutting the door to his mind and feelings.

My lips parted. "How…?"

He merely smiled. "Later." He winked and moved to my mother's side, who gave him a knowing smile.

*My father's still keeping secrets from me,* I marveled, talking to Makayla. That link just automatically came to the forefront, making it easy to speak to her. The others required clear and concise thought. At least, I hoped that was the case, or the pack would be in on a lot of very personal conversations soon.

*Yeah, he is,* Makayla agreed, her own eyes narrowed because he'd shut her out, too.

"We'll let you two… catch up on your sleep," my mother said softly, her expression holding a few of her own secrets.

I almost commented on it, but the idea of being alone with Makayla strongly appealed to me. And from the chuckles in the crowd, several of my wolves knew why.

Rather than comment, I grabbed Makayla's hand to tug her forward. She hadn't anticipated my move, something I used to my advantage by lifting her by the hips and tossing her over my shoulder.

Several of my wolves howled in approval.

Makayla growled.

I slapped her ass and turned toward my cabin, not caring at all what the pack thought of my antics. With this damn link, they'd know exactly what I intended to do anyway. Or maybe they couldn't sense me. I really didn't know. And I wasn't going to stand around and find out. I wanted to play with my mate. Alone. In my bed.

My wolf enthusiastically agreed with my plan. I sensed her wolf panting in agreement as well through our link. However, Makayla wasn't quite so accepting… which only heightened my desire to dominate her.

*Alaric Calder,* she snapped through our connection. *Put me down right the hell now.*

I smacked her ass again, harder this time. "Not going to happen, baby."

The pack disappeared behind us as we entered the house.

Opening and closing the door had required me to divide my focus just for a second—one Makayla took advantage of by whacking me in the kidney with her healed hand.

The blow knocked the breath right out of me, leaving me to wonder what it said about me that I found her behavior incredibly arousing.

My breathless state gave her the opportunity to wiggle over my shoulder. I shouldn't have been shocked when she grasped the waist of my jeans and flipped her legs up and over—essentially doing a backbend and landing on her feet behind me.

I choked out a laugh—just as I finally inhaled enough oxygen—as she sauntered into the kitchen, her hips and luscious ass swaying enticingly behind her.

My body already burned to feel our naked skin pressed together, to taste her delicious pussy, to experience the bliss of sliding in and out of her tight center.

I considered making another grab for her and dragging her back to the bedroom like a caveman, but she headed straight for the coffee maker. I paused to consider her, my instinct to care for my mate overriding my lust.

My wolf pushed hard for me to give in to the animalistic urges, but something about the vibes coming off of Makayla caused him to back off. It had been a long damn day, leaving us both exhausted. I'd been privy to her every emotion during her captivity, and while she'd been her usual badass self, she'd also had moments of terror for herself and for the other girls.

Although, I knew she'd never admit it out loud, so I allowed her a moment to gain comfort from her caffeine addiction. When she finished, I'd comfort her via my preferred method.

I followed her into the kitchen and gently guided her to the table, urging her to sit. She sank heavily into the chair and sighed.

I filled the machine with enough beans to make it black and strong, the way we both liked it.

When I finished and turned around, the lines around her eyes and the pucker on her forehead set my desire to the back of my mind, replaced by worry. While I waited for the machine to brew, I took a seat across from her.

"Are you all right?" Even the toughest person would have scars from what we went through last night.

She nodded, but I wasn't satisfied. I sensed her turmoil through our bond, as well as her need to let it out in order to heal.

"Talk to me," I commanded softly. I wanted to be gentle, but I also wouldn't take no for an answer.

# CHAPTER 37

## ALARIC

MAKAYLA BLEW OUT A BREATH. "Just thinking through everything. The auctions. The girls. I should have picked up on it sooner, you know? It was all related."

"You sensed that relation."

"Yeah, but I didn't follow it all the way through. And to find out the trafficking wasn't even the main scheme?" Her lips twisted to the side, and she shook her head. "It's a bit of a blow. Because it shows there will always be layers to everything. And I've spent all this time focused on one aspect of crime, without factoring in the others. So I missed the obvious link."

"You didn't miss anything," I argued. "You found the initial links. That's what matters."

"But we lost lives in the process."

"And that will always happen," I told her. "That doesn't make it our fault, though. It makes it the faults of the monsters out there like Bortex."

Just thinking about what he did to Savannah, to me, and to Makayla had me wishing we could have prolonged his death.

Alas, he'd died with a hell of a lot of bullets inside him. And Jude would be cremating the son of a bitch to ensure he didn't return.

"Yeah, I know you're right," she said. "I'm just… I'm thinking about how my life is going to change. Not just for work stuff, and jobs, but also leaving my family. I might not have gone home often, but we were still close."

I frowned, afraid of the direction this conversation might take. "Are you considering going back to your old home?"

She'd shared a heartfelt goodbye with Nathan and Asher before we'd left, and I hadn't sensed any hesitation in her. Hell, I'd been the most hesitant of the pair because they intended to take Savannah back to their home realm. They had some advanced therapies they felt would help her. There was also her whole wavering link that I still sensed inside the hive mind, like she wasn't meant to be here.

I wondered if that was what Nathan had felt about Makayla all these years. Had she blinked in and out, too? Her life strand connecting to me and my pack rather than her own?

She fingered the amulet around her neck and moved her head from side to side without hesitation, similar to what I'd observed from her goodbyes earlier. "I have the ability to visit, but I'm still a world away from them. Literally."

*Thank fuck for that*, I thought, momentarily appeased by her acceptance to stay.

Her lips twitched, having heard my relief. But she didn't comment on it, instead inhaling deeply as she considered me.

"It's just a lot at once. The fully developed bond between true mates can be overwhelming, not that I have any regrets. I mean, it's the most real and incredible thing I've ever felt, but it will still take some getting used to. Especially this whole hive-mind thing. Not to mention figuring out how to balance it all—my duties to our pack and my need to help humans."

The coffee maker beeped, and she stood before I could. She headed over to take out a mug and fill it with steaming liquid while I silently observed her graceful movements. One of the most attractive things about my mate was her complete obliviousness to how fucking sexy she was doing even the smallest things.

She poured me a cup as well, bringing both over to the table.

"We really need to master the ability to block our thoughts," she muttered as she sat again. "Pouring coffee is not sexy."

I grinned and sat back in my chair, crossing my arms over my chest. "You're right. Unless the woman pouring said coffee is you."

She rolled her eyes, but I sensed her playful energy returning.

We sat in silence for a few minutes, enjoying our coffees and allowing our minds just to exist with the other.

I felt her acceptance of our situation, just as she sensed mine.

And after several blissful beats, I reached out to squeeze her hand, saying, "Anything you need, Makayla, I will support you. That includes you taking on freelance jobs and venturing to your home realm. Whatever you want, I'll do my best to give it to you."

Her lips curled. "I know. I hear all that in your head."

"Just as I hear similar thoughts in yours." She wanted to support me. To be there for the pack. To be a good alpha, even if her wolf tended to prefer freedom and alone time. "You're not the only one with a lone wolf inside, baby," I reminded her softly.

She studied me as she drank her coffee, her mind running over my words and so much more.

I chuckled when her thoughts slipped south, her body lining with tension for an entirely different reason than before. My wolf perked up at the scent of her growing arousal, his interest a deep-seated need inside me that only Makayla could satisfy.

Yet she seemed rather content with her coffee.

Maybe even a little *too* content.

"If I didn't know better, I'd worry that you loved coffee more than my mouth on you," I teased.

Makayla's blue orbs lit with desire, and the corners of her mouth lifted. "See? Annoying."

I laughed, feeling the rest of my stress melt away, giving the hunger for my mate room to surge to the surface once more.

She drained the last of her drink and stood to make herself another cup of coffee. At the machine, she hesitated. "Maybe I shouldn't have more coffee," she muttered suddenly, her expression torn between longing and resignation. "I just want to collapse in bed."

I stood and walked right up to her, crowding her against the counter, caging her in with my arms on either side of her hips.

"Oh, you're going to bed, Makayla," I whispered in her ear.

She turned around and gave me a dirty look, causing my mouth to widen into a grin.

"Have as much coffee as you want, sweetheart. You're going to need the energy."

Her brow knitted, but she rotated to pour herself another cup, then nonchalantly faced me again. She leaned back against the counter and peered at me over the rim of her mug as she took a drink. "Aren't you exhausted?" she asked.

I pushed my pelvis into her and smirked. "I'm tired, but I'm not *that* tired, baby."

Makayla raised a single eyebrow while the rest of her face remained neutral. Although, I didn't need our link to know she was full of shit. The heat simmering in her eyes gave her away.

"And what if I'd rather get some sleep, Alpha?" A sly smile gradually curled her lips, as if she just couldn't keep it in any longer.

All the blood in my body drained to my cock, and I swelled to painful proportions, while my wolf tried to barge to the surface. When she called me alpha in that tone, it was hot as fuck.

"Guess I'll just have to change your mind." I didn't bother to hide the eagerness in my voice.

"Cocky," she uttered in a low, raspy tone, the simmer having grown into flames.

"You bet your sexy little ass." I took the mug from her hands and set it away from her before catching her around the waist and stepping back.

This time, when I swept her into my arms, she didn't fight me. Her breathing picked up, and I could hear her racing pulse. It turned me on even more as I stalked to the bedroom.

After kicking the door open, I tossed Makayla onto the bed and climbed over her, pinning her to the mattress, my body covering her nearly from head to toe. I stared boldly into her eyes, my gaze burning with the promise of untold pleasures. "You're mine now, Makayla."

Her lips curled. "Yeah?" She licked her lips once, then unexpectedly rose up to sink her fangs into my neck.

I arched into her and growled in satisfaction, the sound

more animal than man. My wolf fought to surface, desperate to be with our mate, but I growled at him. *Mine.* Makayla's claws scratched down my back, and I felt her need mixing with her wolf's as well.

She shredded my shirt, leaving it in tatters on the bed.

My dick pulsed as I rocked into the scorching heat at the apex of her thighs. I dropped my head to her neck and sank my teeth into my claiming mark near her throat. Electricity zipped through me, my body fevered with an intensity that made me think I might burst into flames at any second.

She pulled back and licked over the wound in my flesh, sending a shudder of pleasure through me. When I retracted my own teeth, I dropped my gaze and locked it with Makayla's again.

For a moment, we lay there in complete stillness.

We'd already slept together, but this time would be different, and we didn't need words to know that. Our bond had fully developed, and I could only imagine the rapture we would experience when we physically became one as well.

Makayla's emotions mirrored my own, and her eager response brought our wolves to the surface, nearly breaking through. We gave in to our animalistic desires and aroused bodies. Our need overpowered everything outside the bedroom.

I didn't care who heard us. I didn't care if our pack felt us. I didn't care if her old alpha sensed us.

This was about me and Makayla.

Our bond.

Our mating.

And no one—and nothing—would come between us now.

Teeth and claws made quick work of shredding the rest of our clothes until we were flesh against flesh.

"Alaric," Makayla moaned, rubbing sensuously against me.

I crushed my mouth onto hers, and there was something new in our kiss. Our tongues danced around each other, tasting and fighting for ownership, and it hit me. Makayla wasn't holding back any longer—she'd laid her mind and body bare to me. It was easy to do the same, and something between us shifted, something almost otherworldly.

Our touches became wild and abandoned. Makayla arched her back, pressing her breasts against my chest as she writhed beneath me. My mouth ravaged hers, and eventually I retreated to track shivery kisses down her jaw, neck, and the valley between her breasts.

I paused, and my hot gaze slid slowly and seductively over them. "You are so fucking sexy," I murmured.

She gasped when my tongue caressed one sensitive, swollen nipple. She cried out and growled in approval as she bucked her hips against my hardness. I switched to the other taut bud and gave it the same attention.

Makayla's hands delved into my hair, clutching at it as though it would keep her from flying away, but I felt her continue to spiral upward with every tug and nip from my mouth.

My palms skimmed either side of her body to her thighs, and I gently parted them before gliding down until I stared at her glistening mound. I licked my lips and whispered, "Still fucking sweet, baby."

I didn't tease either of us, just dove in to devour her with my hunger fueling my movements.

As my tongue hit her most sensitive areas, she moaned, soaring higher and higher until she shattered, cascading waves of ecstasy across every inch of her body. Experiencing her release... there were no words to describe it. I growled and nipped at her thigh in appreciation, causing the muscles there to tremble, then I bit her soft flesh, and she shuddered violently while calling my name. It nearly took me over the edge with her, but I wasn't ready for that yet.

"Holy fuck," she gasped when she finally caught her breath.

"I intend to," I said with a smirk.

With one last lick, I worked my way back up, my tongue leaving a shiny trail in its wake. When I reached her mouth, I captured it in a drugging kiss. Knowing she could taste herself drove me crazy, almost forcing my actions, but I was an alpha for a reason. Control lived in my blood.

My hands traveled down over her taut stomach to the swell of her hips, and I held them in place while I coated my shaft in her wetness. Then I shifted my caress to her thighs, guiding her legs up to lock around my waist.

Suddenly, I was overwhelmed with the need to possess my mate, to claim her entirely, to ensure she knew whom she belonged to. Hell, I wanted the entire world to hear her cry out *my* name.

"You're mine, Makayla." My tone left no room for argument. And yet, I needed to hear the words, so I followed them up with a demand. "Tell me that you're mine."

She hesitated, but I felt her laughter in my mind. She was fucking with me.

"Makayla," I growled, sending another shiver through her and causing her heartbeat to speed up.

"I'm yours," she whispered.

Hearing it from her lips snapped my patience, and I could no longer push back the rising tide of hunger and need to be inside her. She rose up and brushed her lips along my jaw and across my lips, to settle over my mouth. Then she nipped at my lip, encouraging me.

My hips moved back, and in the next instant, I'd filled her completely with one thrust. Makayla inhaled sharply and her back arched, rubbing the tips of her breasts against the damp skin of my chest. It added another layer to the ecstasy of feeling my mate wrapped tightly around my cock.

"You make me feel so full," Makayla moaned. I held still, letting her body stretch to accommodate me. The feeling of being whole lingered between us, then grew to cocoon us in our own little world.

Her body clenched, and I groaned as my hands anchored onto the roundness of her hips. I started with a slow, steady rhythm. Now that she'd accepted her place as my mate, I wanted one more thing.

Her submission. It was incredibly hard for a female alpha wolf to submit, and when they did, it indicated a level of trust that was absolute. I didn't question our bond, but I wanted the act anyway. I wanted her to acknowledge that I'd earned it.

Besides, I'd promised to make her crawl.

But I could be magnanimous enough to accept her begging instead.

I continued to torture her with my slow, steady rhythm.

*Yeah, that doesn't work for me,* she snapped, her growl of annoyance an aphrodisiac for my wolf.

She grasped my shoulders and tugged me down so she could bite my earlobe as she clenched her inner muscles again. A secret smile stole over her face when I lost a bit of my control and grunted, speeding up. Raking her claws down my back, she hummed in approval and nipped my throat where she'd left her own mark.

My body froze for a single heartbeat before I dropped my head into the crook of her neck and muttered, "Shit."

I gave her exactly what she wanted, my movements becoming wild. I thrust in and out with a force that had her nearly crying out for release, but at the last second, she swallowed while thinking, *I don't beg.*

*We'll see about that, won't we?*

My hands were everywhere all at once, and she touched as much of me as she could reach. Blood pounded in my ears, and I breathed in deep, soul-wrenching drafts. A buzz floated over my skin, and the world began to spin before my eyes. She was pushing me higher, closer and closer, almost there. No. Not yet.

Abruptly, I ceased all movement.

*What the fuck?* Makayla shouted.

"Beg me," I demanded quietly.

"Excuse me?"

"I didn't make you crawl like I swore I would. So you're going to beg. I want your submission, Makayla."

Hovering right on the precipice of climax, I almost gave in. My wolf snarled at me when I remained silent.

I began to move again, but I returned to the agonizing pace with which I'd begun.

"Oh G—"

"No, sweetheart," I interjected. "Beg *me.*"

My hands searched out the bundle of nerves between her folds. I teased and tantalized until she was ready to kill me. With her teeth clenched tight, she gritted out. "Alaric, if you value your life, you will stop torturing me and give me my fucking orgasm!"

I shook my head. "Beg me, sweetheart. That's all you have to do, and I'll give you everything you want."

My wolf shoved at me, growling, impatient to take our mate to completion. She continued to hesitate, but I could see her fighting for the will to do it. She wanted to; it simply wasn't in her nature.

On instinct, I suddenly said, "Outside of the bedroom, you are my partner in all things, Makayla. But when it comes to fucking…" A devilish smile curved my lips. "I'm in charge." Somehow, I knew she needed those words to submit.

And I felt her acceptance before she said it.

Sensed her capitulation in this one thing.

Here, in our bed, she would let me take complete control.

She swallowed hard, her body shuddering violently beneath mine. Then the sweetest, most beautiful word crossed her lips. "Please."

My wolf surged to the surface, and I knew she could see him in my eyes, both of us filled with satisfaction and pride. He finally retreated and I breathed, "You're mine forever, Makayla." For some reason, I loved hearing that out loud. But it set me off like a bundle of fireworks.

I wasted no time, thrusting in over and over with a fierceness worthy of the animal that shared my soul. Makayla and I both climbed higher and higher, closer to the pinnacle that I knew would change us forever.

I felt her rising passion, sweet and explosive, and it pushed me the last of the distance. I reached between us again and pressed my thumb over her sensitive bud.

I needed her to come. *Right. Now.*

With a scream, she fell over the edge.

As I followed her, I shouted and shattered into a million pieces, each fragment glowing with bliss. Then the world exploded all around me. I'd never felt pleasure so intense, so pure. That feeling of something otherworldly returned, only this time, the power of it hit me like a freight train.

Then it became clear, like a veil lifting from over my

eyes. Our gazes locked, and I knew she'd experienced the same epiphany.

We'd breached both realms. Our crossed fates had merged into one as much as our souls and bodies had. We were bonded metaphysically, shared a passion deeper than many could understand, and belonged solely to each other.

I knew in that moment that even if fate had given me a choice, I would have chosen Makayla over anyone and anything. A surge of emotion filled me as Makayla echoed my thoughts.

*Love.*

Our time together had been too short to truly develop those feelings in full, but it didn't really matter, because we had chosen each other on a soul-deep level.

Words were unnecessary, so I just dropped to the bed beside her and gathered her into my arms. Just days ago, I'd thought I knew my place, my purpose. But I'd had no damn clue, and now, I couldn't understand how I hadn't seen the emptiness inside me.

"You were pretty blind," Makayla said, breaking the silence.

I pinched her delectable ass. "We're not having this discussion, baby," I told her. "If anyone was blind, it was you."

She scoffed, and I decided to shut her up with my mouth.

*Yeah, I could do this forever.*

# CHAPTER 38

## MAKAYLA

My EYES WERE HEAVY, my body still utterly exhausted despite having spent the last day in bed.

Probably because my insatiable mate kept waking me up to "make sure we were really still alive and that all our parts still worked appropriately." I nearly grunted at the excuse.

*Are you complaining?* Alaric asked, his deep voice amused.

My lips twitched. Because of course he was awake and had heard me. *No.*

He chuckled out loud, and I used one elbow to lean up and gaze at his sleepy, satisfied face.

He ran a hand through my wild, tangled red hair, then cupped my neck and guided me up to him for a deep, thorough kiss. Things between us started to heat up again, and I pulled back before we were carried away by it. I needed some sustenance before we engaged in any more acrobatics.

Alaric growled at my retreat, but it morphed into a laugh when my stomach growled loudly back at him. "It seems I need to feed my mate."

"Mm-hmm," I agreed, my insides protesting the lack of food in my system.

Alaric chuckled again and climbed out of bed.

My breath caught in my lungs as he padded over to his dresser. His muscled rippled down his back, and his ass looked like it had been sculpted from marble. Good grief, I was going to burst into flames. Maybe I wasn't hungry after all...for food, anyway.

I shook my head and tried to recapture my rational brain. *This is ridiculous!* I'd seen him naked many times. Touched all that smooth, warm skin, had my mouth all over him. *I should not be distracted by this.*

Then he turned around and bent to pull on a pair of pajama pants, giving me an excellent view of his sculpted torso with that mouthwatering V—which I'd licked every inch of—and his impressive cock. I released an audible sigh when he covered it up, and he gave me a sexy, dimpled smile. The twinkle in his eyes confirmed that he knew exactly how he was impacting me.

*Damn link*, I thought. *Whatever.*

"Breakfast can wait," I decided out loud as I rose up onto my knees.

His blue irises became nearly eclipsed by black as they scanned my body. Good to know I affected him just as much.

Still, he shook his head and reached into another drawer before tossing a shirt at me. "Can't have my mate wasting away. I have plans for her later."

I perked up. "Plans?"

"Now who's insatiable?" he asked with a playful grin.

I returned his expression before pulling the shirt down over my head and sticking my arms through the gigantic armholes. It always amazed me that he could make a tall, strong woman like me feel small and dainty. Even Nathan, who was freaking huge, had never had that effect on me. Maybe it was a mate thing? Regardless, I loved it.

Alaric came to the side of the bed and snaked an arm

around my waist, hauling me close. It knocked me off-balance, and I went tumbling into his arms. Then he kissed me until I melted into a trembling pile of goo.

"Food," he stated against my lips before taking his mouth away, making me frown.

"But—"

Alaric shook his head and swept me up into his arms again.

"I can walk, Neanderthal."

"You could, but we both know you like it when I carry you around."

I sighed. There wasn't any use in denying it. He'd clearly been listening to my thoughts about feeling small and feminine when he manhandled me like a caveman.

He deposited me on the island counter just inside the kitchen and gave me a brief, hard kiss before beginning a search of the cupboards. He located a frying pan and started digging through the refrigerator, only to be interrupted by the doorbell.

I hopped off the marble counter, intending to answer it so he could cook, but his icy glare stopped me in my tracks. His gaze dropped pointedly to my naked legs. Sighing, I rolled my eyes and hopped back up to sit again. The jealousy radiated from him, and I couldn't help feeling sorry for whoever was at the door. They were about to receive the full force of a possessive alpha, and it was my fault, not theirs.

"What?" Alaric snarled, yanking the door so hard it slammed into the wall.

I pressed my legs together, finding his display of strength and dominance ridiculously sexy. His nose lifted just a fraction, and then his eyes darted over to me.

*Shit.*

He could smell my arousal.

His gaze slowly returned to the person at the door, and every muscle in his body tensed. The visitor must have been a shifter, or Alaric wouldn't care about the caller smelling me.

My mate snatched a package from the person and slammed the door in the poor guy's face. Then he spun around and prowled to me, throwing the box on the counter.

"I don't like other men smelling what's mine," he growled as he crowded me with his arms on both sides of me like he'd done the night before.

"Then stop being so damn sexy," I returned.

That seemed to break him out of his jealous fog, and he threw his head back and laughed. "I'll work on it," he promised with a wink.

He stepped away to pick up the rectangular box on the counter. His brow furrowed after a second, and he angled it so I could see whom it had come from.

"E.V.I.E.?" I frowned. "I guess you didn't really give your notice."

Alaric grunted. "Yeah, I don't think a formal resignation is Jude's thing." He ripped open the package and pulled out a thick padded envelope. Inside it was a tablet, a watch, and a note.

*I know how much you'll miss your toys. Consider this a farewell gift. But I expect you to wear that watch and show up when I need you.*
*—Jude.*

"What the hell?" I took the note and read it again.

"Jude collects assets like chess pieces," he muttered, eyeing the fancy watch.

*Sounds like Nathan*, I thought. "Is Jude saying that he's not allowing you to quit?" I wondered out loud.

"I think he's saying that while I'm not officially on the E.V.I.E. payroll, I'll be working as a freelancer." He grinned, his gaze lifting to mine. "Like you. So. it's possible that you won't be the only one called to help people outside the pack from time to time."

The possibility of that didn't sit well with me. I didn't fear for Alaric—he could handle himself, especially now that he was immortal and much harder to kill. But what happened if our missions overlapped and that left the pack without either of their alphas? *Maybe I shouldn't—*

Alaric grasped my hips, yanking my attention to him. "It would have to be a major emergency for me to leave my pack, Mak. But if it happens, we have my dad."

"But he won't—" Then I smacked myself on the forehead. *Duh.* The entire pack had inherited the traits of my pack when Alaric and I mated. His dad would always be there, and the man wouldn't hesitate to step in if both of us were called away. "It's refreshing to have all these similarities to my old pack. Like the immortality thing."

"It's certainly a gift we all appreciate." Alaric set the items on the island, then kissed me quickly before going back to making us some food. He pulled a carton of eggs out and set them on the counter by the stove.

"So you're really okay with me still working as a freelancer?" I asked. Other than a little worry for my safety —which was understandable, as I was his mate—I hadn't sensed any doubt from Alaric. But sometimes it felt better to hear it out loud.

"Makayla, I want to spend eternity with you. If you stop being who you are, who would I be spending my forever with?"

*Well, fuck.* That had been the most perfect answer I could have imagined.

My heart squeezed, and a thought I hadn't considered

crept into my mind. I wasn't sure what love was, beyond the love I had for my family. But romantically? It had never been something I'd experienced or even really considered. It had seemed like a complication, so I'd been glad to avoid it. But now I wondered if what Alaric and I felt for each other would grow into love one day.

Yeah, I was definitely falling head over heels for this man.

Alaric glanced at me, and something passed between us. *Someday.*

I smiled, feeling warm and happy.

"Ok, so what's next?" I asked.

Alaric was quiet for a minute, thoughts floating through his mind too fast for me to grasp them all at once.

"Well, first, I think I need to move. Not just from New York City, but… into Tyler's house. The alpha's house. It's been the alpha's home for generations, and it's where we belong."

I loved that he sounded so sure of his decision. He constantly proved why he was meant to be the alpha of this pack, and I couldn't help but be damn proud to stand beside him.

"Besides," he continued, "I think it will be a comfort to be surrounded by childhood memories of Tyler. Even if I have a feeling he's chuckling at me right now for being so stubborn all these years."

I snorted, and Alaric pinched my outer thigh as he walked by, earning a glare from me. It didn't hurt. Actually, it shot tingles directly to my core. However, apparently, *pinching* was his new thing, just like crowding me into tight places, and I didn't care for it.

*Liar. I know it turns you on,* he murmured into my mind.

Stupid connection. He was right. It did. And that irritated the shit out of me.

I let it go and went back to our conversation. "Okay, so we're moving. We take care of pack business and freelance from time to time."

He nodded.

"Then?" I prompted.

"That's for us to decide together. One day at a time. We have quite a few of them. There's no rush."

I rolled my eyes at his lame joke.

Then he was in front of me again, except this time he didn't cage me in or pinch me anywhere. His expression was thoughtful, and he cocked his head to the side as he considered me.

"Well, one of these days, we could take advantage of a full moon." The suggestion in his tone had my brow popping upward.

*Like... real advantage?* I asked him, my throat suddenly dry. Female wolves, at least those of my kind, went into heat during a full moon. Which meant I could conceive. I'd never asked if it was the same for him or not, yet he somehow knew it about me. Maybe from when I'd pushed all my pack details to him before when our mating connection had snapped fully into place.

*Yeah,* real *advantage,* he murmured.

*Um...* I'd never considered kids because I hadn't expected to ever mate.

"We can wait as long as you need, baby," he said out loud, his palm cupping my cheek. "I just want you to know... I'd be interested."

"Oh. I... I just need some time to absorb the idea," I admitted. "But I think I might like that." Actually, I was pretty sure I would. Because the idea of having little pups with him made some matronly part of me melt into a puddle of happiness.

Alaric grinned and kissed me sweetly.

"Although, there's something you should know about true mates, at least among my kind," I started slowly.

"What's that?" he asked, cocking his head to the side.

"Well, true mates in my old world tend to experience an intense attraction until they reproduce. It's a primal thing because our animals don't understand why we would choose to wait. They mate, fuck, and create pups. From what I understand, we just fuck like bunnies until it happens."

He stared at me. "Sorry, I'm not seeing the problem with this revelation."

I rolled my eyes. "Of course you wouldn't. But I'm telling you… we might end up doing it on a full moon without thinking clearly."

He shrugged. "Yep. I'm good with that." He went back to his food preparation. "Good thing we have my immortal parents to help babysit. Who knows how long the *fucking like bunnies* will happen? I mean, maybe we'll need a whole litter before we're ready for a break."

I laughed. "Yeah, no. Unless you're the one popping them out…"

"Well, you can push the pain to me, right?" He waggled his brows at me, then he turned off the oven and grabbed me by the hips, pulling me over his shoulder again.

"Hey! What about food?"

"I'm suddenly in the mood to eat something else. Something *sweet*," he replied, taking off down the hallway toward the bedroom. "Besides, the next full moon is in a week. We need to practice."

"Practice?" I repeated with a laugh as he tossed me onto the bed. "I thought we were waiting?"

"Waiting just means more practice until we reach

perfection," he murmured, crawling over me. "I mean, you need to work on your begging skills."

"Then you're going to have to up your teasing game," I teased him.

"Hmm." The shirt inched up my thighs, over my hips, and to my belly. "Well, good thing I know exactly where to start, sweetheart."

# EPILOGUE

## SAPPHIRE

DIMITRI's blue eyes glittered in the darkness of my room, his presence imposing and borderline intoxicating. "Sapphire."

"Vampire King," I returned. "There's blood in the fridge for later, and I left a bottle of aspirin under your pillow. You'll need both soon. Not that the aspirin will help. That's more symbolic for your future headache."

*In the form of an avenging slayer,* I thought, amused by the foresight. Oh, the violent fun awaiting his impending choices. I couldn't wait to watch the match unfold.

"Your penchant for riddles is exhausting."

"I know." That was why I always spoke in them. "But if people knew I could speak eloquently, they would ask for more. If I utter nonsense, they just assume I've lost my mind." Such as Makayla calling me a crazy bitch.

I grinned. I really did like that feisty wolf. Maybe I could have been a bit more forthcoming, but she had to realize her fate on her own to accept it. I'd just... nudged her a little.

"Did you tell her about the amulet?" Dimitri demanded.

"Just that it's similar to the ring and has a few additional *gifts.*" What would be the enjoyment of giving every detail away? Honestly, some people just needed to live for themselves.

"Sapphire." He repeated my name in that sexy, dark voice, his presence even more imposing this time. It made me a little jealous of Nikola's future. Dimitri would be dynamite in bed. Alas, I had a growly wolf in my destiny. I couldn't see him fully, just heard his sensual snarls.

*Mmm. More, please.*

"Are you listening to me?"

"No," I admitted. "Caught up in a vision." *Of washboard abs and a sexy little V-line to his hips. I really hope his face matches the rest of the package.*

Dimitri sighed, the sound old and tired. "If you didn't tell her how the signal works, then how will she know to portal here when we need her?"

I blinked at him. "The signal alerts her when there's trouble nearby, Dimitri. Not when we need her."

"*What?* I specifically said—"

"To portal her here when we are ready," I finished for him. "Yes, and it will do that. But the signal is just to help her see the signs around her." I gave him a look. "She couldn't just become a stay-at-home wolf. She's much too aggressive for that. She'll continue her freelance jobs, and I'll send her messages accordingly. But it's kind of you to worry."

I patted him on his muscular arm. He really was a good vampire king. I almost said that out loud but suspected he wouldn't approve.

"I can't decide if I want to kill you, throttle you, or fire you."

"All of the above, I imagine," I mused. Then I smiled to put him out of his misery. "If we need them, they will be here." A strong *if* because the futures kept shifting.

Would Dimitri kill Nikola?

Would Nikola kill Dimitri?

I didn't know.

He was playing a very dangerous game.

*Stakes. Blood. Sires. Oh my!*

But that was a story for another time.

"Makayla and Alaric are where they're meant to be," I told Dimitri. "And I finally have our ring." I held it up for him to see. "Which means I'll know Nikola's location by nightfall. I suggest you prepare yourself, King of Vampires, for you're about to meet your Slayer Queen."

## The End

Curious to learn more about the real Romanov bloodline? Check out the Vampire Dynasty series by Elle Christensen & Lexi C. Foss. This isn't a fairy tale. It's dark, violent, and underlined in brutal betrayal. Stake up. It's going to be a bloody affair.

Read more about the Silver Lake wolves from Makayla's realm in Nathan's book, An Unexpected Claim.

Want more from the E.V.I.E. world? Check out Violet Slays and The Slayer Witch.

Or consider visiting the future with Sapphire in Sapphire Slays. Is Jean-Marc her intended mate?

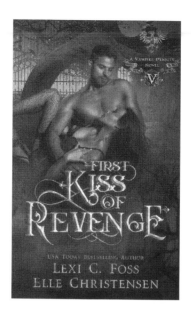

### FIRST KISS OF REVENGE
### VAMPIRE DYNASTY, BOOK ONE

*Three dynasties.*
*Two monarchs.*
*One war.*

### Nikola Romanov
My destiny is paved in blood.

Slayer.
Slave.
Vampire.
Pawn.

All titles apply after a dethroned vampire king turns me into a well-trained pet. Now he wants me to take down the renowned assassin guarding the Vampire Dynasty throne. In exchange for my cooperation, I'll be given my freedom.

All right, Master. I'll dance. And when I'm done, I'll burn the entire f*cking dynasty to the ground.

It's the Romanov slayer legacy, after all.

### Dimitri Ivanov

Grigori Rasputin thinks he's bested me. He's wrong. I've added a new player to the board, and she's going to paint his world in red.

Nikola is mine to train.
She's a weapon.
Maybe even my lover.
Whatever I choose.

By the time we're through, Grigori's entire empire will crumble to the ground. Then I'll pick up the pieces of my former throne.

The Vampire Dynasty will thrive again because nothing will stand in my way of taking back what's mine. Not even *her*.

Be a good pet and do as you're told, Nikola darling. I promise this will all be over soon.

**Authors' Note:** This is a dark paranormal romance trilogy featuring overarching themes that will be resolved over the three books. Each couple has a happily-for-now ending in their respective book, with strings that tie the entire trilogy together in the end.

*USA Today* Bestselling Author Lexi C. Foss loves to play in dark worlds, especially the ones that bite. She lives in Atlanta, Georgia with her husband and their furry children. When not writing, she's busy crossing items off her travel bucket list, or chasing eclipses around the globe. She's quirky, consumes way too much coffee, and loves to swim.

Want access to the most up-to-date information for all of Lexi's books? Sign-up for her newsletter here.

Lexi also likes to hang out with readers on Facebook in her exclusive readers group - Join Here.

*Where To Find Lexi:*
www.LexiCFoss.com

ALSO BY LEXI C. FOSS

**Blood Alliance Series - Dystopian Paranormal**

Chastely Bitten

Royally Bitten

Regally Bitten

Rebel Bitten

Kingly Bitten

**Dark Provenance Series - Paranormal Romance**

Heiress of Bael (FREE!)

Daughter of Death

Son of Chaos

Paramour of Sin

Princess of Bael

**Elemental Fae Academy - Reverse Harem**

Book One

Book Two

Book Three

Elemental Fae Holiday

Winter Fae Holiday

**Immortal Curse Series - Paranormal Romance**

Book One: Blood Laws

Book Two: Forbidden Bonds

Book Three: Blood Heart

Book Four: Blood Bonds

Book Five: Angel Bonds

Book Six: Blood Seeker

Book Seven: Wicked Bonds

## Immortal Curse World - Short Stories & Bonus Fun

Elder Bonds

Blood Burden

## Mershano Empire Series - Contemporary Romance

Book One: The Prince's Game

Book Two: The Charmer's Gambit

Book Three: The Rebel's Redemption

## Midnight Fae Academy - Reverse Harem

Ella's Masquerade

Book One

Book Two

Book Three

Book Four

## Noir Reformatory - Ménage Paranormal Romance

The Beginning

First Offense

Second Offense

## Underworld Royals Series - Dark Paranormal Romance

Happily Ever Crowned

Happily Ever Bitten

## X-Clan Series - Dystopian Paranormal

Andorra Sector

X-Clan: The Experiment

Winter's Arrow

Bariloche Sector

## Vampire Dynasty - Dark Paranormal

Violet Slays

Sapphire Slays

Crossed Fates

First Bite of Revenge

## Other Books

Scarlet Mark - Standalone Romantic Suspense

# ABOUT THE AUTHOR

### About Elle Christensen

I'm a lover of all things books and have always had a passion for writing. Since I am a sappy romantic, I fell easily into writing romance. I love a good HEA! I'm a huge baseball fan, a blogger, and obsessive reader.

My husband is my biggest supporter and he's incredibly patient and understanding about the people is my head who are fighting with him for my attention.

I hope you enjoy reading my books as much as I enjoyed writing them!

Join Elle Christensen's newsletter to receive a couple of updates a month on new releases and exclusive content. To join, all you need to do is click here.

Website
Newsletter Book+Main

ALSO BY ELLE CHRISTENSEN

### *Silver Lake Shifters*

An Unexpected Claim (Book 1) – Preorder Now!

A Promised Claim (Book 2) – Coming 2021

A Forbidden Claim (Book 3) – TBD

A Vengeful Claim (Book 4) – TBD

### *The Slayer Witch Trilogy*

The Slayer Witch (Book 1)

The Wolf, the Witch, and the Amulet (Book 2)

A Witch in Wolf's Clothing (Book 3)

### *Wrath of Angels Trilogy*

Wrath and Ruin (Book 1) – Coming 2021

Where My Demons Hide (Book 2) – TBD

My Kingdom Come (Book 3) – TBD

### *Blue Blood*

Blood Throne (Book 1) – TBD

Blood Prince (Book 2) – TBD

### *Stone Butterfly Rockstars*

Another Postcard (Book 1) – Available Now!

Rewrite the Stars (Book 2) – Coming 2021

Daylight (Book 3) – TBD

Just Give Me a Reason (book 4) – TBD

All of Me (Book 5) – TBD

### *Miami Flings*

Spring Fling – Available Now!

All I Want (Miami Flings & Yeah, Baby Crossover) – Available Now!

Untitled – TBD

### *Ranchers Only Series*

Ranchers Only – Available Now!

The Ranchers Rose – Available Now!

Ride a Rancher – Available Now!

When You Love a Rancher – Available Now!

Untitled – TBD

### *Happily Ever Alpha*

Until Rayne – Available Now!

Until the Lighting Strikes – Available Now!

Until the Thunder Rolls – Coming Summer 2021

### *Standalone Books*

Love in Fantasy – Available Now!

Say Yes (A military Romance) – Available Now!

Bunny Vibes – Available Now!

### *The Fae Guard Series*

Protecting Shaylee (Book 1) – Available Now!

Loving Ean (Book 2) – Available Now!

Chasing Hayleigh (Book 3) – Available Now!

A Very Faerie Christmas (Book 4) – Available Now!

Saving Kendrix (Book 5) – Available Now!

Forever Fate: (Book 6) – Available Now!

### The Fae Legacy (A Fae Guard Spin-off)

Finding Ayva (Book 1) – Coming November 2020

### Books Co-authored with Lexi C. Foss

Crossed Fates (Kingdom of Wolves) – Preorder it now!

First Kiss of Revenge (Vampire Dynasty Trilogy Book 1) - Preorder Now!

First Bite of Pleasure (Vampire Dynasty Trilogy Book 2) – TBD

First Taste of Blood (Vampire Dynasty Trilogy Book 3) – TBD

### Books Co-authored with K. Webster

Erased Webster (Standalone Novel) – Available Now!

Give Me Yesterday (Standalone Novel) – Available Now!

**If you enjoy quick and dirty and SAFE, check out Elle Christensen and Rochelle Paige's co-written books under the pen name Fiona Davenport!**

Fiona's Amazon Author Page

Website

Printed in Great Britain
by Amazon